THE DEVIL'S EDGE

THE DEVIL'S EDGE

Stephen Booth

sphere

SPHERE

First published in Great Britain in 2011 by Sphere

Copyright © Stephen Booth 2011

The moral right of the author has been asserted.

A CIP catalogue record for this book
is available from the British Library.

Hardback ISBN 978-1-84744-479-0
Trade Paperback ISBN 978-1-84744-480-6

Typeset in Meridien by Palimpsest Book Production Limited,
Falkirk, Stirlingshire
Printed and bound in Great Britain by
Clays Ltd, St Ives plc

Sphere
An imprint of
Little, Brown Book Group
100 Victoria Embankment
London EC4Y 0DY

An Hachette UK Company
www.hachette.co.uk

www.littlebrown.co.uk

For Lesley

Acknowledgements

As usual, my first attempt at this book has been improved on by several people. In this instance, they include my agent Teresa Chris, my editor Dan Mallory at Little, Brown, senior desk editor Thalia Proctor and copy editor Jane Selley. Thanks, everyone!

Lines from 'Country Life' by Show of Hands are reproduced by kind permission of Steve Knightley and Hands On Music. More information at: www.showofhands.co.uk

1

Tuesday

A shadow moved across the hall. It was only a flicker of movement, a blur in the light, a motion as tiny and quick as an insect's.

Zoe Barron stopped and turned, her heart already thumping. She wasn't sure whether she'd seen anything at all. It had happened in a second, that flick from dark to light, and back again. Just one blink of an eye. She might have imagined the effect from a glint of moonlight off the terracotta tiles. Or perhaps it was only a moth, trapped inside and fluttering its wings as it tried desperately to escape.

In the summer, the house was often full of small flying things that crept in through the windows and hung from the walls. The children said their delicate, translucent wings made them look like tiny angels. But for Zoe, they were more like miniature demons with their bug eyes and waving antennae. It made her shudder to think of them flitting silently around her bedroom at night, waiting their chance to land on her face.

It was one of the drawbacks of living in the countryside. Too much of the outside world intruding. Too many things it was impossible to keep out.

Still uncertain, Zoe looked along the hallway towards the kitchen, and noticed a thin slice of darkness where the utility room door stood open an inch. The house was so quiet that she could hear the hum of the freezer, the tick of the boiler, a murmur from the TV in one of the children's bedrooms. She listened for a moment, holding her breath. She wondered if a stray cat or a fox had crept in through the back door and was crouching now in the kitchen, knowing she was there in the darkness, its hearing far better than hers. Green eyes glowing, claws unsheathed, an animal waiting to pounce.

But now she was letting her imagination run away with her. She shouldn't allow irrational fears to fill her mind, when there were so many real ones to be concerned about. With a shake of her head at her own foolishness, Zoe stepped through the kitchen door, and saw what had caused the movement of the shadows. A breath of wind was swaying the ceiling light on its cord.

So a window must have been left open somewhere – probably by one of the workmen, trying to reduce the smell of paint. They'd already been in the house too long, three days past the scheduled completion of this part of the job, and they were trying their best not to cause any more complaints. They'd left so much building material outside that it was always in the way. She dreaded one of the huge timbers falling over in the night. Sometimes, when the wind was strong, she lay awake listening for the crash.

But leaving a window open all night – that would earn them an earful tomorrow anyway. It wasn't something you did, even here in a village like Riddings. It was a lesson she and Jake had learned when they lived in Sheffield, and one she would never forget. Rural Derbyshire hadn't proved to be the safe, crime-free place she'd hoped.

Zoe tutted quietly, reassuring herself with the sound. A window left open? It didn't seem much, really. But that peculiar man who lived in the old cottage on Chapel Close would stop her car in the village and lecture her about it endlessly if he ever found out. He was always hanging around the lanes watching what other people did.

Gamble, that was his name. Barry Gamble. She'd warned the girls to stay away from him if they saw him. You never knew with people like that. You could never be sure where the danger might come from. Greed and envy and malice – they were all around her, like a plague. As if she and Jake could be held responsible for other people's mistakes, the wrong decisions they had made in their lives.

Zoe realised she was clutching the wine bottle in her hand so hard that her knuckles were white. An idea ran through her head of using the bottle as a weapon. It was full, and so heavy she could do some damage, if necessary. Except now her fingerprints would be all over it.

She laughed at her own nervousness. She was feeling much too tense. She'd been in this state for days, maybe weeks. If Jake saw her right now, he would tease her and tell her she was just imagining things. He would say there was nothing to worry about. Nothing at all. *Relax, chill out, don't upset the children. Everything's fine.*

But, of course, that wasn't true. Everyone knew there was plenty to worry about. Everyone here in Riddings, and in all the other villages scattered along this eastern fringe of the Peak District. It was in the papers, and on TV. No one was safe.

Still Zoe hesitated, feeling a sudden urge to turn round and run back to the sitting room to find Jake and hold on to him for safety. But instead she switched on the light and took a step further into the kitchen.

She saw the body of a moth now. It lay dead on the floor, its wings torn, its fragile body crushed to powder. It was a big one, too – faint black markings still discernible on its flattened wings. Was it big enough to have blundered into the light and set it swinging? A moth was so insubstantial. But desperate creatures thrashed around in panic when they were dying. It was always frightening to watch.

There was something strange about the moth. Zoe crouched to look more closely. Her stomach lurched as she made it out. Another pattern was visible in the smear of powder – a section of ridge, like the sole of a boot, as if someone had trodden on the dead insect, squashing it on to the tiles.

She straightened up again quickly, looking around, shifting her grip on the bottle, trying to fight the rising panic.

'Jake?' she said.

A faint thump on the ground outside. Was that what she'd heard, or not? A footstep too heavy for a fox. The wrong sound for a falling timber.

This wasn't right. The only person who might legitimately be outside the house at this time of night was Jake, and she'd left him in the sitting room, sprawled on the couch and clutching a beer. If he'd gone out to the garage for some reason, he would have told her. If he'd gone to the front door, he would have passed her in the hall.

So it wasn't Jake outside. It wasn't her husband moving about now on the decking, fumbling at the back door. But still she clung on to the belief, the wild hope, that there was nothing to worry about. *I'm perfectly safe. Everything's fine.*

'Jake?' she called.

And again, louder. Much louder, and louder still, until it became a scream.

'Jake? Jake? *Jake!'*

Six miles from Riddings, Detective Sergeant Ben Cooper turned the corner of Edendale High Street into Hollowgate and stopped to let a bus pull into the terminus. The town hall lay just ahead of him, closed at this time of night but illuminated by spotlights, which picked out the pattern in its stonework that had earned it its nickname of the Wavy House. Across the road, the Starlight Café was doing good business as usual, with a steady stream of customers. Taxis were lining up for their busiest time of the day. It was almost ten o'clock on an ordinary August evening.

The pubs were even busier than the Starlight, of course. Cooper could hear the music pounding from the Wheatsheaf and the Red Lion, the two pubs on either side of the market square. A crowd of youngsters screamed and laughed by the war memorial, watched by a uniformed PC and a community support officer in bright yellow high-vis jackets, the pair of them standing in the entrance to an alley near the Raj Mahal.

Even in Edendale there were often fights at closing time, and drug dealers operating wherever they could find a suitable spot. On Friday and Saturday nights there would be a personnel carrier with a prisoner cage in the back, and multiple foot patrols of officers on the late shift. A change came over the town then; a place that had looked so quaint during the day, with its cobbled alleys and tall stone buildings, revealed its Jekyll and Hyde nature.

'Hey, mate, shouldn't you be out arresting some criminals?'

'Ooh, duck, show us your baton.'

Looking round at the shouts, Cooper saw that the bus was a Hulley's number 19 from the Devonshire Estate. Oh, great. He took a sharp step back from the kerb, turning his body away towards the shop window behind him. There were too many eyes gazing from the windows of the bus, and the likelihood of too many familiar faces, people he didn't want to meet when he was off duty. Half of the names on his arrest record had addresses on the Devonshire Estate. He didn't recognise the voices, but there was no doubt their owners knew him.

Well, this was his own choice. Many police officers opted to live outside the area they worked in, for exactly this reason. When you went for a quiet drink in your local pub, you didn't want to find yourself sitting next to the person you'd nicked the day before, or sharing a table with a man whose brother you'd just sent to prison.

But Cooper had resisted moving to a neighbouring division. He could easily have travelled into Edendale every morning from Chesterfield or Buxton, but that wouldn't be the same. He belonged here, in the Eden Valley, and he wasn't going to let anything push him out. He intended to stay here, settle down, raise a family, and eventually turn into a cantankerous pensioner who rambled on about the good old days.

That meant he had to put up with these awkward moments – the looks of horrified recognition on faces, the shying away as he passed in the street, the aggressive stare at the bar. It was all part of life. *All part of life's rich pageant.* That was what his grandmother would have said. He had no idea where the expression came from, but he knew it would stick inside his head now, until he found out. He supposed he'd have to Google it when he got home. He seemed to be turning into one of those people whose mind collected odd bits of information like a sheep picking up ticks.

As he walked, Cooper checked his phone in case he'd missed a text message, but there was nothing. He carried on towards the end of Hollowgate, ignoring the loud group of youngsters. Not his business tonight. He'd only just come off shift, at the end of a long-drawn-out series of arrests and the execution of search warrants. With six prisoners processed through the custody suite at West Street, there wasn't much of the evening left by the time he finally clocked off.

At the corner of Bargate he stopped again and listened for the sound of the river, just discernible here above the noise of traffic. The council had been talking about making Hollowgate a pedestrianised zone, like neighbouring Clappergate. But of course the money had run out for projects like that. So a stream of cars still flowed down from Hulley Road towards the High Street, forming Edendale's version of a one-way system. 'Flowed' wasn't exactly the right word for it. Half of the cars stopped in front of the shops to unload passengers, or crawled to a halt as drivers looked for parking spaces, the little car park behind the town hall already being full at this hour.

Cooper studied the pedestrians ahead. There was no sign of her yet. He glanced at his watch. For once, he wasn't the one who was late. That was good.

He decided to wait in front of the estate agent's, looking back towards the clock on the Wavy House to make sure his watch wasn't fast. There was always a smell of freshly baked bread just on this corner, thanks to the baker's behind the shops in Bargate. The scent lingered all day, as if it was absorbed into the stone and released slowly to add to the atmosphere. It was good to have somewhere in town that still baked its own bread. For Cooper, it was the sounds and smells that gave

Edendale its unique personality, and distinguished it from every other town in the country, with their identikit high streets full of chain stores.

He turned to look in the estate agent's window, automatically drawn to the pictures of the houses for sale. This was one of the more upmarket agents, handling a lot of high-end properties, catering for equestrian interests and buyers with plenty of spare cash who were looking for a country residence. He spotted a nice property available not far away, in Lowtown. An old farmhouse by the look of it, full of character, with a few outbuildings and a pony paddock. But six hundred and fifty thousand pounds? How could he ever afford that? Even on his new salary scale as a detective sergeant, the mortgage repayments would be horrendous. He had a bit of money put away in the bank now, but savings didn't grow very fast these days, with interest rates still on the floor. It was a hopeless prospect.

'So which house do you fancy?' said a voice in his ear.

It was totally different from the voices that had shouted to him from the bus. This one was warm, soft and caressing. A familiar voice, with an intimate touch on his arm.

Liz appeared at his side, laid her head against his shoulder, and slipped her hand into his. He hadn't seen her approach, and now he felt strangely at a disadvantage.

'What, one of these?' he said. 'Chance would be a fine thing.'

She sighed. 'True, I suppose.'

Cooper looked beyond the pictures of houses and caught their reflections in the glass. The pair of them were slightly distorted and smoky, as if the glass was tinted. Edendale's traffic moved slowly, jerkily behind them, like a street in an old silent film. And not for the first time, it struck him how well matched they looked. Comfortable together, like an old married couple already. Liz looked small at his side, her dark hair shining in the street lights, her face lit up with a simple, uncomplicated pleasure. It delighted him that she could respond this way every time they met, or even spoke on the phone. Who wouldn't love to have that effect on someone? It was a wonderful thing to bring a bit of happiness into the world, to be able to create these moments of joy. A rare and precious gift in a world where he met so much darkness and unhappiness, so many lonely and bitter people.

'Kiss, then?

He bent to kiss her. She smelled great, as always. Her presence made him smile, and forget about the gaping faces. Who cared what other people thought?

They crossed the road, squeezed close together, as if they'd been parted for months. He always felt like that with Liz. At these moments, he would agree to anything, and often did.

'So, any progress on the big case?' she said.

'The home invasions, you mean?'

'Yes. The Savages. That's what the newspapers are calling them.'

Cooper grimaced at the expression, sorry to have the mood momentarily spoiled. It was typical of the media to come up with such a sensational and ludicrous nickname. He knew they were aiming to grab the public's attention. But it seemed to him to trivialise the reality of the brutal violence inflicted on the victims of these particular offenders.

'No, not much progress,' he said.

'It must be awful. I mean, to have something like that happen to you in your own home.'

'The victims have been pretty traumatised.'

The gang of burglars the papers were calling the Savages had struck several times this summer, targeting large private houses in well-heeled villages on the eastern edges. E Division was Derbyshire Constabulary's largest geographical division by far, and those long gritstone escarpments in the east marked its furthest fringes, the border with South Yorkshire.

Cooper wondered how he would feel if he owned that nice house in Lowtown, and someone broke into it. He'd been told that owning property changed your attitude completely, made you much more territorial, more aggressively prepared to defend your domain. Well, he'd seen that at first hand. Because it had certainly happened to his brother. He'd watched Matt

8

turn into a paranoid wreck since he became responsible for the family farm at Bridge End. He patrolled his boundaries every day, like a one-man army, ever vigilant for the appearance of invaders. He was the Home Guard, ready to repel Hitler's Nazi hordes with a pitchfork. That level of anxiety must be exhausting. Was owning property really worth it?

'Do you think the Savages are local?' asked Liz, voicing the question that many people were asking. 'Or are they coming out from Sheffield?'

There were few people he could have discussed details of the case with. But Liz was in the job herself, a scene-of-crime officer in E Division. She'd even attended one of the scenes, the most recent incident in Baslow.

'They know the area pretty well, either way,' said Cooper. 'They've chosen their targets like professionals so far. And they've got their approaches and exits figured out to the last detail. At least, it seems so – since we haven't got much of a lead on them yet.'

They had a table booked at the Columbine. It was in the cellar, but that was okay. In Edendale, there wasn't much of a choice of restaurants where last orders were taken at ten. And even at the Columbine that was only from May to October, for the visitors. Edendale people didn't eat so late.

Cooper was looking forward to getting in front of a High Peak rib-eye steak pan-fried in Cajun spices. Add a bottle of Czech beer, and he'd be happy. And he'd be able to forget about the Savages for a while.

They opened the door of the restaurant, and Cooper paused for a moment to look back at the street, watching the people beginning to head out of town, back to the safety of their homes. If anyone's home was safe, with individuals like the Savages on the loose.

'Well,' he said, 'at least they haven't killed anybody yet.'

In Riddings, a figure was moving in the Barrons' garden. Barry Gamble was approaching the house cautiously. The last time he'd been on the drive at Valley View, it hadn't been a happy experience. Some people just didn't appreciate neighbourly concern. He hoped there was no one hanging around outside, no chance of seeing any of the Barrons. He would just have a quick check, make sure everything was okay, then get back to his own house a few hundred yards away in Chapel Close.

Gamble tutted at the roof trusses and window frames stacked untidily against the wall. That was asking for trouble, in his opinion. It gave the impression the house was empty and vulnerable while construction work was going on. The improvements seemed to have stalled, though. The area that had been cleared behind the garage was supposed to be an extension for a gym and family room, so he'd heard. But the foundations were still visible, the breeze-block walls hardly a foot high where they'd been abandoned. Perhaps the Barrons had run out of money, like everyone else. The thought gave Gamble a little twinge of satisfaction.

He wondered if some item of builders' materials had made the noise he'd heard. A dull thump and a crash, loud on the night air. And then there had been some kind of scrabbling in the undergrowth. But he was used to that sound. There was plenty of wildlife in Riddings at night – foxes, badgers, rabbits. Even the occasional deer down off Stoke Flat. The noises animals made in the dark were alarming, for anyone who wasn't used to them the way he was.

Gamble skirted the garage and headed towards the back of the house, conscious of the sound of his footsteps on the gravel drive. He tried to tread lightly, but gravel was always a nuisance. He'd learned to avoid it whenever he could. A nice bit of paving or a patch of grass was so much easier.

He began to rehearse his excuses in case someone came out and challenged him. *I was just passing, and I thought I heard . . . Can't be too careful, eh? Well, as long as everything's all right, I'll be getting along.* He couldn't remember whether the Barrons had installed motion sensors at Valley View that would activate the security lights. He thought not, though.

The house was very quiet as he came near it. The younger

Barron children would be in bed by now. He knew their bedrooms were on the other side of the house, overlooking the garden. Their parents tended to sit up late watching TV. He'd seen the light flickering on the curtains until one o'clock in the morning sometimes.

Gamble peered through the kitchen window. A bit of light came through the open doorway from the hall. But there wasn't much to see inside. No intruders, no damage, no signs of a break-in or disturbance. No one visible inside the house, no soul moving at all.

In fact, there was only one thing for Barry Gamble to see. One thing that made him catch his breath with fear and excitement. It was nothing but a trickle. A narrow worm, red and glistening in a patch of light. A thin trickle of blood, creeping slowly across the terracotta tiles.

2

Wednesday

Ben Cooper arrived under the Devil's Edge as the morning was already getting warm. He followed the directions of a uniformed officer and parked his Toyota on a narrow verge behind a line of vehicles that had reached the scene before him. He unbuckled his seat belt, pressed redial on his mobile phone, and stepped out of the car into the smells of new-mown grass and horse manure.

'Gavin, it's Ben. Did you get the message earlier? See if you can round up Luke and Becky and get them out to Riddings asap. Drop everything else, mate. This is a priority.'

As he put his phone back into his pocket, Cooper was wishing he'd got a call-out earlier. He couldn't deny that the adrenalin was flowing. This was his first big challenge as a recently promoted detective sergeant. He had to do a good job, make sure he got his team focused and producing results. Results were what everyone demanded. But you had to be on scene early, and get in at the start, if you were going to play a leading role. Otherwise you started to look like an extra.

He began to walk towards the blue and white tape marking out the crime scene. According to a street sign, he was on Curbar Lane.

Cooper wasn't too familiar with Riddings. In normal times, these villages weren't usually the focus of crime. Expensive houses and affluent middle-class residents, by and large. A few months ago, this road had appeared on a list of the most expensive places to buy property in the East Midlands, along with a similar location in Curbar. Decent houses were pricey everywhere in the Peak District. But Riddings and its neighbouring villages seemed to have an appeal all of their own. *A highly desirable location*. He could almost write the estate agent's details himself.

The villages of Froggatt, Curbar and Riddings lay on the banks of the River Derwent, between the bigger communities of Grindleford and Baslow. From all of these Derwentside villages, the view to the east was blocked by a series of high gritstone edges – Gardom, Baslow, Curbar, Froggatt. Created through glacial action twenty thousand years ago, they formed a great curve of rock faces swinging away to the north and south, a formidable barrier protecting the clusters of grey-roofed houses in the valley and the wooded dales to the west. An almost continuous twelve-mile-long wall of rock.

Cooper paused for a moment when he reached the outer cordon and looked up. Riddings Edge was considered a mecca for climbers, with routes up to seventy feet high. He knew a few rock climbers, and they told him it presented some of the most testing challenges, comparable to the popular sections of Stanage Edge. Sheer perpendicular faces were split vertically like shattered teeth, angles shifted suddenly to steep slabs or overhangs. Some stretches of rock were said to be notorious for crumbling unexpectedly under the fingers, so that a hold that seemed perfect one second disappeared into thin air the next. Climbers looking for something easier tended to head a bit further north, to Froggatt.

With one hand Cooper shaded his eyes against the sun to study the edge itself. Grotesque, twisted outlines of weather-worn gritstone. Jutting outcrops, misshapen boulders, broken shards of stone, so dark that they seemed to absorb the light. Against the sun, some of the rocks were impossible to distinguish from watching human figures.

He pictured what was beyond the edges. Desolate expanses of scrub known as flats, and vast tracts of moorland beyond

13

them. Above Riddings Edge was the biggest area of moorland, known simply as Big Moor. If you took the trouble to walk to the highest point of the moor, you would see what lay beyond – the suburbs of Totley, Dore, Beauchief, the first tentacles of the city of Sheffield, reaching out towards the Peak.

Cooper gave his name to an officer at the inner cordon, just inside an impressive entrance with electric wrought-iron gates and a long driveway leading up to the front of the property. A Land Rover Discovery stood on a paved parking area, next to a brick-red Beetle Cabriolet. Beyond the house, he saw land-scaped gardens, a water feature with a fountain, shrub borders, a lawn containing a children's trampoline.

He headed towards a group of figures and made out his DI, Paul Hitchens, who nodded to him briefly.

'Ben.'

'Sir.'

Hitchens was looking well fed these days, or maybe losing a battle against middle-aged spread. He was always dressed smartly, though – in a suit and tie, like a middle manager in a large insurance company. Cooper brushed automatically at his own leather jacket, wondering whether he should think about changing his image.

The DI's expression was serious and preoccupied. Cooper decided he ought to make an effort not to let his excitement show too much.

'House invasion?' he said.

'And a bad one.'

August had been a hell of a month under the Devil's Edge. Warm weather and long evenings tempted people to leave their windows open at night, a back door ajar, their house unattended. It was an opportunist thief's dream.

But these weren't opportunist thieves. Their attacks were planned. They had everything so well worked out that they seemed to disappear after the event. Disappeared without a trace, the newspaper reports said. Well, almost.

'Ben, suppose we were looking at this scene without any preconceptions,' said Hitchens.

14

'Yes?'

'Well, if the children had been harmed, we might be thinking murder-suicide. Father kills the wife, the kids and then himself. It happens.'

Cooper nodded. 'Too often.'

They were both silent for a moment, watching the crime-scene examiners go about their work. The circus had arrived early this morning, the SOCOs and medical examiner, the photographers and CID, and the task force officers in their overalls conducting a fingertip search. They were all here promptly, arriving like magic. It was as if everyone had already known where to go, as though they were expecting something like this to happen. Well, it was that kind of summer. One where death had been inevitable.

'Or it can be the mother. That happens too,' said Hitchens, as if as an afterthought.

'No. The mother does it differently. A woman sets fire to the house, so she doesn't have to see them die.'

'Yes. And these children are unharmed anyway.'

'We know, though, don't we?' said Cooper at last.

'Yes, I suppose so. The Savages.'

'If you like that name, sir.'

'Well, this was definitely savage. They've upped the stakes, Ben. This is a deliberate escalation.'

As he listened to Hitchens, Cooper was trying to absorb the atmosphere of the house. There was always a lingering atmosphere after a violent crime – a sense of the shock and fear, the impact of death echoing from the walls.

'Maybe it was deliberate,' he said. 'But perhaps it all just went wrong for them this time.'

SOCOs were busy everywhere, dusting for fingerprints, hoovering up trace evidence, examining the garden for shoe marks. Cooper realised that he'd arrived only just in time to see the body in situ. A black van was already waiting on the drive to take it away.

'Besides,' said Hitchens, 'the husband isn't dead. Not yet. Want to take a look?'

Cooper could see the body from the back door. It lay on the kitchen floor, the face turned slightly towards him. A woman, wearing jeans and a white T-shirt stained red at the shoulders. A woman lying in a pool of darkening blood. The stain had spread right across the floor and soaked into the tiles.

There were always a lot of people around at a murder scene. Many of these officers would never have attended a violent death before. Some of them were trying to avoid looking at the body, in case they couldn't forget it afterwards. It was different if you had an immediate job to do. If you walked into a crime scene with a professional attitude, thinking about carrying out your work, it really focused the mind. Then you were able to concentrate on looking at the evidence, assessing the circumstances of death, planning what should be done next. Sometimes it was only later, when you saw the photographs of the scene, that reality hit you.

'The victim's name is Barron,' said Hitchens. 'Zoe Barron, aged thirty-six.'

'The husband?'

'Jake.'

'Okay.'

When she was attacked, Zoe Barron had been clutching a bottle of wine. Château d'Arche Sauternes, according to the label. It had smashed on the tiles as she fell. The golden liquid had formed thin streams through her blood, and now the smell of wine was turning sour on the morning air. The back door stood open, and flies were starting to converge on the kitchen.

It was the sight and smell of the wine that made Cooper feel suddenly nauseous, the way that blood and the presence of a corpse no longer did. He felt guilty at the excitement he'd experienced on the way here, the adrenalin that had been surging through his body and heightening his sensations as he stepped out of the car. Zoe Barron's dead eyes stared like a reproach.

'You know we're already taking a lot of flak over these incidents,' said Hitchens quietly.

'Yes, sir.'

16

'Well, take it from me, Ben – that was nothing. The shit is really going to hit the fan now.'

Because the Barron family were far from the first. There had already been four attacks in the space of a few weeks. All the incidents had taken place in villages along the eastern edges, with high-value properties targeted in Hathersage, Padley and Baslow. Aggravated burglaries, with at least two cases of GBH if they ever came to court. Two people had suffered injuries at the hands of ruthless offenders who showed no hesitation in using violence to get in and out quickly. No sneaking through windows while the occupants were asleep for these men.

Yet from the way the Barrons were found, it seemed as though they had expected nothing. For them, it had probably been a normal day. A spell of warm weather meant a chance to tidy up in the garden, a spot of maintenance on the back fence before the autumn began. There were probably no signs of danger as twilight fell in Riddings – only the late-afternoon sun catching the edge, picking out those grotesque, twisted gritstone shapes.

And inside the house? The kitchen was the most dangerous place in any home, the room where more people were killed or injured than any other. But most of those cases were accidents. A fire, a fall, or a faulty electrical connection.

Zoe Barron's death looked at first glance as though it might have been an accident. The dropped wine bottle, the slippery floor, the hard tiles. And that head injury, oozing blood. But the circumstances were different. The husband, for example. Jake Barron had been found in the sitting room, sprawled in front of a fifty-inch plasma TV.

'He was lucky,' said Hitchens.

'So he's alive, you say?'

'Just about. He has serious head injuries. If he survives, there's a high probability of brain damage.'

'What about the children? There are children, aren't there? In a house this size . . .'

'Yes, three. Social Services have taken custody of them while

17

some relatives are tracked down. There are grandparents living in Sheffield, and a sister somewhere in Nottinghamshire, I think. None of the kids seems to be injured, but they're in shock, of course.'

'Did they see anything? Or is it too early to interview them?'

Hitchens shrugged. 'It doesn't seem likely that they did. They were all upstairs in their bedrooms. The youngest was already asleep, and the older two were watching TV, listening to their iPods, chatting to their friends on their mobile phones. All at the same time, as far as we can tell. I suppose it's one of the advantages of giving kids all those electronic gadgets to use. Personally, I've always thought it cuts them off from the real world too much. But sometimes . . .'

'Sometimes that can be a good thing,' said Cooper.

'Exactly.'

There was a stir behind them in the doorway, and Cooper turned. Detective Superintendent Branagh had arrived. There was no doubt who would be Senior Investigating Officer on this one, then. The inquiry was getting the superintendent's personal touch. Of course it was. A major, high-profile case like this. A sergeant would be a long way down the pecking order.

Branagh brought an air of authority on to the scene. She had a physical presence that made other officers step back. Cooper sometimes thought it was the shoulders that did it. She was built like a professional swimmer, broad and flat across the shoulders, an effect emphasised by the cut of the jackets she wore. She moved like a rugby player ploughing through the opposition, her face set in a determined glower. Cooper knew he would hate to get on the wrong side of her. But so far he seemed be in her good books. It was to Superintendent Branagh he owed his promotion.

After Hitchens had briefed her, Branagh cast a sharp eye around the immediate scene, then walked to the sitting room window.

'Neighbours?' she said.

'Not so as you'd notice, ma'am,' said Hitchens.

'What? This isn't an isolated farmhouse. We're in a village. There were plenty of houses visible as we came up the road.'

'Well, take a look for yourself.'

Each property in the area was screened by high hedges or thick banks of conifers, with long drives and gates to separate them from the road. A desire for privacy was a double-edged sword. In other villages, where smaller cottages clustered together, no strangers could have got too close without the neighbours seeing them. Here, some of these homes were as isolated from prying eyes as if they stood alone on the remotest plateau of Kinder Scout. More so, actually, when you considered the number of walkers scattered across open-access land.

'You're right,' said Branagh. 'There must be houses nearby, but we can't see them from here.'

'Yes, they chose their target well.'

'And that's good news, in a way. It suggests they must have checked out the location in advance. Someone will have seen them.'

'Maybe.'

Branagh was trying to strike a note of confidence, but Hitchens sounded unconvinced. No one was mentioning the word 'Savages' now. Everyone knew the superintendent wouldn't like it. She loathed the media. More than one officer had felt the strength of her disapproval after quoting something from the press. Besides, it hardly seemed necessary. Standing in this house, and with all the incidents that had happened in the last few weeks, the conclusion seemed obvious.

'We keep an open mind,' said Branagh. 'Until the evidence points one way or the other.'

Everyone nodded. But everyone had their own ideas.

Hitchens nudged Cooper.

'Take a look round outside, Ben. See if you can get any ideas about their approach.'

'Okay.'

'Then we need to start talking to the neighbours. Can you get your team organised on that as soon as?'

'We're a bit thin on the ground, sir.'

19

'You'll get more help. I've got at least one more pair of hands on the way for you.'

Cooper went back out and walked around the house. Roof trusses and window frames were stacked against a wall, presumably ready to go in the extension he could see was being built at the back. He nudged one of the timbers. They were heavy, too heavy for one person to move on their own.

The parking area provided access to a garage block big enough for four cars at least. To the rear, a terrace led via a decked walkway to a large balcony with wrought-iron railings. Doorways led out of the house on to the balcony from the kitchen and a games room.

It was a breathtaking position, with spectacular south-facing views across to Stoke Woods and down the Derwent Valley as far as Chatsworth.

Across a lower deck he found himself looking into a pool room and gym. The garden sloped away to a weeping willow on the boundary. Near a dense coppice of beech trees he could see a greenhouse, a polytunnel, a pergola. Among the beeches he thought he could make out a large tree house.

He was about to start making more phone calls when he saw with relief that his team were starting to arrive. Divisional CID would have an important part to play here. He aimed to make sure of that.

Detective Constable Gavin Murfin was the first to plod his way up the drive, chewing ruminatively on a soft mint and wiping sweat from his forehead.

'Nice gaff,' he said. 'They tell me it costs a fortune to buy a place like this. I might move here when I retire.'

'Really?'

'Yeah, and I'll start breeding flying pigs.'

Of course, there were bigger and better houses than these in Derbyshire. Properties with more bedrooms, higher-specification kitchens, larger grounds and longer swimming pools. But here, location was the factor that raised the price so high. *Location, location, location.* The estate agent's mantra was accurate. People were willing to pay big money for a view like this. It was why

20

those who'd grown up here found it so difficult to afford properties in the Peak District.

Murfin peered through the French windows into the lounge.

'Look at this furniture. I bet they didn't buy this on eBay.'

Cooper wondered what had been stolen in the break-in. It was too early to know, even if there was anyone here who could tell them. There were no obvious signs. He'd noticed a retro-style DAB radio standing on a kitchen work surface, and an iPad lying on the table. Easy pickings for a burglar. Who could have failed to snatch up the iPad? Unless they were panicked by the violent confrontation with the householder and fled empty-handed. Or maybe they were looking for something specific. A safe, perhaps, where the Barrons kept their most valuable possessions.

The house itself was nothing special, as far as Cooper could see. Not architecturally, anyway. It had been added to many times over the years, and had lost any character it might have possessed when it was built. Most of it was stone, but it failed even to blend in with its surroundings. The size was impressive, though. It seemed to go forever, stepping down on to a lower level and constantly revealing another extension. Guest bedrooms, a gym, a sauna. It seemed to have everything.

'I wonder what the mortgage is like,' he said. 'It makes me shudder just to think about it.'

Murfin grunted. 'Don't talk to me about mortgages. I've got one as big as a planet. As big as Alpha Centauri. We went for a fixed rate just at the wrong time, like. Typical.'

'Alpha Centauri?'

'My lad's getting keen on astronomy.'

'Your son is doing wonders for your education, Gavin.'

'I have to help with his homework. Just one of my many jobs.'

'Speaking of which . . .'

'Yeah, I know. Start knocking on doors. Just call me the tally man.'

'I'm not sure how many adjoining properties we'll have.'

'I can tell you,' said Murfin.

21

'Really?'

'Did you think I'd been wasting my time until I got here? Oh ye of little faith.'

'So you didn't have time to call at that baker's in Hollowgate?'

'I was a model of restraint. No, I've rounded up information on the immediate neighbours. Modern technology is wonderful. Saves me a bit of leg work, anyway.'

Who did they have to start with? The Barrons' house was called Valley View for good reason. This whole section of Curbar Lane enjoyed views down into the valley of the Derwent. Along the lane Cooper had noticed a sign for Fourways, and he could just see the roof of another property beyond the trees.

'Yes, Fourways is the nearest,' said Murfin, consulting his notebook. 'The people there are called Holland. On the other side we need to talk to a Mr Kaye at Moorside House, and Mr Edson at Riddings Lodge. Across the way are Mr and Mrs Chadwick. Their house is called The Cottage. Irony, I suppose. There are also two properties backing on to this one from The Hill. A Mrs Slattery at South Croft, and a family name of Nowak at Lane End.'

'Nowak?'

'That's what it says here.'

'Well, when Luke and Becky arrive, we can divide them between us.'

'Looks like the lass is here now,' said Murfin.

DC Becky Hurst was just passing through the cordon, ducking to get under the tape. She was sensibly dressed in jeans and sweater, as if she'd known when she got up this morning that she was scheduled for a day in the country. Her hair was very short and a colour that Cooper would probably call coppery red. He was fairly sure it wasn't the same colour she'd had last week.

Hurst walked briskly up the drive with that businesslike air with which she approached every job, clutching her notebook and phone in her hand, her expression alert and eager. When she and Gavin Murfin were working together, they often looked like a young Border Collie shepherding an aged ram. Sometimes

Cooper felt like calling 'Come bye' to get her to steer him into the right pen.

'Morning, boss,' she said brightly. 'Has Gavin given you the information I pulled out on the neighbours?'

Murfin coughed quietly, as if a piece of mint had gone down the wrong way.

'Oh, you did that, Becky?' said Cooper.

'Of course. Gavin had to call in somewhere on the way.'

'And is there anything else you've done for Gavin?'

'Yes, I checked with the hospital on the condition of the householder, Mr Barron. They say he's on the critical list.'

'In hospital-speak, that means they don't think he'll make it,' said Murfin.

'Thanks, Gavin.'

Hurst looked at the Barrons' house for the first time, running a keen eye over the façade as if she was counting the windows and doors.

'So it could be a double murder we're dealing with,' she said.

'Very likely.'

A flash of colour caught Cooper's eye. On the edge above Riddings, two climbers were clinging to the rock face. From here, their grip on the rock looked impossibly precarious. But inch by inch, foot by foot, they were making their way up towards the edge itself. The clang of karabiners reached him clear on the air.

The rock climbers who'd told him about Riddings Edge had mentioned that many of the routes up those gritstone faces had been given names that reflected a climber's view of the challenges they presented. There was Torment, Hell's Reach, Satan's Gully, Demon Buttress. The message was pretty clear.

Those names alone would be enough to explain why this particular escarpment had become known as the Devil's Edge. But this summer, they weren't the only reason.

3

Detective Sergeant Diane Fry was starting to feel suffocated. And it wasn't just the heat, or the airlessness of the conference room. The suffocation went much deeper. It was a slow choking of her spirit, the draining of life from her innermost being. In a few more minutes she would be brain dead. Heart dead, soul dead, her spirit sapped, her energy levels at zero.

And her bum was numb, too. This was purgatory.

Fry had spent the whole morning in Nottinghamshire Police headquarters at Sherwood Lodge. At the front of the room, someone whose name badge she couldn't read was sticking Post-it notes on a sheet of brown paper that had been Blu-Tacked to the wall. The Post-its were all the colours of the rainbow, which apparently had some significance. A few of them had already moved position several times during the session, making determined advances or strategic retreats, like military units moving around a simulated battlefield. She supposed there was some kind of overall narrative to the presentation. It might even be explained in the handout she hadn't read. But she'd lost track half an hour ago. Now she was losing the will to live. She could feel her eyes glazing over, a well-known clinical side effect of staring too long at yellow Post-it notes.

When the speaker turned his back for a moment to move another Post-it, she leaned towards the officer sitting next to her.

'What is this kind of presentation called again?' she whispered. 'A Sellotape brainstorm?'

'No. A brown-paper workshop.'

'Of course.'

If she remembered rightly, her neighbour was an inspector from the Leicestershire force. Mick or Rick, something like that. They'd all had to do ten-second introductions at the start of the session. *Tell us who you are and what you hope to get from today.* Cue a bunch of po-faced lies.

'The Sellotape comes at the end,' said Mick or Rick with a conspiratorial smile. 'When we fix the Post-it notes in their final position.'

'I'll be on the edge of my seat by then.'

'You and me both.'

Fry sighed. She was almost starting to miss Edendale. Unlike Derbyshire Constabulary, their neighbours in Nottinghamshire had an extra assistant chief constable, whose sole responsibility was Strategic Change. And change these days meant cooperation between forces to save money. So here she was, in this conference room in Sherwood Lodge, forty miles from Derbyshire E Division and starting to feel nostalgic for the company of DC Gavin Murfin and his colleagues. She would never have thought it possible.

She wondered idly which she would prefer right now – a nice restful spell in the private hospital she'd seen on the other side of the trees as she came down the drive, or a visit to the pub a little way back down the road.

She caught Mick or Rick looking at her. He pointedly checked his watch, and made a gesture with his wrist suggesting the act of drinking. A soulmate, then. Or at least close enough for now.

'Seven Mile Inn,' he said.

'I saw it. Just by the lights.'

These working-group sessions were supposed to be interactive. That meant she couldn't entirely escape joining in. At strategic moments she had found herself blurting out phrases that sounded right. *Methodical workforce modernisation. Greater interoperability*. She tried to say them while other people were shouting out suggestions, so that her words were swallowed in the general verbiage. The best place to hide a tree is in the forest.

The frustrating thing was that she knew she could do this stuff. She could do it standing on her head, write the entire report for them if that was what they wanted. You didn't get far in the modern police service without learning those skills. It was just that her heart wasn't in it. This wasn't how she should be spending her days, trapped in a stuffy conference room.

And then the facilitator said the words she'd been waiting for.

'Okay, people. We'll break for lunch. Please be back promptly at two.'

Some of the attendees had brought their own sandwiches. Packed lunches, like schoolchildren. There was a civilian, a techy type from an IT department somewhere in the region, who was drinking Coke through a straw while he listened to an iPod and scrolled through messages on his iPhone.

You would have thought they'd supply lunch, at least. But this was the age of austerity. No such thing as a free lunch. Whoever said that had got it dead right.

Fry wondered what the others had done wrong to be sent here. When she stood up, her body ached. Not just from the ordeal of sitting still for so long. She physically craved action.

Somewhere in the world, something must be happening. There must be people who needed her. Mustn't there?

The village of Riddings had no pubs, and no shops. Not a sign of a café or a craft shop, or even a farmhouse selling fruit at the side of the road.

Yet Cooper could see that the place still attracted tourists. Perhaps they saw some quaintness in its narrow lanes and stone houses, or enjoyed the smell of horse manure. But the people who lived here clearly had no interest in tourism. Unlike

26

other villages in the Peak District, they made no effort to encourage visitors. They provided no facilities, not even anywhere to park a car.

Driving through the centre of the village, he noticed a few smaller cottages standing on The Green, where a hand-written sign advertised horse manure at a pound per bag. But the only people he saw anywhere were women walking their dogs.

The lanes really were *very* narrow. Where cars were left parked at the side of the road, their offside wing mirrors had been folded in to avoid getting knocked off by passing vehicles. A lesson learned from experience, he supposed.

The property neighbouring Valley View was called Fourways. This one was probably worth barely a million. Through more black wrought-iron gates, a drive ran straight up to a double garage, and the house was below it, approached by a set of steps. It was much smaller than Valley View, maybe no more than three bedrooms. But the views alone would add a lot of value to the property.

On the way to the front door, he passed a window and saw a woman emerging from the kitchen and walking towards a split-level dining room. Through the kitchen door, Cooper glimpsed Shaker-style units, lit by a dozen spotlights. A cream Persian cat sat in a basket by the Aga. When it saw him, it gave him a look of pure contempt.

He thought of his own moggy back at home in his flat in Welbeck Street, a rescue from the local animal sanctuary and happy just to have a back yard to sit in when it was sunny. There were cats and cats, just like there were different people.

When he rang the bell, the same woman answered.

'Mrs Holland?'

'Yes.'

'Police. I'd like to have a few words about your neighbours. Have you heard what happened?'

'Oh, the Barrons, yes. Terrible.'

Inside the house, the entrance hall was floored with slate, which Cooper had always liked the look of. Wherever it was used, it seemed to bring a bit of the natural world into a home.

The feel of it underfoot was so different from synthetic flooring. He liked the way it changed colour in different light, and even the smell of it when it got wet. One day he would own a house with slate floors. One day.

The Hollands were a couple in their late sixties. Comfortable-looking was the expression that came into his mind. Well settled into retirement, but fit enough to be active. The husband was a bit overweight. Perhaps he ought to play more golf, and eat fewer good dinners. Compared to him, his wife was like a slender bird, forever moving here and there, steel-grey hair cut straight around her face.

'I feel so sorry for the children,' said Mrs Holland. 'At their age, it must be terrible. At any age, I suppose. You know what I mean.'

'Yes.'

'I wouldn't wish a thing like this on anyone, no matter what I might think of them personally.'

'How do you get on with the Barrons, then?'

'Oh. Fine, you know. We don't see all that much of them. It's not as if we're right on top of each other.'

'We hear them more than see them, I suppose you'd say,' said Mr Holland.

His wife gave him a look, but Cooper couldn't quite interpret the message.

'The children play in their garden, of course,' she said. 'What children wouldn't love to have a garden like that to play in?'

Cooper gazed out of the window, trying to orientate himself in relation to the Barrons' property.

'Those trees there. They must be on your neighbours' side.'

'Yes, that's right.'

'I think I noticed a tree house when I was at Valley View.'

'Oh, you saw it.'

'The most expensive tree house ever built,' said Mr Holland. 'When I was a child, my dad built us one out of bits of spare timber, and we loved it. Not Jake Barron. He brought in a tree house designer. Can you believe it?'

'I don't think Sergeant Cooper wants to hear about tree houses,' said Mrs Holland firmly.

Her husband shrugged and wandered away a few feet, making a show of examining the rose bush outside the window.

'Actually, I was wondering if you might have seen anything last night,' said Cooper.

'Oh, anything suspicious? That's what you say, isn't it?'

'Yes. Any unusual activity, strangers hanging around, vehicles you didn't recognise?'

She looked disappointed. 'No. We would have told someone already if we'd seen anything like that.'

'How long have you lived here in Riddings?'

'About five years,' she said. 'Martin was a very successful commercial lawyer. He still does a certain amount of consultancy work, but at least I get to spend time with him now. And there's the house. It's lovely, isn't it?'

'Oh, yes. Very nice. It must be a wonderful place to live.'

'All this business is very worrying, though. Nowhere is safe, is it? Not these days. We thought a place like this, in the country . . .'

'Unfortunately, it's not the case.'

'I suppose it's the times we live in. People need money badly. And they look at houses like ours and think we have more than our share. That must be what makes them do things like this, don't you think? It's envy, isn't it? Envy, pure and simple. It's an emotion that can really eat into people.'

She sounded as though she was speaking from experience. Cooper was about to ask her why, when his phone buzzed. There was a text message from Becky Hurst, asking to speak to him when he was free.

'I'll have to go,' he said. 'But if you do happen to think of anything, here's my card.'

Mr Holland had turned to look at him again with a glower, his hands thrust into the pockets of his corduroy trousers. Cooper handed his card to Mrs Holland, simply on the basis that she seemed to be the one who was most interested.

'Well, you ought to check on the people who go up on the edge at night,' she said.

'Which people?' asked Cooper.

'You'll see them. There are always cars parked up at the gap, no matter what time of night you go past. Goodness knows what they do up there. I wouldn't care to think.'

'We'll be checking on everything.'

'Be sure that you do.'

Cooper thought he was probably going to have to get used to people telling him what to do. Here, everyone would think it was their right.

On his way out on to Curbar Lane, Cooper had to squeeze past a gardener's van drawn up in the gateway with a trailer full of freshly sawn branches. There must be plenty of work for gardeners in this area. Maintenance of all these lawns and flower borders had to be an endless task, like painting the Forth Bridge.

Working near the van was a gardener with short-cropped blond hair. The young man failed to look up as Cooper passed, which was odd. The natural thing would be to show curiosity about what was happening. A few yards down the lane, when his car was out of sight round a bend, Cooper pulled over and wrote down the name of the company from the side of the van. AJS Gardening Services.

While he was stopped, he called Becky Hurst.

'What's up, Becky?'

'I thought you should know, Sarge. I took the side lane by the Methodist church. Chapel Close? Mr Gamble lives at number four. He's the member of the public who called the incident in.'

'Oh, yes. Mr Gamble.'

'Well, his wife was in. Her name is Monica.'

'Where's her husband?'

'She didn't know.'

'Didn't know?'

30

'She told me she often doesn't know where he is. Sorry.'

'He should never have been allowed to wander off from the scene,' said Cooper.

'He did make a statement to the FOAs.'

'The first officers to arrive didn't know what sort of incident they were dealing with. We really need to speak to Mr Gamble again, and soon. I don't like the fact that he's disappeared, Becky.'

'No, that's why I thought you ought to know straight away.'

'You were right. Thanks, Becky.'

'The good news is that he can't have gone far. He hasn't taken their car, so he's likely to be on foot. I've got his mobile number from his wife. I'm trying to call him, but there's no answer so far.'

'Okay. Keep at it.'

Cooper started the car and drove on. He really didn't like Mr Gamble being missing. He liked even less the knowledge that before long, someone was going to ask him about Gamble. Either his DI or Superintendent Branagh would want to know where the informant was. *I don't know* wasn't a good enough answer.

The Chadwicks' home, The Cottage, was a barn conversion with big Velux windows installed in the roof. As Cooper approached, two herons took off from behind the house and flapped ponderously away over the village, their feet trailing clumsily below their bodies. You didn't often see two herons together. He felt sure there must be a pond behind the house, nicely stocked with fish.

He passed a Nissan Qashqai and a Mercedes Kompressor standing close together in front of a double garage. A small boat trailer was parked on the drive. He looked for the burglar alarm, and found a yellow box high on the front wall. There was also a security light at the bottom of the drive.

The Chadwicks were outside, enjoying the sun, seated on garden chairs under a parasol. Mr Chadwick rose to greet him. He was a tall man with anxious eyes and a balding head shiny with perspiration.

31

'Bill Chadwick. This is my wife, Retty. Marietta, that is. We call her Retty.'

Cooper showed his warrant card, even though they hadn't asked to see it. It was odd how some people were so trusting when he said he was a police officer. No matter what was going on around them, they still felt no reason to be suspicious of strangers.

'You'll have heard . . .?' he began.

'At Valley View, yes. The Barrons.'

'It's so close,' said Mrs Chadwick. 'Ever so close. Just across the lane.'

They all looked instinctively towards Valley View, though it wasn't even possible to see Curbar Lane from here, let alone anything of the Barrons' property. Trees and the corner of a wall, then more trees. And beyond the trees, Riddings Edge. So close? Cooper wondered if the Chadwicks knew what it was actually like to have neighbours living practically on top of you, packed in cheek by jowl, so close that you could hear them clearly through the walls on either side of you. There were lots of people in Edendale who knew what that was like. His own ground-floor flat in Welbeck Street sometimes echoed to the slam of a door from the tenant upstairs, the clatter of feet on the stairs, the blare of old Mrs Shelley's TV set next door.

'Obviously you're some of the Barrons' closest neighbours,' he said.

'And you wondered if we might have noticed anything,' said Chadwick. 'Obviously. But I'm afraid we didn't.'

'But you were at home last night?'

'Actually, we went out as soon as it got dark,' said Chadwick.

'Where to?'

'Up on to the edge.'

'Really?'

Cooper couldn't keep the surprise out of his voice. He'd been warned only a few minutes earlier about the people who went up on the edge at night. But he hadn't thought the Chadwicks were the sort of people Mrs Holland was referring to. From her tone of voice, he'd been picturing a dogging site, where people had sex in public while others watched. The growing number of such sites was a regular cause of complaints from residents in secluded parts of Derbyshire. But they didn't attract people like the Chadwicks, surely?

'Yes, we were out for a couple of hours,' said Chadwick.

'In the dark? Why?'

'Well, it has to be at night-time. It needs to be dark, to watch properly. You can't see anything in daylight, of course.'

'Ah,' said Cooper, still hoping that he was wrong.

Chadwick nodded. 'Yes, we were watching the Perseid meteor shower.'

'Of course you were.'

'It was one of the best nights for viewing. A nice clear sky – but not much moon. We saw lots of shooting stars. A wonderful experience to watch them from a place like that.'

'While you were up there, you didn't notice anything at all?' asked Cooper.

'Well, we gathered there was some trouble. Lots of sirens and flashing lights disturbing the peace during the night. We don't get that here very often. I see it in Sheffield, yes. But not in Riddings.'

'Oh, you work in Sheffield, sir?'

Chadwick shuffled his feet and blinked nervously. A trickle of sweat ran across his temple.

'Yes. Er . . . in a way.'

Immediately Cooper began to study him more keenly. It was unusual to see someone thrown into confusion by such a simple question. You either worked in Sheffield or you didn't. Unless your job involved travelling around the country, and you were only in Sheffield sometimes. But in that case, why not just say so? What was the cause of the embarrassment?

'I'm a head teacher,' said Chadwick. '*Was* a head teacher.'

'So you're retired?'

'I'm on gardening leave.'

Cooper glanced instinctively at the manicured lawn and neat flower beds around them, before he recognised the euphemism.

'What happened?'

Chadwick shrugged. 'I lost it. Simply as that, really. It all just became too much one day. Oh, it had been building up for a while. Quite a few years, actually, when I look back. There was a time in my career when I used to get up in the morning and think *Great, I'm going to work today*. It was exciting. I relished the challenge. I thought only about what I could achieve each day. But gradually it all changed. I began to wake up in the early hours and feel sick. Sick to my stomach at the thought of having to face school. And it wasn't just the kids, either. God knows, they were bad enough. But there were all the whingeing staff, the stupid parents, the endless, endless hassle, everyone expecting me to do something to solve their problem, to make their life easier, to produce some magic solution out of a hat to make their child more intelligent, better behaved, more talented at music or football, or less of a bully. It was always my fault when things didn't happen the way they wanted. And . . . oh God, I don't really want to think about it. It makes my guts churn even now.'

'So you were suspended.'

'Not exactly. It was . . . a mutual arrangement. A spell away from the job, while things are sorted out. Or that's what they said. Maybe it's just to allow the governors time to find a new head to replace me. My deputy will be happy enough with that, I dare say. Or they could be hoping I'll give up the fight and resign. It would save them money.'

'I see.'

Chadwick screwed up his eyes and gazed into the distance, staring at something that Cooper couldn't see.

'Or maybe . . .'

'What?'

'Well, I wonder sometimes. Perhaps everyone is just waiting for me to do the decent thing, and top myself.'

Too surprised to know how to respond, Cooper watched Chadwick turn away and walk slowly into the house, as if seeking the shade. He moved like a wounded animal, creeping away to find somewhere quiet and dark.

34

Cooper looked at Mrs Chadwick. She smiled sadly.

'I'm sorry. He's been like that for a while. It doesn't seem to get any better.'

'Do you have any family living here?'

'We have a daughter, Bryony. She's seventeen, nearly eighteen.'

'Where would she have been last night?'

'Oh, she was out.'

Mrs Chadwick became more relaxed now that she had been steered on to a different subject.

'Bryony got her A level results last week,' she said. 'So she was out celebrating with her friends from school. She'll be off to uni in September.'

'Good grades? All A stars?'

'How did you know?'

'Sometimes I think I'm the only person who never got any,' said Cooper.

The woman was becoming more animated as she spoke of her daughter. This was a far more comfortable topic, something to be seized on gratefully when life was going wrong.

'We wanted her to do a gap year,' she said. 'The way we both did ourselves when we were students. It was a terrific experience for us. And, of course, it helped us to work through in our minds what we really wanted to do with our lives. I don't think you can do that without seeing a bit of the world, do you?'

'Perhaps.'

'But Bryony wasn't interested in a gap year. She says she knows what she wants to do. She's set out her plan, and she needs to get on with it and earn her qualifications if she's going to meet her goals. A gap year would just be a waste of time and set back her schedule. She's very driven, you see. Very ambitious. Obviously we're giving her all the support she needs. We're *very* proud of her.'

'I'm sure you are.'

A shadow of anxiety passed across her face, and she glanced back towards the house. It was sad that a few moments of silence was enough to cause that apprehension. But she saw her husband pass in front of a window, and the concern eased.

'She's chosen her university herself, too,' she said. 'I went to Oxford. St Hilda's. But Bryony wanted to go to Bristol for some reason. She insisted on putting it down as her first choice. Something about them having the best reputation in her subject. As I said, she's very . . .'

'Driven?'

'Quite.'

A very slim girl with long dark hair appeared round a corner of the house. She saw Cooper, and walked quickly away again.

'Was that your daughter?' he asked.

'That's Bryony, yes.'

Mrs Chadwick escorted Cooper to his car. Usually people were only too glad to see him leave, and shut the door behind him as quickly as possible. But this woman seemed to want to linger. Did she want to talk more about the achievements of her daughter? Or was there another subject she longed to discuss, but was afraid to force on him? Something she might be ashamed of. That self-conscious, embarrassed look again. She was a person afraid of showing too much emotion, yet struggling to hold it inside any longer.

'So what actually happened, Mrs Chadwick?' asked Cooper.

'Happened?'

'To your husband?'

She nodded, and her shoulders seemed to slump, as if a great weight of tension had been lifted from her.

'A child pushed him too far one day,' she said. 'A fourteen-year-old kid. Student, we're supposed to call them, aren't we? Cocky little devil he was, by all accounts. Everyone knew he was trouble. He just kept pushing and pushing to see how far he could go, wanted to find out what he could get away with. You know the type. You must see them all the time in your job.'

'Yes, of course. Usually when they're a bit older.'

'Well, perhaps you wouldn't see so many of them if teachers like Bill were allowed to keep proper discipline in our schools.'

36

Cooper knew that a lot of police officers would agree with this view. More than one of them had gone the same way as Mr Chadwick when they'd been pushed too far. There was only so much you could take, after all. Everyone had a breaking point.

'Is your husband getting help?' he asked.

'Oh, yes. Regular counselling sessions. Medication for his depression. I don't think the medication is working properly yet.' She paused. 'That, or he's stopped taking it.'

Cooper glanced at her, saw the strain in her eyes. 'It must be a difficult thing to live with.'

She smiled through a sudden welling of tears. 'Thank you,' she said. 'Yes, it is. We just hope that we can all rely on some support when we need it, don't we?'

Cooper drove back along Curbar Lane to Valley View and took a look at the Barrons' property with new eyes, trying to see it as a passer-by might.

One thing immediately struck him. At the front, everything seemed to have been done to advertise the fact that there was plenty worth stealing inside – electric gates with an entry-phone system, a security camera pointing at the gate, little yellow signs warning of an electric fence topping the dry-stone wall. Yet at the back, the property had been pretty much left open, the fences low and the trees cleared to provide a view of the edge from the patio and balcony. Whoever designed this landscape had seen the edge as an attraction, not a threat.

He supposed most of the residents of Riddings would be commuters, or well-off retired people like the Hollands. These weren't the seriously rich, just the affluent and comfortable. Definitely not a tourist-friendly village, though.

Many of these people would have come here from the city, seeking peace and quiet, looking for a refuge from noise and traffic – and an escape from crime. Perhaps they had encoun-tered violence on the streets of Sheffield and Manchester, or become nervous at the stories of robberies and shootings every week in the newspapers, feared the monsters stalking their cities. So they had sought refuge in a rural haven. The village of Riddings, in the eastern edges. Secluded properties, respectable neighbours. Yet it seemed that for some of them, their monsters had followed them to their sanctuary.

Of course, everyone had monsters in their lives. Most people left them behind in their childhood, locked away safely in a fading corner of memory. Some kept them with them, all the way through their lives. Cooper was one of those people, so he knew all about it. His monsters were always close by, glimpsed from the corner of his eye, forever lurking in the darkness, breathing quietly in the silent hours of the night.

He paused outside the Barrons' back door, watching the sunlight catching the windows, hearing the birds singing in the trees, listening to the quiet engine of the black van as it took Zoe Barron's body away.

He knew that most people never met their monsters in the flesh.

But a few were not so lucky.

4

Handymen, gardeners, tree surgeons. The village noticeboard advertised all of their services, alongside the times of mobile library visits, instructions for the council's blue bag recycling scheme, and a poster announcing the attractions of Riddings Show, which was due to take place on Saturday.

Cooper was waiting for his team to rendezvous and compare notes. They had arranged to meet in the centre of the village, where an ancient stone horse trough provided the central feature on a few square yards of cobbles. From here, he could see Union Jacks flying over several properties.

For some reason, many of the house names in Riddings included the word 'croft'. There was South Croft, Hill Croft, Nether Croft. It made them sound more like remote homesteads in the Scottish Highlands than homes in an affluent middle-class Derbyshire village.

Every few yards, steel posts were sunk into the verges to prevent cars parking on the grass. In one place, someone had exercised a bit of artistic interpretation and used giant imitation toadstools instead. All the mail boxes he'd passed seemed to be decorated with illustrations of post horns or stage coaches. He couldn't imagine that little touch on the Devonshire Estate.

Throughout the village, rose hips hung over the road, and long banks of unpicked blackberries were ripening at the wayside. What a waste.

Just beyond a sign warning of horse riders, Cooper saw a gate with a cattle grid to keep the sheep out. There might have been sheep in Riddings once, but there wasn't much sign of them now. Apart from horses, the nearest livestock would be the Highland cattle roaming the flats above Baslow Edge, so often photographed by tourists against a backdrop of the Eagle Stone or Wellington's Monument.

Nearby, a woman in a pink sleeveless top was kneeling on the grass weeding a flower bed, watched by a West Highland terrier. In a small orchard, speckled hens pecked among windfall apples. Life seemed to be going on as normal in Riddings.

'The Barrons have been here for three years,' said Gavin Murfin, sweating his way to the meeting point and peering at the scum-covered water in the horse trough. 'One of the neighbours told me that Valley View was on the market for nearly two and a half million. I guess prices have fallen a bit since then, though.'

'Not in this village.'

'Oh?'

'So where did the Barrons get the money to move into Riddings, I wonder?'

'I know what you mean. Not forty years old yet, and three kids to bring up. You'd think they'd be on the breadline like the rest of us poor saps who have families draining every penny from our pockets. But Jake Barron is in line to take over the family business. The Barrons have a chain of carpet warehouses across South Yorkshire – Sheffield, Rotherham, Doncaster, all those places. His dad is still company chairman, but Jake is chief executive. I guess he's taking a fair whack out of the company.'

'Hasn't the carpet trade suffered from the recession?'

'No, the opposite. People have been spending their money on home improvements instead of moving house. New furniture, new carpets, that sort of thing. There's no recession so bad that somebody doesn't benefit from it. They say the pound stores are booming.'

Detective Constables Becky Hurst and Luke Irvine arrived

together, and shared the results of their interviews with neighbours. No one had seen or heard anything, it seemed. As far
as the residents of Riddings were concerned, the Barrons'
assailants had come and gone like ghosts.

'Who has details of the Barrons' children?' asked Cooper.

Hurst held up a hand. 'I can tell you that. There are three
of them. Their names are, let's see . . .' She consulted a notebook. 'Melissa, Joshua and—'

'Fay,' said Murfin. 'Melissa, Joshua and Fay.'

He couldn't resist a note of satire in his voice as he read out
the names. His own kids were called Sean and Wendy.

'But I don't suppose they were in a position to see or hear
anything. I bet none of them even went near a window to
look outside.'

'We need to keep knocking on doors, then,' said Cooper.

Murfin wiped a hand across his brow and fumbled in his
pockets for sustenance. 'We need more manpower to do all
this door-to-door.'

'I've been promised there's more coming.'

'Some people have got out from under anyway,' said Murfin
grumpily.

'Like who?'

'Diane Fry, that's who. The Wicked Witch of the West
Midlands. Let's face it, she's just phoning it in these days.
Secondment to a working group, I ask you. It should be *me*
phoning it in. I'm the one who's done his thirty. I'm the one
who's so close to retirement it's practically singeing my arse.
But look at me – still pounding the streets, knocking on doors.
It's cruelty to dumb animals.'

'Gavin, I really don't think you'd want to be on a working
group. *Implementing Strategic Change*? Think about it.'

Murfin chewed his lip ruminatively. 'Okay, I thought about
it. And I fell asleep.'

Cooper thought of the Barrons' house again. They were
getting nothing from the neighbours, so the answers must lie
at Valley View. Everything would depend on forensics from
the scene, and he was missing out on that.

'Better keep knocking on doors, Gavin.'

'Yeah, I know.'

Murfin looked at the main street that ran through the village.

'I'm not walking up that hill, though. Someone will have to drive me to the top, and I'll work my way down.'

It was true that Murfin had never been cut out for country treks. No matter how many memos were sent out by management about the fitness of officers, he had been unable to lose any weight. From time to time he'd compromised by taking his belt in a notch, which had only succeeded in producing an unsightly roll of spare flesh that hung over his waistband.

His wife Jean had been putting him on diets for years, but they never worked. Now he was so near to completing his thirty years' service and earning a full pension that he didn't really care any more, didn't feel the necessity to meet the fitness requirements or respond to emails on the subject. It was odd, then, that the prospect of approaching retirement hadn't made him more cheerful. Instead, he was becoming more and more lugubrious, like an overweight Eeyore or Marvin the Paranoid Android.

A woman came past walking a terrier. Surely the same woman Cooper had seen gardening only a short time earlier.

'How're you doing, duck?' said Murfin with forced brightness.

The woman glared at him coldly.

'What are you selling?' she said. 'Whatever it is, we don't want any.'

Murfin sniggered as if she'd told a dirty joke and sidled up to her to show his warrant card.

'Police,' he said. 'Oh, I know – I can't believe it either. They take anybody these days. Can you spare a minute, duck?'

'Okay,' said Cooper. 'While Gavin is out ingratiating himself with the locals, let's get some real work done.'

'Ten to one he'll end up being offered a cup of tea,' said Hurst, watching Murfin with a hint of admiration.

'Fresh coffee,' said Cooper. 'But if I know Gavin, it'll be the biscuits he's interested in.'

A car pulled alongside, a metallic blue Jaguar XF with the number plate RSE1. The passenger window hummed down, and man leaned towards it from the driving seat. Iron-grey hair swept back, a sardonic eyebrow, a loud and commanding tone of voice.

'Police?'

'Yes, sir,' said Cooper.

'You know what's going on around here, I suppose?'

'Yes. We're aware of it.'

'So what are you doing about it? Anything? Or nothing?'

He didn't wait for an answer, but put his car back in gear and accelerated off down the hill.

'Great.'

'Nice to know we have the support of the public,' said Hurst as she watched him drive away.

'When people get upset and frightened, they need someone to blame.'

'Surely they should be blaming the thugs responsible for the crimes?'

'But no one knows who they are, do they? So we're the nearest target. That's the way it works, Becky.'

'That's so unfair.'

'It happens.' Cooper glanced at her. 'You're going to have to get used to our relationship with the law-abiding public.'

While Fry waited in the garden of the Seven Mile Inn, she checked her phone and saw she'd missed a call from Angie. There was a voicemail message.

Hi, sis. We haven't talked. We need to talk, you know? Call me.

She saw Mick or Rick coming back towards her with their drinks.

He smiled as he handed her a glass. 'A boyfriend?'

'No, my sister.'

'Right.'

His smile became a smirk, as if he'd just been given some kind of signal. Fry gritted her teeth. Just because the call wasn't from her boyfriend didn't mean she hadn't got one. But that was the way some men's minds worked. They read an invitation in the slightest thing. She supposed it must be some instinct from their primitive past, sniffing the air to detect the presence of a rival, then mating with anything that stood still long enough.

He sat opposite her, gazing into her eyes, his mind evidently searching for the right conversational gambit. Best to stick an oar in straight away.

'So, what do your people down in Leicestershire think about the plan for elected police commissioners?'

She lifted an eyebrow at him over her glass. For a moment, he looked pained, as if she'd just kicked him under the table. But he recovered well.

'The scrapping of performance targets and minimum standards is okay. But locally elected police commissioners? That's not so welcome. Everyone thinks that, don't they?'

Fry supposed that was true. As with all kinds of amateur interference, the role of elected politicians tended to be viewed with suspicion. Most officers preferred the idea of power resting in the hands of the chief constable. After all, he or she was a police officer, a colleague who had come up through the ranks.

That said it all really. It was 'us and them' again. The police and the public. The constant blurring of the lines was viewed as a threat. Even creeping civilianisation was regarded as an insidious disease.

'Politics has no place in the police service. The idea of an elected commissioner with the power to sack the chief constable makes my blood run cold. Are police numbers sustainable in the face of budget cuts? Who knows? Who wants to wait around to find out?'

With eighty-three per cent of the policing budget being spent on staffing, it seemed likely that numbers would be reduced in the coming months. More than likely. If Fry had been a gambler, she would have called it a racing certainty.

So the big idea was to save cash through structural reforms, exploring the possible mergers of specialist units and back-office functions, sharing the purchase of expensive equipment and IT systems, forensic and legal services. Any merging of functions would have to be low profile, though, and needed spinning in the right way when it was announced.

An overtime and deployment review had been under way for some time. The police authority's audit and resources committee was already looking at ways of providing value for money in policing. The addition of government budget cuts meant an ideal opportunity to look at streamlining costs. At least that was what the management team had called it in their emails – 'an opportunity'.

It was all spelled out in the document currently sitting on Fry's desk back in Edendale: 'Policing in the Twenty-first Century: Reconnecting police and the people'. Her head resounded with phrases about mobilising neighbourhood activists, implementing radical reform strategies, stripping away bureaucracy in the partnership landscape . . .

The partnership landscape. Well, it was certainly a different kind of scenery from the one Ben Cooper harped on about endlessly. These days, her hills were mountains of paperwork, her valleys contained rivers of jargon, endlessly flowing. The only thing her landscape had in common with the Peak District was the number of sheep involved, and the amount of shit they left behind.

She was hearing more and more buzzwords as each day passed. *Sacrifices, restraint, institutionalised overtime.*

Fry looked at her companion. She really ought to get his name right, but he'd taken off his badge when they left Sherwood Lodge.

'You know, when you've been in the job for a few years, everything seems to come full circle,' he said. 'It's funny to watch the pendulum swinging. Take the question of force mergers . . .'

Force mergers. If she ever heard that phrase again, she would probably scream. Back in 2005, HM Inspector of Constabulary had pointed out that poor information-sharing

45

between police forces had led to serious crime that crossed regional boundaries slipping through a gap. HMIC said that the forty-three-force structure was no longer fit for purpose, and proposed the creation of 'strategic forces'. The result had been the government's 'superforce' merger plan, which had soon been abandoned in the face of local opposition and the cost of restructuring.

Full-scale force mergers were seriously unpopular with voters. The suggestion for a huge East Midlands Constabulary covering Derbyshire, Nottinghamshire, Leicestershire, Lincolnshire and Bedfordshire had been dropped like a hot potato. No one wanted to see their local force disappearing into an unaccountable monolith.

Now they were discussing another report, which had also declared the structure of forty-three forces obsolete. But the answer to the problem was different. They pointed to figures showing that small police forces caught more criminals than larger ones. They suggested that the current forty-three forces should be split into around ninety-five, more than twice the present number, so that police forces could properly reflect their local communities. No mention of restructuring costs there. But Fry was willing to bet the budget cuts would count that one out too.

'What's your task after the working-group sessions?'

'Demand management reports on control room processes for all five forces.'

He shrugged. 'Good luck. Control rooms will probably be contracted out, like payrolls.'

'You think so?'

Fry knew that payrolls had been contracted out to a business services company with a brick and glass office block on the waterside in Lincoln. Sorry – not an office block; a human capital management facility.

'And, of course, we wait to hear the good news about front-line services. How many sworn officers will *your* force lose?'

It struck Fry that this was the only reason he'd wanted to go for a drink with her, the chance to talk to someone from

46

another force about all his worries. A soulmate, in a way. But she'd hoped for a different kind of conversation.

She took a drink. 'I'm leaving Derbyshire anyway,' she said.

'Oh? Where to?'

'I thought I might try for EMSOU.'

The East Midlands Special Operations Unit had been set up nearly ten years ago to provide operational support for the Regional Intelligence Unit, helping to tackle serious and organised crime. It had initially covered only Nottinghamshire and Leicestershire. But the chief constables of the region had got together and agreed to expand it from two forces to five. The unit now employed officers and staff from all five areas, but there might be vacancies.

Then Fry remembered that the Home Office funding package for EMSOU and the Regional Intelligence Unit had come to an end this year, leaving Derbyshire and the four other forces responsible for all future funding. Probably not many vacancies then.

And then there were the effects of the recession. According to Human Resources, attrition rates had shown a sharp dip. That meant fewer officers leaving the job, and fewer openings to replace them. Candidates for recruitment to the police service were being told there were no vacancies at the moment due to the 'economic conditions'.

Normally, candidates who successfully completed a two-day recruitment process and achieved a mark of at least sixty per cent in the National Recruiting Standards test were given a start date to attend their first day of training. But for some time now, such candidates had been told that their applications were going to be rescinded, and there would be no start dates for at least two years.

So a move back to the West Midlands, which had looked so easy a couple of months ago, was becoming a distant hope.

How many years had she been in Derbyshire now? Well, it was too many, anyway. Far too long since that transfer from Birmingham had brought her here, and a return to her old patch was way overdue.

Trouble was, while she waited, she was afraid she was losing her edge. After a while, you began to find yourself accepting second best.

Fry looked at her companion as he drained his drink.

'Better get back, I suppose.'

5

There were older properties in Riddings, though they only dated from the first decade of the nineteenth century. Not old at all in Derbyshire terms. The Iron Age settlements on the moor above the edge made these cottages on The Green look almost futuristic.

To reach number four Chapel Close, Cooper had to park on The Green, leaving the Toyota angled awkwardly on the verge, right up against the steel posts that prevented him getting any further off the road. He supposed there would be complaints, but in Riddings it couldn't be helped.

At least Barry Gamble was home now. He looked innocently surprised when he was asked where he'd been, as if he had no idea that anyone would want to speak to him again. He'd done his bit, and that was it. Cooper was amazed how often he had to disillusion people in these circumstances. Surely everyone must know by now that it wasn't so simple?

'I'm afraid not, Mr Gamble. There will probably be a lot more questions.'

'Well, I suppose I'm an important witness.'

'Absolutely.'

Gamble had bushy eyebrows that made him look as though he was permanently peering through a hedge. He wore a cowboy hat pulled too low, making his ears stick out, and he carried a stout walking stick, though Cooper could see no sign of a limp. When Gamble turned to lead him into the house, Cooper saw tufts of hair sprouting from his ears to match his eyebrows. The crown of the cowboy hat was circled by wooden beads.

'The Barrons,' said Gamble. 'You'll want to know everything I can tell you about the Barrons.'

'Well, you and . . .'

He indicated Mrs Gamble, who sat in a corner of their little sitting room; so far she had hardly said a word. But her husband didn't even notice the interruption.

'The Barrons. They're not really local people,' he said. 'I don't just mean that they aren't from this area – hardly anyone in Riddings is. But they don't support local businesses either. They bring everything in from outside. I don't think that's right, do you? We should support the place we live in. But *they* do their weekly shop at the big Waitrose store in Sheffield, rather than using the Co-op in Bakewell or somewhere more local. Sometimes *she* goes shopping at nearly nine o'clock at night even.'

Cooper remembered the bottle of wine Zoe Barron had been carrying when she was attacked. He wasn't sure she would have bought that at Waitrose.

'She did,' he said. 'She won't be doing it any more.'

'Oh, yes. Sorry and all that.'

Mrs Gamble sat listening quietly to her husband. She was a worn-looking woman with a mouth that turned down at the corners, taking all the warmth out of her smile and replacing it with a shadow of bitterness. She looked at Cooper with sad eyes, like an abandoned dog in an animal sanctuary hoping that someone would take her to a new home.

Gamble didn't remain chastened for more than a few seconds. He jumped up and stared through the front window as a car passed slowly along the street towards the Methodist chapel. He grunted as if confirming some suspicion to himself.

'Caretaker at the chapel.'

'The Barrons, sir?' said Cooper, beginning to get irritated.

'Oh, yes. I talked to some of the builders working on their

extension,' said Gamble. 'Just passing the time, you know. They said the Barrons were really fussy, wanted everything just so. They imported all kinds of fancy things, and still they were constantly complaining.'

He shook his head sadly, as if despairing at the ways of the world.

'You've been inside the house, I suppose?' he said.

'Yes.'

'Have you seen their furnishings? Italian. It's all Italian. They had a man over from Rome. Guido, he was called.'

'You even interrogated the Italian designer?'

'Interrogated? What do you mean? That's *your* job.'

'So what would you call it?'

'I just talk to people. I call it making conversation.'

'So do people know each other well in Riddings?'

'No, I wouldn't say that. It's not a village in the way I used to think of it,' said Gamble. 'I grew up in Bradwell, just across the bridge from Town Gate.'

'Not far from me, then.'

'Aye.' Gamble peered at Cooper more closely, suddenly resembling a startled sheep. 'I think I might have known...'

'My father, I expect. Yes.'

'That's it. Well... like I was saying, that was a proper village, the sort of place where you know everyone, because folk join in. You know them because your parents knew their parents, and so on.'

'I understand.'

'Here, it's not like that. You can see it just by looking at the place. These newcomers, they know how to keep their privacy all right. So you get the walls, the cameras, the long drives, the locked gates. All of that stuff.' Gamble smirked again. 'And when you look at those things, you've got to wonder, haven't you?'

'Wonder what?'

'Well... you wonder what it is they've got to be so private about.'

'I see.'

51

Cooper thought for a moment that Gamble was going to wink at him. Instead he leaned closer, with a sly grin and a lift of one bushy eyebrow. Then he nodded in the general direction of Valley View and Moorside House.

'What secrets have these people got? What is it they're trying so hard to hide?'

'I don't know,' said Cooper. 'I have no idea. But perhaps you do?'

'Ah,' said Gamble, delightedly. 'Now we're really on the same wavelength. You know what the Bible says. *There is a God in Heaven that revealeth all secrets.*'

'Are you a churchgoer?'

'Yes, I am. But none of *them* ever go to chapel. That would be the day.'

'You're a Methodist, then?'

'Certainly. Someone has to be. There aren't many of us left.'

'Mr Gamble,' said Cooper. Then, seeing that he wasn't getting the man's attention because of some sound outside the house, he repeated it more loudly. 'Mr Gamble!'

Gamble jumped. 'Yes? What? Have I told you enough? Have you got the information you need?'

'Not at all.'

Cooper glanced at the man's wife, who seemed to shrug helplessly, using only her eyes. He wondered if it would be possible to get the chance to speak to her on her own. And, if he did, whether she would cling to his leg, whimpering pitifully.

'Tell me again what you saw last night.'

'I did all that.'

'A preliminary statement. We'll need more, I'm afraid.'

'I didn't see much, not really. Not until I looked through the window.'

'You'd heard a noise, is that right?'

'Yes, a thump or a crash. Perhaps both, I'm not sure now.'

Cooper stifled a sigh. Somebody who already couldn't be sure the day after an incident probably wasn't going to make a great witness in court.

'Tell me exactly where you were when you heard the noise.'

'It was dark,' said Gamble.

'So?'

'I was in the lane.'

His answers had become suddenly terse. Cooper wished he had someone else with him for this interview. Becky Hurst, preferably. Someone to watch for reactions and absorb impressions, to chip in with an unexpected question. A partner he could discuss the visit with afterwards. But right now he couldn't spare Becky or any of the other members of his team. There were too many people to speak to, and too many doors to knock on. The first twenty-four hours were so crucial.

'Which lane do you mean?' said Cooper. 'Curbar Lane?'

'No, at the back.'

'There's a small lane running up to Riddings Lodge. Do you mean that one?'

'Yes, it goes as far as Lane End, the Nowaks' place. We call it Croft Lane.'

'Croft Lane? Is that where you were?'

Gamble nodded. 'Thereabouts.'

Cooper gritted his teeth. *Thereabouts* wasn't good enough.

'We're going to have to take you back there and let you show us the exact spot,' he said.

'Does it matter?'

'Yes.'

'There was a tree,' said Gamble. 'I was standing near a tree. But it was dark, you see.'

'And what were you doing near this tree?'

'Just . . . standing. I'd been out for a walk.'

'And you heard . . .?'

'A thump or a crash.'

'Which?'

'A thumping crash. A crashing thump. I don't know. Both.'

'And what did you do?'

'I looked towards the house. The Barrons' place, Valley View. That was where the noise seemed to come from.'

Cooper leaned forward, deliberately pressuring Gamble to come up with an answer. 'And what did you see?'

'I saw a light on.'

'Where?'

'In the kitchen.'

'Was that where the noise came from?'

'It seemed so to me.'

'So you went to investigate.'

'Exactly. Neighbourly concern. Anyone would do the same.'

'And when you investigated, you saw . . .?'

'I looked through the window and realised there was something wrong.'

'Wait. Before you looked through the window . . .?'

'I didn't see anything. No one around. It was dark, though, like I said. There might have been people in the garden, among the trees, watching me. I thought I was quite brave, actually.'

Cooper had to admit that was true. In those circumstances, Mr Gamble could have been putting himself at risk. He started to feel a bit guilty about questioning him so closely.

'What do you know about the Barrons?' he said.

'Well, everyone knows they have plenty of money,' said Gamble, visibly relaxing. 'Rolling in it, they are. You should see the stuff the children get. Mobile phones, those iPod things. New trainers every week. We have grandchildren, and they don't get anything like that. It doesn't make them any less happy. And they'll grow up knowing the value of money. The Barrons' kids are just ruined.'

'Was it generally believed that the Barrons had valuable items in the house?'

'Obviously. The builders knew it, the neighbours knew it, anyone coming to the house knew. They never tried to make any secret of how rich they were. Far from it. She told me once how much the taps in their bathroom had cost. It was enough to buy me a new car.'

'I wasn't really thinking of bath taps. Antiques, maybe. Or a lot of cash in the house?'

54

Gamble looked at Cooper thoughtfully, giving him his full attention for the first time.

'Well, if you're asking me, I'd say yes. People like that don't make their money by paying income tax, do they? I wouldn't be surprised to find a cupboard stuffed with cash. And I bet they wouldn't keep quiet about it, either.'

'What about the Barrons' neighbours?'

'Well, you've got the Hollands on one side, at Fourways. They're mostly harmless. Spend their time walking and picking flowers, or some such. There's the Kaye bloke at Moorside. He arrived in the village like the Queen visiting the natives. He's never spoken to me yet, the stuck-up bugger. I never got inside the gate either.'

'Interesting. And the Chadwicks? They're nearest to you, but you haven't mentioned them yet.'

Gamble's lips tightened. For once, he seemed to be reluctant to answer.

'Mr Chadwick is a teacher, I believe.'

Still Gamble was silent. His expression suggested that he was searching his memory for something to say. Something that would give the right impression, perhaps. Finally Mrs Gamble offered some information.

'The Chadwicks are having a party tomorrow night,' she said. 'Their daughter has just got her A level results.'

'A stars,' burst out Gamble. 'She was screeching about it to her friends on her mobile phone all day long. A stars. They all get A stars these days. It doesn't mean a thing. In my day, you were lucky to get a few O levels.'

'Well, perhaps not everyone . . .'

'The bloody Chadwicks think their child is an intellectual and artistic miracle, of course. Gifted at everything. A genius, but perfectly normal at the same time.'

'And Mr Edson at Riddings Lodge?'

'Oh, the lottery winner. We don't see much of him.'

'Lottery winner?'

'So they say. Won millions on the rollover, he did. Bought Riddings Lodge and some place in Tuscany. Took on a housekeeper and moved his mother in to live a life of luxury. You see him swanning about in a brand-new Jag, or sometimes a vintage MG in the summer.'

'Oh, I think I might have met him.'

'Lucky you.'

Cooper thought of the man who had stopped his car in the village earlier to offer a piece of his mind.

'It's about time I had a word with him, I think. On his own territory.'

Gamble was wearing brown corduroy trousers that were getting rather baggy at the knees. When he stepped outside to follow Cooper to the gate, he pulled on a dark grey fleece over his faded checked shirt.

At the gate, he gazed up and down the street, his protruding ears almost flapping, the beads on his cowboy hat rattling quietly. He was like a Native American scout, scenting buffalo.

Cooper moved closer to Gamble. He noticed that the sleeves of his fleece were covered with small burrs and thorns that had snagged in the wool. He thought of suggesting that a woollen fleece wasn't the best garment to wear when squeezing through hedges or climbing fences. But he decided against it.

Cooper drove the Toyota up the hill and turned up the small lane that ran past the back of Fourways. He was immediately faced with 'Private Road' signs and warnings that there was no public right of way. He slowed the car almost to a crawl as he reached a blind bend between high hedges. You wouldn't want to meet something coming the other way.

At the end, a driveway went off to the left towards Lane End. On his right, he was facing a set of gates.

These gates weren't just black wrought iron like the others he'd seen. They were decorated with gold highlights, and had gilt finials and scrollwork. It was as if they had pretensions to be the entrance to Buckingham Palace. They exuded an air of having gone one better than their neighbours. There would have been no doubt in Cooper's mind who lived behind them, even if the name of the house hadn't been prominently displayed. Riddings Lodge.

Cooper pressed a button on the entry phone and waited for an answer.

'Yes?'

'Police, sir. Detective Sergeant Cooper, Edendale CID.'

'Do you have identification?'

'Yes, of course. But—'

'There's a camera.'

'Okay, I see it.'

Cooper held his warrant card up towards the lens of a camera mounted so that it was pointing directly at the area in front of the gates. After a moment, he heard the click and hum of the gates beginning to open.

'All right.'

The voice didn't sound very welcoming. But not many people managed to give a good impression through the speaker on an entry phone.

Cooper drove on to a vast paved area around a central water feature, with a fountain and stone cherubs. It was like driving into a Roman piazza. Well, a Roman piazza with imitation Victorian gas lamps. When he saw the house, at first it looked modern. Everything shiny and new, like an illustration from a high-end property brochure. He was thinking of an upmarket country hotel. Then he noticed that it featured several decorative arched leaded windows, as if the owner had changed his mind and decided to live in a bishop's palace instead.

Although he couldn't see the extent of the grounds, he sensed that they must be enormous. All he could make out from the piazza was a large monkey puzzle tree, its shape suggesting a mature specimen, with deep green leaves forming dense clusters at the top. A male tree, judging by the cones.

He was greeted at the door of the house by a woman in an apron, who introduced herself as the housekeeper. She led him into a hallway, watched him carefully as he wiped his feet, then escorted him across an expanse of carpet so soft and springy that he felt as though he was walking on a trampoline.

57

A good jump and bounce, and his head would almost touch that crystal chandelier.

He entered a room filled with a confusingly diverse range of furniture and ornaments. Porcelain vases, a brass barometer, a large tapestry showing figures against a background of stylised foliage and towers. There were so many items he felt as though he'd just walked into an antiques shop.

The man he'd seen in the metallic blue Jaguar XF was sitting at a large round glass table. His image was reflected perfectly in its surface, as if he was looking out over a pool of clear, still water. Iron-grey hair swept back, a sardonic eyebrow, a loud and commanding tone of voice.

'Russell Edson. This is my mother, Glenys.'

Edson didn't bother getting up, didn't offer to shake hands. The gesture towards the plump lady with the blue rinse was fairly perfunctory too. He seemed supremely confident about who was important in this room, and who wasn't. So far, he was only counting himself in the first category.

'I'm sorry to trouble you, Mr Edson.'

'Well, I hope you have some news, Sergeant. Made a quick arrest, have you? No, I suppose that would be too much to hope for from our local constabulary.'

'It's early days yet, sir,' said Cooper, falling back on a stock phrase to cover what he would really have liked to say.

'Early days? Of course, I expect you like to take your time. Judging from the speed that things happen around here, we'll all be in our graves by the time you crack the case.'

Cooper recalled the number plate of the Jag that Edson had been driving – RSE1. He could think of a few possibilities for what 'S' stood for. He could hear Gavin Murfin's voice in his head. *Russell Soddin' Edson.*

'I just need to know if you saw or heard anything out of the ordinary last night, sir,' he said.

'Well, I suppose you've talked to the old man of the woods? He can't be hard to find, at least. You only need to follow the smell.'

'Who?'

'Gamble, for heaven's sake. Barry Gamble.'

'Oh, Mr Gamble, yes.'

'I mean, he was the only person who saw anything, so far as I'm aware. Not that he would be my idea of a reliable witness. But I suppose you have to make do with what you can get. There's a definite shortage of evidence, from what I hear. The police are baffled, and all that.'

Edson snorted loudly, and Cooper realised he was laughing.

'How do you know about Mr Gamble being a witness, sir?'

'Well, if there was going to be a witness, it would be him, wouldn't it? It's rather stating the obvious. Besides, he was here.'

'Here? At your house? When?'

'Last night, of course. The idiot came running up our drive and banged on the window. He frightened the life out of my mother, I can tell you. She can do without shocks like that at her age. So I went out to see what was going on, planning to give him a piece of my mind, and he was standing there on the drive, with the security lights on him, gibbering about Zoe Barron being injured. When I finally got a proper story out of him, I offered him the use of my mobile phone to dial 999. But it turned out the old fool had his own phone with him all the time.'

Cooper glanced at Glenys Edson. She hadn't spoken, but had stared at him so fixedly throughout his visit that she was starting to make him feel uneasy. When he looked more closely, he could see that she was heavily made up, and probably well over seventy. Perhaps she was afraid to speak in case the make-up cracked. Or perhaps she had tried to conceal her age with Botox treatment, and couldn't move her face anyway.

'So Mr Gamble ran to your house first,' said Cooper, 'before he called the police or an ambulance?'

'Yes,' said Edson.

'Why would he do that?'

Edson shrugged. 'Why do people do anything? In *his* case, I'd suggest insanity.'

'I don't think he mentioned that he came here – either to me, or to the officers who took his initial statement.'

'Well, Sergeant,' said Edson. 'If you're going to spend much time in Riddings, you'll find that people never tell you more than they think you need to know.'

'Really?'

'Yes, really.'

Edson seemed to look at him properly for the first time, perhaps detecting something in his tone of voice.

'I'm sorry, would you like a drink?' he said. 'My house-keeper will—'

'No thank you, sir. I have some more visits to make.'

Cooper could have drunk a coffee right now. But he would have been afraid to put his cup down on that glass table. It must take someone hours to polish it to such an immaculate shine, without a streak or a smear. Even with a coaster, the danger of spilling just a drop of liquid on the table was too great. It would be like splashing acid on the *Mona Lisa* and expecting da Vinci to paint it all over again tomorrow.

'In that case, if I can't help you any further . . .'

'Do you have many staff at Riddings Lodge, sir?'

'The housekeeper, Mrs Davis, and a girl who helps her in the kitchen. A couple of cleaners. And an odd-job man I get in to maintain the property – there's quite a lot of work, as you can imagine. Why do you ask?'

'We'll need to speak to them too.'

'I'll make sure they're available.'

Cooper gazed out of the window of the lounge. He was looking at a vast expanse of garden, sloping lawns leading down to a pond so large that it might have been described as a lake. The monkey puzzle tree stood in a prominent position, dominating the foreground.

'The tree is splendid,' he said.

'Do you like it?' asked Edson. 'There are male and female trees, I'm told. You need both sexes for the seeds to be fertile, but there isn't another one of this species for miles.'

Beyond the tree, a long bank of rhododendrons formed a

backdrop and blocked out any sign of the neighbouring properties. To Cooper's eye, the flower beds on either side looked regimented and weed-free.

'Are you a keen gardener, sir?' he said.

'No, of course not,' said Edson. 'I get a man in to do that, too.'

6

Gavin Murfin was humming to himself when Cooper met him on the corner of Curbar Lane and The Green. When he got closer, he recognised the tune. *Neighbours. Everybody needs good neighbours.*

'You're not going to sing, are you, Gavin?' he said.

'Not in this life.'

'Thank heavens for that.'

'Right,' said Murfin, settling down on the horse trough with his notebook. 'I thought you might like to share my insights, honed to perfection over many years as an experienced detective.'

'Who have you talked to?'

'I've been on the back lane there, behind Valley View.'

'Croft Lane.'

'There's no street sign, but if you say that's the name . . .'

'It's a private road, I think. But that's how it's known locally.'

'Okay, Croft Lane. I spoke to Mrs Slattery at South Croft. She's the widow of a local GP, Doctor Slattery, and she lives alone now, though there seems to be a son in the background. Then there's Mr and Mrs Nowak at Lane End. I got nothing from either of them. They can barely see the Barrons' property from their houses, you know.'

'No. Too many trees, too many walls, too much distance.'

'The women were nice,' said Murfin. 'Very helpful. Or at

least, they seemed to want to help, and were sorry they didn't know anything.'

'But . . .?'

'Mr Nowak. Not the helpful type. If I was a cynical person, I'd say he was quite pleased about what had happened to the Barrons.'

'You *are* a cynical person, Gavin.'

'But I'm usually right, all the same.'

'So you think he has some grudge against the Barron family?'

'If he does, he wasn't telling. You might want to check him out for yourself. Get a less cynical view, like.'

'I will, Gavin.'

'He's Polish, by the way. In his origins, at least.'

Murfin turned a page. 'You did Riddings Lodge yourself, didn't you?'

'Yes, the Edsons.'

'I get the impression nobody likes the Edsons very much. Nothing was said out loud, like, but my nose was twitching like mad.'

'I know what you mean.'

'Luke and Becky are still wearing out the shoe leather. I made them go up the hill.'

'Of course you did.'

'It's the privilege of my great age.'

Cooper watched a couple of cars go slowly through the village. A huge four by four, a sporty Mercedes.

'So what do you make of the people round here, Gavin?' he asked.

'Everyone's so middle class,' said Murfin. 'They've got middle-class houses, middle-class kids and middle-class attitudes. Even their dogs are middle class. I thought the poodle at Hill Croft was going to ask me where I went to school.'

Cooper tried hard to stifle a laugh. He shouldn't encourage Murfin. He was a bad example to the youngsters.

'Wait a minute. Are you eating, Gavin?'

'No.'

Cooper glanced at him; his mouth was still, though his eyes were bulging slightly with the effort not to chew.

'It's only a chocolate truffle.'

'I hope you weren't eating while you were doing interviews.'

'I might have been.'

'Gavin, show a bit of respect.'

'They don't mind. But if they ask, I'll tell them it's organic Fairtrade chocolate from Waitrose.'

Cooper sighed as he looked round Riddings. The Union Jacks fluttered, a dog barked, the hens in the orchard clucked quietly. A trio of horses clopped down the hill to their stables. The smell of manure drifted on the breeze again.

'There's still a lot to do,' he said. 'So many doors we haven't knocked on, for a start. Even in a village this size.'

'I can't do overtime tonight,' said Murfin. 'I've only just told Jean that I'm going to the football on Saturday, and I have to get home in time for the row.'

'Okay. Well, there's no money for overtime anyway. It just means more for us to do tomorrow, and the day after.'

Murfin offered him a chocolate.

'No thanks.'

'Suit yourself. So what about you, Ben? Are you doing anything tonight?'

Cooper hesitated. 'Nothing special.'

Murfin gave him a sceptical look. 'You're lying.'

'What?'

'Years of experience have honed my skills of detection. I can sense when someone is telling me a porky. Especially you. You're as transparent as my new double-glazing.'

'Yeah, yeah.'

'So . . . how are things going with that nice dark-haired little SOCO?'

'She's a crime-scene examiner.'

'Civilian all the same,' sniffed Murfin.

'Her name's Liz. And things are fine.'

'I like her, actually. I think you've made a good bargain there. Better than I ever did.'

'One of these days I'm going to tell Jean what you say about her.'

'I'll let you know when I'm feeling suicidal.'

Below Riddings lay the theological college and the hamlet of Stanton Ford, where the Baslow road skirted the banks of the Derwent.

Cooper saw a car with a window sticker: *Christ for all – all for Christ.* A student or member of staff from the bible college at Curbar? He could just see the buildings from here, where students would be wrestling with their bibles right now.

Or would they? The college ran residential courses, he was fairly sure. They took students from all over the world, trainee evangelists from Africa and South America. But most institutions were on holiday in August. Students went home for the summer, or did vacation work to raise money. Was Cliff College closed this month, or did they run summer courses?

'When does their term start down there?'

'I don't know, but we can find out.'

Cooper nodded. *'There is a God in Heaven that revealeth all secrets.* Who said that, Gavin?'

'It's in the Bible, isn't it? It sounds biblical anyway.'

'Yes, but who said it?'

'I don't know. Matthew, or Mark. Or Malcolm. One of those.'

'Oh, of course – the Gospel according to St Malcolm. I know it well.'

'Well . . . right. Last time I went to church, it was all in Latin.'

On the road below Curbar Gap, there were three stones close to the roadside, with biblical references carved on them. Visitors often parked with their car wheels right up to the stones without even noticing them. He'd heard it claimed that zealous students at Cliff College had made the inscriptions at some time. In another version of the story, they were carved in the nineteenth century by a mole-catcher who worked for the old duke. He was said to have been a devout Wesleyan, and inscribed the biblical quotations as a thanksgiving for recovering from a serious illness.

On his way down the road, Cooper pulled over on to the

verge and looked at the nearest stone. He must have remembered the story wrong. He'd thought there was actually a quotation carved on the stone, and had even hoped it might have sent him some useful message. But all it said was: *Isaiah 1:18*. That meant he would have to find someone with a Bible.

Another woman was passing with her dog, this time an arthritic black Labrador. She stopped and stared at them for a moment, then seemed to lose some kind of internal battle.

'I don't mean any disrespect,' she called. 'But the police need to get a grip.'

Cooper sighed as she stamped away.

'Thank you.'

Back at Valley View, Cooper skirted the crime-scene examiner's tent and walked round the back of the house. He wanted to get an idea of the layout on this side of the property.

When he reached the back garden, he realised how easy it was to be distracted by the edge. It was a great looming presence that cut off the light from the east. Its high rock faces dwarfed everything nearer to hand, made the trees look smaller, the fences less solid. The distance from here to the edge was compressed, a trick of perspective caused by the sheer difference in scale.

He felt a cold shudder. His mother would have described that feeling as *like someone walking over your grave*. As a saying, it had never made much sense to Cooper. For someone to walk over your grave, you would have to be dead. So it could only be said by a ghost. And ghosts didn't shudder with cold. On the contrary, that was supposed to be the effect they had on the living. So it was another of those baffling aphorisms with which his life seemed to be filled when he was growing up. They were passed on as mystical wisdom, but they were meaningless when you stopped to think about them even for a moment.

He turned and studied the garden. The intruders must have come this way. They had surely entered from the back, from the direction of the edge, rather than approaching through the village.

He bent to inspect the lawn. The grass was cut too short to show any sign of footprints. In fact, it was very neatly trimmed. He made a note to find out who mowed the lawns, whether Jake Barron preferred to do it himself, or if one of those gardening contractors was employed here. And if so, when they had tended to the garden last.

As he crouched in the garden, Cooper noticed something strange. It stood out on the perfectly trimmed grass. It was only a fragment of stone. But if it had lain here for long, it would have been thrown up by the mower.

He worked his way carefully across the lawn to the drive. There was another bit of stone, and another. A small trail of them, leading from the back fence towards the house. It was as if the Devil's Edge itself had been here, and left its tracks behind. Only small chips and splinters, a mere scattering of gritstone dust. But it seemed out of place amid the neatness of the trimmed grass and swept gravel.

Cooper looked up. The edge looked much the same. Ragged and broken, split into cracks and fissures, still dotted with the figures of climbers drawn to their favourite playground. He assumed that it looked the same from one day to the next, but it was impossible to be sure.

He shook himself, trying to shrug off the feeling that something had passed through the garden even as he stood there. A presence both invisible and cold. Like someone walking over his grave.

Last night, the Barrons had met everyone's worst nightmare, the fiends who invaded their home and destroyed their lives. No wonder these offenders were being referred to as the Savages. They seemed to come from outside civilised society, and were ruthless in their use of violence. No home was safe any more.

Cooper bagged the fragments of gravel and began to walk back towards the house, unsettled by the same dread that everyone had, the fear of never being safe in your own home.

At the gate, he stopped and looked up at the edge again. This time he saw it not as a playground for rock climbers, but as the battered wall of a stone fortress. The Devil's Edge had the air of a battlement that had withstood centuries of siege. Cracked and broken, but still standing firm, holding the invaders at bay. Or was it?

That afternoon, after the working-group session had ended, Fry had to make her way through the northern outskirts of Nottingham to reach the M1. Then it was three junctions north up the motorway before heading across Derbyshire via Chesterfield. It was the most direct route, and she preferred driving through the town. The only alternative was a tortuous crawl through country lanes, which was fine if you enjoyed scenery.

It was the sense of dislocation that was bothering her. One minute she'd been in inner-city Birmingham, confronting violence and dealing with gang members, recalling all too vividly her time with West Midlands Police, in the days before she transferred to yokel land. Then suddenly she'd been back here, in the midst of the rural idyll, bird shit on her car and straw sticking to her shoes. And not only that, but sidelined too. Somehow she'd found herself in this horrendous limbo, a world of business speak, living in sheer torture. What had she ever done to deserve this?

At least she had learned a few figures to use. Sixteen thousand officers and police staff were employed across the East Midlands region, serving over five and a half million people in an area of sixteen thousand square kilometres, half the size of Belgium. She had no concept of how big Belgium was, but it made a change from measuring size in comparison to Wales or a football pitch, which also meant nothing to her. Statistics were good. They had a nice, clean feel, free of the messy ambiguities and uncertainties that came with the package when you were dealing with human beings. If you trotted statistics out at the right moment, they impressed people. And they were grateful, because you gave them something they could write down and memorise. It allowed them to convince themselves that they hadn't just wasted the last two hours of their life. Just as Fry was trying to convince herself now, in fact.

During the course of the day, someone had also claimed that the population of the East Midlands region was growing thirty-three per cent faster than elsewhere in England. That 'elsewhere' had worried her. It didn't seem to mean anything. It wasn't the same as 'thirty-three per cent faster than anywhere else in England'. That would be more specific, a claim that could be checked against the official figures. But 'elsewhere'? Where was that, for heaven's sake? Elsewhere was nowhere. Elsewhere might be some place, but it was nowhere definite. So the region was growing faster than the Isles of Scilly, maybe? Or the Outer Hebrides?

It was a vagueness that bothered her as she drove back towards Derbyshire, crossing the M1 junction at Heath. She couldn't make use of a fuzzy claim like that. She would be challenged on it immediately. Now she was starting to feel cheated. Who had perpetrated that fraud? Which member of the Implementing Strategic Change working group? She had the urge to go back and grab whoever it was by the lapels and make them justify the statement. By the lapels? Yes, she was sure it must have been a man. A man wearing a suit and a brightly coloured tie. Tomorrow she would identify them and sort them out.

Her heart sank at the thought. Tomorrow. Another day of brown-paper workshop. And it was still only the middle of the week.

Next week she had to organise a Challenge Day to examine the various options. Damn it, she could hear the comments now. She could imagine the derision that would be flying around the CID room in Edendale, feel the buckets of scorn dripping on her head as she invited her former colleagues to her Challenge Day. Gavin Murfin would laugh so much he'd choke on a pork pie or have a heart attack.

Fry stared ahead at the approaching Derbyshire signs. How

on earth had she got herself into this mess? Her dreams and ambitions in the police service had never involved becoming mired in jargon, or trapped in working-group meetings. Right now, she felt as though her career was already in its grave and being buried under an avalanche of consultation documents.

By the end of the day, a mantra had been drummed into her. *Joint thinking, joint working.* It echoed around her skull right now, as she drove towards Derbyshire.

Of all the phrases she might want in her head, that wasn't the one. During her time in E division, there were so many things that hadn't been said, relationships left unexplained. She wondered if anyone would bother about her, now that she'd been sidelined. Or would they just forget her as quickly as they could, let someone slip in and replace her quietly and completely, as if she'd never been there?

If only she knew what they really thought of her. If only once someone in Edendale had said: *We'll be sorry to see you go.*

7

Things were changing at Bridge End Farm. Well, that was nothing new. The farming industry had been in a state of change for decades. But now the pace was speeding up so much that it had become a revolution, instead of evolution.

Dairy farmers like Matt Cooper were leaving the industry every week. It had become inevitable, ever since supermarkets reduced the price per litre of milk to the same as the cost of producing it. It had become impossible to make a living from milk production. Instead of the UK being self-sufficient, a large percentage of milk supplies were imported from Denmark or the Netherlands. Presumably those were countries where the market still allowed dairy farmers to earn a livelihood.

Bridge End Farm stood five miles out of Edendale, in a stretch of the Eden Valley where the land was good. The farm was reached down a rough, winding track that was dry and dusty in the summer, full of potholes that had been hastily repaired with compacted earth and the odd half-brick. When winter came, the first heavy rains would turn the track into a river, washing mud into the farmyard as water came rushing down the hillsides in torrents.

But now, in August, the tyres of Cooper's Toyota threw up clouds of dust as he bounced the last few yards and rattled over a cattle grid into the yard.

The yard was still wet, where Matt had hosed away the

freshly dropped cow manure left by the herd on their way back to pasture after afternoon milking. Ben had noticed that he wasn't quite so particular as he used to be about cleaning up. Sometimes he even left the job until morning if he was called away to do something else.

But tonight there were visitors. Kate would never have let her husband get away with leaving the yard dirty. She knew that Ben was bringing Liz. There were a lot of things that Kate knew, without anyone having to tell her. Ben always went to his sister-in-law if he wanted to know anything. And he was fairly sure that his nieces, Amy and Josie, were growing up just like their mum. Wise beyond their years, those girls. They missed nothing.

He parked close to the farmhouse, opposite the Dutch barn and the tractor shed where Matt's latest John Deere stood. An old grey Fergie used to live in the shed, too – Matt's pride and joy, the object he had lavished more time and attention on than he did Kate. But the Ferguson had gone the way of so many things. It was too much of a luxury. The cost of its restoration just couldn't be justified in the farm accounts.

Matt could often be found tinkering with a bit of machinery at this time of the evening, but there was no sign of him outside. Ben felt sure he would have been cajoled into getting cleaned up for the evening and changing his clothes, and would now be waiting uncomfortably in the sitting room, itching to get his boots and cap back on, but too obedient to Kate's wishes to rebel.

Of course, he wouldn't have done it if it was just his brother arriving at the farm for dinner. But Liz was treated almost like visiting royalty. It always made Ben smile, yet feel the tug of grief and sadness at the same time. This was just the way his mother would have welcomed her, if she'd still been alive. But she hadn't lived to see this moment.

As always, the big farmhouse kitchen smelled of cooking. Tonight he scented herbs and garlic, and the aroma of meat roasting in the oven of the range.

Matt was starting to look tired and middle-aged. Ben worried about the amount of stress his brother was coping with.

'Well, I could have done without the extra work today,' said Matt. 'I mean, it's harvest time. I'm out in the fields all hours as it is.'

'Problem?'

'Some bloody ramblers climbed the wall in the bottom field and knocked the coping stones down. They couldn't be bothered walking down to the stile, I suppose. It's all of a hundred yards away, after all. Ridiculous. They think open access means they can do whatever damage they like, and poor sods like me will go round after them picking up the pieces. If I'd caught them at it . . .'

He trailed off. It was a habit he had got into recently, and came with a sly sideways glance at his younger brother, a look that suggested he was afraid of saying too much. Ben was beginning to hate that look. It seemed to suggest more loudly than any words that his brother didn't really trust him.

'Didn't you say that section of wall needed repairing anyway?' he asked.

'That has nothing to do with it.'

Ben raised a placatory hand. 'Okay, okay.'

At one time, he would have spent a rest day helping to repair the walls at Bridge End. It was one of the jobs he could help Matt with around the place. But since he'd moved out of the farm and into his flat in Edendale, that habit had lapsed, just slipped out of his life without him really noticing.

Perhaps Matt had noticed, though. He hadn't said anything about it, of course. They'd never said much to each other, had never really needed that form of communication, not since they were boys growing up at Bridge End together. They had come to understand each other without the necessity of words. A look was enough, a touch, or a shrug of the shoulder. So what had Matt understood from the fact that his brother no longer showed any interest in the farm?

Matt's thoughts had been diverted, though. He started off on a long rant about the cost of everything these days. Fuel, feed, fertiliser . . .

But Kate wasn't so easily distracted.

'Ben, it's good to see you both. But I've a feeling there's some particular reason you've called.'

He and Liz glanced at each other. She gave him a small nod, and squeezed his hand encouragingly.

'We're getting engaged. We're going to be married.'

'Well, I thought you were never going to announce it. You've taken your time,' said Kate. 'Congratulations.'

'Thank you.'

She jumped up, kissed Ben and then Liz.

'Matt . . .?'

'Oh, yes. Congratulations.'

'Of course, I'd like you to be best man, Matt.'

Matt's mouth was hanging open, like a bull calf shot through the head with a captive bolt pistol. That stunned second before the legs gave way. But surely the possibility must have crossed his mind at some time?

'He'll be delighted,' said Kate, trying to cover the silence. 'I told him ages ago that you'd ask him. But I don't think he believed me.'

'When will it be?' asked Matt. 'Not in September?'

'Matt, it couldn't possibly be so soon.'

'Or November?'

'No, of course not. Look, I know what you're saying . . .'

'It'll be next summer, probably,' said Liz.

Ben turned to her. 'Will it?'

'Well, no one wants a winter wedding. It's too cold to do the photographs outside. And it always rains.'

'It rains in July and August too,' said Matt. 'Chucks it down, just when we're getting ready for harvest. You can't rely on the summer.'

'No, I suppose not.'

'And is it . . .?' began Matt.

'Yes? What?'

'Not a church wedding,' said Liz. 'We've decided it will be in a nice hotel somewhere. There are so many places that do civil weddings now, and it means we can have the reception at the same venue, so there's no running around.'

Ben nodded. He couldn't remember deciding that, but it sounded like a good idea.

'I meant, what we will all be wearing?'

Now Ben laughed. That was typical of his brother. He was mostly worried about having to get out of his cap and overalls and put on a suit and tie.

'Top hat and tails, of course,' he said. 'We've got to do it properly.'

'Oh, shit.'

And then Ben noticed that Liz and Kate weren't laughing, but nodding vigorously.

'Absolutely,' said Liz. 'The full works.'

After dinner, Ben excused himself and left the dining room to go to the bathroom. On his way back, he stopped, reluctant to rejoin the noise.

The passage that ran through the centre of the house had once been a gloomy place. In his childhood, the woodwork had been covered in dark brown varnish, the floorboards painted black on either side of narrow strips of carpet that ran down the passage and up the stairs. That carpet had long since lost any trace of pattern under the dirt trampled into the house by humans and animals alike. But now, this part of the house was almost unrecognisable. Kate's influence had brought light and colour into the farmhouse, with fitted carpets and woodwork stripped to its original golden pine. Mirrors caught and emphasised the light, creating illusions of movement and life in the passage.

Almost unrecognisable – but not quite. Ben paused at the bottom of the stairs, seizing the chance of a quiet moment on his own away from the family. Even though the house was so changed, there were certain spots where the memories were too strong to be erased by paint and fabric. Here, at the bottom of the stairs, was one of those places. When he stood here and looked up towards the bedroom doors, he knew he would see his mother. He would hear the swish of her dress and the scuff of her slippers as she moved across the landing. She was always there, even now. There in his imagination, at least.

One day, he hoped he might stand here at the foot of the stairs and see his mother coming towards him, instead of always moving away.

He wanted to talk to her, but was too conscious of the crowd in the sitting room to speak out loud. Instead he found himself just giving a little nod towards the landing. She would understand.

In Riddings, the Chadwicks were watching their daughter Bryony getting ready to go out. They knew there was no point asking her what time she'd be back. She would never tell them, always said she didn't know, because it depended how good a time she was having that night. She had her own key and she knew how to operate the burglar alarm, so they could go to bed if she came in late. But both of the Chadwicks were aware, without mentioning it to each other, that there would be no sleep for them tonight. They would lie awake worrying about Bryony, and who she might be spending time with. They had a feeling she'd fallen into bad company, and was developing a relationship with quite the wrong sort of person. They had always dreaded the phone call in the middle of the night.

Russell Edson and his mother sat down to dinner in silence, just the two of them in the huge dining room, surrounded by antiques Russell had collected, random items he'd picked up whenever they took his fancy. A pair of Royal Worcester porcelain vases, a William IV brass barometer, an Aubusson tapestry. They didn't give him the same satisfaction as the old cars, particularly the MG. People didn't see his antiques. That was because they didn't get many visitors any more at Riddings Lodge. He and his mother had held parties at one time, when they first moved to the village. They put on champagne receptions out on the lawn in the summer, elegant suppers here in the dining room in the winter. But he'd gradually lost touch with his old friends in Sheffield, and the neighbours no longer replied to his invitations. Snobs, all of them.

Martin and Sarah Holland were walking up through the village towards the edge. They, too, were silent, holding hands until the slope became too difficult or they had to use their torches to light the way. At the top, they stopped to get their breath, and looked down at the village. They searched automatically for the lights of their own house on Curbar Lane. Strange that they should feel so much safer out here, on the edge in the dark, than down there in their own home. There was an advantage to being in the dark. No one knew that better than the Hollands. Fourways was right next door to Valley View, and violence had come too close to their lives.

Across the lane, Vanessa Slattery had made up a bed in one of the spare rooms for her son. He'd insisted on staying overnight, saying that he was concerned about her being in the house at South Croft on her own. And it was true, it did help a bit. But what about tomorrow, and the day after? Alan had his job to go to, and she couldn't expect too much of his time. She watched him patrolling the garden, putting on all the outside lights and checking every door and window before he locked the house up for the night. She was slightly troubled by the fact that he seemed to be enjoying this so much. She'd always known he had an aggressive streak, and it didn't take much to bring it out. And he was likely to be far too free in what he said, even to the police, if they asked him questions about the Barrons.

Richard Nowak had drunk too much, and he intended to drink more yet before the night was over. Not vodka – he hated the stuff – but good single malt Scotch whisky. He had his own miniature bar at Lane End, and he made sure it was always well stocked. Alcohol was the only thing that helped him deal with the stress. And these people certainly made him feel stressed. God knew, he needed to unwind. His father Adam had already gone to bed, and Sonya was on the phone to one of her friends. She'd been on the phone all evening, and most of the day. Talking about him, no doubt. Complaining how awful her life was, hoping that one of her friends would give her the right advice. Of course, there was another day to face tomorrow. And who knew what might happen then?

Behind number 4 Chapel Close, Barry Gamble was in his shed. He felt he ought to be out and about in the village, but he knew Monica was keeping an eye out from the sitting room. She'd drawn the curtains back so that she could see the door of the shed, and she was sitting with her armchair turned towards the window. She didn't trust him, that much was obvious. But all he ever intended was to make sure everyone was safe and behaving in a civilised manner. He thought of himself as the guardian of Riddings. The police were useless, after all. If anything was going on that shouldn't be, he was the one who would know. But he was wasting his time trapped in his shed. All he could do was check through his collection, pausing for a moment at one particular item.

Another person was up and about in Riddings. If Barry Gamble hadn't been stuck in his shed, he might well have seen the figure creeping cautiously along the edge of Curbar Lane, ducking behind a tree when the lights of a car went by. He might have seen the person, but he wouldn't have experienced any feeling of recognition. As far as most of Riddings was concerned, this was a total stranger.

Diane Fry had stopped at the services on the M1 at Tibshelf. A TV was on in the restaurant, a news bulletin with some story about a murder. She heard a mention of Derbyshire, and found herself glued to the screen.

As she watched the item, her coffee grew cold on the table. Behind the reporter on the screen she could see blue crime-scene tape. And beyond that, crime-scene examiners whom she recognised, officers she'd worked with often.

Oh my God. What a time to be sitting on the sidelines.

8

Thursday

The CID room at Edendale was full this morning. As full as it ever was, anyway. Ben Cooper looked around the room, and smiled. The team had a more settled look than it had done for a long time. It was strange to be thinking that, with everything else that was going on at the moment – the cost-cutting and uncertainties, the feeling of walking on a tightrope day by day, not knowing whether your job would still exist next month, or even the division you worked in. But it was true. Somehow, a shadow had been lifted.

Cooper was particularly pleased with the two youngsters, Luke Irvine and Becky Hurst, who were settled in and doing well. A steady lad, Irvine. He reminded Cooper a bit of himself when he was a few years younger. Fair enough, Irvine wasn't Derbyshire through and through. He came from a Yorkshire mining family, with Scottish blood a generation or two back. But he would do, as they said round here.

Dependable as Irvine might be, it was Becky Hurst who was proving to be the best of the new recruits to Edendale CID. She was like a little terrier, keeping at a task until she produced a result, no matter what the assignment. She seemed to have no ego problems, no reluctance about doing the less glamorous jobs. That was a drawback with some of the more ambitious young officers, the ones who thought they were too good for the routine stuff, but not Hurst. Cooper had to check himself sometimes, to make sure he was resisting the temptation to let Becky do all the legwork. She deserved better than that.

This was what his mother had dreamed of for him, the promotion to sergeant. For her, it had been the culmination of an ambition. Her son had achieved the same rank as his father. Young Ben had finally come up to the standard set by Sergeant Joe Cooper, the great local hero. He remembered the moment he'd lied to her as she lay in her hospital bed. He'd told her he'd been promoted, when in fact he had just learnt that he'd lost out to the newcomer, Diane Fry. One of the most difficult moments of his life, the decision to tell his mother what she so much wanted to hear, instead of the truth.

And now the promotion had finally come, it was too late. Isabel Cooper had died before her hopes could be realised. He couldn't go home and tell her the news. The lie he had told would have to stay a lie. Too late. They were the saddest two words in the English language.

More bodies trickled in as the time for the morning briefing approached. There wasn't a room anywhere in the building that had enough chairs, so officers would be perched on desks, leaning against walls. It looked a bit chaotic, but somehow it added an air of activity and urgency. It was as if they were all too busy to sit down, but had just paused for a moment, eager to get on with their important tasks.

The E Division headquarters were said to have won an architectural design award once. But that was back in the 1950s, practically beyond living memory. The building in West Street was ageing badly now, with a constant need for maintenance, an inefficient heating system, and water coming through the flat roofs in the winter. No amount of redecoration could take away the institutional feel of the corridors on the upper floors. A lot of money would have to be spent on providing a new headquarters building – money that just wasn't available now, of course.

Last year, the loss of A Division in a cost-cutting restructure had really thrown a spanner in the works and focused the minds of the management team. The territory that had once formed a separate Basic Command Unit in the south-east of the county had now been divided up between C and D Divisions. Who knew how long E Division would last, when it had started to look so alphabetically surplus to requirements?

Detective Superintendent Hazel Branagh was Senior Investigating Officer on the Riddings murder. A major inquiry was anticipated. That was because there were no obvious suspects, and no apparent leads that might produce one in a short time frame. A HOLMES incident room was being activated next door right now, the technicians and HOLMES operators arriving to set up the system. From now on, the pattern of the operation would be governed step by step as laid down in the protocols for the Home Office's Large Major Enquiry System. A collator would arrive from headquarters, and a specialist DS to task teams of detectives.

Besides, the division was already facing a constant barrage of criticism, and everyone was aware of it.

'These villages are quiet, peaceful communities,' said Branagh, opening the morning's briefing. 'We can't allow violent incidents like these to make people living in this area feel unsafe. It's our job to keep them safe, and to make sure they *feel* safe. One way we're going to do that is with a visible police presence. Our uniformed colleagues will ensure there are patrol cars, and officers on the street.'

It was funny, reflected Cooper, how a visible police presence seemed to be the answer to so many issues. Were the public really so reassured by the sight of a uniform, even when the officer inside clearly wasn't catching any criminals? Well, that seemed to be the current wisdom. He supposed detectives would be put back into uniform before too long. Plain clothes were contrary to the spirit of high-visibility policing, after all. He was rarely a visible police presence, until he pulled out his warrant card.

'There's a big confidence issue here, in more ways than one,'
Branagh was saying. 'You all know that we face upheavals,
and the possibility of some restructuring. So we have to demon-
strate that Derbyshire Constabulary are up to the job of dealing
with a major inquiry. In particular, we have to prove that we
here in E Division are as capable as anyone of policing our
own area. I don't have to spell that out for you any further.
I'm sure you all understand what's at stake. It could be your
entire future. All of our futures. I'm relying on you all to show
exactly what you can do.'

'No pressure, then,' whispered Murfin to Cooper. 'Should
be a doddle.'

'Shush, Gavin.'

'Oh, sorry, boss.'

Cooper wondered how many of the other officers in the
room were feeling the same excitement that he was. The older
hands, like Gavin Murfin, put on an air of world-weary resig-
nation, as if to suggest they'd seen it all before. Been there,
done that. Nothing new in the world for those who were
approaching their thirty. But he bet they still had that feeling
deep inside, that guilty thrill of a high-profile murder case.

'I don't care how secluded the houses on Curbar Lane are,'
said Branagh. 'The neighbours in the village must have seen
something. It's just not conceivable that our suspects could
have reconnoitred their target in advance, then come in and
gone out again – all without anyone seeing them or noticing
any suspicious activity, even a strange vehicle. We need to
canvass all the neighbours. And I mean all of them. It's not a
big village. We have the manpower available, and we're going
to get round every household, however long it takes. They're
not getting away from this one without leaving some traces.
A sighting. Something.'

'What about the neighbours we've already talked to, ma'am?'
asked Luke Irvine.

'We visit them again. Make them account for where they
were, and who they saw. We can piece this together bit by bit.
Even negative information could be useful.'

'Right.'

'And bear this in mind,' said Branagh grimly. 'The pattern of events suggests that they'll be back. Unless we bring this inquiry to a swift conclusion, we can expect the perpetrators to strike again. Where, we can't predict. When, it's impossible to say. One thing I'm sure of, though – time isn't on our side. So get your teams up to speed, pick up your tasks from the incident room, and let's get out there finding some leads.'

DI Hitchens took over and outlined the facts known so far. Zoe Barron had apparently been attacked by an intruder or intruders who had entered the house from the back door shortly after ten o'clock, when it had only been dark for an hour so. The door had been locked, but the deadbolts had not been closed, and none of the security alarms were active. The lock alone had not been strong enough to resist a determined assault.

'Mrs Barron was in the kitchen, so she encountered the suspects first. She was attacked with a heavy metal object, something like an iron pipe,' said Hitchens. 'She was struck with some force and suffered a fracture to the skull. So far as we can tell, there was no resistance from her, no scuffle or physical contact. Just the one blow, inflicted before she had time to react or escape. Preliminary post-mortem report shows that she died of head trauma from a blunt object.'

'So if they didn't make contact with her, there would be no traces for forensics,' said someone.

'Only one kind,' said Hitchens grimly. 'The suspect who struck the blow would almost certainly have Mrs Barron's blood on him. Or at least on his clothes.'

'How do we know there was more than one suspect?'

'We're making a reasonable assumption, based on the fate of the husband, Jake Barron.'

Photographs of both the Barrons were stuck on the white-board behind the DI.

'At the time of the attack, Mr Barron was in the sitting room, watching TV. He must have heard the noise made by the intruders entering the house. We assume that his wife screamed or called out. Yet he seems to have been struck down before he could move more than a few paces towards the kitchen. He hadn't even reached the door of the sitting room when he suffered a similar blow, again with a metal object.'

Cooper tried to imagine the scene inside Valley View, and the speed with which events must have happened. There was always that moment of shock, when the body and brain were frozen, and refused to respond. Fear drove all logical thought from the mind and paralysed the muscles.

A determined and ruthless assailant knew to take advantage of that. They would aim to get in quick and close down the resistance. It was only if you hesitated that things began to go wrong. Amateurs often messed things up at that point. They were reluctant to use violence except as a last resort, and tried to control the situation without it.

But these weren't amateurs. They had hit hard and fast, shown no mercy and no hesitation. They had given their victims no time to react or raise the alarm, no chance of offering the slightest resistance.

'The children,' said Hitchens. 'Obviously, once we were on the scene, one of our main concerns was for the children. The Barrons have a son and two daughters. The oldest, Melissa, is aged thirteen. At the time of the attack, they were all in their separate bedrooms upstairs. Valley View is a large property, and the bedrooms are in another part of the house, well away from the kitchen and sitting room where the assaults on their parents took place. One of the children told Social Services that it was quite normal for them to call their parents on their mobile phones rather than go downstairs to speak to them.'

A small, restless mutter went through the gathered officers, many of them parents themselves. They were constantly bombarded with advice on talking to their children, monitoring their activities, spending quality time together. Here was a family that seemed to spend its time in separate parts of the house, children isolated from their parents. There was a danger of losing sympathy for these victims.

The DI tried to override the wave of mutterings.

'In any case,' he said, 'the youngest child, Fay, was already asleep, while the two oldest, Melissa and Joshua, were engaged in activities that would have drowned out any extraneous noise. An iPod and a computer game respectively. It seems the boy also had the TV on. As a result, they weren't even aware of what had happened to their parents until the FOAs and paramedics arrived.'

This was taking insulation from the real world to extremes, Cooper thought. Your mother was killed and your father seriously injured in a violent assault right there in your own house, and you were unaware of it. At least one of the children might have been in some fantasy world they preferred to the real one. When the emergency services arrived at the house, it would have seemed like an extension of the fantasy, a TV drama brought right into the home. Cooper wondered how the children had reacted when they discovered what had happened to their parents. It was a shocking way for reality to intrude. The worst possible way. How long would it take for it to sink in for these kids?

'Because the children didn't hear much,' said Hitchens, 'we can't be sure how long the offenders spent inside the house. The only thing we can be fairly confident about is that they didn't go upstairs. In the downstairs rooms we can find no fingerprints that don't belong to family members. It's almost certain they wore gloves. If not, they were incredibly careful. And this was never planned as a slow, careful operation. They went in fast, and we can assume that they wanted to get out fast, too. So they wouldn't have wanted to be worrying about leaving prints or DNA traces.'

'What is missing?'

'Mrs Barron's purse, which was in her bag, and her mobile phone – which might have been left on a table, either in the kitchen or the sitting room, we're not sure.'

'It's not much of a haul for such a risky enterprise.'

'You can say that again. A couple of hundred pounds at most. They seem to have made no attempt to take anything else – neither jewellery or watches from their victims, nor anything kept in a drawer or cupboard. There was very little disturbance, not of the kind you might expect in a rapid search of the premises.'

That was an understatement, too. Cooper remembered the pristine state of the rooms at Valley View. They hardly looked as though they were lived in, let alone just been the scene of a burglary. He would have expected belongings scattered around, furniture overturned, the contents of drawers tipped out. But none of that was evident. It was what had made the blood, and the body of Zoe Barron, seem so incongruous.

'Is there a safe somewhere in the house?'

'The children don't know, and the rest of the family say not. We've got Jake Barron's father and his wife's sister at the house to take a look. The whole family wanted to come, but we managed to divert them. We don't need a crowd.'

'Check with the company who installed the security systems anyway. Jake Barron might not have told anyone, not even his family.'

'The forensic examination will continue for some time,' said Hitchens. 'But as of this moment, we can only be sure of the suspects entering one part of the house – the kitchen, via the decking and the utility room, and the sitting room, with a short length of passage in between. If they went into any other area of the house, there is no evidence of it so far. So all we have are some shoe marks, and those aren't too clear. A few faint impressions on the tiles in the kitchen, where Mrs Barron was attacked. Nothing in the sitting room, except for small deposits of soil from the garden. The carpet has retained no footwear impressions. The weather was dry, so there are no muddy prints.'

Hitchens was starting to sound a bit desperate now. His tone of voice quietened the restlessness as officers realised the magnitude of the task ahead of them. At this stage, the hopes would be of some early suspects, and a bit of help from forensics. Or at least a sighting of a suspicious vehicle.

'Also, we have yet to establish the route the attackers took to approach the house,' he said. 'Forensic examinations will

86

be going on for some time, given the size of the property. So it would be very helpful to us if we could get an angle from someone who saw or heard anything in Riddings last night. Anything. It would at least give us a line of inquiry to follow.'

'Can we establish a definite connection with the earlier assaults, sir?'

That was Becky Hurst. A good question. So far, it had been an assumption in everyone's minds.

Hitchens shook his head reluctantly. 'Nothing specific enough to rely on in court. Only a similarity in the choice of target – a high-value property in the eastern edges.'

'Within striking distance of Sheffield.'

Cooper turned round, but couldn't see who had said that.

Hitchens ignored the comment. 'And, of course, the MO is comparable to the previous incidents. The difference is that a higher level of violence was used. It's a standard pattern of escalation when suspects of this nature are able to continue their activities over a period of time.'

That was an uncomfortable fact, too. If the Savages had been apprehended after any of the first four incidents, the attack in Riddings would never have happened. Zoe Barron would still be alive, and her husband wouldn't be critically ill in hospital. Three children wouldn't be facing the loss of their parents.

If the same attackers were responsible, anyway. Cooper was still waiting to hear the evidence for that.

'Meanwhile,' said Hitchens, 'all the available information from the earlier incidents will be referenced by the HOLMES databases to establish any firm links. As you all know, we don't have descriptions of the offenders, except that they're male. In previous incidents they wore masks. In this latest assault, we have no one who is capable of telling us what they saw. It could be that they became concerned about being identified. That might actually help us, if we can find out what led to that concern.'

'You mean they might have been seen earlier? Maybe in Riddings?'

'It's a possibility. DS Cooper's team have been interviewing

87

the Barrons' immediate neighbours. Want to give us an idea of the lie of the land, Ben?'

Cooper stood up. This was the part of the briefing he'd been preparing for. A map of Riddings had been projected on to a monitor so that the whole room could see it. The names of properties and householders had been written in.

'This is Curbar Lane, where our inquiry is centred. The Barrons live here, at Valley View. As you can see, the grounds are quite extensive. No neighbouring property overlooks the house, or the drive. If you were going to choose a location where you wouldn't be seen by the neighbours, this is certainly it.'

He consulted his notes, making sure he was absolutely accurate. It would be bad to get confused at this stage.

'Just along Curbar Lane, we have the Hollands at Fourways,' he said. 'Martin and Sarah. He's a retired commercial lawyer. No connection with the Barrons, so far as we can tell. Then here we have the Chadwicks at The Cottage. Last night, they were out on Riddings Edge.'

'In the dark, Sergeant?'

'Watching for shooting stars,' said Cooper. 'It was supposed to be one of the best nights for observing the Perseid meteor shower.'

There was a bit of laughter. For some reason, it made Cooper feel more relaxed.

'The Chadwicks' property is shown on the map as Nether Croft, but they renamed it. William Chadwick is a head teacher, currently on suspension following an incident with a pupil.'

'Which school?'

'Black Brook High.'

'In Sheffield.'

That was the same voice, the person who'd mentioned Sheffield before. Cooper could see him at the back now – a detective he didn't know, probably drafted in from C Division. He looked like a veteran, one of Gavin Murfin's generation, with an expression that suggested he'd seen it all before.

'Yes, Black Brook High School is in Sheffield,' said Cooper. 'In the Fulwood area, to the west of the city. Only eight miles from Riddings, if it's relevant.'

'Well, we don't know what's relevant, do we?'

Cooper wondered if he'd encountered the detective before, maybe rubbed him up the wrong way somehow. But it was more likely that he was this way with anyone. There always had to be the awkward squad.

'At the back, we have Mr and Mrs Nowak at Lane End, and a Mr Russell Edson at Riddings Lodge. The Nowaks' property can be accessed from The Hill, which is the main road through Riddings. But there's also a lane here, which leads past the Chadwicks' gate to Riddings Lodge, then on to Lane End.'

'Russell Edson is rumoured to be a lottery winner,' chipped in Murfin.

'I hate him already,' said the voice at the back.

'The one immediate neighbour we haven't spoken to is Mr Kaye at Moorside House. That's the biggest property on Curbar Lane, the other side of the Barrons. There's a housekeeper in residence, though. She says Mr Kaye is in Florida.'

'It's all right for some.'

'But he's due back in the country later this week, so we might get a chance to speak to him. I doubt he'll be able to tell us much if he hasn't been around.'

'Tyler K,' said Irvine.

'I'm sorry?'

'That's his professional name. He started off as a rapper and DJ on the club scene in Sheffield. Then he opened his own club and went into promotion and management. I heard he has five or six clubs now. Manchester, Leeds, Birmingham. He's done really well for himself, considering he was just some kid off the Manor Estate.'

'Could he have criminal connections?'

'Well, I don't think you can assume that,' said Irvine defensively.

'It's possible, though. Likely, even. We'll do some checking.'

'He wasn't even in the country.'

'That's the best sort of alibi. It's a question of known associates.'

Irvine went quiet and slumped in his chair, casting a

89

frustrated glance at Becky Hurst. He looked sorry to have spoken.

'As you can see, those properties cover all the possible approaches to Valley View, with one exception. If our suspects approached along Curbar Lane, they would either have to pass Fourways, which would mean coming through the centre of the village, or they would have to come from the direction of Curbar, past Moorside House. The back of the property borders on to the garden of Riddings Lodge, with The Cottage and Lane End directly across this lane. From any one of these directions, the suspects must have known they were likely to pass witnesses.'

'And the one exception?'

'It's obvious.' Cooper pointed to the eastern boundary of the Barrons' property. 'On this side, there are no neighbours. There isn't anybody. On this side, there is nothing. It leads only to the edge.'

DNA and trace evidence had gone to the lab. Normally, results would take a week, but the extra expense had been approved to make them a rush job, so they might expect something within forty-eight hours or so.

Fingerprints ought to be back tomorrow, even with a complete search of the national database. It was good to have a shortlist of suspects to compare prints against, but there was no list in this case, not even a shortlist of one.

'It'll be the husband,' said Murfin as the briefing came to an end. 'You'll see, it's always the husband.'

'The husband is in hospital with serious head injuries,' pointed out Cooper.

'That's a minor quibble.'

'You don't believe in the Savages, then?'

Murfin snorted. 'There are plenty of savages out there. Some of them work in this building. Have you seen that custody sergeant?'

'Are you with us on this, Gavin? Because it has to be everyone pulling together.'

Murfin looked startled. 'Of course. I was only kidding.'

'Yeah, okay.'

Murfin was still regarding him curiously.

'What?'

'I've never noticed before,' said Murfin.

'What are you on about?'

'Since you got to be DS, I've never noticed how much you're starting to sound like Diane Fry.'

The divisional CID teams would get the legwork, of course. As expected, Cooper was put in charge of house-to-house in Riddings. The SIO wanted a detailed map of the village showing all the properties near the Barrons, every lane, every footpath and every rabbit track. The attackers must have approached and left by some route, however obscure. And with a bit of luck, someone might have seen them.

'If they knew the area, they must have been in the village before,' said Cooper, as Irvine came over to join them. 'An earlier visit to get an idea of the layout, the routes in and out. Make sure you ask about the last few weeks. Any strangers acting in a suspicious manner, or asking questions. They might have posed as inquisitive hikers, or as potential house buyers looking to move into the village. You know the sort of thing, some trick to get information out of the residents.'

'The thing is,' said Irvine, 'you can get a lot of what you need online these days. All they had to do was log in to Google Street View. And there are plenty of aerial maps on the internet.'

An aerial view was of limited use, though. It might show you the layout of buildings and where driveways ran. But it didn't tell you anything about the lie of the land, whether you would be hidden from view by those trees, what windows were on this side of the house, whether there was a dip in the terrain to conceal your approach, or would you be marching downhill in full view of the whole world?

So what about Street View? But that only showed the public roads. And in Riddings, the view of many of the properties was hidden from the Google camera van. If Cooper was a burglar, he thought, he wasn't sure he would get what he needed from it.

'If we can pin down where everyone was and what they saw,' he said, 'we might get an angle on the route the attackers took. In and out. We've got the approximate times.'

'They must have used a vehicle, surely,' said Irvine.

'If they did, it wasn't on the Barrons' property. The gates were closed, and they can only be opened from inside. There's a lane running along the back here, though. It borders on part of the Barrons' property. It's only a track really, but it would be possible to get a vehicle up there.'

'Who else in the village knew the Barrons?' asked Irvine.

'Uniforms are doing a trawl right now,' said Murfin. 'But my guess is that it'll be a short list.'

'What about this Barry Gamble? First on the scene, and all that. He has to come into the frame. Did he have a justification for being at Valley View?'

'We'll be talking to him again today, Luke,' said Cooper.

Zoe Barron's sister was on TV, being interviewed on behalf of the family. It was a routine that seemed to be demanded by the media after any personal tragedy.

'She was a good mother, and a good wife. A very bright, loving woman. She was just in the wrong place at the wrong time. If she hadn't disturbed those intruders, she would still be alive and with us today.'

'Did she disturb them?' said Cooper afterwards. 'Is that the way it went?'

Murfin shrugged. 'They came in across the decking and through the back door into the utility room.'

'Yes, they came into the kitchen, where Zoe was already standing. They came to her, not the other way round. Something about that doesn't feel right. And, as I asked before, what's missing?'

'A motive,' said Murfin. 'That's what's missing.'

'Not to mention a clear idea of how they got in and out,' added Irvine.

'Right. All we have on that are the views of the loony tendency.'

There were certainly plenty of theories being floated around, if you followed the news sites on the internet, or simply did a Google search. After the attack on Valley View, some members of the public suggested the attackers must have abseiled down the rock face like the SAS. Others claimed they flew in by hang-glider launched from the edge. They didn't bother to explain what had happened to the glider after it had landed in the Barrons' garden.

The thought of Google made Cooper remember the biblical reference carved into the stone below Curbar Gap. He didn't need to find someone with a Bible, of course. Google could come up with it for him in an instant.

He typed in *Isaiah 1:18*, and the quotation appeared:

Come now, and let us reason together, saith the LORD:
though your sins be as scarlet, they shall be as white as snow;
though they be red like crimson, they shall be as wool.

Wool? He was puzzling over the simile when DI Hitchens appeared by his desk.

'Ben, you've got a new addition to your team,' said Hitchens.

'Oh?'

'She's just on her way up from reception.'

Cooper had been waiting for a new recruit ever since he'd become DS. He'd been starting to think that it would be a long wait. Cost-cutting meant that staff wouldn't be replaced. 'Natural wastage' it was called. Nobody had said anything, but he knew how these things were done. Now it seemed that he'd been wrong.

Murfin grinned at him and tapped the side of his nose.

'Gavin, do you know something?' asked Cooper.

'My lips are sealed.'

'Mr Hitchens said *she*. Tell me it's not Diane Fry come back to join us.'

Murfin's laugh was more of a hysterical bark, too high-pitched and nervous for genuine amusement.

'Oh God. Shoot me now if it is.'

Hitchens came back into the room.

'Ben, this is your new colleague, DC Villiers.'

Cooper stood up, ready to hold out a hand in greeting. But he froze when he saw who was with Hitchens, walking calmly into the CID room with a smile. She was a bit older, leaner, more tanned than when he'd last seen her. And there was something else different, an air of confidence, a firm angle to her jaw and a self-assurance in the way she held her head. Her pale hair was pulled back from her face now. But he recognised her immediately.

'Carol,' he said.

'Hello, Ben. It's been a long time.'

9

Riddings had originally consisted of a dozen estate workers' cottages, built by a local land-owning duke. Not the Duke of Devonshire, for once, but some rival aristocrat. The Duke of Rutland, perhaps. One of those people.

He had also built a tiny Wesleyan Reform chapel in the village, but there was no parish church. Several villages in this area were served by All Saints down the hill at Curbar, with its four-hundred-year-old poor box and Jacobean pulpit of black bog oak.

'It seems strange,' said Cooper. 'Strange that we're colleagues now. Last time we spoke, you were in the RAF Police.'

He'd taken Carol Villiers with him from Edendale to ease her into the inquiry, and they were parked up in the centre of the village on The Green, near the horse trough. It felt odd having her sitting next to him in the car. They had gone to school together, studied for their A levels at High Peak College at the same time, got a bit drunk with a group of mates in a local pub when they received their results. She had been a good friend, to whom he'd been sorry to say goodbye. Her parents lived in Tideswell, so it was a bit of a surprise that he hadn't heard she was back in the area.

Seeing her earlier, Cooper's mind had been thrown back several years, to the time when he'd seen another new DC coming towards him from the far end of the CID room. She had moved with a cool deliberateness, not meeting his eye, but glancing from side to side as she walked past the desks. He remembered thinking she was far too slim – slimmer than he'd grown up expecting women to be. His mother would have said she was sickening for something. Yet she had possessed a wiry look that suggested she was no weakling, no wilting violet. And so she had proved. That had been Diane Fry.

Carol Villiers was completely different. Isabel Cooper would have approved of her, for a start. She looked strong and fit, a woman who worked out in the gym regularly two or three times a week, and never found an excuse to miss. She had an outdoor colour too, not the deathly pallor he remembered when Fry first came. And her attitude was confident, but not belligerent. He felt no hostile vibes. He knew immediately that she didn't need to be aggressive in her style. Her self-confidence went deeper.

'Yes, I was an RAFP corporal,' said Villiers. 'Here. This is me as a Snowdrop.'

She showed him a photograph of her in her uniform, with black and red flashes, her corporal's stripes on her sleeve, an MP badge, and a white top to her military cap. The cap was what gave the RAFP their nickname.

Cooper remembered her back in their school days as a lively, sports-obsessed girl who was also surprisingly ready to let her hair down. She had been into swimming and running half-marathons, had talked a lot about some female role models who had been prominent in athletics at the time, but whose names he had now forgotten.

And she hadn't been called Villiers in those days either. She had been Carol Parry, the daughter of Stan and Vera Parry, who ran a bed and breakfast in Tideswell High Street.

'I knew you were planning to join the police when you left the forces,' said Cooper. 'But I didn't recognise the surname. Villiers? What happened?'

'I got married,' she said simply.

'Oh.'

For a few moments they sat in silence, watching Riddings quietly coming to life. Opposite The Green there were still some of the original cottages standing near the chapel. But over the years, the older part of the village had been swamped by all those expensive detached houses, their paddocks and gardens carving out the lower slopes below Riddings Edge.

Cooper looked around him at the narrow lanes, no more than a car's width, the stones embedded in the grass verges, the women walking their dogs, the high banks of trees screening every house. It wasn't the best place for surveillance. A stranger sitting in a car stood out like a sore thumb. Indeed, there was hardly anywhere to park without blocking up the whole village. And all those trees hiding the big houses meant you couldn't see a thing anyway.

A visible police presence? You could drive a marked response vehicle up and down these lanes all day with its beacons flashing like Blackpool Illuminations, and no one would even see it from behind those hedges and walls.

'I never heard about the marriage, Carol. You kept it pretty quiet. Who is he? Someone you met in the RAF?'

'Yes, he was a colleague.'

Cooper hesitated. He caught the word 'was' and the tone of voice that went with it. He'd heard them often enough from the families of victims.

'Here.'

Another photograph. Carol again. But next to her was a tall, well-built man in a similar uniform. He had taken off a pair of sunglasses, which dangled from one hand, and was staring into the camera lens with eyes narrowed against the glare of the sun. Behind them, Cooper could see the background of a military compound – vehicles, stores, a high boundary wall. The ground was dry and dusty, baked by heat. He could almost feel the grittiness of the sand on his skin.

'That's Glen.'

'Your husband?'

'Yes.'

Cooper hadn't really needed to ask. His eyes had been drawn

directly to the name badge stitched on the man's uniform. *Villiers*, it said. Carol's badge was marked *Parry*.

'Before you were married, though.'

'Yes.'

'You look happy.'

'We were. Very happy.'

She had certainly changed a lot, but Cooper realised he'd noticed it happening a while ago. On the few occasions he'd seen her or spoken to her in the intervening years, the old Carol Parry had developed a brisk professional air, a confidence that few of his old school friends possessed. He supposed that was what the services did for you, instilled discipline and self-confidence. Especially if you had a team looking to you for decisions, men and women you were responsible for.

But now there was an extra dimension – a shadow in her eyes, a darkness behind the professional façade. He'd noticed it straight away when DI Hitchens had brought her into the CID room in Edendale this morning. He'd looked into her eyes and seen a different Carol Parry. Part of that darkness might be explained by the loss of her husband. And perhaps there were other experiences, too, that she would be unwilling to talk about.

Cooper wondered if she was still the 'work hard, play hard' type. It seemed to go with the territory, when he thought of the squaddies in garrison towns getting drunk and picking fights with the locals. They came back from a conflict zone and needed to let off steam.

But Carol had served as an MP. It had been part of her job to control those drunken squaddies, surely? Or whatever their equivalent was in the RAF. That had to be good practice for dealing with some of the customers they scooped up for a spell in the custody suite.

'I was aiming to come to E Division anyway, if I could,' said Villiers. 'But they moved my posting forward a bit, in view of the major inquiry you've got on here. I guess I was lucky to get in just before recruitment was frozen.'

'We're glad to have you,' said Cooper. 'Very glad. Especially right now.'

'A detective sergeant, then? I always knew you'd get on. Nice to have you as my boss, Ben.'

'Are you up to speed? Do you know what's going on here?'

'Yes, I've read the bulletins. Not to mention the newspapers. It's causing a lot of media attention, isn't it?'

'All these stories being put around are just frightening the public,' said Cooper, shaking his head. 'It's making everyone unnecessarily paranoid. We ought to be calming the mood down, not allowing it to be whipped up.'

'You can't do anything about stories on the internet,' said Villiers. 'It's unpoliceable. Like gossip over the garden wall, there's no way of stopping it. Facebook and Twitter just make the stories spread all the faster.'

'I know. But when people get as jumpy as this, something bad is likely to happen.'

'Really?'

Cooper started the car and drew away from kerb.

'You'll see,' he said. 'There'll be some idiot who decides to take the law into his own hands, and a random passer-by will get hurt. It's inevitable, the way things are going.'

At Valley View, E Division's Crime Scene Manager Wayne Abbott had just completed a full review of the Barrons' security systems.

Cooper introduced Abbott to Villiers, and asked him whether the Barrons had a monitored alarm system. False alarms had become so common that most police forces no longer attended call-outs from non-monitored systems, unless they also had first-hand indication of a crime in progress, either from the owner of the property or a member of the public. An alarm signal routed via a monitoring centre was a different matter.

'Yes,' said Abbott. 'They have a monitored twenty-four-seven response system. There's an external system panel, and a decoy siren box. A door entry system on the gate. Intruder alarms, passive infrared motion sensors, CCTV. They did pretty much everything they could.'

'I thought most burglars avoided properties with an alarm system,' said Villiers.

'That's because they don't understand them, or don't know how to do deal with them.'

'So these were professionals? They knew how to disable the alarms?'

'No,' said Abbott. 'They didn't bother with that. They chose the other option. The one that's only available if you're completely ruthless and foolhardy.'

'What are you saying?'

'They came into the property before the alarms had been set. Simple when you think about it.'

Villiers looked at Cooper. 'But that could only have been when the occupants were at home, and before they'd gone to bed, too. They must have known people would be around.'

'Exactly, Carol,' said Cooper. 'They didn't care if they were seen by the family. They came in fully prepared to use violence. Probably planned it that way.'

Abbott called back as he walked away: 'Like I said, ruthless and foolhardy.'

'You get an idea of what we're up against now,' said Cooper.

Villiers looked grim. But she wasn't shocked, didn't start talking about how horrible it must have been for the family. Cooper wondered what she might have seen elsewhere that made the incident at Valley View seem unshocking.

He took her inside the house, walking carefully on the stepping plates left by the scenes-of-crime team. Now that many of the crowd had left, it seemed very quiet inside Valley View. The windows were closed, and no sound penetrated from the garden. There was no birdsong, no sigh of the wind through the trees, no clang of karabiners from the climbers on the edge. It was good double-glazing, maybe even triple. The outside world was just that – sealed out.

Inside, Cooper found that every movement he made was deadened against the carpet, every dash of colour flattened by the stark white walls. It felt unnatural, and uncomfortable. He was used to entering houses where a TV set was babbling constantly in the background, a dog was barking in the yard, a couple of children crying upstairs. Noise and life. Funny how the two seemed to go together. But this place was like a morgue. A chapel of rest, waiting for the next body.

He turned to Villiers. 'Seen enough?'

'Yes.'

Outside, they paused, and Villiers squinted against the sun as she looked up.

'And that – that's the edge?'

'Of course. Don't you know the edges at all?'

'I've never been up there. It's funny, when I grew up not far away. But I suppose you take these things for granted. You tend to think they're just for tourists. So I've only ever seen them from down here, and never so close. Standing on the ground looking up, that's me.'

She seemed to have become thoughtful. Cooper wished he could tell what she was thinking. He supposed they would have to get to know each other properly all over again. There might be things she didn't want to talk about. But now that he was her supervisor, he had to be there and ready to listen in case she *did* want to talk. It could be a bit of a minefield.

Villiers looked at him, and smiled.

'Will you show me the edge sometime, Ben?' she said.

Cooper raised his eyebrows in surprise. 'Of course, if you want me to. Have you got a pair of boots?'

'Are you kidding? I was in the military. Of course I've got boots. And don't start worrying about my fitness, either – I'll race you up that slope any time. What is it like up there?'

'It's a whole different world,' said Cooper.

Villiers lowered her hand and touched him gently on the arm.

'I'll look forward to you showing me, then.'

Across the garden, Cooper saw a cluster of SOCOS in their blue scene suits. They were well away from the house, but had set up a route marked off by crime-scene tape. They had put an aluminium ladder against the high stone wall that formed the boundary on that side of the Barrons' property.

One of the SOCOs was over the ladder and examining the far side of the wall.

Cooper approached cautiously, not wanting to get in the way. Wayne Abbott saw him and held up a hand to stop him getting any closer.

'What have you found?' asked Cooper.

'Handprints. Two white handprints on the wall.'

'White?'

'Two prints, clear as day,' said Abbott. 'They look almost as if they've been made in chalk.'

'Good work.'

Watching the SOCOs at work photographing the wall, Cooper fingered his bag of stone chippings, deep in thought. What sort of person left white handprints? It didn't make sense.

But then, that was par for the course. Nothing the Savages did made sense either. Only in some twisted logic of their own, anyway. They were fearless and audacious. And no one knew where they would strike next.

Lane End had a drive of freshly laid gravel, thick and crunchy under the Toyota's tyres. Two convex mirrors mounted on the gateposts provided drivers leaving the property with a view round the blind bend to warn of oncoming traffic. This was certainly an area to drive with care, thought Cooper. The lane was only wide enough for one vehicle, and those stone walls looked pretty unyielding.

He drew up in front of the house and parked next to a brand-new Mini Clubman.

'Who lives here?' asked Villiers as she got out of the car.

'Some people named Nowak,' said Cooper. He checked his notebook. 'Richard and Sonya, and Mr Nowak's father, Adam.'

'Polish?'

'At some time.'

Villiers shaded her eyes as she studied the house. Cooper couldn't resist the impression that she was scanning the horizon for potential enemies. A group of insurgents, a suspect vehicle on the skyline.

'They are only possible witnesses at the moment,' he said. 'We're canvassing all the immediate neighbours in the hope that one of them might have seen or heard something on the night of the attack on the Barrons.'

'Yes, I understand.'

'The grounds of Valley View are just across the lane there. That wall is their boundary. We don't know which way the attackers came in, but this lane is one of the possible approaches. And, as you can see, it ends here.'

'At Lane End.'

'Exactly.'

Richard Nowak was older than Cooper had anticipated. He didn't know why he'd expected to meet someone in their thirties or forties, but Nowak was clearly in his early sixties. Well, that wasn't old these days. And he was undoubtedly fit and healthy. He had sandy hair cut very short, and large hands with a powerful grip as he shook Cooper's.

'It's so nice to see police officers flocking to the premises,' he said with a sardonic smile.

'Sir?'

'When we had our shed broken into a while ago, the police didn't even come. They said there would be no forensic evidence, so there was no point in investigating. When we had the quad bike stolen, they didn't do anything then either. Oh, they were happy to counsel us as victims of crime, but they made it clear that they weren't going to try to find out who'd stolen the bike, let alone get it back. But when you're driven to take the law into your own hands, they arrive in force and arrest you. They treat us as if we're the criminals.'

'You should have had a visit from a scene-of-crime officer.'

'Yes, a civilian.'

'Most of them are. They're just as professional.'

'And yet now we have a crime at my neighbours', and the

police are out in force. Three detectives have been to my house in the space of twenty-four hours. I'm so lucky.'

'Well, we're doing our best, sir.'

'That *was* a detective you sent yesterday?' said Nowak. 'He ate a lot of my wife's chocolate cake.'

'Detective Constable Murfin. He's very experienced.'

'Yes, his experience shows in his waistline.'

Cooper introduced Carol Villiers and watched as she returned Nowak's firm handshake. He found that he was looking forward to getting her impressions of the man. He already knew he could trust her opinion.

'We're sorry to bother you again, sir,' said Cooper. 'But the fact is, your property is in a very strategic position here, from the point of view of our inquiry.'

'I know, I know. You think the people came up this lane. And if they did, I ought to have seen them. And if they came in a car, they would have turned round in my driveway. But I can't tell you whether any of that happened. I didn't see anything, nor did my wife.'

'Your father also lives here?'

'My father was already in bed at that time. He's not in the best of health.'

Cooper looked at the front of the house. 'What sort of view do you have from your front window? Can you see the gate?'

'Not quite.'

'And you don't have CCTV, I noticed.'

'No, unlike some of my more wealthy neighbours. So, as you can see, we would not be able to tell if someone drove up this lane and turned round.'

'Would you mind if we take a look along the boundary on this side, sir?'

'Help yourself.'

Villiers accompanied Cooper as he followed a flagged path towards the right-hand corner of the property. According to his sketch map, the house he could just see through the trees was South Croft, home of Mrs Slattery, the doctor's widow. Croft Lane ran just behind the hedge towards Nowak's. But the lane was so narrow and empty of traffic, he wouldn't have known it was there.

'What are you looking for?' asked Villiers.

'I want to get a good idea of the layout in this area, the way the properties adjoin each other. Who neighbours who, and how well they can see the approach roads.' Cooper looked at her apologetically. 'I realise that might sound a bit strange.'

'Not at all. You need to know the ground. It's vital.'

They walked back past the gate, where the gravel drive swept up to the house. Cooper glanced out on to the lane, then back up at the Nowaks' house. Richard Nowak was still watching them from his front door, his arms folded, sleeves rolled up over muscular forearms.

'He's not missing much now,' said Villiers quietly.

Cooper restrained a smile. 'Have you noticed that there's one feature we can see from here? If you look down the lane . . .'

'Another set of gates. Rather grand ones.'

'It's the entrance to Riddings Lodge. Mr Edson. Quite a statement, aren't they?'

'And he has CCTV, I imagine?'

'Oh, yes. Why?'

'Mr Nowak's comment. *Unlike some of my more wealthy neighbours.*'

'Ah. A little bit of envy creeping through there.'

'Aren't those gilt-edged gates all about provoking envy?'

Cooper nodded. 'Of course. I wonder if there's any envy of the Barrons, too?'

'Can we see Valley View from here?'

Cooper pointed down the lane. 'It's close to where the road takes a bend there. See the big bank of rhododendrons?'

'Yes?'

'Those mark the boundary of the grounds at Riddings Lodge. Valley View and Fourways are on the other side of them.'

'We'd better move, before Mr Nowak starts getting nervous,' said Villiers.

The last section of boundary was a stone wall, which ran

right up to the rough ground at the foot of Riddings Edge. Over the wall was more Edson territory. But the Nowaks and the Edsons had made sure they couldn't see each other along this section. The wall was too high for that.

'What next?' asked Villiers.

'I need to speak to Barry Gamble again. And I'm glad to have someone with me this time.'

'Someone?'

'Actually,' said Cooper, 'I'm glad to have you.'

When they left Lane End, Cooper noticed that his tyres had pushed the gravel up into waves like the wake of a boat. It was laid so deep and soft that every vehicle, no matter how small, must leave this impression. The marks of the Mini Clubman's tyres would be just as visible as those of his Toyota. He supposed someone must rake this stuff back into place regularly to keep it looking neat. Otherwise there would soon be wheel ruts worn into the drive, and bare earth exposed. And that would never do.

Bare earth? Cooper looked back at the drive again as he reached the gate. If there was bare earth under this gravel, he could see no sign of it. No weeds broke the white surface – not a single blade of grass trying its luck. Someone with a rake and a tank full of systemic weedkiller, then.

A few yards down Curbar Lane, he saw a smart blue van, the signage on its side advertising *Garden Landscaping and Design Services, Paving and Driveway Specialists*. He stopped when he saw a man in a matching blue overall, and got out to speak to him, showing his warrant card.

'Excuse me, do you maintain many of the driveways in this area?'

'Oh, yes. We installed quite a few of them, too.'

'At Valley View, for instance?'

'Stone paving, right? A very nice design, that. Expensive, but it lasts well. We installed that about three years ago, when the new owners came in. Oh, isn't that the people . . .?'

'Yes. There's no gravel on their property, is there? I couldn't see any.'

He shook his head. 'Gravel. no. Not at Valley View.'

'I thought gravel was making a bit of a comeback.'

'Well, gravel driveways cost less to build, but they need more maintenance. Over time, tyre tracks appear, hollows fill with rain, the surface breaks down. And keeping down weeds and grass is a never-ending job. I'm working on the drive of the house across the road there. If it were me, I'd have put a weed barrier down under the gravel when it was laid. But I didn't build this one. I just got the maintenance. I'm not complaining, though.'

'There must be plenty of work.'

'Oh, aye.' The man looked at Cooper more closely. 'My name's Brian Monk, by the way. This is my company. Well, it belongs to me and my brother. But we thought Monk Brothers sounded odd for a trading name.'

'A bit too monastic.'

'Maybe.' He removed a blue baseball cap and scratched his head. 'Well, if you're interested in Riddings, it's a bit funny round here. You'd think gravel would be a good material to use in a place like this. It matches the predominant stone colouring of the area. Nicely rural, like. And a lot of people just like the crunch of it under a car's wheels. Some even go for it as a security measure, too – you can hear people coming, you know. But the thing is, you can't use gravel on a site that has any gradient to speak of. It needs regular top-up, and can be really tricky to keep in place. And there are lots of gradients here, as you can see.'

'Any other problems with it?'

'Well, it sprays out everywhere, especially if you like to spin the wheels on your posh convertible.'

Cooper laughed, recognising the view that a tradesman must get of the people he worked for.

'I bet they complain a lot, don't they?'

'You can say that again,' said Monk. 'See, I tell them – if you have a lawn next to your gravel driveway, you're going to have to pay for expensive repairs to mowing equipment. Not to mention the potential damage to people and property if gravel gets spat out at speed by a mower. Then if you get it spreading on to pathways, there's another hazard. Granules will roll underfoot, and you get people slipping and falling over. Some of these folk are paranoid about getting sued for injuries. If you're laying gravel, you don't lay it any deeper than two inches, otherwise cars sink in. It does depend on the size of the granules, though.'

Cooper produced a piece of the stone he'd collected and bagged from the Barrons' lawn.

'What about this, sir?'

Monk peered at it closely. 'Too small. If it came from a drive, anyway. No, I doubt we laid that stuff. Not here in Riddings.'

'Why?'

'Well, it's a personal choice, but ten-millimetre gravel like this tends to move around more and get stuck in car tyres. We advise people to use a fourteen- or twenty-millimetre stone on driveways.'

'I see. Thank you, Mr Monk.'

The man looked at him curiously. 'Is it important?'

'I don't know.'

'Well, I'm not saying it *isn't* from round here. Just that it's unlikely my firm laid it. There are a few other outfits around. I wouldn't call them cowboys exactly, but not they're not as well qualified, if you know what I mean. Not so particular about their work. A couple of lads out of a job might decide to set up a little gardening business, mowing lawns and that sort of thing. Then they start branching out. When people ask them if they can do drives or tree surgery, they don't want to say no. That's how it happens. I'm not naming any names, you understand. But you might find some around here that answer the description.'

Cooper nodded. 'Thanks again.'

'No problem.'

The landscaper went back to work on the house across the road. The driveway looked quite smart to Cooper, but he could

108

see there was an occasional burst of green where a weed had dared to come through.

'Gravel?' said Villiers when he got back in the car.

Cooper could hear the laugh in her voice, and turned in his seat, ready to justify himself. Then he saw her face, and he couldn't help laughing with her. For the first time today he was seeing the old Carol, the one he'd known before she went off to join the services and experienced all the bad things that he was sure must have happened to her.

'Well, that's what we're like in Derbyshire Constabulary,' he said. 'We leave no stone unturned.'

10

Monica Gamble greeted Cooper and Villiers with a sour expression, a resigned look, as if she was always expecting this kind of knock on the door.

'Mrs Gamble. Is your husband in?'

She hesitated, not sure what the best answer would be. 'Well . . .'

'Oh, I forgot,' said Cooper. 'You often don't know where he is.'

'That's right.'

'I expect that can be quite convenient sometimes.'

He could see Mrs Gamble trying to figure out what was safe for her to say. She must be wondering how long he'd been outside the house, watching. What were the chances that he had seen her husband through the window? If she lied, he would know. Not worth the risk.

'He was here a moment ago. He's probably gone to his shed.'

Cooper hadn't realised the extent of the back gardens in Chapel Close. It wasn't obvious, when the front doors of the houses opened almost on to the road. There was certainly room behind number four for a large wooden shed, though.

Gamble met them at the door of the shed, no doubt alerted by their footsteps, and his wife's slamming of the kitchen door. Inside, Cooper glimpsed the usual gardening equipment – a lawn mower, forks and spades, a few hand tools hung on racks.

A workbench ran along one wall, fitted with a vice, the wooden surface pitted and scarred.

Further back, in the darkest part of the shed, Cooper could see that there was another room partitioned off, a makeshift door firmly closed against prying eyes.

Gamble had been boiling a kettle when they arrived. A small cloud of steam trickled out of the door into the open air. A large white mug stood on a table with a tin of tea bags.

'More questions?' he said, settling his cowboy hat over his ears. He glanced at his wife, as if expecting her to go, but she showed no signs of leaving.

'Just a few,' said Cooper.

'Go on, then.'

'It's about Tuesday night, of course. When you were at Valley View.'

'Yes?'

'After you heard the noise from the Barrons' property, you mentioned seeing a light on in their kitchen.'

'That's right.'

'Did that strike you as odd, Mr Gamble?'

'Odd? I . . .'

'Because according to your initial statement, it was when you saw the light on in the kitchen that you decided to go and investigate.'

'Well, there wasn't usually . . .'

'Yes?'

'Er . . . yes, it struck me as odd.'

Gamble had developed a stubborn expression, his thick eyebrows bunched together.

'Let's be honest,' said Cooper. 'You'd watched the Barrons' house at that time of night before. You knew what their habits were.'

'I don't know why I thought it was odd,' he said sullenly. 'I just heard the noise and saw the light, and I thought I ought to see what was going on. I was being neighbourly. Concerned.'

'Concerned. Of course. And was that also why you ran to

Riddings Lodge before you called the emergency services? You were concerned for Mr Edson's welfare?'

'Signal,' blurted out Gamble.

'What?'

'I couldn't get a signal on my mobile phone. You know what it's like in these places.'

'Ye-es.'

It was true that this landscape made it difficult to receive a signal from a mobile phone mast. That high wall of rock to the east would block any mast located on the Sheffield side of Riddings. There was an area up on the Snake Pass that for years had possessed neither mobile phone reception nor coverage for the police radio network. For a long time it was a spot where you would want to avoid having an accident or emergency. The only way to get assistance was to leave the scene. In that case, the national park authority had finally given planning permission for a radio antenna on an existing pole, with an equipment chamber underground to reduce the impact on the environment. It was perfectly possible that Mr Gamble had been obliged to leave the scene of the Barrons' assault to make his call.

Gamble had noticed Villiers trying to edge closer to the doorway to see inside the shed, and he stepped smartly in her way.

'What network are you with, sir?' asked Cooper.

'O2. You can check.'

'I know.'

It bothered Cooper that the answer about the mobile phone signal had come so quickly. It was as if Gamble had been expecting the question for days, and the reply had been bottled up inside him, under so much pressure that it burst out of its own accord when the button was pressed.

He couldn't help the feeling that he should have asked this question before. Yet how could he, when he didn't know Gamble had gone to Riddings Lodge until he got that information from Russell Edson?

'Mr Gamble, why didn't you tell the first police officers you spoke to that you went to Riddings Lodge before you made the emergency call?'

'It didn't seem, well . . . relevant.'

Cooper heaved a sigh. 'Also, I need to ask you again whether you saw anyone else around Curbar Lane at that time? Please think carefully. This is very important.'

Gamble considered for a moment, glancing at his wife out of the corner of his eye, fingering the brim of his hat.

'Yes,' he said. 'I saw the Chadwicks. You know, the people from over there, at Nether Croft.'

'The Cottage,' said Cooper.

'That's what they call it now. It was always Nether Croft to me. But I saw them, the Chadwicks. They were walking up The Hill, just as it was getting dark.'

'They were going to watch the meteor shower,' said Cooper.

'Oh?' He sniffed. 'Aye, well, if they say so, I suppose.'

'Anyone else?'

Gamble lowered his head and fixed Cooper with a keen gaze from under his eyebrows.

'Yes, the Hollands. I don't know where *they* had been until that time. You should ask them, I reckon.'

Gamble moved slightly, and Cooper noticed a digital camera on the table in his shed. Not a cheap pocket camera, but quite a decent SLR model.

'Are you interested in photography, Mr Gamble?' he asked.

'Oh, just in an amateur way.'

Cooper wished he could get a look at what was on the camera. But he didn't have any justification at the moment.

'You'll be around, sir, if we need you again?'

'I'm always around,' said Gamble.

As they left Chapel Close, Cooper's phone buzzed. It was a text from Liz.

Hiya. forgot to ask u last nite, what did matt mean abt not marrying Sept or Nov?

He looked at the screen for a while, knew he couldn't possibly explain it in a text message, and finally typed:

Will explain tonite.

It was funny, but he'd rather assumed that Liz had understood what his brother had meant, why nothing like a wedding could be planned for those months. Anniversaries had always been important in the Cooper family. Their mother had died in September, their father in November. The anniversaries of their deaths were always marked by a visit to their graves in Edendale cemetery. It was a tradition that neither he nor Matt would ever want to be the one to break.

The memory of his mother's death was still too clear in his mind. He had been the only one there at her bedside in the hospital, after her fall. He remembered waiting outside among the trees, while Matt and their sister Claire sat with their mother, watching the fading light as the day came to an end. He'd spent the previous few days talking to people about the death of their loved ones, encountering all kinds of ways of dealing with death, and accepting it. He hadn't been sure how he would react himself, what other people would expect of him. He became terrified that when the reality of dying came close enough to touch him personally, his mind would go into denial. How could he face the physical truth? The slow process that began with the final breath. Surely, when the moment came, it would be too much to cope with. He'd be frozen with fear, unable to express a thought or emotion in case it burst a barrier that held back the demons.

And then the moment had come when he'd found himself holding his mother's hand as she slept, and realised that she wasn't asleep, but dead. Her fingers felt limp and cold. Her stillness was beyond sleep.

He'd expected to go through all kinds of emotions, but none of them seemed to come. There was only a spreading numbness, an emptiness waiting for something to fill it.

He remembered walking down the corridor to the nurses' station. A young nurse in a blue uniform looked up at him, and smiled.

'Yes, sir? Is there anything I can do for you?'

'It's my mother,' he'd said. 'I think she's dead.'

And that had been it. Now he would never be able to tell her about his engagement. The two things she'd hoped for, his promotion and his marriage, had both evaded her in life.

'The Hollands,' said Villiers. 'I guess that's where we're going next.'

Cooper jerked, drawn back into the here and now by her voice.

'Fourways,' he said. 'Right on the corner of Curbar Lane, and next door to the Barrons. He's a retired lawyer. They seem pretty harmless, but . . .'

'You never know, do you?'

'Not here,' said Cooper.

As they entered Fourways, Cooper noticed something he hadn't seen on his previous visit, perhaps because he'd been distracted by a phone call or a text, he couldn't remember which. A stone feature had been constructed in the front garden, a sort of vertical rockery built from the local gritstone. It seemed to be intended to echo the view of Riddings Edge beyond the house. On top of smooth slabs someone had balanced jagged and weathered stones, apparently chosen to suggest animal shapes. Cooper gazed at it for a moment, trying to fathom its significance. He didn't know what it meant, but he knew what it was. This was the Devil's Edge in miniature, right here outside the Hollands' front door.

'Mrs Holland. This is my colleague, DC Villiers.'

'Hello. What can we do to help?'

'Just a quick question.'

Sarah Holland looked expectant, but she was smiling. Her expression suggested she was alert, and ready to help. Quite the opposite of Barry Gamble.

Cooper gestured first at the rockery. He needed to satisfy his curiosity.

'Who built the stone feature in your garden, Mrs Holland?'

'Oh, I did,' she said. 'Though Martin collected most of the stones for me, on his walks.'

'Mr Holland is a keen walker?'

'He likes to keep fit. And walking is wonderful exercise at our age. Good for the heart, isn't it?'

'I believe so. Does he go walking on the edge?'

He didn't feel the need to specify which edge he meant. She must be as conscious as he was of the gritstone battlement looming over their heads.

'Yes, of course. It's a great place to walk. It's quite flat on the top, you know – once you get up there.'

Cooper looked at the small-scale version of the Devil's Edge again.

'Do you do your own gardening, Mrs Holland?'

'What?'

'It's a big garden. Do you do all the work yourself?'

'No, we have a couple of young men who come in now and then to mow the lawns, do the weeding, all the heavier work. They work at quite a lot of properties in Riddings. They're good boys. Hard workers.'

'AJS Gardening Services?'

'Yes, that's them.'

Martin Holland came through the house to join them.

'Ah, glad to see you're still on the job,' he said. 'Nothing like a police presence. How can we help you?'

'Where were you both on Tuesday?' said Cooper. 'I'm not sure I asked you before.'

'Oh, we'd been out balsam bashing,' said Mrs Holland, with a smile.

For a moment Cooper thought he must have misheard her. 'You'd been out . . .?'

'Balsam bashing.'

No, he'd definitely heard it right. And she sounded proud of it, too. So it probably wasn't a euphemism – not for the sort of thing he was imagining, anyway. There were all kinds of quaint local customs in Derbyshire, of course. Well dressing, garland ceremonies, Shrovetide football games. But balsam bashing was not one he'd heard of before.

'Himalayan balsam,' said Mrs Holland.

'Oh.'

Now she looked disappointed in him. He'd failed some kind of test, and that didn't happen to Cooper very often where local knowledge was concerned.

'It's an invasive species,' she said. 'It smothers riverside habitats, harms native plant life and erodes the riverbanks. It needs to be rooted out by late August, before its seed pods explode.'

'I see.'

'It was on TV.'

'Was it?'

'Central News. That was when the schoolchildren helped to clear Calver Marshes. Everybody's been helping along the Derwent. Cub scouts, conservation volunteers, Duke of Edinburgh Award people. Everybody.'

'I must have missed it,' said Cooper. He actually was surprised that he hadn't known about it. Normally he would have been aware of a project like that. Living in the town was somehow disconnecting him from what was going on in the villages.

'So anyway, there was a working party. We were clearing the stretch of river from Froggatt Old Bridge down past Calver Mill and around the weir. It was quite a big party of volunteers, maybe three dozen or so. We were there most of the day, from about ten o'clock in the morning. Hard work it was, too. But it's all in the interests of the community and the local environment.'

'Who else was there from Riddings?'

'Well, Barry Gamble, of course. A few of the other people from Chapel Close. Old Mrs Slattery drifted by, but she didn't stay very long. She's not too strong, from the look of her.'

'How about Mr Edson?'

Mrs Holland sniffed. 'You're joking. Edson wouldn't get his hands dirty with a job like that. He wouldn't even think it was

117

worth getting a speck of mud on his green wellingtons. Though I'm surprised he didn't send the gardener down to do some work on his behalf.'

'Anyone else you knew?'

'I think they were mostly people from Calver or Froggatt. Plus a couple of national park rangers.'

'What time did you come back?' asked Villiers. 'You weren't working in the dark, I'm sure.'

Mrs Holland laughed. 'Oh, no. Most of us went for a drink at the Bridge Inn afterwards. It's thirsty work, you know. And it was our last session together, so it was a kind of celebration drink. Or two.'

'Or three,' said her husband.

'Well, some of us, perhaps.' She looked at him accusingly. 'Anyway, that meant it was dark when we came home. So it was after nine o'clock, I suppose. Possibly nearer ten.'

'Is the balsam bashing finished, then?' asked Cooper.

'Until next year. Why, were you thinking of volunteering?'

'I don't think I'd have time.'

'That's what everyone says.'

'I suppose they do.'

'Do you know many of the residents of Riddings?' asked Villiers.

'Quite a few,' said Holland. 'More than most do, I'd say. We're quite gregarious, and like to say hello when we're passing. But you don't get people coming together much in this village.'

'That's right,' said his wife. 'There's no pub here, or anywhere else to meet. We only have the chapel, and that's just for a few particular individuals. The annual show is about the only time you see people together.'

'Oh, Riddings Show?' asked Cooper.

'Yes, it's this Saturday, as it happens. Always on the bank holiday weekend. For some folk in this village it's the one day of the year that they actually see each other. It's funny, they might have spent the previous twelve months avoiding someone, but everyone goes to the show. Everyone. You have to put in an appearance.'

118

'A question of being accepted, looking respectable?'

'Not everyone is all that respectable,' said Holland.

'Yes, we do have the Russian mafia living in Riddings,' said his wife.

Cooper raised an eyebrow. 'Do you?'

'Mr Nowak at Lane End. You must have spoken to him.'

'Yes. His family is Polish.'

Holland shrugged. 'Sarah rather likes the idea of having a criminal as a neighbour. As long as he's a major drugs baron, or the head of an organised crime syndicate. Nothing petty, you know. But then he'd have to be a particularly successful criminal if he can afford to live at Lane End.'

'We don't know much about him,' Mrs Holland admitted.

Cooper nodded, noting that she knew enough about him to pronounce the 'w' in his name as a 'v'.

'You must see a few strangers around in the village,' put in Villiers.

'Of course, there are all kinds of people hanging around Riddings at times. Tourists. They walk through the village and take photos of almost anything. Sometimes I see them with their cameras pointing apparently at random, and I want to ask them what on earth there is to photograph. I mean, what? A tree? A wall?'

Cooper nodded, thinking: *Or a burglar alarm?*

'We're quaint,' said Mrs Holland. 'That's what it is.'

Her husband snorted. 'Quaint. Nonsense.'

'I bet we are if you live on a council estate in Sheffield.'

'Thank you,' said Cooper, as he and Villiers turned to go.

Before they were halfway down the drive, Mrs Holland called after them.

'It'll be in the paper this week. The balsam bashing, I mean. We all had our photograph taken before we started.'

Cooper started the car, and waited for a white van to pass on Curbar Lane, heading towards the centre of the village.

'This is getting quite exciting,' said Villiers. 'Meteor showers, balsam bashing, gravel . . . I hardly know what's going to come up next.'

'Sarcasm,' said Cooper.

'No. Actually, I'm really starting to get into it.'

Cooper shook his head. 'Unfortunately, I don't think we're making progress quickly enough.'

'Well, there should be some results coming in from forensics soon, shouldn't there? That ought to provide some lines of inquiry. I presume there's been a thorough forensic sweep at Valley View?'

'Of course,' said Cooper. 'But . . . well, I could be wrong.'

She looked at him curiously. 'Are you often wrong, Ben?'

'No comment.'

'You're enjoying yourself, aren't you?' she said. 'Having a murder case to work on gives you a kick.'

'It does,' admitted Cooper. 'I think a lot of officers would say that, if they were to tell the truth.'

She nodded. 'I always felt like that. Even when you know people around you are getting killed, the excitement of the moment carries you along. There's nothing like it, really. It's not something the public back home get to hear about, but I saw a lot of guys really high on the adrenalin rush of being shot at. And being able to shoot back, of course.'

'In my case,' said Cooper, 'I think it's the shooting back that I like. Speaking metaphorically, obviously.'

'Catching the bad guys.'

'Or at least making life difficult for them.'

'So where to now, then?' she said.

'South Croft. Mrs Slattery, widow of Dr Slattery.'

Cooper pulled out into Curbar Lane and turned past the horse trough into The Green, where the mobile library was parked. It was right what he'd said, that they didn't seem to be making any progress. For some reason, a phrase that Superintendent Branagh had used was running through his head. *Time isn't on our side.* Cooper's subconscious had rephrased it and set it to the tune of the old Stones song. It seemed to change the emphasis, refine the meaning. *Time is not on our side. Time is NOT on our side.*

A woman walking her dog turned to watch them go by. A few yards further on, the driver of the mobile library stared at them until they'd passed. A pair of hikers stopped abruptly on The Hill and gaped as if they were members of a travelling circus.

Forget about surveillance. In this village, Cooper had the feeling that *he* was the one being watched.

11

Mrs Slattery was ill. She'd taken to her bed, sedated by her GP as a result of the stress she was going through. All this business in Riddings had really upset her. If the police didn't sort it out soon, it would kill her.

At least that was what her son said. He faced Cooper and Villiers on the doorstep of South Croft, his arms folded, an aggressive scowl on his face. The very image of a perfect guard dog.

'She didn't see anything, anyway,' he said. 'On Tuesday she'd been down at some community effort that she was keen on. I don't know what . . .'

'The balsam bashing?'

'Something like that. Well, Mum's not up to that sort of malarkey, not anything physical. She soon got tired, and one of the organisers brought her home. She went straight to bed and she was fast asleep by the time it all kicked off. Never heard a thing.'

'I see.'

Slattery looked from Cooper to Villiers challengingly. 'Since then she's been frightened out of her wits thinking that it could have been her that got attacked, worrying about what might happen next. That's why I came down to stay with her for a bit. The tablets are helping, but I don't want her being harassed by you lot. Or any of those pillocks in the village either.'

'Who do you mean, sir?' asked Villiers politely.

'Any of them. They're all cut from the same cloth. If my dad was still alive, he wouldn't have taken any nonsense. But Mum is on her own, and she can't cope with it all.'

'The Barrons?'

'Well, that Jake Barron is a real piece of work. Mind you, I could say the same about a lot of people in Riddings – look at the teacher who beat up one of his own pupils, the gangster from Moorside House who drives round in the BMW, the dodgy East European businessman, the mad character at Riddings Lodge . . .'

'What about the Hollands? Nothing against them?'

'Pussies.'

'What?'

'They let themselves be intimidated. I wouldn't allow that to happen to Mum. If one of them tried to bully her with their fancy lawyers, they'd have me to deal with.'

'You know it's never wise to take the law into your own hands, don't you?' said Cooper.

'Oh, yeah. Like the law is doing such a great job of protecting people round here.'

'Was there some kind of legal dispute?' asked Villiers.

'It's nothing to do with my mum. And I'm not having you asking her questions. If you want to know about it, ask Jake Barron – or that Nowak person.'

Slattery slammed the door. Cooper and Villiers looked at each other.

'Well, that told us,' said Villiers.

'It told us *something*,' said Cooper.

Gavin Murfin and Becky Hurst were on The Green, comparing notes at the horse trough. It had become an unofficial meeting place in the village, given that there was no pub or shop, or any other facilities at all, apart from the phone box a few yards down the hill.

'Gavin. How is it going?'

'Deadly,' said Murfin.

'Have you both met Carol?'

'Yes, at the office. Good to have you on board,' said Hurst.

'Thank you.'

'So what have we got?' asked Cooper. 'Anything or nothing? Tell me we have something, please.'

'I spoke to some walkers,' said Hurst. 'They're regulars in this area, often go up on the edge in the evening and come down when it starts getting dark.'

'They were up there on Tuesday night?'

'Yes. And they walked back down through the village, so they passed the corner of Curbar Lane. I asked them if they saw anyone around.'

'And?'

'All they can remember was seeing someone in the phone box on The Green, making a call. It was about the right time.'

'That doesn't help very much. Did they see who it was? Any description?'

'No, he had his back to them. Making a call, like I said.'

'A man, then.'

'Probably.'

'If we could find out who that was, he might be a good witness. Even when you're on the phone, you notice things from a kiosk. They're glass on all sides, and you can't help looking at people and cars going past.'

Hurst shook her head. 'We'd have to go round the whole village again to stand a chance of identifying him. And he might not have been local anyway.'

'No, you're right.'

'It's clutching at straws, Ben.'

Cooper sighed. 'What about Cliff College?'

'I spoke to someone on reception,' said Murfin. 'Their registration date is the first of September.'

'No students, then?'

'There are just a few staff on site.'

'Okay. So what do we have from the neighbours, really?'

'No one saw anything,' said Murfin. 'Not a thing. No suspicious vehicles, not even a person they didn't recognise.

124

We have no evidence that anyone came in via the front of the property.'

'So . . . if the attackers didn't come through the village, they must have come the other way.'

Cooper found himself looking at the edge. It was certainly hard to ignore. His eyes were drawn to it irresistibly. He saw a ledge of rock jutting out into space at the top of the cliff face. There were many of those spurs and outcrops. They looked precarious, not a place to stand for too long if you had a problem with heights or sudden drops. A very similar location had been used by a film crew for an iconic shot in the filming of *Pride and Prejudice*. Keira Knightley posing almost in mid-air, with an immense panorama of the Peak District spread out in front of her. It struck Cooper that he could get an incredible bird's-eye view of Riddings from one of those outcrops – a perspective even Google couldn't achieve.

'Did you talk to the lottery winner, Ben?' asked Murfin.

'Yes, Russell Edson. Why?'

'I was just wondering – what does this Russell Edson do with himself all day?'

'Not much, I suppose.'

'And his mother – what's her name?'

'Glenys. She does even less, I should think. Unless you count a couple of hours a day having facials and applying make-up.'

'One of those who needs scaffolding and a truck full of cement, is she? But otherwise it's a life of idleness, like?'

'There's a housekeeper at Riddings Lodge. And Mr Edson gets a man in to do everything else. Or a woman, maybe.'

Murfin shook his head. 'That's not possible,' he said.

'What isn't? Getting a man in?'

'No. I mean, doing nothing all day. I don't care who you are, or how much money you've got – you can't just sit and do nothing for hour after hour, day after day. You'd go mad. You'd start tearing up the furniture.'

'Or the antique tapestries,' said Cooper.

'Exactly.'

'Well I think you're right, Gavin. The brain can't stand total inactivity.'

'And I bet he's not a stupid bloke, is he?'

'No, definitely not.'

'So he must do something,' said Murfin. 'Stands to reason. Even if he doesn't actually *do* anything, he must be thinking about something. Planning.'

'Right. Planning what?'

'I don't know.'

'Well. Thanks, Gavin.'

'Gavin Murfin seems . . . experienced,' said Villiers as they got back into the car.

'He's close to his thirty,' said Cooper.

'Ah.'

'You know what that means?'

'Yes. He's one of the lucky generation. While poor Luke and Becky . . .'

'Best not to mention it.'

For police officers looking forward to retirement, thirty had always been the magic figure. Having paid in a compulsory eleven per cent of their salary for three decades, that was the moment they could claim their full pension.

But times changed. The younger officers would have to put in thirty-five years' service now to earn their pension. No wonder Gavin Murfin was looking so smug about his approaching landmark.

'I was lucky too, I suppose,' said Villiers. 'Coming in from the services.'

'Yes, you were. These days new recruits are expected to work for nothing as special constables for eighteen months, or pay for their own training.'

'Would you have done that, if it was the system when you signed up?'

'I'm not sure,' said Cooper. 'Well, to be honest, I don't think I could have afforded to.'

126

He started the car. Villiers had put her finger on something he hadn't really thought about. That would have been a really tough decision to make. But he couldn't imagine what else he would have done. If he hadn't been able to join the police when he left High Peak College, he might have ended up as one of those jobbing gardeners or handymen, finding work wherever it came from. He didn't have qualifications for anything else in particular.

'I gather your team have talked to some of the neighbours already,' said Villiers.

'Yes,' admitted Cooper. 'But I want to get round them all myself. I need a good idea of who these people are. You can't get that at second hand, no matter how well Becky and Luke do their jobs.'

'Or Gavin.'

'Yes, or Gavin.'

'Can I ask you something, Ben?' said Villiers.

'Fire away.'

'Well, we always had a clear command structure in the services,' she said. 'Briefing, debriefing, rules of engagement. And keeping lines of communication open was vital. We never did anything or went anywhere without someone else knowing exactly what we were doing.'

'Your point is?'

'I thought it was a bit like that in the police. There's an SIO in charge of the case. There are collators and action managers in the incident room. Aren't they the people who establish the lines of inquiry and allocate tasks?'

'Of course.'

'Yet you're following a theory of your own,' said Villiers. 'Isn't that a dangerous game?'

'If I'm right, it'll be worth it.'

She nodded, smiling quietly to herself. Cooper waited for another comment, a challenge or a cautionary word. He expected her to question what he was doing. She was quite right to do so.

But he waited, and she said only one more word.

127

'Interesting.'

It was then that Cooper saw AJS Gardening Services again. Their van was white, and looked a bit older and more battered than the vehicle belonging to the landscape contractor down the road, Mr Monk. The signage on the sides of this one had probably been done by hand from a DIY kit.

Cooper got out of his car and walked up to the van. Two men were in deep conversation at the back doors, discussing something about their equipment. A preference for a petrol or electric mower, perhaps. Comparing the size of their dibbers.

Cooper identified himself. One of them was the blond young man he'd seen the previous day, while the other was a bit older, and darker, with a few days' growth of beard.

'Did I speak to you before?' asked the younger of the two.

'I don't think so,' said Cooper.

'You're police, right?'

'Yes. Detective Sergeant Cooper.'

'I spoke to one of your pals, then.'

'Is this your company, AJS?'

'That's me. AJS Gardening Services. Adrian J. Summers, see. Great name for a gardener, isn't it? Summers? Gives just the right image. This is my mate Dave.'

The other man nodded awkwardly. Cooper studied him for a moment, feeling a flicker of recognition. If he was local, there was a chance he'd encountered the man during the course of his duties. Perhaps not an arrest – he usually had a good memory for the faces of people he'd nicked. He was more likely a witness, or even a victim.

'Just routine, but I'd like a list of names from you. Yours, and all the staff you might have had working for you in Riddings during the past week or so.'

'There's not many of us,' said Summers. 'I'm only a small outfit. But, yeah – no problem.'

'If you could do that list for me now, I'll send an officer along to collect it shortly.'

'Sure.'

'You might also note which houses you work on in this area.'

He left them to it and went back to his car. Their names could be put through the HOLMES indexes, along with AJS Gardening Services, to see if there was any common link with earlier attacks. That was what HOLMES was good at, sifting through mountains of data for connections. It wasn't beyond imagining that these same gardeners had worked at properties in Hathersage, Baslow and Padley. If they had, it would be flagged up as something rather more than a coincidence.

'Want me to collect that list?' asked Villiers.

'No, it's okay. I'll get Luke or Becky to do it when they're free.'

'It's not about gravel again, then?'

'No,' said Cooper. 'It's about knowledge.'

A movement caught his eye, and he looked up. A red hang-glider was sweeping down from Riddings Edge, banking as it caught a thermal and rising high into the air again.

Hang-gliding and paragliding had become increasingly popular over the last ten years or so, and on summer weekends the skies seemed full of them, buzzing around like enormous flies.

The sport needed a breeze and an updraught, so Mam Tor near Castleton was generally considered the ideal spot – the ridge caught the wind from all directions. But some of these eastern edges were popular too. Like most flying, the hardest parts were said to be taking off and landing. Once in the air, they could glide for ages on a good day, and if they caught a thermal it was possible for experienced pilots to travel as far as the coast. Though they didn't look it, hang-gliders were claimed to be capable of flight speeds up to seventy miles an hour.

There were licensed training schools in the Peak District, but Cooper knew it wasn't a cheap sport. He'd heard that the training cost eight hundred pounds or more, on top of the two to four thousand you would pay for a hang-glider or paraglider canopy, and a few hundred more for personal equipment. If you could afford to live in a place like Riddings, that probably wouldn't be a problem. But he couldn't imagine any of the

129

inhabitants he'd met so far being tempted to launch themselves out into space from the edge with nothing but carbon-fibre spars and a few feet of polyester cloth to support them.

He thought of the theories being bandied about in the media and on the internet about thieves who flew down on their targets by hang-glider. It was complete madness. For a start, those things must weigh around thirty kilos, even when they were packed in a bag for carrying.

Cooper watched the trajectory of the hang-glider as it swooped over the valley and passed in front of the edge. Totally impractical as a means of transport. Still, you would get a really good view of what lay below, even better than from an outcrop on the edge. You would be able to look directly down on the climbers who were still clinging precariously to the rock faces as the afternoon drew to a close.

He looked back at the climbers again. Watching them inching their way up the rock one hold at a time, he felt like slapping himself on the forehead. He'd been a complete idiot. But at least he knew now where those white handprints had come from.

Remnants of quarrying activity were scattered all over this area. Half-formed millstones lay below Riddings Edge, some of them covered in lichen as if slowly being reabsorbed into the landscape. Quarrymen had come to the eastern edges looking for the coarse sedimentary rock known as gritstone.

Now, for climbers, gritstone possessed friction properties that compensated for a lack of holds on the sheer faces. It was best climbed in the autumn or spring, when the sun was out, the midges were on holiday, and the moisture had seeped off the rock. Like at Stanage Edge, on a fine weekend there were cars parked along the side of every road, and so many people climbing that the only sound was the cacophony of karabiners.

Cooper had no trouble finding what he needed. Near the car park at the top of The Hill, a foam crash pad had been left at the foot of a boulder – the sort of thing a climber placed on the ground in case of a fall, to reduce the risk of serious injury. A man was standing at the foot of the rock face coiling a length of rope, and Cooper interrupted him to ask him about the equipment that was used on the edges.

'We're trads,' said the climber. 'Traditional rock climbers. We don't use bolts on gritstone. We respect the rock.'

He was wearing a helmet and rock boots, and was hung about with a full rack of gear – rope, harness, karabiners, belay devices, wires, hexes, cams. And there on his harness was the item Cooper was most interested in – a chalk bag.

'Our aim is to leave the rock as we found it. There's been a spate of chipping on these faces recently – where people create a hold artificially, you know? When we see that, we report it to the Access and Conservation Team at the British Mountaineering Council. It has no place on gritstone.'

'But what about the white handprints?' asked Cooper, looking up at the rock. 'They're all over the place.'

'Yes, it is rather a lasting visual sign. But we only use what we need, and we clean up any spillage.'

And they were certainly visible from here. White marks showed up in every spot where a climber had sought a hold. Some of the chalk had faded as it weathered; some marks were still clear and fresh.

'The chalk is used on the hands to combat sweat and improve grip, right?'

'That's it. Some of these faces barely have even crimps, small fingerholds. If your hands are sweating . . .'

'Yes, I see.'

'It helps if you happen to do a highball off the face.'

'A what?'

'A highball. A fall.'

Cooper looked at the sheer face of the edge.

'If you were far enough up the face when you did a highball, you'd be killed.'

'Oh no,' said the climber. 'We call that a deathball.'

Above them, a climber was reaching the end of a traverse and completing the mantelshelf – the final move of the route, where he had to press down with his hands until his arms were straight and get his legs up behind him to place a foot on the shelf. It looked difficult to do if you were tired after a climb.

'These climbing routes,' said Cooper. 'They have names, don't they?'

'Yes. This one here is Hell's Reach. My favourite is Torment. That's a real challenge. Torment is an E1, at least.'

'E1?'

'Most routes are graded from Moderate to Extremely Severe. E1 is at the Extremely Severe end. It has an overhang – one up from sheer on the steepness scale.'

'Sounds dangerous to me,' said Villiers.

'We had a guy who nearly died in a highball on this face,' said the climber. 'Well, he would have died, if he hadn't got medical attention fast. That was thanks to the mountain rescue team.'

Cooper looked at Villiers. Neither of them bothered to remark how surprising it was that there weren't more deaths in Hell's Reach.

They drove back towards Edendale. For Cooper, it was a constant pleasure to escape into these hills, where the changing moods of the scenery never failed to fascinate him. Edendale sat right at a point where the areas known as the Dark Peak and the White Peak met.

The White Peak, to the south, was a human landscape of limestone farmland, dotted with wooded valleys and dry-stone walls, settled and shaped by people, and still a place where thousands of years of history might be expected to come to the surface. The bleak, empty moors of the Dark Peak to the north looked remote and forbidding, an uncompromising land-scape that was anything but human. The bare, twisted faces of hardened gritstone appeared to absorb the sun instead of reflecting it as the limestone did. They seemed to stand aloof and brooding, untouched by humanity.

At the top of a hill just outside Edendale stood a pub called the Light House, with stunning views across both limestone and millstone grit. Rumour had it that the Light House, like so many rural pubs, was struggling financially. Village after village was losing its centre of community life. Cooper expected to drive past the Light House one day and find it permanently closed and boarded up, a depressing backdrop to the view.

He looked at his watch as they began the descent into the town.

'I have to go back to the office for a while,' he said. 'But your shift is over, Carol. No overtime.'

'All right.'

'I'll meet you later, then.'

'What?'

'You wanted to see the edge, didn't you? The evening is a good time.'

'You're sure it's okay?'

'Yes. Trust me, a breath of fresh air is just what I need right now.'

At West Street, Cooper headed to the DI's office to report, conscious that he hadn't been keeping in touch as he ought to have done. But Hitchens was just about to go into a meeting with Superintendent Branagh, and hardly seemed to listen.

'Yes. Great, Ben. Get your team to write everything up and feed it into HOLMES, won't you?'

'Of course, sir. Are we making any progress?'

'We think we've got some promising leads from the forensic sweep. Right now, we're setting up a joint operation with South Yorkshire. Hoping for some arrests. Taking the Savages off the streets. The super has the headlines written already.'

'Really? Can I—'

'Later, Ben. Keep up the good work.'

Cooper nodded as he watched Hitchens disappear.

'Okay, fine. So perhaps I'm wrong more often than I thought.'

12

It was one of those peculiar transitions that Cooper experienced from time to time in the Peak District. Within a few minutes, he'd passed from a secluded cluster of affluent twenty-first-century homes into an alien stone landscape. Pools of peat-stained water, traces of primitive habitation.

Often the shift could be quite sudden. In this case, it had been the point where he turned the corner of a rocky outcrop and found himself on the far side of the Devil's Edge. The wind had dropped, the sound of traffic fell away, the last sign of human habitation disappeared. It all happened in a second, within a distance of two or three steps. But he'd been concentrating on keeping his footing on the smooth rock, and he hadn't noticed the exact moment of change.

He turned to see if Villiers was still behind him. He felt as though he'd walked through an invisible doorway by accident. Maybe he'd never be able to find it again to return to the twenty-first century. Would that be such a bad thing?

From the edge, he found himself looking eastwards across an expanse of scrub on Stoke Flat towards Big Moor. Big Moor was a kind of no-man's-land, a buffer zone wedged between the Peak District National Park and the city of Sheffield. Out here on the moors, you stumbled across mysterious locations every few hundred yards. Isolated guide posts pointed the way across empty moorland, patterns were burned into the heather like UFO landing strips, memorial cairns commemorated long-forgotten deaths. And there were so many of those dark, twisted outcrops of rock, sculpted by centuries of wind and rain into bizarre shapes. and marked on the map by sinister names.

For Cooper, this was a landscape infested with evil. Hobs and boggarts, and all kinds of monsters. Ahead of him, the ground was scattered with curious lumps and hollows that his grandmother would have said were hob holes. You wouldn't go walking across this moor at night, for fear of what might climb out of those holes and grab at your ankles with sharp claws. Of course, they were rabbit burrows, most likely. Or the remains of ancient mine shafts. But they could break your ankle just the same in the dark. They were as lethal as a hob any day.

Villiers was close behind him, hardly even breathing heavily from the climb. But her face was glowing and her eyes were bright as she gazed over the valley, sharing his pleasure at the panoramic view.

'This is terrific,' she said. 'You know, I was never based anywhere in the world that compared to the Peak District.'

'I suppose this kind of country doesn't lend itself to air strips.'

He'd never really been able to explain the appeal that a landscape like this had for him. In a way, he felt it must mirror some hidden landscape inside his head. Those stories from local history and folklore were permanently lodged in his sub-conscious, a legacy of tribal memory. But it was here, in the physical environment of the edges and moors, that they came to life and were acted out by ghostly figures. Their spirits were caught and preserved in the ancient stones and trackways, their names immortalised on the map, their shapes and faces still vividly re-created in the imagination.

People talked about the mists of the past, as if history was wrapped in a gentle haze of nostalgia. But when Cooper thought about some aspects of his ancestors' lives, the images in his mind tended to be swallowed by an evil fog – a swirling miasma of fear and superstition, a bitter smog of poverty and suffering.

They walked part of the way along the summit track, stopping whenever a new view opened up of rocks and valley. Dusk was falling quickly, changing the light every few minutes as the sun played among low clouds on the western horizon.

Seen from the valley, these gritstone edges resembled the long, broken battlements of an old fortress. One of Cooper's nieces, seeing the edges one day, had said they were like the ruins of Helm's Deep after the siege of the orc army. But from up here, high on the moors, there were fantastic views over the rooftops of the Derwentside villages, right out across the Peak District, with the Kinder plateau and Bleaklow in the far distance.

Turning to the south, he glimpsed a magical vision – a vast mansion gleaming gold in the midst of a green landscape. Chatsworth, of course. The home of the Duke of Devonshire, a favourite destination for millions of tourists. Its gilded window frames made the whole house glow in the evening sun.

He knew that Chatsworth was literally packed to the rafters with priceless antiques. Old Masters and oriental porcelain had been collected by dukes over the centuries. Da Vincis and Rembrandts hung on its walls. Delft vases and Blue John bowls mingled with Roman statues and precious silver. But security on the estate was top notch. Most of the thefts they experienced at Chatsworth were the result of tourists taking plants from the gardens.

'This track was a millstone road, made by seventeenth-century quarrymen,' said Cooper. 'Then it was owned by one of the dukes, and he set gamekeepers to guard it against pesky ramblers. Now the public has access. It must be one of the best stretches of scenery in the country.'

'No argument there.' Villiers took a deep breath. 'No matter how often I came home on leave, I never really felt I was back properly.'

'It gets in the blood, doesn't it?'

'Like a virus. But in a good way.'

From the edge, they could see the steep, wooded slopes below, with a dense covering of rotting silver birch. You could make your way down to the woods, but only if you had good stability and the right footwear.

Riddings Edge was also littered with prehistoric sites. Ancient settlements, burials, field systems. To the north, the Stoke Flat stone circle was only a few yards from the main path. And old maps showed a network of packhorse trails crossing the moors, from a time when they provided the only route from north Derbyshire to the towns and cities in the east. It must have been a wild and lonely place for packhorse men and traders to navigate across in safety.

Yet these moors were within such easy reach of Sheffield, Chesterfield, Derby and the M1 motorway that they were possibly the easiest wild place in Britain to access from a major city. There were good footpaths too, and parking close to the top so that people could enjoy the views without a long walk.

The moors had originally been shaped by farming, tree clearance and grouse shooting. There was the purple haze of heather, and the strange, cackling call of the red grouse. And maybe a fleeting glimpse of a common lizard basking on weather-worn rocks. Here and there, under a tree, Cooper saw little mounds writhing with brown ants. There were hairy wood ants, fearsome creatures that squirted formic acid at you if you came too close. The smell of vinegar was the warning sign. There were adders here too. The snakes hibernated for winter. But in May, as the weather warmed up, they came out on to the moor to sun themselves.

No adders or lizards were out at this time of day, not even a deer. Cooper saw only a Coke can lying in the bracken. An aluminium can outlived most people. If it wasn't picked up, this one would still be lying here in sixty years' time. Maybe seventy or eighty. It wouldn't have rotted or decomposed. There was nothing biodegradable about it. By the end of the century, this can would still be weathering slowly, its bright red surface faded to a dirty brown that matched the dead bracken. Yet the entire population of Riddings would be dead and gone. The human body was different. In the High Peak mortuary, Zoe Barron's body was doing more than just fading.

He jumped as a pheasant burst from under his feet in an explosion of noise and feathers. He had failed to see it, been completely unaware of its presence as it lay motionless in the heather.

On other moors, the shooting season had started on the Glorious Twelfth. But Big Moor was owned by the National Park authority and designated as a Site of Special Scientific Interest for its rare plants and wildlife. Despite the ease of access, this moorland had been left pretty much undisturbed since prehistoric times.

'You think a lot, don't you?' said Villiers. 'You'd forgotten I was here for a while – I could tell by your face. I don't remember that about you, Ben.'

'Sorry,' said Cooper.

But she was right. He'd started to feel so relaxed with her that he hadn't felt it necessary to concentrate on acknowledging her presence, the way courtesy demanded you had to do with strangers.

'How long is it, then?' he said.

'Since we saw each other?' she guessed.

'Yes, sorry. That's what I mean.'

'When I was home on leave once, visiting the old folks. Maybe five years.'

'Yes, I suppose it would be about that. So . . . five years ago. Does that mean you've not been given any leave in the last five years?'

'Well, you know . . .'

'You had more interesting things to do.'

'We move on, don't we?'

'Of course,' said Cooper. 'Just not always in a good way, I suppose.'

'No.'

'So which was it for you?

He watched her eyes as she thought about the question, saw the doubt and pain pass across her face, the conflicting memories of love and grief written as clear as any words could express.

'Both, perhaps,' she said. 'Is that possible?'

'I don't know.'

Villiers was silent for a moment, and Cooper thought he'd said the wrong thing, hurt her by poking into all those darkest corners of her life that she was trying so hard not to remember.

'What about you, Ben?' she said finally. 'Moving on in a good way?'

Cooper hesitated. His first instinct was to tell her everything, to spill out all his feelings, explain exactly what he felt about his family, about his job, about Liz. Everything, for good or bad.

But then he looked at her again, noticing once more how changed she was. No, the time wasn't right. Not quite yet. He needed to be sure that he still knew her as well as he'd always thought he did.

He pointed away from the edge towards the flats. Large expanses of these would be covered in bright red reeds in the autumn. The colour would merge with the purple of the flowering heather like a swathe of dramatic fabric. The furthest hills were already carpeted in heather. To stand on a rocky outcrop on the edge and look westwards was like gazing out over a red sea, crimson and magenta waves moving gently in the breeze like an ocean of blood.

'Let's walk that way for a while, across the moor towards White Edge. There's a Neolithic settlement called Swine Sty. We should be able to reach that and get back again before the light goes.'

'Okay. You're the boss.'

'Watch out for the hob holes,' said Cooper.

Villiers laughed. 'Hob? Are you kidding.'

'You know about hobs?'

'Yes, from my childhood fairy stories.'

The footpath towards White Edge crossed an area of grassland that gleamed gold even on a day of mist and rain. They headed towards a solitary tree standing in forlorn isolation on the moor.

'I spend most of my time in this country, of course,' said

Villiers. 'I served with an RAFP flight at a station in Cambridgeshire after I came back from Afghanistan. Mostly community policing, but you'd be surprised how much drug detection work we did, not to mention more recently breathalysing military personnel suspected of drink-driving.'

Cooper noted that her breathing was getting a bit ragged now. But the strenuous activity didn't stop her talking. It was as if these wide-open spaces, the empty landscapes above the Devil's Edge, had given her the freedom to express what she might not have said down in the valley, among strangers.

'My last posting was with Number Five Squadron at RAF Waddington,' she said. 'In April last year, my unit was deployed to Santander after the Icelandic volcano closed air space. We were assisting stranded British troops from Afghanistan, and some UK civilians. They came back to the UK on board HMS *Albion*.'

'I remember that in the news.'

'Outside unit level, I had a spell in the investigations branch, the Specialist Police Wing. That's plain clothes, the investigation of serious crime. CID work, in fact. Some of that time with the SPW was spent in Germany. I even liaised with the Forensic Science Flight on forensic investigations.'

'Your CV must have read like a dream for the interview panel,' said Cooper.

She laughed. 'Yes, I think I had everything. A local girl who knows the area, has life experience and leadership abilities. Not to mention the training. Our basic training includes on- and off-road driving, weapons training, lines of communication . . .'

'And good physical fitness.'

'We were tested every six months. That doesn't happen here, I guess.'

Cooper remembered the way she'd looked at Gavin Murfin. 'No.'

They were climbing now, towards the highest point of Big Moor. Beyond Swine Sty, the county boundary ran right along a stream called Bar Brook. The moors they could see in the middle distance lay in South Yorkshire.

'This stuff is difficult to walk through,' said Villiers.

'It's peat, but it's shallow peat. Not like the depths on Kinder or Bleaklow.'

The result of the peat's shallowness on these eastern moors was a mass of coarse, tussocky grass interspersed with boggy areas. Villiers was right – it was a difficult landscape to walk through. In places, it felt like wading through drifts of snow, with no idea what lay underneath. Blankets of dead bracken stems choked everything.

'And you met your husband in the service?' asked Cooper.

'Glen had a posting to the Tactical Provost Squadron. The TPS take on forward policing tasks in conflict zones. He served with his unit in the Gulf – Iraq, you know.' Villiers paused, seemed to reflect for a moment on something. 'The rest of his guys are still in a conflict zone now, in Afghanistan. Those are just the more publicised taskings, though. Most of our work doesn't get in the news.'

'Close protection duties?'

'Not me personally. But I was given the training. We all were. So stick close to me and you'll be safe, Ben.'

'Great.'

'Mind you, I'm used to carrying a Browning nine-millimetre. An extendable baton doesn't quite feel the same on the hip.'

As they reached the top of the moor, Villiers gazed across the valley that opened up to the east.

'I was trained not far from here, you know. Until the training school moved down south, we were based at RAF Newton in Nottinghamshire. We used to have a Hawker Hunter at the entrance, as our gate guardian.'

'Over the river, then,' said Cooper. 'I think I know the site. The buildings are an industrial estate now, though. The airfield itself has gone back to being arable land. They grow oilseed rape.'

'Shame.'

She hesitated. 'I keep saying "we" and "us", don't I? I keep forgetting I'm not in the RAFP any more. When you've been a member of a tight-knit unit for so long, it's hard to make the break. Especially if you've served in a conflict zone. You learn to depend totally on your mates, to watch each other's back. Being part of a team under pressure, there's nothing like it.'

'I understand,' said Cooper.

'That's why so many leave the services and find it impossible to adjust to civilian life. They suddenly find there's no one to watch their back, no mates to depend on. No buddy at their side.'

Cooper could think of nothing to say. He could tell from the catch in her voice that she was no longer talking just about her colleagues in her unit, but about a much more personal loss. It was a loss that she might never recover from, no matter how often people told her that time was a healer.

'You might not think so yet, Carol,' he said, 'but we can be like that too. A close-knit team. People you can depend on to watch your back.'

She smiled. 'Thanks, Ben.'

In the distance, Cooper saw the antlers and head of a stag outlined against the moor. The animal itself stood motionless, listening. Its ears were erect, its nostrils quivering. What was it listening for? What scent had it detected? Could an animal sense the presence of evil on the moor?

'How long were you actually in the services?' asked Cooper as they reached the edge. 'It can't be more than – what? Nine years?

'Yes. The standard contract.'

'It seems such a lot to have crammed into nine years.'

'Well, that's the armed services for you. You never know what you're going to be doing next, or where you're going to be posted. It's not like being a copper in sleepy old Derbyshire.'

She smiled, and Cooper knew he didn't have to tell her that it wasn't like that. But he said it anyway.

'It *can* get quite exciting,' he said. 'Some of the time, anyway.'

'From what we hear in the media, all you do is fill in paperwork for an entire shift.'

'So Snowdrops spend their off-duty time reading the *Daily Mail*, do they?'

'Oh, and I forgot – maybe the odd spell of planting false evidence, too.'

'Well, that's true.'

They began to trudge back towards the edge. As he walked through the expanse of reeds and cotton grass, Cooper noticed the way the distant rocky outcrops seemed to change shape. They slid slowly sideways, merged and divided, their outlines shifting from smooth to jagged to a distinctive silhouette.

It was all the effect of altering angle and perspective. With each step, a transformation took place in the landscape, a gradual reveal like the slow drawing aside of a curtain. At a point halfway across the flats, a split rock he hadn't noticed before came into view. As it emerged from behind a larger boulder, its two halves slowly parted and turned, like the hands of a clock creeping past noon.

Of course, his logical mind told him that he was the only moving object in this landscape. It was his steady strides across the flats that were causing the change in perspective. But his senses were sending him a different message. With no nearby landmarks, and in this peculiar light, the effect was deceptive. Despite what he kept telling himself, it really seemed to be the rock that was moving.

Some people studied these rocks in minute detail, mapping the strata and analysing their structure. Cooper supposed it was important to understand the geology, to explain in cool scientific terms how these eastern edges had come into existence. That was one way of dealing with their presence. But he couldn't help feeling that a logical approach took away the mystery. Didn't analysis always destroy romance, and drain the life out of poetry? Why not just stand and gaze, and let the imagination wander? He preferred the edges this way – wild, and full of magic.

'Afghanistan,' he said. 'You mentioned it once, but . . .?'

Villiers stared out over the valley. 'Yes, we were both in Afghanistan. We were there for two months, instructing new Afghan police recruits in Kabul. That was fairly uneventful, actually. There are lots of other duties that people never get to hear about back home. Back in 2002, Glen was injured in Cyprus, during demonstrations against a new radio mast at RAF Akrotiri. He got a commendation from the Provost Marshal for that.'

Cooper waited, knowing there was more, but not sure of the right question to ask, or even if he should be asking.

Finally Villiers spoke again, more quietly. Cooper had to strain to catch her voice, before her words were swept away in the wind blowing across the Devil's Edge.

'But then he went back to Afghanistan,' she said. 'Two years ago, he was shot and wounded in Helmand Province, when Taliban insurgents opened fire on his patrol one night. He died from his injuries before they could fly him back home.'

They stood silently together for a few minutes as the light faded and dusk settled on the valley. Riddings was directly below them, and Curbar could be glimpsed in the south.

Northwards, the village of Froggatt lay below its own grit-stone edge. The main part of the village was on the other side of the A625, with a tiny, ancient stone bridge that crossed the river to reach the Grindleford road. That bridge must have stood on another packhorse route, Cooper felt sure. Probably the route that snaked up the slope behind the Chequers Inn and zigzagged to the top of the rock-strewn edge. It was a steep track, worn into ruts over the centuries by the hoofs of the laden horses. It boggled the mind to imagine how they had managed it. Cooper had always thought it was difficult enough going down without losing your footing, let alone carrying a couple of millstones. Those packhorse men must have been tough characters.

Where were the packhorse trains heading when they went over the edge and crossed the moor? Towards Chesterfield. And, of course, to Sheffield. They carried grindstones for the city's steel and cutlery manufacturers.

Tonight, mist hung in the valley bottom, masking the lights of the villages. As with any of these edges, the best light was in the evening, as the sun started to descend in the west and bathe the stones with warm light. Cooper liked to wait to see the afterglow, then walk back to experience the moors in the dark. There was nothing like starlight and moonlight, and there was plenty of it up here on the edge. As long as you tried to ignore the orange glow from Sheffield in the east.

On the slopes below the edge, the houses of Riddings and its neighbouring villages were taking on their own distinct shapes in the dusk. Tonight they looked like frightened creatures crouching in the hollows of the hillside, an occasional light winking on and off as if a cautious eye was opened to check for danger.

Cooper pictured the inhabitants huddled inside their homes. For some reason, the image in his mind resembled an illustration he'd seen once in a children's history book – a primitive tribe of *Homo sapiens* crouching in their caves around smoking fires, their shadows thrown on to rock walls decorated with drawings of wild animals.

It must be so difficult, sitting in your home, or lying in your bed at night, knowing you were a potential victim. How did you run your life with the knowledge of lethal danger lurking outside the door? You huddled together in that primeval instinct for safety. It was the same fear that cavemen must have felt, listening to wild beasts crashing through the forest at night, picturing in their minds those unseen terrors in the darkness beyond the cave. A completely primitive dread.

There was one thing Cooper did know – the Savages didn't belong in a village like Riddings. They belonged up here, on the moor. They were, after all, wild beasts who walked on two legs.

'Carol,' he said, 'have they shown you how to access the PNC and use the intelligence system?'

She looked at him in surprise, her mind no doubt following a completely different train of thought.

'Yes, I'm fully trained,' she said. 'I did all that in Ripley before I came up to E Division.'

'I've got some jobs I'd like you to do in the morning, then.'

'In the office?'

She sounded disappointed. Cooper sympathised, but it couldn't be helped.

145

'I'm afraid it's where most of our work is done,' he said.

'Oh, I know.'

They were looking down on Riddings from the outcrop, poised in space, conscious of the empty air around them. It was the God position, everything below them laid out and visible. Cooper saw the headlights of a vehicle travelling along Curbar Lane, the beams sweeping across the trees and catching a reflection from the convex mirrors outside Valley View. He watched for the vehicle to reach the corner at The Green and turn up or down the hill. But the lights vanished before they reached that point. The driver must have stopped or pulled into one of the houses close to the junction. He wondered if that had happened on Tuesday night, too.

Tuesday. From their account of that night, William and Retty Chadwick had stood around here, watching for shooting stars as the Perseid meteor shower passed overhead. On the surface, it didn't sound like much of an alibi. But how many other star-gazers were out on the edge that night? If it was a good night for viewing meteors, there were probably many people who'd driven out from Sheffield or Chesterfield to get away from the city lights and take advantage of the darker skies over the Peak District. Had that night been overcast, though? Or was it clear and cloudless, perfect for watching shooting stars?

So the Chadwicks had been standing here in the dark, looking upwards at the sky. But surely they must have looked down, too? They couldn't have resisted this God-like sensation of being able to see everything from above, gazing down on their village and watching their neighbours coming and going.

Down there, the residents of Riddings would not have been able to see anything from behind their walls and hedges. The Chadwicks were the only people who might actually have witnessed what happened. Whether they realised it or not, their position had been unique.

Cooper wondered who else knew that the Chadwicks had been on the edge that night, watching the Perseids. That knowledge might be critical. Because if his theory was correct, it put the Chadwicks at risk of being the next victims.

146

Villiers shivered. 'Is it me, or is it getting a bit cool now?'

'Yes, the rocks lose their heat very quickly when it goes dark. And there's always a cold wind up here. It's a totally different place in the winter.'

'I can imagine. Not the most hospitable landscape in the cold and rain, I guess.'

For a moment, Cooper took one last look at the rooftops of Riddings, spread out below him. He was reminded of the case of a serial killer who had chosen his victims on the basis of where they lived. When he was caught, he'd told his interviewers that the shape of a house roof told him something about the people living there. Told him whether it was their turn to die, he supposed.

Cooper was just thinking it was time to go home, when the ear-splitting screech of a burglar alarm shattered the silence.

13

Today there had been a cool atmosphere in the conference room at Nottinghamshire Police headquarters. Fry had noticed that the facilitator's expression was stony as they arrived. They were even made to turn off their mobile phones before the session started. Somebody had been naughty in class. But who?

During the coffee break, word went round. It turned out that the youth from the IT department had been using Twitter on his iPhone during yesterday's session, sending out disparaging tweets about the working group at regular intervals. Everyone knew the hierarchy didn't like communication with the public. Look at all those police officers with anonymous blogs who'd been tracked down and eliminated. Deblogged, anyway. Too much honesty was contrary to official policy. Even civilians couldn't get away with it.

Fry looked at the IT guy with new respect. She was starting to feel warmer towards her colleagues.

It might have been that feeling that made her accept the invitation from Mick or Rick, the Leicestershire inspector who sat next to her in the session. Lunch with him yesterday had been pleasant enough, a relief from the tedium of the conference room. Besides, anything seemed preferable now to the drive back over to Edendale and her empty flat.

'We can't risk lunch again today,' he'd said. 'But how about when we finish the session tonight? When they give us our freedom back.'

She'd nodded without much thought of the consequences. 'Okay.'

Fry knew she mustn't drink and drive, so only one glass of wine would be acceptable. God forbid that she should get breathalysed by her colleagues on her way back to Derbyshire.

When they got to the pub, it was her turn to buy the drinks.

'There you go, Mick,' she said.

'Rick,' he said. 'My name's Rick.'

'Oh, right. Rick . . .?'

'Shepherd. I'm stationed in Leicester.'

'Of course. I remember.'

He smiled, apparently unaffected by her lapse. Fry wondered if she could say anything she liked to him and he would just keep on smiling. He looked to be that sort of man.

'So, tell me about yourself,' he said.

'What's to tell? Right now, I'm based in Derbyshire E Division. Edendale.'

'In the middle of the Peak District.'

'You know it?' said Fry in surprise. In her head, Edendale was such a backwater that she didn't expect anyone outside Derbyshire to have heard of it.

'Everyone must have visited the Peak District at some time. Don't they say that half the population of England lives within an hour's drive?'

'If they do, I don't know why they're all driving in that direction. There must be more interesting places to go.'

'You think so? Don't you like it?'

'It's a desert,' said Fry. 'No culture, no shops, no proper transport facilities. It takes forever to get to a motorway. And the nearest airport is way down past Nottingham. So you can't even escape the place easily.'

'I often go walking in the Peaks,' he said. 'We've got a little hiking group together in my section. We head out towards Kinder Scout or somewhere at the weekends.'

'Walking,' she said.

'Yes.'

'Just walking?'

'What else? It's great to get out of the office, away from work for a while. To feel the wind in your hair. Physical exercise, a few hours in the open air. It helps me to relax.'

He was starting to sound like Ben Cooper. Besides, he didn't actually have much hair for the wind to blow through.

'There must be other ways to relax,' she said.

He smirked at her, fondling his beer bottle. 'I'm sure I could think of a few.'

A burst of laughter from a nearby table gave Fry an excuse to look away. A group of office workers were having a drink on the way home. They might even be civilian staff from across the road at Sherwood Lodge. She didn't recognise any of them. But then, a civilian was a civilian.

She looked back at Rick Shepherd. It was Rick, wasn't it? Not Mick, or Dick. He was smiling at her again, one eyebrow raised. Some unspoken message was being conveyed. Fry knew what the message was. She ought to respond, knew deep down what she should do. She ought to act now, before it went any further.

And yet a great weariness had come over her. None of this really mattered, did it? Perhaps there might be a moment when she felt something, a brief response that was more than the deadly worthlessness she'd been feeling for the past few weeks. Rick Shepherd wasn't the greatest thing she'd ever met. But he was there, he was available, and she had his attention.

He took another drink, laid a hand on the table, toying with a coaster. He frowned, seemed to search for a line of conversation. Perhaps he was as unaccustomed to this as she was. He didn't wear a wedding ring, but that meant nothing. People slipped them on and off like raincoats these days. And many couples chose to live together for years without bothering to marry. He could have a partner back in Leicester. Would he tell her, if she asked? Did she want to know?

'We'll be merging soon anyway, I guess,' he said.

'Will we?'

'Nottinghamshire, Derbyshire, Leicestershire, maybe a couple of others. It's inevitable, sooner or later.' He shook his head. 'I know it would save millions of pounds on headquarters costs and all that. But I'm starting to think it would create too big an organisation.'

'Really?'

Fry thought of West Midlands Police, the force she'd moved from when she came to Derbyshire. With almost thirteen thousand officers and staff, it was bigger than Notts, Derbyshire and Leicestershire combined.

'Maybe some people don't know what big is.'

'You know, the East Midlands region is growing faster than elsewhere in the country,' he said.

Okay. Now she had her ID. He'd been wearing a different tie today. In fact, he'd taken it off altogether when they came to the pub. But the words were identical, and the tone of voice was the same. The exact tenor of complacency and laziness, a lack of concern about accuracy and rigour. Just the sort of qualities she hated.

Fry finished her drink and stood up. Her companion hastily drained his beer, picked up his jacket and his phone, suddenly eager to leave. They walked back towards the pub car park together, and stopped when they reached her Peugeot. Rick leaned casually on the roof.

'I'm sure we could work closely together, you and me,' he said. 'Don't you think? A bit of mutual assistance, Diane? I know a nice quiet spot in Sherwood Forest where we could explore our personal merger options. I can promise you I always come up to my performance targets.'

He was standing a bit too close now. Well inside her personal space. Fry felt herself tense. It was that instinctive reaction she couldn't control, an automatic response of her muscles triggered by a suppressed memory. She always knew it would happen. But she couldn't explain the reason for it, not to someone like Rick Shepherd.

He was close enough now for her to smell the beer on his breath, the deodorant clinging to his shirt. She was frozen, her limbs so stiff that they hurt. A long moment passed, when neither of them spoke or breathed. Just when it seemed that nothing would happen, he made his move. And Fry felt his hand touching the base of her spine.

The shriek went on and on. In Cooper's mind it was a despairing wail, the scream of a dying victim. A call for help he was unable to respond to.

'Oh God. Which house is it?' he said. 'Can you see?'

'It might be nothing. A false alarm.'

'Do you really think so?'

You couldn't easily pin down the direction of a burglar alarm. It was one of those elusive noises. Its high-pitched shriek bounced off everything – the houses, the trees, the rock faces of the edge. Cooper stared apprehensively down at the village. He was looking for the telltale red flash of the light on an alarm box. He felt an anxious sweat breaking out on his forehead despite the cold wind.

'Can you see it? Carol, can you see where it's coming from?'

'No.'

'Nor me. Damn.'

With shaking fingers, he used his phone to alert the control room – though there were units in the immediate area who ought to be responding even as he began to make the call. Thank goodness he was on top of the edge, and within signal range.

'There are people running,' said Villiers when he finished the call.

'Where?'

She pointed. 'Over there, behind the trees.'

'That's on the other side of Curbar Lane. Yes, it must be The Cottage. It's the teenagers' party at the Chadwicks.'

Voices drifted clear on the air now from the village. Screams, shouts, a smashed glass, bodies crashing through undergrowth. Distantly a siren started – the two-tone wail of a police vehicle. Too distant, though. Why weren't they in the village already?

'How do we get down?' said Villiers.

'There's only the old packhorse route. But for God's sake be careful.'

'You go first then. I'm right behind you.'

Their progress down the slope from the edge was frustratingly slow. The stone was uneven and dangerous, worn smooth and slippery in places by centuries of passing feet. Cooper cursed under his breath many times as he stumbled, or felt his feet begin to slide on the rock. He wished he could have gone faster, but there was no point in breaking an ankle or hurtling head first down the slope. An injured police officer was no use to anyone.

'Be careful,' he called at every corner or steeper section. 'Carol, be careful.'

'I'm *being* careful,' she shouted back. 'Would we have been better going back to the car?'

'Too late now,' said Cooper. 'Too late.'

Finally the slope grew less steep, the ground levelled out, the track became more grass than rock. They were on the outskirts of the village, covering the rough terrain between the edge and the boundaries of the first properties.

But now they could see almost nothing – a dark wedge of trees directly in front of them, indistinct shapes further away in the dusk, a brief glimpse of a light from a window, appearing and disappearing among the trees.

Cooper was breathless now, his lungs burning and his legs tiring. He glanced over his shoulder to see Villiers still close behind him.

'I'm not sure where this track comes out,' he said.

'Oh, great. I thought you knew where we were going.'

'You know what?' gasped Cooper. 'I think I must be mad.'

'No argument from me.'

Over a stile, they found themselves running through a field, passing a large property to their right.

'This is Moorside House,' said Cooper. 'Tyler Kaye.'

A horse snorted in the dusk, and Villiers skidded sideways in surprise.

And then they were on Curbar Lane at last, emerging on to tarmac and stumbling to a halt. Cooper stared around, trying to regain his breath, clutching his phone in his hand but not knowing now which way to go. He could still hear the burglar alarm, but the sound was lost in the trees, less shrill and distinct than it had been from the edge. There was music too, loud and pounding, a background to many voices still screaming and shouting.

'How many kids are at that party?' said Cooper. 'Has she invited the whole school?'

'Maybe it's on Facebook,' said Villiers.

But at least there was a police vehicle, a marked response car at the end of the lane, with its blue lights flashing.

'We're responding to a call about an intruder,' said one of the uniformed officers when he saw Cooper. 'It's a high-priority response in this area. They called out the cavalry.'

'Which house?' asked Cooper.

'The Cottage, Curbar Lane. Name of Chadwick. But we can't find it.'

'It's right there. You've probably got it as Nether Croft on the database.'

'Okay, I see it.'

The officer's radio crackled, and he acknowledged.

'Air support is on scene,' he said.

'What? They were quick.'

'It's the South Yorkshire air support unit, Sierra Yankee 99. It was already in the air, and a lot closer than the unit in Ripley.'

Cooper could hear the helicopter now. If it had been deployed for a suspect search, it would already be using its thermal-imaging camera to sweep the ground along the edge of the village.

'Are you in contact with them?'

The officer from the response unit had an Airwave radio, while Cooper had only his phone.

'Yes, the observer is in direct communication. He can give us a commentary.'

154

The officer joined Cooper and Villiers on the lane. Nearby somebody, or something, had bulldozed a way through the undergrowth, leaving a trail like the charge of a rhinoceros.

'What the heck has been going on here?' said Cooper.

The noise of the helicopter overhead drowned out everything else. Cooper felt the downdraught of the blades stirring the bushes along the edge of the lane. Then a powerful light burst from the sky and dazzled him, lighting up the area for yards around.

'Please tell Sierra Yankee there are police officers on the ground – and to get their damn light off us!'

'They're reporting multiple individuals going through the gardens at The Cottage,' said the officer.

'Multiple? How many?'

'A dozen, at least.'

Cooper could still hear music thumping from the house. If the speakers were inside, they must have all the doors and windows open.

'It's the party. Can't someone tell those kids to stop running around like maniacs and get back in the house? They're only confusing the situation. They're creating far too many heat signatures for the thermal imager.'

'We spoke to them earlier, when we had complaints from their neighbours. They've been drinking all evening.'

'So?'

'Well, they're not taking any advice from us. No doubt they think all this is a great laugh.'

'Idiots.'

Villiers had pushed her way through the undergrowth and found a gate standing open.

'Whoever they are, I think they went this way.'

They could see figures milling around now, many of them simply running round in circles. Solar lights had been set up in the Chadwicks' garden, and teenagers were charging backwards and forwards, in and out of the lights, creating a chaos of shadows. Some were shaking bottles of beer and spraying liquid into the air.

155

'How are we going to get this situation under control?' said Villiers.

'Without a lot more bodies on the ground, we're not.'

Cooper grabbed a passing youth and held on to him.

'Hey, who are you?'

'Police. What's going on here?'

The young man laughed. He was flushed and pouring with sweat, and his shirt was soaked with beer.

'Intruder,' he said. 'They chased him off.'

'Which way?'

He stared wildly around. 'That way. Some of the guys went after him.'

Cooper looked at the PC, who was listening to his radio.

'The helicopter crew are tracking the heat signature of a single figure running from the scene.'

'Okay. Come on.'

The three of them had only gone a few yards towards the corner of the Chadwicks' property, close to The Green, when the officer reported again.

'The suspect has disappeared from the thermal imager. Gone to ground somewhere, or got inside a house.'

'Where?'

'In the vicinity of Chapel Close.'

'This way, then.'

'He's on the move again. The observer on Sierra Yankee 99 is directing us to the second house on the right in Chapel Close.'

Cooper grimaced. 'Oh God. That's the Gambles' house. I've got a bad feeling about this.'

He could tell from the noises around him that more officers had arrived in Riddings, and were closing in on the location under the direction of the helicopter's observer. Torch beams flashed towards him and away again. An Alsatian barked excitedly, and he pictured it straining against its handler's lead.

He grabbed Villiers' arm and pointed.

'There he goes,' he said. 'Over the wall and running through that orchard. If we cut across the lane, we can catch him at the other side.'

'I'm ahead of you.'

Villiers sprinted off, and was there first. She caught up with her quarry, grabbed an arm, kicked out a leg and flipped him on to the floor. Coming up behind, Cooper heard the breath go out of his body in a long whoosh.

By the time he arrived, Villiers already had handcuffs on and had patted the suspect down. She sat him up and Cooper gazed down at him, trembling with anger.

'Mr Gamble. What the hell do you think you're doing?'

Gamble had lost his hat, and his hair was standing out from his head in a wild tangle. For several moments he could do nothing but gasp and wheeze. He stared around him in shock, as if he'd suddenly found himself in the middle of some surreal fantasy. His bushy eyebrows waggled in alarm, and he looked down at the cuffs on his wrists.

'I wasn't doing anything,' he said plaintively.

'What?'

'That isn't true.' Cooper gestured at the activity – the running officers, the flashing lights, the swinging torch beams, and the helicopter hovering overhead. 'You were the cause of all this.'

Gamble gazed up at him. His voice was feeble and wretched.

'I was just watching.'

Straightening up, Cooper took a deep breath to calm himself down.

'You know what? You do too much watching, sir. Far too much. You should spend more time at home, with your wife.'

They handed Gamble off to a pair of uniformed officers, who escorted him to his house. Other officers were trying to calm the teenagers and shepherd them back to the party. It was unclear what offence Gamble might have committed yet, until they could get a coherent account from someone, a few details about what had happened. Judging from the state of some of the participants, that might not be until morning.

Cooper looked at Villiers. 'Thanks, Carol.'

'It's okay.' She brushed her hands together. 'But what's this

157

spend more time at home with your wife? Are you turning into a marriage guidance counsellor now?'

Cooper shook his head.

'This village is turning me into something, though. And I'm not sure I like it.'

He turned away from Chapel Close and looked across the gardens of The Cottage. Finally, he could tell the direction the burglar alarm was coming from. The sound was much clearer now, screaming high-pitched and urgent across the village, calling endlessly for attention while all these people ran madly around in circles.

He could see it, too – a small red light blinking and blinking high on the corner of a wall, no more than fifty yards from Valley View.

He knew now that the alarm wasn't at the Chadwicks', where the party had been taking place. It was sounding at Fourways, the home of the Hollands.

It was already dark when Diane Fry drove into Edendale and turned into Grosvenor Avenue. She found a space at the kerb and parked outside the house.

When she pulled out her key to enter her flat, she noticed that she had streaks of blood on her hands. Strange that she hadn't see it while she was driving back from Nottinghamshire. Her mind must have been on other things.

She closed the door, shrugged off her jacket and headed for the shower. Blood on her hands. That was something not everyone could cope with. But right now, for her, it felt good. The sight of blood was exactly what she needed.

14

Friday

By the following morning, a scene-of-crime team had moved into the Hollands' house. SOCOs were checking any items with a smooth surface. Doors, worktops, kitchen utensils, anything the offenders might have touched. If they had, there was a possibility of the items being fingerprinted.

Cooper had managed only a few hours' sleep before he found himself back in Riddings. Last night already seemed like a strange dream. By the time he returned, much of the circus had been and gone, leaving a team conducting the forensic search and an examination of the garden in daylight.

DI Hitchens was there, marshalling resources, snapping at people on the phone, urging the press office to restrict the amount of information released to the media. If they weren't careful, there would soon be a danger of panic,.

'It appears there was an earlier 999 call,' said Hitchens when he saw Cooper arrive. 'The call handler told the householder to follow the usual procedure for a burglary report.'

'Don't touch anything that the offenders might have touched.'

'Right.'

Cooper nodded. The instinct of most householders was to tidy up. Clear away the broken glass, close the drawers, mend the damaged door hinges. And wipe away those fingerprints from the windowsill, of course. In retrospect, they realised their mistake. But by then it was often too late.

'It wasn't given a high enough priority, obviously.'

'Obviously.'

Sarah Holland wouldn't have been thinking logically anyway. Not once her husband had been taken away in the ambulance, with a paramedic frantically working on him all the way to the hospital.

'People are getting very jumpy, Ben,' said Hitchens.

'I know.'

'At times like this, people start to see crime all around them. And the press – I think they've gone mad. They're just reporting stuff off the internet as if it was fact. Blogs and so on. Some of the rubbish going round takes the breath away.'

Hitchens turned away to take a phone call. When he finished, his face was grim.

'Any news?' asked Cooper.

'Martin Holland has died in hospital.'

'Damn. What was the cause of death?'

'There were no visible injuries. It seems likely he had a heart attack. The post-mortem will tell us for sure.'

Cooper remembered Mrs Holland talking about her husband walking on the edge for exercise. *Good for the heart, isn't it?* He ought to have realised that Martin Holland had a heart condition. He was the right age, and came from a fairly sedentary profession. A classic case. A cardiac arrest just waiting to happen.

'Did Mrs Holland see anything?'

'A masked figure. She hasn't been able to give us any further description. She's too upset.'

This was the woman who liked the idea of having a criminal as a neighbour. A Mafia lover, Gavin Murfin might have called her. Maybe she'd watched *The Sopranos* too often on Channel 4. It was a middle-class attitude towards crime. He bet she'd never experienced serious crime herself in her life. Not until now.

'Mr Holland confronted the intruder, then.'

'That's the way it seems. But there was no actual physical contact, so far as we can tell.'

'That's very different from the attacks on the Barrons, sir.'

'Probably they were just disturbed sooner. They got scared off and legged it.'

'The Savages aren't the type to be scared off,' said Cooper.

'We'll see.'

'I don't think it's all down to the Savages,' he said. 'It doesn't make sense for them to come back to the same area so soon. It doesn't fit in with their pattern.'

'So what, then?'

'I think someone has been exploiting the panic over the Savages. I think the answer lies much closer. Here, in Riddings.'

Hitchens looked at him. 'Prove it, Ben.'

'If only I could . . .'

The DI nodded. 'Everything comes down to "if only". By the way, Murf is here somewhere. Make sure he's not causing a nuisance, will you?'

Hitchens walked away to talk to the crime-scene manager, and Cooper cautiously entered the house. The slate floor in the hallway was scattered with plastic wrappers, the detritus of the paramedics' attempts to stabilise Martin Holland before his trip in the ambulance.

The spotlights were on in the kitchen, illuminating the Shaker-style units with a harsh, cold light. The cat's basket by the Aga was empty. Cooper wondered where the Persian was. Probably taken offence at all the strangers in the house, and gone to hide in the garden.

Normally a neighbour would step in to look after any animals in a case like this. He wasn't sure there was a neighbour in Riddings who would think of it. Next door, Valley View was empty, while Russell Edson and Richard Nowak seemed unlikely sources of support.

'Cute,' called Murfin from a doorway.

'What?'

'This downstairs bathroom.'

Cooper looked in, and saw a cast-iron rolltop bath with clawed feet, his and hers hand basins.

'And look at this,' said Murfin from the hallway a minute later.

'What now?'

'Mail. They get mail. Proper letters in envelopes, with their name and address typed on them. Most people only get advertising leaflets through their letterbox these days. That's what's been keeping the Royal Mail in business since the internet was invented.'

'Are you doing anything useful, Gavin?'

'Yes, keeping everyone's spirits up.'

Cooper watched the SOCOs dusting the door handles and laying down stepping plates in the hall.

'We're not being much use here,' he said.

They retreated to the garden. Cooper found himself standing near the miniature version of the Devil's Edge. He noticed that a stone had fallen off the top and lay shattered on the drive.

'Actually, I got a letter the other day,' said Murfin.

'Oh? Good news?'

'They sent me my pension statement. It was like a first draft of the inscription on my tombstone.'

'Gavin, you really enjoy being miserable, don't you?'

'It's the only pleasure I get.'

'That must be why you insist on supporting the Rams, then.'

Murfin sniffed.

'Why don't these people have guard dogs?' he asked.

'Guard dogs?' said Cooper.

He'd seen plenty of dogs in Riddings, but none of them looked much use for guard duty. The fashion seemed to be for geriatric golden retrievers and pampered spaniels. Not a German Shepherd or Rottweiler in sight.

'It's a good question, Gavin. I don't know.'

'Perhaps it's too common.'

'I think we'll be more use back at the office,' said Cooper.

'What, no house-to-house, boss?'

'All the information that could be got out of neighbours was collected last night. Nobody was taking any notice of what was going on at Fourways. Thanks to a bunch of drunken teenagers and Mr Barry Gamble.'

'Oh, Gamble. The local vigilante nut job?' said Murfin.

'I don't think he's a total nut job.'

'He's a good actor, then. He gets my vote for the Oscar.'

'I know what you mean. But he's just eccentric. There used to be one in every village. But he seems particularly out of place in Riddings.'

Murfin shoved his hands in his pockets, considering the property in front of them.

'No house-to-house, then. I'm devastated. What about my hill?'

'I'll find you a mountain of paperwork to climb instead,' said Cooper.

'Oh, thanks.'

They went back down the drive to where a long roll of crime-scene tape had been used to cordon off another gateway. Murfin paused, and looked back at Fourways.

'You know what, Ben? If I lived in Riddings, I'd have my house on the market by now,' he said. 'Too many murders bring down the tone of an area. It really ruins the character of a place.'

One of the SOCOs glanced round from the back of the crime-scene van as Murfin walked past. They all tended to look a bit indistinguishable in their shapeless blue scene suits, especially with their hoods up and masks on. But Cooper recognised this SOCO from her size and the way she moved. He didn't have to wait to see her eyes over the top of her mask.

'Hi.'

'Hi, you.'

'One day we'll stop meeting like this.'

They both spoke in lowered voices, conscious of the comments they would get if colleagues saw them chatting at a crime scene.

'So, where were you?' asked Liz.

'When?'

'Last night. You said you were going to explain something. But I never even saw you. Never heard a peep from you all evening.'

'Look at this,' said Cooper. 'This is where I was.'

'But I heard you were already in the area when it happened.'

'Yes, I was,' admitted Cooper.

She came a bit closer.

'Ben,' she said, her tone switching from accusation to concern. 'You're not . . .?'

'What?' he said, suddenly afraid of what she was going to say.

'You're not getting obsessed with the case, are you? I know what you're like. You'll be letting it take up every minute of your time if someone doesn't stop you. And no one will thank you for it, you know.'

'I don't think it's like that.'

'I hope not. Because I'm the one who'll have to stop you. I need some of your time for myself.' She lifted a case of equipment from the van and gave him a wink. 'Besides, you definitely can't be like that when we're married.'

'Shush.'

'It's not going to be a secret for long. We need to talk . . .' She broke off as the crime-scene manager came out of the house to look for her. 'Later.'

Carol Villiers and the rest of the team were already at their desks in West Street, busy with phone calls, following up contacts from residents in Riddings during the night. Most of them were complaints about noise from the party, or the police helicopter frightening their horses. But they all had to be checked out.

'Well I don't know about you, but I've been busy,' said Villiers. 'All the work is done back at the office, like you said.'

'Yes, it is. Sometimes I think it would be nice to have a desk job.'

She studied him more closely. 'Actually, you look shattered, Ben. Didn't you get much sleep?'

'No, I couldn't get last night out of my mind.'

'It wasn't your fault.'

'If I'd been able to take control of the situation, instead of letting that chaos go on . . .'

'It wouldn't have made any difference to Mr Holland.'

'Maybe not. But we might have been pursuing the real suspects instead of letting Barry Gamble and a bunch of drunken kids lead us on a wild goose chase. Damn it.'

'Well, let's put that aside. I got the intel you wanted. And a bit more besides.'

Luke Irvine and Becky Hurst came over and joined them, forming a tight-knit group around Cooper's desk.

'There was one thing I was thinking about,' said Cooper. 'Mr Nowak said they had a break-in at Lane End a while ago.'

'Yes, I found the incident log.'

'What was the outcome?'

'Finalised at source,' said Villiers.

'Oh, great.'

'Finalised at source' was the current euphemism for a decision not to investigate a crime. A lack of evidence, low priority, a judgement that there was no prospect of a successful outcome. Whatever the reasons, the report could be signed off, provided the victim was notified of the decision within five working days and issued with a Victim of Crime leaflet. That was the Code of Practice, by the letter.

Cooper sighed. When you did things by the book, the results could depend on which book you were using. It was hardly an unusual story, though. At the serious end of crime, money was rarely a major issue. But at the bottom end, forensic resources were considered too expensive to be justified.

'They did get a visit from Victim Support,' said Villiers.

'What about Richard Nowak?' said Cooper. 'Any convictions?'

'Nothing on him.'

'Really? So much for the Russian mafia theory, then.'

'Definitely a red herring,' laughed Villiers. 'It might almost have been intended to distract us from the real villain in Riddings.'

Detecting a tone of significance in her voice, Cooper looked up and caught the smile on her face. A bit self-satisfied, perhaps. But right now, he was glad to see it. That smile suggested that someone had made some progress. If Carol had discovered a new lead, she was entitled to feel as pleased with herself as she wanted to be.

'Come on. Spill it.'

Villiers nodded. 'Mr Kaye.'

'Wait.' Cooper located Kaye on the map of Riddings. 'Tyler Kaye at Moorside House? What about him?'

'He's well known.'

Now Cooper was interested. 'Well known' in this context meant only one thing – an individual with a substantial criminal record, whose name cropped up frequently in the intelligence system.

'He's a Sheffield villain,' said Villiers. 'And a major player, by all accounts. I'm just waiting for a return call from the Regional Intelligence Unit.'

'But he's a celebrity,' protested Irvine. 'He runs a string of clubs across the north of England. He puts on gigs. His company manages some well-known bands.'

'And your point is?' said Hurst.

'Okay,' said Cooper. 'I can see he's likely to have some form from way back. Drugs, I suppose? Links to organised crime? It seems to go with the territory. But it's not what we're looking for, is it?'

Villiers looked at him with a frown. 'Unless the Barrons and the Hollands had both upset him at some time. It sounds as though he's the only one who might have the right contacts.'

That made Irvine laugh. 'What, to put a hit on his neighbours?'

'It's not what we're looking for,' repeated Cooper.

'Oh, do we actually *know* what we're looking for?' asked Villiers.

'Well . . . maybe not. But I think I'll know it when I hear it. What about the others?'

'There's nothing on the PNC – none of them has a criminal record.'

'Shame.'

'But . . .'

'But? Have you found something, Carol?'

'Yes.'

'Brilliant.'

'It's a county-court hearing.'

'A civil case, then? Is it relevant?'

'Yes, I think so.'

Cooper felt the familiar surge of interest, sparked by the tone of her voice. 'Which of them was involved?'

'Nowak and the Barrons,' said Villiers. 'It was a dispute over ownership of a piece of land. The judge said it was ludicrous to drag a petty argument between neighbours into court. It must have cost them both a fortune in legal fees. The lawyers are the only winners in a case like that, aren't they? But you know how these things go. Nobody wants to back down.'

'So who won?'

'Well, that's debatable. Reading the reports, it sounds as though they both thought they'd lost the case. Neither of them really got what they wanted, you see. Not completely. The judge thought he was achieving a reasonable compromise, but neither of the parties involved seems to have been in any mood to find a middle ground.'

'That's the problem with the Judgement of Solomon. The baby tends to die in the process.'

She nodded. 'Well, strictly speaking, the Barrons were given the judgment. They weren't awarded any costs, but in the letter of the law they were the successful party.'

'So . . . Did Nowak seem to you like a man who would bear a grudge?'

'I don't know. But it certainly must have cost him a lot of money.'

Cooper stood up, his tiredness forgotten.

'Well, I think we'd better talk to Mr Nowak again,' he said.

'Ah. So now we *do* know what we were looking for, do we?'

On the way back into Riddings, Cooper came to a traffic jam on Curbar Lane. A couple of uniformed officers were trying to marshal a media posse into a convenient cluster. Of course, there had been a lot of press attention ever since the Savages first started operating in the eastern edges. Yet now, with two fatal attacks in the same village, all the photographers seemed to be clustered around the gate of Moorside House, hoping for a glimpse of Tyler Kaye.

'This isn't helping at all,' he said.

'Nothing we can do about it,' said Villiers.

'We haven't heard that Mr Kaye is back yet, have we?'

'Last we heard he was still in Florida. But I'll check.'

'Thanks. I wouldn't like to think the press knows more than we do.'

Cooper turned into Croft Lane and slowed the car to a crawl. Many of these lanes around Riddings petered out into rough tracks that meandered upwards to the moors. Several times already in the last few days he'd had to stop where the tarmac ran out and struggled to turn the Toyota in someone's gateway.

He stopped at a point where he judged the back of the Hollands' property met the Barrons'.

'I won't be a minute, Carol. I just want to take a look here.'

He went through the back gate into the garden of Fourways. In the copse at the back of the house, he came across an area that had been left wild, perhaps to encourage wildlife. Pushing his way through the undergrowth, he came to the remains of a dry-stone wall, so overgrown and covered in moss that it was invisible until he was practically touching it. The wire fence that surrounded the Barrons' property ran along the top of this wall too. Or at least, it had at one time. Now there was a gap. He found the broken end of the wire, and could see from the glint of the metal that it had been cut cleanly, and quite recently too.

He turned to go back to the gate, thinking he ought to send scenes-of-crime down here. He could see that Villiers had got out of the car and was waiting for him, a puzzled look on her face. Perhaps he ought to explain himself too.

It was then that he noticed the remains of the old gravel

path under the foliage. Small granules of gravel, too small to be used on a drive where vehicles would compact it. Small enough to stick in the soles of your boots, especially if you were running.

Cooper stopped. The hairs on the back of his neck crawled as he sensed movement in the undergrowth at the bottom of the garden. A surreptitious rustle, the faintest of sounds, almost inaudible against the sigh of the wind.

Keeping his back to the garden, he spoke to Villiers.

'Carol, I think we're being watched. Go back round the house and out into the lane. Quietly, without any fuss. Make it look as though you're leaving.'

He pretended to be checking messages on his phone, while he waited a couple of minutes to give Villiers enough time to get out and round the corner into the lane. Then he turned back to the garden and strode rapidly across the grass.

Now he saw a face in the bushes. It almost merged with the undergrowth, and bits of foliage seemed to sprout from it like whiskers. It reminded Cooper of one of those stone gargoyles you saw on old churches. A living image of the green man.

'Mr Gamble?' he said. 'You might as well come out.'

There was a moment of silence, then a loud sniff and more rustling in the undergrowth. Finally a figure pushed aside the branches and stepped on to the grass.

'I heard something going on,' he said. 'So I came to have a look. You can't be too careful. Especially at the moment. That's right, isn't it?'

'Of course.'

Gamble made a half-hearted attempt to brush the twigs and burrs from his jacket, apparently oblivious to the privet leaves in his hair. For a moment Cooper saw him as a kind of elemental figure, something from a children's folk tale. A mischievous goblin or ancient woodland sprite. The boggart in the flesh. But what mischief was he up to now?

'So you were just passing, were you, Mr Gamble?'

'Yes.'

Cooper nodded. 'Again?'

Villiers pushed her way through the bushes behind him.

'Do we need the handcuffs again?' she said, straightening her jacket.

'No,' said Cooper. 'Not this time.'

He turned back to Gamble. 'You never learn, do you, sir?'

Gamble shuffled his feet. 'I'm not doing anything wrong.'

'This is a crime scene. You shouldn't be here.'

'Oh well, I'd better be off then. So, er . . . what happened to the Hollands?'

'I've no doubt you'll find out in due course.'

'Only I saw the ambulance.'

'I'm sure you did.'

'You don't give much away, do you?'

'No. But if you happen to stumble across any information, Mr Gamble, I'm sure you'll come and share it with us, won't you?'

'I don't know anything. Not a thing,' said Gamble. 'Shall I just . . .?'

'DC Villiers will escort you off the property,' said Cooper.

'Fair enough.'

'No – wait a minute.'

Gamble stopped, his eyebrows waggling uncertainly.

'Perhaps you can help,' said Cooper. 'What do you know about a dispute between Mr Nowak and the Barrons? An argument over a bit of land.'

'Oh, that. Everyone knows about that. It was the boundary, you see. Just along there, on Croft Lane.'

'How did it start?'

'Well, when Nowak bought Lane End, there was no wall or fence there, not even a hedge to mark the boundary between the properties. There was just a grass verge bordering the lane.' Gamble removed his hat and scratched his head. 'It had been that way for decades, I suppose, and the previous owners had never bothered about it. But when the Barrons moved in at Valley View, they decided to lay claim to the verge. Jake Barron said he wanted to create an access into the pony paddock.

Their daughters are into horses, you know. Gymkhanas and stuff. They wanted to get a trailer in without going through the main entrance and past the garage block.'

'So they claimed the land they needed?'

'Aye. Trouble was, there were no maps with the deeds, to show the exact line of the boundary. If you ask me, I think it might actually have been common land, dating from the time when the original village was built by the duke. I don't suppose anyone worried about boundaries back then, being as how the whole village belonged to one person. It would just have been shared by the community.'

'I see.'

Gamble smiled ruefully. 'Those were the days, eh? Not much community spirit now. Not between those two, anyway. Not anywhere, really.'

'So they ended up in a dispute that went as far as a court hearing.'

'That's right. You know, if they'd got on better, it might have been settled amicably. But they hated each other on sight, I reckon. Nowak and Barron, they were like two bulls at a gate. They locked horns, and that was it. Neither of them was ever going to give in. Not in this life.'

'And the Barrons won, in the end?'

'So they say.'

'Did anybody else take sides in this dispute? Any of the other neighbours?'

'No. They just sat back and enjoyed the show. It was a few months ago now, of course.'

'Thank you, sir.'

Cooper realised Gamble was looking at him eagerly, as if he suddenly felt like part of the team and might be employed for his natural detection abilities. There was nothing worse than an interfering amateur who felt they'd been given some encouragement.

He nodded to Villiers, who took Gamble's arm.

'We know where to find you if we need to speak to you again, Mr Gamble.'

'I'll be around,' said Gamble.

'I'm sure.'

Villiers was smiling when she returned from escorting Gamble away.

'Lovable eccentrics. You can't beat 'em.'

'Well, it's surprising what good sources of information they can make,' said Cooper.

'Fair enough. Is it Mr Nowak now?'

'In a minute.'

He remembered Barry Gamble's account of the way he'd discovered the attack on the Barrons. He had been here in Croft Lane, he'd said. No. What he'd actually said was *thereabouts*. He was standing near a tree when he'd heard a noise. *A thumping crash*. He had looked towards the Barrons' house, Valley View. And what did he see? A light on in the kitchen.

From Croft Lane, Cooper walked down the garden as far as the hedge, turned and looked at Valley View. He was in no doubt now. There was no way Gamble could have seen the light in the kitchen from here.

Well, when you were looking for a suspect in a murder investigation, there was always the person who found the body. In this case, Barry Gamble.

15

'My neighbours? My neighbours? You know what? I wouldn't lift a finger to help those people. If I saw their house being burgled, I wouldn't bother to phone the police. In fact, I'd help the thieves load up their swag myself.'

Cooper was looking at Richard Nowak's large, powerful hands. They were gripping a glass and a half-empty bottle of whisky. Nowak already smelled of alcohol and his face was flushed.

'We're thinking about a particular set of neighbours,' said Cooper. 'The Barrons.'

'Jake Barron. He's such an aggressive man. Have you spoken to him?'

'He's still critically ill in hospital, sir. Serious head injuries, following the assault on Tuesday night.'

'Oh, yes. Of course.'

'Had you forgotten?'

'I don't think about the Barrons all the time. Why would I?'

Nowak put the bottle down on the table in his kitchen and looked at the glass thoughtfully. Perhaps he wasn't so drunk as he'd appeared at first. It was very early in the day, after all.

'Last time we spoke to you, you talked about how the police might react if you took the law into your own hands.'

'Not me personally. I was speaking theoretically.'

No one could pronounce those words so clearly if they were drunk. Cooper began to relax. Nowak's reaction must have been due more to emotion than alcohol.

'We know you were involved in a dispute with the Barrons, sir. It went on for quite a long time, didn't it?'

'You don't give in to people like that. Appeasement never works. They just walk all over you, if you let them.'

Nowak put the glass down as well now. He didn't even bother to finish the whisky in the bottom of it. His wife, Sonya, appeared behind him, her expression cold. Perhaps it was the sound of her footsteps that had sobered her husband up.

Through the open door, Cooper glimpsed what looked like a well-stocked bar. If he wanted to, this man could probably go on drinking all day and all night, without leaving the house. Yet he didn't look like a habitual drunk. He had the appearance of a strong, fit man who had given in to stress.

'I know what my rights are,' said Nowak. 'Why shouldn't I stand up for my rights? This is a free country, they tell me. What's mine is mine, and I'll take it. Jake Barron was in the wrong from the start.'

'So you never accepted the court's decision, sir.'

'No, and I never will.'

There was silence for a moment. Nowak turned to the window, and pointed in the direction of Riddings Lodge.

'Listen to that awful noise,' he said. 'Just listen to it.'

Outside, a chainsaw was whining in the coppice. Cooper had to admit it was one of the most irritating sounds that you could ever hear. It had a nasty, angry pitch to it, like a huge mutant wasp. If that sort of noise went on all day outside his flat, he'd be climbing the walls. But perhaps it did. He wasn't at home during the day, so he wouldn't be aware of it. Here, people were at home. They were all too conscious of what was going on at the edge of their territory.

'They're cutting trees down,' said Nowak. 'Mature, well-established trees, not some bit of birch scrub. I don't know what they're thinking of, despoiling the environment like that. It ruins the area for all of us. But there's no preservation order

174

on that coppice, and the council aren't interested, so they just do what they like.'

'Does the noise go on for long?' asked Villiers, frowning.

'All day. Sometimes it lasts right into the evening, until it gets dark. We've spoken to them about it, but they just blank us, pretend they can't understand what the problem is. I'm telling you, after a while it starts to feel like a deliberate provocation.'

Cooper looked at him more sharply. 'Have you taken steps against your neighbours, other than speaking to them?'

Nowak's expression was suddenly wary. 'Not like you're thinking of.'

'And what am I thinking of?'

'I wouldn't do any damage or resort to violence. I might take legal action, if necessary. That's what I did over the land. And that's my right as a citizen.'

'All right.'

Sonya moved closer, not quite touching her husband, but a supporting presence nevertheless. Nowak looked up and met Cooper's eye.

'I wouldn't do anything like what happened to the Barrons. I wouldn't be involved in anything violent. It's not in my nature. Not in my history.'

Mrs Nowak spoke then for the first time since Cooper and Villiers had arrived.

'Richard was born in a refugee camp in East Germany,' she said. 'None of us can understand what an experience like that does to a child. But my husband has a horror of violence, I can tell you that.'

'It's true,' said Nowak. 'I was part of the displaced people of Europe. But my family came here, to Sheffield, when I was very young.'

He laughed ruefully, fingered the whisky glass, but didn't pick it up.

'As a small child, I spoke only Polish,' he said. 'Like my parents. But my older brother was already bringing English into the house. I remember hearing how different it sounded when he spoke. And, of course, when I went to school I learned to talk just like my classmates. A Polish accent did no favours in those days. We weren't so multicultural then.'

Cooper nodded. He was thinking how interesting it was that Mr Nowak had said 'here, to Sheffield' when he was actually living in the Peak District. Many of the people living in this area came here because it *wasn't* Sheffield. It was as different to Sheffield as they could get and still be within commuting distance. But for a child born in an East German refugee camp, this was all part of the country he'd come to. For Mr Nowak, Riddings was as much Sheffield as Pond's Forge or the City Hall. They were all one place in his imagination – the sanctuary he'd escaped to.

They walked out of the house, and Nowak took a deep breath. The noise of the chainsaw was even louder out here – a nagging, intermittent sound that could set the teeth on edge and induce a headache.

'Look at these people here,' said Nowak with a wave of his hand. 'They don't have the least bit of consideration for their neighbours. Rude, arrogant, ignorant, offensive, supercilious, inconsiderate, selfish, vulgar, nasty, self-obsessed . . .' He took a deep breath. 'Words fail me.'

'So I see.'

Nowak smiled, in a moment of self-awareness. 'Well, I could think of a few more names, given time.'

'Those will do. We get the general impression.'

'It's a shame,' he said. 'This would be such a nice place to live, without . . .'

'Other people?'

'Yes, I suppose so. It sounds bad when you say it out loud, doesn't it? Very antisocial. But we – my family and I – we value our privacy, you see. Our peace and quiet is very precious to us. There are some things that you have to be prepared to fight for. Don't you think that's true, Sergeant?'

Cooper and Villiers left the house and found their way back down the drive of Lane End to where Cooper had parked his car. A builder's van was squeezing past, and he wondered whether he ought to emulate the residents of Riddings and fold his offside wing mirror in to avoid damage. But the van driver seemed to be used to the narrowness of the lanes, and he made it through without any problem.

It was funny how different the attitudes of Barry Gamble and Richard Nowak were towards their neighbours. One seemed to be a self-appointed vigilante, and claimed to be concerned about his neighbours' welfare, while the other admitted openly that he couldn't give a damn.

Well, that was what they said. The difference might only be on the surface. Underneath, their level of hostility could be exactly the same.

As he started the car, Cooper thought about the last thing Nowak had said. Everyone had a different idea of what was worth fighting for in their lives. Many people would say their families were the most precious thing they had, that they would fight to the death to protect their children. But it depended what sort of life you lived. He saw many individuals in the course of his job who had thought it worth fighting over a perceived insult, a lack of respect, a spilled drink, or a casual glance at their girlfriend. What seemed trivial from the outside could take on an immense importance in someone's else's mind. It was all a matter of perspective.

Murfin, Hurst and Irvine were waiting by the horse trough. No sooner had Cooper and Villiers arrived than a black Audi drew up alongside, with the passenger window already lowered.

'I don't mean any disrespect,' said the driver. 'But . . .'

'We need to get a grip, I suppose?' said Cooper.

'Pretty much.'

'Thank you, sir. I'll bear it in mind.'

'Are you being impertinent? I'll speak to your superiors.'

'Supervisor, sir. We don't have superiors any more.'

Cooper turned back to his team.

'Carol, I want you and Becky to visit Mr Gamble on Chapel

Close. Seize his dark grey fleece, his brown corduroys and his fell boots.'

'Why?'

'We're going to have them analysed for trace evidence.'

'Okay.'

'Then we're going to take him with us to Valley View. I'll meet you at his house.'

'What about me?' said Murfin. 'Not more house-to-house. I'm dying here, Ben.'

'Gavin, you can't die until I tell you to.'

Murfin sighed. 'Okay, boss. But it's that hill. Let the kids do the uphill work. That's what they're for.'

'They're not packhorses.'

'What?'

'Never mind. Just something I was thinking about. Anyway, Gavin, you can come with me to Riddings Lodge to talk to Russell Edson.'

'Oh, it'll be a pleasure. Some of his luck might rub off on me.'

'Why, do you play the lottery?' asked Cooper.

'No. But I can get lucky in other ways, can't I?'

'What, at your age?'

'Ha, ha.'

Russell Edson was watching a man in waterproof trousers wash his metallic blue Jaguar XF. The door of one of the garages stood open, and Cooper glimpsed a shrouded shape. A vehicle so precious that it couldn't be exposed to dust or sunlight.

'My handyman, Stanley. You have his name on your list. I gave all the information I could to your colleague here.'

Edson nodded towards Murfin, somehow managing to instil an immense depth of disdain into a simple gesture.

'Yes, we have all that, thank you.'

'So what else can I do for the constabulary?'

'I think you said you employ a gardening contractor, sir.'

'Of course. Look at these grounds. They need to be kept immaculate.'

'Would it be AJS Gardening Services?'

'Are you joking? They might be all right for some people. But I expect something a bit more professional. We do have standards.'

'So . . .?'

'I have a contract with Mr Monk.'

'And for the driveway?'

He smiled. 'The same. It applies to everything here. If it needs maintenance, I get a man in.'

'I presume you also have security procedures.'

'Naturally. However – I'm sorry, but I'm not prepared to discuss my security arrangements, even with the constabulary. You can never be entirely sure that information won't be passed on.'

Murfin had become very silent and still. Although Russell Edson hadn't looked at him at all, there was a palpable tension between them. This was one of the things Cooper had wanted to see. You couldn't get a proper impression of somebody until you saw them interacting in different situations, with a number of different people.

'There was one thing I don't think my colleague asked you, sir,' he said.

Edson was frowning at the handyman, as if he wasn't polishing the hub caps of his Jag brightly enough.

'Yes?'

'Just for the record, sir, where were you on Tuesday evening?'

'What, when the incident took place at Valley View?'

'Yes, sir.'

'Is there a necessity for me to have an alibi?'

'For the record.'

Edson sighed. 'Well, we were out for dinner.'

'Oh? Where did you eat?'

'Bauers, at Warren Hall.'

Cooper knew the place, and was impressed. 'Very nice. Special occasion?'

Edson raised an eyebrow. 'No.'

Okay, so that sounded like a put-down. And it probably

wouldn't be the last, either. Cooper decided to probe a bit further and see what sort of reaction he got.

'Can you remember what you had to eat, sir?'

'Oh, let's see. We've been so many times it's difficult to recall.' Edson smiled. 'But I think I had the Gressingham duck, glazed in roasted hazelnuts, with breast of quail for the first course. Mother had . . . yes, I think she chose the pan-fried sea bass. She tends to change her mind a couple of times when she's looking at the menu, you know. But I think that's an accurate recollection. Oh, I haven't told you what she started with.'

'It doesn't matter.'

'No, no, we must be accurate. For the record.'

Cooper stifled a sigh. 'Right.'

'Well, she's particularly fond of the foie gras. It's one of the reasons we go to Bauer's so often. They have a strict policy on their foie gras. It comes only from one specific French supplier, who produces it from Moulard ducks. The Moulard is a migratory breed that naturally gorges itself to prepare for long flights, and it's totally free-range. So there's no force-feeding, you see. The bird has a naturally large liver as a result of its lifestyle. These things are very important to us. We're particular about where we eat. We don't exactly go for the standard pub lunch.'

'And plenty of alcohol consumption, I imagine.'

'Sophisticated alcohol. We're not lager louts.'

Cooper closed his notebook with a snap, restraining his irritation.

'By the way,' said Edson, his eyes sweeping contemptuously over the two detectives. 'We also like Bauer's because they have a dress code. No jeans, no trainers. Otherwise, you get turned away. And quite right, too.'

'I know a lot of people like that,' said Murfin as they reached the gate.

'What, like Mr Edson? You're kidding.'

'No, people with naturally large livers as a result of their lifestyle. There are quite a few of them down at my local.'

*   *   *

Monica Gamble was waiting to grab Cooper as he arrived at Chapel Close. She was agitated about the appearance of police at her door again.

'You can't think Barry has anything to do with what's been happening to people in Riddings,' she said. 'He's an old fool, I know. But he's harmless.'

'What concerns me is whether we're being told the complete truth,' said Cooper.

'There's nothing to hide.'

'We'll see.'

'It's just because Barry raised the alarm. It's always the person who finds the body who gets suspected by the police, isn't it? I've seen it time after time on the TV.'

Cooper wanted to point out that what she saw on TV was just fiction. But sometimes it did come a bit too close to reality for comfort. People who reported the finding of a body often turned out to be involved in the death. Either they thought it would signal their innocence, or they did it out of a desire to be involved in the investigation in some way. You couldn't rule it out. Not even with an old fool like Barry Gamble.

'There must be more witnesses,' said Monica appealingly. 'Someone else must have seen something on Tuesday night.'

'Well . . .'

She grasped his sleeve desperately, clutching at any possibility.

'They did, didn't they?' she said. 'Someone?'

'There was a party of walkers coming down The Hill from the edge. They recall seeing someone in the phone box, but that's all.'

'The phone box in the village?' she said.

'Yes. Why?'

She stared at him for a long moment, as if she was working something out in her mind.

'Oh, nothing. It's nothing,' she said finally.

Cooper turned as Gamble was brought from the back of the house, where he had no doubt been lurking in his shed.

'All right. Would you come with us, Mr Gamble?'

181

'Are you arresting me?'

'No. We're going to take you to Valley View. I want you to show us exactly where you were on Tuesday night, and explain what you saw.'

'I've told you all that.'

'Well, make it easier for us to understand, would you?'

Gamble settled his cowboy hat on his head, pulling it down over his ears as if that made him ready for anything.

'Have it your way,' he said.

'And remember that Valley View is a crime scene, Mr Gamble. While you're there, please don't touch anything.'

'Fair enough. Lead on, Macduff.'

There was a hold-up at the end of the road, where the access into Chapel Close was blocked by a van and trailer being turned round in the narrow space. This must happen all the time in Riddings. One man was trying to do a twelve-point turn while another stood behind and shouted a warning when he came too near a wall.

Finally they managed to complete the manoeuvre and drew into the side to let Cooper's car pass.

When Cooper saw who the van belonged to, he wound down the window of the Toyota.

'Mr Summers.'

'Oh, hello.'

'I see you have a different assistant today.'

'Eh? Oh, yeah. This is Alek. I only employ the lads on a casual basis, you see. As and when needed, you know.' He glanced at Cooper. 'It's all legit. All the paperwork is in order. I don't employ illegals or anything like that.'

'No, I'm sure you don't.'

'And I pay all my taxes. None of that cash-in-the-back-pocket stuff. Me and Customs and Revenue are like best mates.'

'Fine.'

Cooper didn't really believe it. Summers had been too eager to bring the subject up. Small-scale tradesmen like him took cash in hand all the time, gave the householders a lower rate for the job to keep it off the books. It was nice to see that

Summers had a bit of a guilty conscience about it. But it wasn't something Cooper was interested in right at the moment.

Valley View was quieter now. The crime-scene tape was still in place, and a uniformed officer had been assigned to deter curious passers-by. But much of the attention had moved to Fourways next door, where the forensics activity was taking place.

The officer on duty looked bored, but his face lit up when he saw the detectives arriving. He made quite a performance of signing them in, as if this one task might justify his pay this week.

'Have you had much interest from the public?' asked Cooper.

'What public? No one pays any attention to me. The media go past here sometimes, but they're all heading further along the road.'

'I've seen them. They're outside Moorside House.'

'Bloke there is a pop star, they say.'

'Something like that.'

'Well, help yourself, Sergeant. Spend as long here as like.'

Cooper started to feel sorry for the officer. He'd done plenty of duties like this himself when he was in uniform. They could be mind-numbing.

'Let us know if we can get you anything,' he said.

'A cold beer would be nice.'

'DC Murfin might give you a wine gum.'

'Oh, cheers.'

For the next few minutes, Cooper watched Barry Gamble going through something that resembled a pantomime rehearsal. He was such a bad actor that it was impossible to believe anything he said or did. But he hammed up it for his audience as if he was playing the Dame in *Jack and the Beanstalk*.

'And I went "Ooh, what was that noise? I do hope there's nothing wrong. I'd better go and have a look." So I decided to walk this way a bit to see what the trouble was. And I saw – a light.'

Cooper glared at Villiers and Hurst as they tried to stifle laughter. The sound of a giggle only made Gamble act up more. His version of 'walk this way' became a cross between Danny La Rue and Captain Mainwaring from *Dad's Army*. If you could look pompous and camp at the same time, Barry Gamble managed it. He marched purposefully towards the house, his arms waving in dramatic semaphores.

'It was coming from this window here.'

Before they could stop him, Gamble had stepped towards the wall of the house and put his hand on the window pane. A flat hand, palm against the glass, all four fingers and thumb pressed on to the surface. That would leave a perfect set of prints.

'Mr Gamble, please – I asked you not to touch anything.'

'Oh, sorry.'

He took his hand away from the glass and looked at it, as if it might be possible to withdraw the touch of his fingers.

Cooper cursed quietly to himself. That was his own fault. He shouldn't have allowed Gamble to get so close to anything.

'I'm not sure that told us anything,' said Villiers, after Gamble had been taken home. 'But you've got your own methods, obviously.'

'Details,' said Cooper. 'It's the details.'

And that was true, very often. But as he drove out of Riddings and passed under the Devil's Edge, he had the feeling that it wasn't the case in this village. He was beginning to suspect that there was something right under his nose, but written in letters too big for him to see.

16

Everyone had been called back to West Street for a briefing. The air of expectation was tangible as the meeting room filled up. Was there some progress in inquiries in South Yorkshire, where a joint operation was targeting the Savages? Did they have a person of interest?

Apparently not. DI Hitchens made no reference to South Yorkshire, but wanted to go over the two incidents in Riddings.

'Thanks to the parents and the oldest daughter, we've finally established what's missing from the Barron house,' he said. 'It seems extraordinary they would go to those extremes for such a small haul, but still . . . we haven't been able to add anything to the list, no matter how hard we try. And as you'll see, it's a very short list. An iPhone in a pink case, belonging to Zoe Barron. A women's Gucci wallet with an interlocking "G" charm. I'm told it's made of rose peony guccissima leather, whatever that is. It was a gift to Zoe from Jake Barron. Two small, high-value items, easy to grab hold of. The wallet alone is worth three or four hundred pounds. We don't know how much cash was in it.'

'The phone . . .?'

'It hasn't been used since it was stolen. It was switched on, but it went off the network some time on Tuesday night, after the theft. Probably the battery just ran out.'

Information sheets were passed round, showing specifications and photographs of similar items to those stolen in the attack on the Barrons' house. For a few minutes there was a general murmuring among the assembled officers.

'That wallet has twelve card slots,' said Murfin to Cooper. 'Made for someone who might actually possess twelve credit cards, then.'

'Hardly surprising, Gavin. The wallet is worth three or four hundred pounds, remember.'

'They'll have taken the cash and ditched the wallet. Even if they knew how much it was worth, it's too distinctive for them to try to sell it.'

'If they knew what they were doing,' said Cooper.

'The Savages are pros. That's why we've never got near them.'

'Yes,' said Cooper. '*They* are.'

Murfin looked at him, then at Villiers. He grunted. 'Why do I get the feeling that you're about to make it all too complicated? All I want is a nice quiet life, you know. I want to do exactly what I'm told, no more and no less. Another few months of keeping my head down and my nose clean, and I'm free and clear.'

'Ah, but Gavin – is retirement what you really want? Remember, it's impossible to do nothing all day. You'd go mad.'

Someone raised a hand, and Hitchens hushed the room.

'Isn't it right that the Barrons had alarm systems in place at their property?'

'Yes, of course,' said Hitchens. 'Why?'

'Well, don't burglars normally choose properties without alarms?'

'It wasn't an option once they decided to target a village like Riddings. All of these homes have security systems. Some of them are more sophisticated than others, but you'd have to be an expert to know that from the outside, just from looking at the alarm box. A number of them have automatic response from the monitoring centres. But apparently the only householder in the Curbar Lane area who has thought it necessary to install a panic button is Mr Tyler Kaye at Moorside House.'

'There could have been some inside information.'

'We've got lists of names and run checks on them. Nothing is presenting itself at the moment.'

'The gardeners would be favourite, I reckon. Or a cleaner.'

'Sometimes you can get the information you want online anyway. No need to hand out any cash.'

Cooper shifted restlessly in his chair as he listened to officers going over the arguments. Everyone knew the methods to use. At one time, burglars could buy information from the milkman or the postman about who was away on holiday, and which properties would be standing empty. It enabled them to get into a property at the start of a vacation, so that any loss might not be noticed for two weeks or more. That left plenty of time to fence the stuff and stash the proceeds before the police came knocking.

These days, some professionals used the internet. People gave away all sorts of information on Facebook, boasting about where they were going for their hols, tweeting from their villa on the Costa, posting messages to their friends to let them know when they'd be back. Dead handy, that was. There were other high-tech methods. Last year, thieves had broken into a couple's car while they were on holiday in the Peak District, and stolen their sat nav. Then they'd plugged the device into their own car and set it to 'home'. The sat nav had led them straight to the family's empty house in Liverpool. Simple.

'No, the gardeners. I'd take a bet on it.'

Yes, the old-fashioned ways still worked, too. The milkmen had disappeared, and the postmen were more cautious. But in neighbourhoods like Riddings, there were always the gardeners and cleaners, the folk who came and went unnoticed and unappreciated. Better still, they were often paid peanuts. Minimum wage or less, cash in hand and not a word to the tax man, or the Immigration Service either. They sometimes found they could earn a decent bonus for a bit of information. And why not? It was all part of the free-market economy, wasn't it?

Finally Cooper could bear it no longer.

'We should check the Barrons' background,' he said.

Silence fell. To his surprise, Hitchens looked at him as if he'd just broken wind.

'Why, DS Cooper?'

Cooper hesitated now, feeling the force of his DI's disapproving stare.

'Surely it's standard procedure in a murder inquiry? To establish the victim's connections and relationships. To find out what was going on in their life.'

'If we were looking for a more personal motive for murder, yes.'

'But aren't we?'

Hitchens took a couple of steps towards him.

'So you don't believe in the Savages, DS Cooper? You don't think all those other incidents took place in Hathersage, and Baslow, and Padley? You doubt the existence of householders injured by violent assailants in a series of aggravated burglaries? These offenders are looking for financial gain and the thrill of violence. At Valley View they just went a little bit further down that road. They could see that the Barrons had money and lived in an expensive property, and were likely to be vulnerable. I don't think they needed any more motive than that.'

There was a moment of silence in the room after the DI's speech. No one seemed quite sure what had happened to provoke the outburst. Cooper kept quite still, in case a movement from him caused any further provocation. But inside he was feeling wounded by the unfair treatment. He was sure he was right. But it was difficult to explain why, especially in this atmosphere, and in a room full of his colleagues.

'Actually, DS Cooper has a point.'

The voice was Superintendent Branagh's. She hadn't moved from her position at the front of the room, but she took control of the situation without any effort. Hitchens stepped back, and the officers nearest to Cooper visibly relaxed.

'There are a number of features about the attack on the Barron family that trouble me particularly,' said Branagh. 'For

188

a start, their home life doesn't seem to have been entirely idyllic.'

'How so?' asked Cooper.

Branagh looked at the DI. 'Paul?

'Yes.' Hitchens turned over a few pages of his file. 'Well, the oldest Barron girl, Melissa, has been able to talk to us a bit about Tuesday night. She's told us that she heard her mother shouting, and then glass smashing downstairs.'

'But she didn't go down to see what had happened?'

'No. She says she thought her parents were fighting. So she turned her music up a bit louder.'

'What sort of childhood is that?' said Cooper, shocked. 'Isolated from your parents, spending all your time alone in your own room. And then – she was so used to hearing them arguing and throwing things at each other that it just seemed like a normal evening. Something to shut out with more noise.'

Hitchens threw out his hands in a helpless gesture, suggesting that he was unable to explain it.

The briefing moved on.

'There were white handprints found by scenes-of-crime on the rear wall. DS Cooper has suggested that these could be from rock climbers, who use chalk to improve their grip. There are many climbers who visit Riddings Edge. It could be a long job, but we're going to try to establish which of them might have been in the area on Tuesday evening.'

Cooper could sense a few black looks coming his way at that. Whoever got the frustrating job of tracking down the climbers would not be thanking him for the suggestion

'Others we haven't identified include a person seen by walkers in the public phone box on The Green. At present, no clues to identity, though probably male.'

Finally Superintendent Branagh clapped her hands, like a primary school teacher organising her class.

'We need to be able to eliminate some of these people from our inquiries,' she said. 'So let's get on with it.'

* * *

'I'm not sure whether that went well or not,' said Villiers when they were back at their desks in the CID room. 'Do you think you can get people here to come round to your opinion?'

'Not in one meeting,' said Cooper. 'Not in a single day. Not even in a week.'

'You need something more convincing, I guess.'

'Yes. The trouble is, we can't get a handle on the relationships between these people.'

'These people? Oh, you don't mean your colleagues now. You mean the inhabitants of Riddings.'

'There's Riddings Show on Saturday. They're all going to be there. If Mrs Holland is right, that's probably the one occasion in the whole year when we might get an opportunity to see them together.'

'A chance to assess the strength of the enemy.'

Irvine signalled Cooper urgently.

'We've got the CCTV footage from the Barrons,' he said. 'They have a camera pointing at the gates, and one at the garage.'

'Okay, let's run it.'

'This is the first one, from around the right time, just before the attack. There's nothing happening, though. The gates are closed. Not even any cars passing on Curbar Lane.'

'Wait a minute. Did you see that?'

'I didn't see anything.'

'A movement.'

'At the gate?'

'I'm not sure.'

Cooper stopped the recording, and ran it back a few seconds. There was still no one visible at the gate. But he was looking at the convex mirror on the gatepost. He ran the tape forward again, watching closely. Now he was sure of the movement. He zoomed in towards the gate. What *was* that reflected in the mirror? He squinted, tilted his head on one side, then sent the image to print, in case it was clearer on a hard copy. It might be his imagination, but he felt sure he was looking at the reflection of a human figure, twisted out of shape by the distorting effect of the mirror. One side of the body looked normal, but the other side was swollen and out of proportion where it was caught in the centre of the reflection. They were like the halves of two different people. Or something that wasn't entirely human at all, but part man, part monster.

'Add another unidentified individual to the file,' said Cooper. 'Along with our mystery man in the phone box.'

'They could be one and the same person, of course.'

'Maybe. The time is right, and the two locations are only a few yards apart.'

Cooper pictured the short stretch of road along Curbar Lane from The Green to Valley View. He wished there had been CCTV in Riddings, the way there was on streets in Edendale town centre. A suspect emerging from the phone box and lurking outside the Barrons' gates would immediately have been picked up and identifiable.

He remembered Luke Irvine's comment about using Google to get a view of Riddings. The HOLMES staff would have done it already; would have produced a detailed image of the village to plot sightings and incidents.

Cooper opened Google maps, and typed 'Riddings' into the search bar. In an instant he was looking at a detailed satellite view of the village, with all the roads overlaid on to the map. When he zoomed in, every house was visible, every field boundary, even cars that had been left parked on drives. He could see who had a swimming pool, and who had a tennis court. So much for walls and security cameras, when anyone with internet access could peer into your back garden and see the layout of your property.

These large, expensive homes and their grounds had spread out from the centre of the old village, transforming acres of rough ground into upmarket suburbia. But the satellite image made it obvious that the battle for dominance over the landscape wasn't all one-sided. Above the village, the cover of bracken and heather could be seen encroaching on to the old field systems, like a brown tide. Dry-stone walls seemed to be no barrier to the spread of vegetation from the direction of

Riddings Edge. Given time, it would engulf those fields, erasing all signs that civilisation had ever been here. But for now, humanity was still in control of the lower slopes.

He clicked on the full extent of the zoom facility and centred the screen on Riddings Lodge. Details were clear now that he hadn't been able to see when he was right there on the ground. He could calculate the best angle of approach from the back fence to the house without coming in sight of a window. He could see exactly how far away the neighbouring houses were, and how dense the trees were in between. He was surprised to discover a manège at the rear of the Edson property, and a small paddock set out with jumps. Those hadn't been evident from his brief tour of the boundary. But it was clear now that there was access to them from behind the stable block.

When he scrolled the map towards the north-east, the rough ground at the foot of Riddings Edge became visible. The transition from rock-strewn slope to landscaped garden was quite startling at this point. The entire colour and texture of the image changed suddenly along a dead-straight line, as if the village existed in a bubble, cut off from the wilderness beyond it by an invisible barrier.

Cooper was reminded of a science fiction story he'd once read, in which a small community found itself isolated from the rest of the world by an alien force field that appeared overnight. The story went on to explore how the inhabitants behind the barrier dealt with the isolation, the power struggles and vicious infighting that developed. New hierarchies formed in the absence of authority, law and order gradually collapsed, and individuals with extreme beliefs came into their own. One religious fanatic proclaimed that their enforced isolation was a punishment from God for the community's sinful behaviour.

Looking down on Riddings, through a camera mounted on an orbiting satellite, he felt a bit like God casting his eyes down from heaven, knowing all about the activities of the inhabitants in this little place on the edge of Derbyshire. If he was God, would he have delivered a punishment on them like this? Let some of them die? And made the rest of them live forever in fear?

Well, of course he didn't know everything about what went on in Riddings. He knew far too little, in fact. But down there was someone who knew more. Someone who *had* decided to take on the role of God, and had handed out the punishments. Did that person see the village as clearly as Cooper did now on his Google satellite image?

Along the corridor in the superintendent's office, Hazel Branagh looked up at DI Hitchens, and raised an eyebrow.

'Detective Sergeant Fry, you say?'

'Yes, she's a good officer,' said Hitchens. 'And her skills are being wasted at the moment.'

'Possibly.' Branagh picked up a memo. 'But there's a small matter of a Leicestershire officer with a broken nose.'

'What does that have to do with anything?'

'Well, like DS Fry, this officer is also a member of the Implementing Strategic Change working group. And it seems Fry was the only, er . . . witness to the incident in which he suffered his injury.'

Hitchens smiled. 'I imagine it was self-inflicted.'

'According to his own statement, he tripped over the kerb in a pub car park and struck his face on the bonnet of his own car.'

'It's easily done,' said Hitchens. 'I've lost count of the number of times I've seen that happen.'

Branagh replaced the memo on her desk. 'It used to be suspects who fell down the stairs on the way to the cells,' she said. 'Even when the custody suite was all on one level.'

'So I've heard. Those were the days, eh?'

'Mmm. But now it seems to be our own officers who suffer mysterious injuries.'

'Times change,' said Hitchens. 'But there are accident-prone individuals in every walk of life, I imagine. Besides . . .'

'What?'

'I thought you said he was from Leicestershire?'

Branagh's lips twitched, the closest she came to a smile. For her, it was practically a belly laugh.

'Good point,' she said.

'Anyway, we've been asked to withdraw DS Fry from the working group.'

'She was never right for it,' said Branagh.

'About as right as a pit bull in a poodle parlour.'

'Perhaps we'd better find her something more meaty to get her teeth into, then.'

'You're going *where* tomorrow?' Gavin Murfin was saying.

'Riddings Show,' repeated Cooper. 'Do you fancy coming?'

'Look,' said Murfin, pointing at his chest. 'This is me. Add Saturday afternoon, plus the start of the football season. And what do you get?'

'Pride Park,' said Cooper.

'Correct.'

The new season had started, and Murfin was a hardcore Rams fan. So dedicated that he'd even recovered from relegation and the arrival of American owners. His threats to transfer allegiance to Nottingham Forest had never translated into action. It was inconceivable, anyway. He was a true Derby County fan.

'Take Carol with you,' said Murfin. 'Why not?'

Cooper looked at Villiers, and saw her expression immediately become eager.

'You don't have to come,' he said. 'There's no overtime, remember.'

'What else would I be doing?' she said. 'I haven't been back in the area long enough to get a social life sorted out for myself yet.'

Murfin opened his mouth to make a suggestion.

'And I don't like football,' said Villiers.

'Riddings Show it is, then. I'll buy you a choc ice.'

In a corner of the CID room, a TV news programme was

194

replaying a clip from Superintendent Branagh's earlier press conference, following the incident at Fourways.

'Yes, we are connecting the inquiries,' she was saying. 'We believe the people who carried out this attack are the same offenders currently being sought for a series of previous incidents in other villages in this part of the county.'

Listening to her words, Cooper couldn't help shaking his head.

'You still think they're wrong,' said Villiers.

'I can see why they're thinking this way,' said Cooper. 'But it feels wrong to me.'

'But you can't go to Hitchens or Branagh and say you have a feeling, right?'

'No.'

Villiers smiled. 'I think I'm getting the hang of the way things work here. I thought there might be a bit more freedom to use your own initiative, but maybe not. It's okay, it's what I'm used to. But still . . .'

'You think I ought to do something about it,' said Cooper.

'It's not for me to say. You're a newly promoted DS, you want to keep your nose clean. At least until you've got your feet properly under the table. I understand that.'

Cooper looked at her. 'It was one of the things that held me back for so long, my tendency to act on feelings, to follow an instinct when all the evidence pointed in a different direction. Otherwise I might have been a DS long before now.'

Villiers said nothing. But he could see from her face that she was disappointed in him. He couldn't help that. This case was starting to irritate him.

'One thing I really don't understand is this obsession with Sheffield,' he said. 'Why does everyone keep talking about Sheffield? It's as if they might be able to shift responsibility for a problem by pointing a finger at the nearest city. I'm telling you, Sheffield is just a distraction. It means nothing.'

Down the room, Luke Irvine had answered a phone call, and looked across at Cooper.

'Ben, there's a reporter downstairs from the local paper.'

'The *Eden Valley Times*?' he said. 'They want a press officer, then. There's someone in the building, Luke. Try the incident room.'

'No, she wants to speak to a detective involved in the Riddings case. She thinks she might have some useful information to pass on.'

'Oh, really?'

'That's what she says.' Irvine pointed at the phone. 'Does the address Sheffield Road mean anything to you?'

17

As she passed through the corridors of E Division headquarters towards the end of Friday afternoon, Diane Fry felt like a ghost. It was as if there were people here but she couldn't see them. And, of course, they couldn't see her. She was only a dim memory to them, a presence forgotten in every way but for her fading signature on a file.

In the CID room, she saw a woman talking to Ben Cooper. A woman who seemed at home, occupying a desk that had once been hers. She guessed this must be the new DC.

At least Cooper had tidied himself up a bit. Maybe becoming DS had done that for him, or perhaps the serious girlfriend, the little SOCO with the dark hair. When she'd first worked with Cooper, Fry had stifled a constant urge to tell him to straighten his tie, push his hair back from his forehead, get rid of that boyish look.

She'd always thought of Cooper as the social-worker type of police officer – the sort who thought there were no villains in the world, only victims; that people who did anything wrong must necessarily be in need of help. When she arrived in Derbyshire, he had obviously been well settled and popular, with friends and relatives around him, helping him out, smothering him with support. And preventing him from standing on his own two feet, the way she did herself.

But when she looked at him now, from beyond the doorway,

Fry could see that the change in him went deeper than she'd thought. There was a different set to his shoulders, a firmer tone to his voice, and a new confidence in his eyes as he gazed around the room. He had the air of a prince surveying his domain. So he was maturing. She'd never really noticed it before.

And another thing. What was it that she detected in his manner when he spoke to the new woman? A fleeting expression, an exchange of glances, a suggestion of familiarity in the body language.

Fry's eyes narrowed. She'd known there was a fresh addition to the E Division CID team. No one had bothered to tell her, of course. That was so typical. Before she'd gone to Nottinghamshire for the working group, she'd just overheard their DI, Paul Hitchens, say something like *when the new DC arrives*. And he'd given a meaningful nod towards one of the empty desks.

Now the new DC was here. Fry managed to hold her tongue for a while so that she didn't look as if she was desperate to know about her. Then she turned to Gavin Murfin.

'So who's the new girl?'

'Carol? You mean Carol Villiers, the new DC, I guess.'

'Where has she come from?'

'She's ex-military. RAF Police.'

'Really?'

Murfin smiled. 'Apparently she's a friend of Ben's, from way back. An old school pal.'

'Oh.'

'From what I've seen of her, she seems great.'

'I'm sure she is.'

The reporter's name was Erin Byrne. She was one of the senior staff at the *Eden Valley Times* – though that wasn't saying much, in Cooper's experience. The turnover in the editorial department of the *Times* seemed to be very rapid, as anyone with two or three years' experience moved on to better things. And for reporters on Edendale's local paper, 'better things' didn't necessarily mean the excitement of Fleet Street. It often meant a move into public relations, or the press office at Derbyshire County Council.

Byrne was dark and angular, with a soft Irish accent that made Cooper think of some rural county in the west of Ireland. Galway or Mayo. She was dressed all in black, like a high-powered businesswoman. One of those destined for a career in PR, perhaps.

'We've been getting these messages,' she said. 'At first we didn't take any notice. We get our fair share of loonies, you know.'

'I'm sure you do.'

She smiled. 'Some of them complaining about the police, of course.'

'So what did these messages say?'

'It's a male caller. He claims his call is connected to the Riddings murder inquiry, and he says, "Tell them Sheffield Road." He's called three times now.'

'Just Sheffield Road?'

'That's what he said. The trouble is, he's been put through to a different person each time he's called, and we all wrote him off as a nutter. It was only when someone mentioned it that we realised three of us had received similar calls. Mine was the most recent one.'

'And they were all exactly the same?'

'It certainly seems to have been the same man each time. He sounded as though he was calling from a phone box some-where, too. Probably had an idea that we might trace his call. People get exaggerated ideas of what journalists can do.'

'*Tell them Sheffield Road.* That's it?'

'Well, my call was a bit different. He was getting cross by then. He didn't like being passed from person to person, and thought we weren't taking him seriously.'

'Which you weren't.'

'True.' She laughed. 'Anyway, when he got me, on the third occasion, he was very unhappy. Maybe because I was female,

I don't know. He might have thought he'd been fobbed off with the secretary or something. He ended up slamming the phone down. But before he did, he said he would put it in writing.'

Cooper's ears pricked up. 'And has he?'

'Not yet. Are you interested?'

'On its own, the message doesn't seem to mean anything.'

'It didn't to us, either. But I thought there might be some significance in the context of the inquiry. I mean, you must have gathered a lot of information that we're not aware of. There might be a significant detail that you haven't chosen to share with the press.'

Byrne raised an eyebrow and looked at him expectantly. He knew she was fishing for a titbit, an angle that she could turn into an exclusive story for her paper. Her charm probably worked on some people. But in this job, you learned to be close-mouthed when it came to giving out information to the public.

'There's a Sheffield Road out of Baslow,' said Cooper. 'The A621. Not many houses on it, though. A couple of farmsteads down at Far End, near the roundabout. And a big house in the woods across Bar Brook, just under Jack Flat. But that's about it, I think.'

'That's the only one I know of, too.'

He pictured the road as it climbed out of Baslow. Gardom's Edge on one side, Baslow Edge on the other, two pincers of rock squeezing the road into a narrow gap. It was a busy route, though – the main road up to the junction at Owler Bar, and on into the city via Totley. Many people thought of Owler as the gateway into the Peak District. At that curious elliptical junction sandwiched between two pubs, you could choose to head north towards Hathersage and the Hope Valley, or southwards to Baslow and Bakewell. Either way, you had to work your way round the edges and the expanse of Big Moor. If you were travelling by car, at least.

'Well? Any thoughts?'

Cooper shook his head. 'I can't think what significance Sheffield Road has. It might be the route the attackers took if

200

they came from Sheffield, but so what? There are only two possible routes to Riddings from the east anyway. It's that, or the A625.'

'I don't know what to make of it, then. I thought you might understand what it meant.'

'I wish I did.'

'I'm sorry, I seem to have wasted your time, then.'

'No, that's all right. And if you do happen to get a written message . . .'

'I'll let you know what it says.'

'It might be helpful if I could see the actual message,' he said.

'Helpful how?'

'I don't know. But seeing the original can often make quite a difference to its interpretation.'

'Okay. If that happens, I'll see what I can do.'

'Thank you.'

'I'm on duty this weekend. If a letter arrives in the morning . . .?'

Cooper gave her his card. 'Don't wait until Monday. Call my mobile number, or email me.'

He escorted Byrne back into reception. In the entrance, two sets of double doors faced the reception desk, looking out on to the visitors' car park. A van came through the barrier, carrying a prisoner to the custody suite behind the station.

He held the door open for her, but she hesitated.

'I might see you again, then,' she said.

'It's possible.'

She gave him a small wave as she went down the steps to her car, and Cooper smiled automatically. It was only as Byrne pulled away that he noticed a crime-scene van waiting for the barrier to rise. It was inevitable that it should be Liz who was driving it.

On his way back to the CID room, Cooper glimpsed Diane Fry in the doorway, and wondered if she had come to see him.

201

But a moment later, she was gone again. He shook his head in incomprehension. It was strange how Fry always seemed to be in a doorway, forever passing through from one place to another.

'I see Diane Fry is back,' said Hurst.

'Is she? I thought it had turned cold suddenly,' said Murfin.

'I wonder what happened to the Implementing Strategic Change working group.'

'There are rumours,' said Murfin darkly.

Cooper turned towards him. 'There are always rumours, Gavin. Usually being spread by you.'

Murfin tapped the side of his nose. 'But this is from a reliable source, like.'

Cooper sighed. 'Go on, then.'

'Well, they say that something happened in Nottinghamshire, after one of the meetings. An *incident*. Some occurrence that upset the deliberations of the Incessant Sodding Change working group.'

A few minutes later, Cooper turned a corner in the corridor and found himself face to face with Fry, who was coming the other way. They both stopped, uncertainly.

'Hi, Diane.'

She nodded briskly. 'How are things going?'

'Busy, you know.'

'Absolutely. I do know.'

'You've heard about the attacks in Riddings? The home invasions?'

'Yes, of course.'

Cooper looked at her more closely. She fidgeted from one foot to the other, as if she was anxious to sidestep him and get on with whatever she was doing.

'I suppose you're anxious to get involved,' he said.

'Not particularly. I'm sure you're on top of things. You surely don't need any help from me. You never did, Ben.'

He took a step back, stung by her tone. He'd thought it might be different, now that they were no longer under each other's feet.

'Diane . . .'

'I have a meeting with Superintendent Branagh,' she said. 'That's why I'm here, if you really want to know.'

'Oh, okay. So it's nothing to do with the incident, then?'

'Incident?'

'Well, I heard . . .'

'Yes, I can imagine what you heard. There are too many people who can't keep their mouths shut.'

'Things don't change much here,' said Cooper.

'There's one lesson you really should learn, Ben, if you never learn anything else. Places don't change. If you want things to change in your life, you have to make it happen yourself.'

'Well, thanks for that. I wasn't expecting a thought for the day.'

He made to move past her, but she stopped him.

'So, how is GI Jane getting on?' she said.

'Who?'

'The female Rambo. Your new DC.'

'Carol Villiers. Have you been checking up on her?'

'Why would I do that?'

'I have no idea. But it sounds that way from your sarcastic references. Otherwise, how would you know she was in the services?'

'I'm not totally out of touch, you know. You haven't quite got rid of me from Edendale yet. It's all around the section who the new DC is. Old pals, aren't you? You went to school with her, right? It must be nice to reminisce about the old days together whenever you feel like it.'

'I suppose you've been talking to Gavin,' said Cooper as he brushed past her. 'I wish you wouldn't try to interfere with my team.'

He knew Fry was watching him as he walked away, but he didn't look back.

'It used to be *my* team,' she said. But he pretended he hadn't heard her.

* * *

When Cooper returned to the CID room, Diane Fry was still there. And she'd met Carol Villiers. The two were sitting at desks opposite each other, though they didn't seem to be speaking.

Murfin was watching Fry and Villiers sizing each other up.

'Who do you think would win in a fight?' he said when he saw Cooper. 'Well, I suppose there's only one way to find out . . .'

'Gavin,' said Cooper warningly, knowing he was wasting his breath.

'Go on. I bet you've wondered. Do you think Villiers knows those SAS death grips? Can she kill someone with nothing but a ballpoint pen? Only, I've got a spare one, if she needs it.'

Cooper couldn't help following Murfin's gaze. The sight of the two women drew his attention irresistibly. They seemed to be talking to each other now. He strained to hear what they were saying, but Villiers was sitting with her back to him, and Fry was speaking too quietly to be heard against the background noise of ringing phones. That was unlike her, too. She had never been one to whisper or mumble. And she had certainly never been afraid of letting people hear her opinions.

'Wishing you could lip-read?' said Murfin.

'What? Of course not,' said Cooper, though it was exactly what he'd been thinking.

'Mostly swear words, I reckon. A bit of sarcasm. Ritual abuse.'

Cooper looked at Fry's expression again, saw a raised eyebrow that accompanied a murmured question.

'No, Gavin,' he said quietly. 'I don't think so.'

Becky Hurst had been busy working on her PC, but she stopped when an officer brought in a copy of the Sheffield evening paper to show her.

'I can't believe this,' she said.

Cooper caught her outraged tone.

'Becky?'

'People are starting to treat the Savages as some kind of heroes.'

'What is it?'

'This story in the Sheffield paper. It's as if they're Robin Hood and his Merry Men or some rubbish. Unbelievable.'

Murfin chuckled. 'Stealing from the rich and giving to the poor? But they're only doing the first part, surely?'

'How do we know?' said Cooper.

'Well . . .'

'We don't know, do we? We don't know anything about them.'

'Still, whoever they are – they're not heroes.'

'It's the way they're managing to come and go at will,' said Murfin. 'Evading capture, eluding the police. The public love all that. It makes them think they're watching a Hollywood film. You'll see, they'll be built up into legends if we don't catch them soon. There'll be stories told about them, all kinds of exaggerations. Songs, jokes – it'll all happen.'

'There's already a Facebook fan page,' said Irvine.

'A what?' asked Cooper.

'A fan page. On Facebook.' Irvine looked at him as if that was enough explanation for anyone.

'Show me,' said Cooper.

Irvine called up the page. It was headed *We all luv the Savages.* Cooper read through a few of the messages before he could stand any more.

These guys are legend.

Just brilliant the way they're giving the f***ing cops the runaround. Ram it to the pigs!

You said it, dude. More power to the Savages.

'Who *are* these people?' he said.

'All kinds of folk. It's been building up ever since the first attack. Not the first one in Riddings, I mean the first one attributed to the Savages.'

'In Hathersage.'

'Right. That guy they robbed was a banker.'

'No, he was a financial adviser,' said Cooper.

'Still. You know how people feel. That was enough for public support to come down on the side of the Savages. And then, with them sticking it to the police the way they have . . .'

'So these are their groupies. Criminals with a fan club. Pity we can't shut them down.'

'We could try. Facebook might cooperate.'

'It's freedom, though, isn't it?' said Irvine. 'That's what the internet is supposed to be about, the freedom to express your own views and share information.'

'Freedom can be used as a weapon, too,' said Hurst.

Surprised, Cooper looked round at her. He was seeing a side of her he hadn't noticed before.

Hurst flushed slightly at his look.

'Well, it's true,' she said defiantly. 'Sometimes you have to protect people from themselves.'

Irvine laughed. 'Listen to Maggie Thatcher. It'll be *no such thing as society* next. Roll on the Fourth Reich.'

'That's very offensive,' said Hurst, going redder.

'Well, lighten up.'

'All right,' said Cooper firmly. 'That's enough. You two can continue your political debate in your own time.'

Hurst and Irvine went back to their desks in silence. Hurst ostentatiously picked up her phone and turned her back to her colleague to make a call. Cooper looked round the office, wondering where the suddenly sour atmosphere had come from. But Fry was no longer there. She seemed to have faded into the background, vanishing as unexpectedly as she'd arrived.

Carol Villiers placed copies of her reports on Cooper's desk for him to check, along with an envelope of crime-scene photographs from Riddings.

'Not much love lost there, then,' she said. 'That was a surprise.'

'They're okay,' said Cooper. 'I think they like each other really.'

'Some people have a funny way of showing it.'

'Yes, they do.'

Cooper opened the envelope and spread the photos out on his desk. Some of them still made him flinch. For some reason, the scene of a violent crime always looked so much more sordid in the photographs than in real life. It might be because the victim was no longer a person, but had been reduced to a tangle of pale, dead limbs, an untidy heap of clothes, a drying bloodstain on the floor. The small details of that person's life were just so much rubbish scattered in the background, every item marked with a crime-scene number.

Many murder scenes were sordid in reality too, of course. Grubby bedrooms heaped with dirty washing, sitting rooms stacked with leaking plastic bags and cardboard boxes, filthy back alleys jammed with waste bins, stinking of rotten food and infested with rats.

Zoe Barron's kitchen was nothing like that. Cooper remembered its gleaming newness, its almost clinical cleanliness – a spare, minimalist lack of clutter that seemed unnatural. Definitely not the way he thought of a kitchen, anyway. A long, long way from the kitchen he recalled in his childhood at Bridge End Farm, his mother surrounded by pans and cooking smells, a huge pine table without an inch of clear space.

And yet these photographs had reduced the kitchen at Valley View to the same sordid level as a rat-infested alley. Blood and violent death could do that. Zoe Barron would be appalled. Muddy footprints, the cold light of the camera's flash, the peculiarly dead quality of a digital image. All the gleam of the steel and marble had been sucked out, drained away the way Zoe's life had been.

Cooper stared for a long while at the sprawled body. Zoe Barron was no longer a human being with a past, a present and a future, an individual with a life and relationships and all the human hopes and fears. She was no longer even a name, but a series of numbers.

Finally he could look no longer. He felt the anger growing inside him, like a surge of acid through his veins. His hands began to tremble, his ears buzzed with the rush of blood as an overwhelming desire took hold of him. The need to hit out, to lash out at anything that came within range.

He gritted his teeth in his effort to fight back the rage.

'Some Robin Hood,' he said. 'Some bloody Robin Hood.'

* * *

Monica Gamble was tired. She'd been tired for years now. Not because she was ill – well, not all the time anyway. She was exhausted from the ordeal of living with her husband. Thirty-five years they'd been married. It was a life sentence. Two or three life sentences. From what she'd read in the papers, some murderers got out after twelve years.

Monica didn't know what crime she'd committed to end up lumbered like this. Barry was the equivalent of the most annoying cell mate you could imagine getting banged up with in prison. She supposed anyone could get irritating after thirty-five years of close contact. But Barry made a special art of being annoying.

'It's a mistake to lie to the police, though, isn't it?' he said that night. 'They always find out you're lying, one way or another. They just keep on and on asking questions, until they catch you out.'

'But they haven't asked us anything important yet. So we're not lying.'

'No,' said Barry doubtfully.

'Well? We're not, are we?'

He shook his head, still looking worried. 'It makes no difference. They'll be annoyed with us if they find out.'

'Let them be annoyed.'

'We'll be in trouble.'

'For God's sake, Barry, do you think you can live your whole life avoiding trouble? That would be so boring, even if you could. It's the thought of getting in trouble that makes life interesting. It's the excitement of the risk. Don't you see that?'

Monica gazed into his face, and sighed. Clearly he didn't see it. She could read it in his puzzled eyes and wrinkled brow.

'Look, just answer their questions as briefly as you can, and don't volunteer any information. You can do that, surely?'

She flinched as she felt her nails digging into the palms of her hands. What had she done to deserve this?

Barry wandered off to his shed and left her standing in the garden in the dusk. Instead of going back into the house, she stayed out for a while. She was gazing upwards, beyond the village, watching the edge as the rocks were painted in vivid colours and shaped by the evening light.

In earlier years, Monica had often heard Barry point out those shapes to the children, encouraging them to picture faces or the outlines of animals in the rock. He said it developed their imaginations. It was true that if you watched the rocks in the setting sun, they seemed to move as perspectives changed, the shadows shifted and lengthened, and darkness filled a crevice to form the suggestion of a mouth or an eye. If you stared long enough, you could see a dragon turn its head to gaze across the valley, a giant dog rise from the ground, a cruel profile sink slowly into the dusk until it was lost from sight.

The children had asked once whether all those creatures came to life at night, when no one was looking. And Barry had said yes, they did. She supposed there was no harm in it. Nothing wrong with letting kids exercise their imaginations. It was better for them than all that sitting in front of TV screens and Game Boys, all that squinting at text messages on their mobile phones.

When she was a child herself, Monica had pictured all kinds of beasts roaming the flats, those wide plains of heather and mat grass that filled the space above the edges. She knew the stories were just folk tales to frighten the gullible. No one would go walking up there in the dark, would they? No one with any sense. Not if they had an ounce of imagination.

Monica had her own theory about those folk stories. She figured they represented natural common sense, a little bit of sound psychological strategy. After all, it was better to place your demons right out there in the dark, and leave them wailing mournfully on the edge. So much better than to keep them prowling endlessly inside your head.

18

Saturday

Above the villages of Riddings and Froggatt, the A625 swung up the hill and climbed through dense trees until it emerged again on to open ground near the Grouse Inn and reached the Longshaw Estate. At a triangular junction just below Longshaw was one of the Peak District's quirkiest tourist attractions. It was a strange one, even for an area known for its quirkiness. It was a wooden pole, standing upright in the middle of a field.

Cooper knew that many visitors thought it was a joke. They came away convinced that the National Trust tourist sign that just said 'Wooden Pole' must be a fake – a hoax perpetrated on them by a local farmer. Yet thousands of them still came every year to look at the pole, and take photographs of it.

It was actually a packhorse route marker from the eighteenth century, marking the way up from Hathersage towards Dronfield. The track in a hollow just below it was the old road itself. The present pole wasn't the original, but it had been there many years. It was so much of a landmark that the area around it was now known locally as Wooden Pole.

There was no explanation of all this on the sign, though. Cooper liked that. A bit of mystery in the landscape was good. Let the tourists go home wondering. A little further north there was another pole, above Stanage Edge. Carvings in the rocks at its base dated back four centuries to 1550, when it must have been a bit different around here.

He sat with Liz on a grassy slope overlooking the Longshaw Estate and Padley Gorge. Somewhere a long way below them ran Totley Tunnel, carrying the railway line from Sheffield that emerged at the little station down there in the gorge.

'When we were children, Grandad Cooper used to tell us that there was a penny on top of this pole,' he said. 'He said if one of us climbed up to collect it, we could have it.'

Liz murmured comfortably. Her eyes were closed, her face turned up to the sun.

'It used to be considered okay to tell kids anything in those days, I suppose.'

'Yes. Except one afternoon, a couple of years ago, I over-heard Matt telling his girls there was a pound coin on top.'

'Well, that's inflation for you.'

Cooper laughed. 'Worse than that. They didn't believe him for a second. Kids are much smarter now than we ever were.'

'Less gullible, anyway.'

'Some people say it's a boundary pole, marking the spot where Yorkshire becomes Derbyshire, or vice versa. I seem to remember there was an old man who lived near here who claimed that lots of poles were erected on the moors during the Second World War, to prevent the Germans landing gliders full of troops to invade Sheffield.'

'That's the way it goes around here. You make up your own stories, and people choose which they want to believe.'

'You're right. It's always been like that, I think.'

The National Trust sign was pretty much as Cooper remem-bered it. When you went up close to see what it told you about the pole, all it said was: *Keep to the paths, do not climb the walls, keep dogs on leads. Observe the by-laws.*

The pole stood about twenty feet high, but it was rather a knobbly-looking affair. In fact, it had the appearance of a failed totem pole, one that had been abandoned before the proper carving had been done. Basically, it was the trunk of a spindly tree, possibly a silver birch.

'I'm glad we got this time together,' said Liz. 'I suspect you'd

211

only be thinking about the Riddings case otherwise. You do get a bit obsessive, Ben.'

'There are two Riddings cases,' said Cooper.

'Oh?'

That was one of the things he liked about her. She worried about him getting obsessed with particular cases, but she couldn't hide the fact that she experienced the same surge of interest. It was evident in her voice, just that one word.

'It's not really clear yet,' he said. 'Too few obvious lines of inquiry to follow. But I think the hunt for the Savages is misguided. Well – not misguided, but not relevant to Riddings, or to the death of Zoe Barron.'

Liz sat up. 'Have you told your DI?'

'No. It would be the wrong thing to say at the moment.'

'Mmm. You have to toe the party line.'

'Yes.'

'Or appear to be doing so, anyway.'

'I can ask appropriate questions. But I can't tell Mr Hitchens and Superintendent Branagh that they're wrong. Not without some evidence.'

'You'd better find some evidence, then. What's your theory?'

'I don't have one yet,' said Cooper. 'I just have the feeling that the answer lies over there, in Riddings. There's an awful lot of hate in that village.'

The words sounded wrong and out of place in this location, with the sun beating down on them, the hills rolling gently away to the west, the sound of sheep quietly bleating to each other in a field down the valley. But Cooper knew what he'd said was right. He could sense it wherever he went in Riddings, and not just from Richard Nowak or Alan Slattery. They were open about it. Those who concealed their feelings were the most worrying.

'This latest attack,' said Liz. 'Mr and Mrs Holland?'

'Yes. You were there, at their house. Fourways.'

'We found very little in the way of forensic evidence, you know.'

'I heard.'

'So unless the lady can provide any information about the intruder . . .?'

Cooper hadn't been present at the interviews with Mrs Holland, but he'd read the transcripts. She'd told her interviewers that she had caught sight of a single figure in the garden of their home, no more than a glimpse of the intruder through a window. She couldn't say whether he had been heading towards the house, or away from it. She couldn't even say for certain that it was a he. When pressed, though, she swore that the intruder was wearing a dark mask. Otherwise she would have been able to see a face, wouldn't she?

'Nothing of any use so far,' said Cooper.

'Perhaps she'll remember something later.'

'She thinks the intruder she saw wore a mask.'

'Like the Savages do.'

'But there was only one intruder at Fourways, so far as we can tell. The Savages always operate in a group, two or three of them at least.'

'I see.'

'I wish you wouldn't make me call them the Savages,' he said.

'Oh, sorry.'

'Besides . . .'

'What?'

'There's really no evidence that anyone was trying to break in at the Hollands' place.'

Liz nodded. 'No, that's what we found, from a forensic point of view. No tool marks on the doors, no broken windows, nothing. The intruder was outside. And even then, he was careful not to leave footprints on soft ground.'

'Careful, or lucky.'

'The result is the same.'

'Apparently the Hollands even set off their own burglar alarm,' said Cooper. 'They activated the motion sensors and didn't turn the alarm off.'

'Well, it would be the last thing on your mind, with your husband breathing his last on the doorstep.'

213

'Oh, yes. If Mr Holland hadn't rushed out to confront the intruder, the outcome would have been quite different,' he said. 'A 999 call would have been far better. Well – on most nights, it would.'

Cooper stared across the valley, not seeing the trees or the hills, but trying to picture the scene at Fourways that chaotic night. Had someone taken advantage of the noise and disturbance in the village to undertake a risky mission of his own?

'What about the suspect you pursued on the night?' asked Liz.

'Barry Gamble? He was questioned, of course, but there was nothing to place him at the Hollands'. We found no mask on him, or anything else incriminating. Besides, some of the teenagers at the party identified him positively as the man they'd seen lurking in the bushes at The Cottage. Theoretically, it would be possible for him to have been in both places within a few minutes – they're close enough together. But why would he hang around after the confrontation with Mr Holland? Why wear a mask at one place and not the other? And there isn't the remotest suggestion of a motive. No history between him and the Hollands. We never had any hope of a case against him. He got a bit of a scare, though.'

'A dead end, then.'

'It seems so.'

Yes, that was an understatement. At the moment, it felt like running into a stone wall. Like running face first into the Devil's Edge itself.

Cooper found a bottle of water, and passed it to Liz. He looked over his shoulder towards the edges. The closest one was Froggatt Edge, with White Edge forming a higher terrace above it. He could see the outline of White Edge Lodge, standing isolated and sinister like a Gothic castle. Dark clouds were building up in the east, massing over Big Moor.

'So,' said Liz slowly, 'I know why we can't marry in September or November.'

'You do?'

'Since you weren't available to explain when you said you would, I asked your sister-in-law.'

'You spoke to Kate?'

'It seemed preferable to trying to get anything out of you, or your brother.'

'It's because of the anniversaries,' said Cooper. 'Our mother died in September, and our father in November.'

'I know.'

'It might seem a bit unnecessary, but anniversaries like that have always been important in our family.'

'I understand, really. November was out anyway.' She shuddered. 'Just imagine. Rain, wind, mud. A nightmare.'

They were silent for a moment, enjoying the sun. A small group of tourists walked along the track from the road to look at the pole, then walked quietly back again.

'And . . . the full works?' said Cooper hesitantly.

'Of course.'

'Right.'

'Which means we have a lot of planning to do, Ben.'

Cooper knew that he ought to sound enthusiastic. No doubt it was expected of him. But when he looked inside himself, he was forced to admit that what he wanted was to be married to Liz, not to have an actual wedding. Not a wedding with all the fuss – the morning suits and bridesmaids' dresses, the confetti and cake, the speeches and the endless group photographs. The full works.

He felt Liz take his hand in hers.

'Don't worry,' she said. 'I know it's not your kind of thing. My parents are just itching to organise it all. What we do is let them have their day, then we can sneak off somewhere nice and be ourselves. That's what we both want, isn't it?'

Cooper's phone buzzed in his pocket.

'Sorry, Liz.'

She sat up. 'Oh, Ben . . .'

He looked at the screen. *Letter arrived this a.m. from sheff rd man. U want to see it?*

'Work?'

215

'Yes.'

'It's Saturday.'

'I know, but . . . you understand.'

She sighed. 'Yes, I suppose I do.'

Erin Byrne lived in a two-bedroom apartment in Calver Mill, with rooms on three levels connected by an original stone staircase.

At the top of the stairs, Cooper found a small office space, with a desk and a computer, and a few bookshelves along the wall, all brightly lit by a generous expanse of skylight. This felt like a real eyrie, almost an ivory tower, a sanctuary raised clear of any neighbours, with a distant glimpse across the Derwent Valley towards the hills on the other side. Cooper could imagine working here if he was an artist or writer, or some kind of creative person. It felt a long way from the real world out there on the streets.

'Thanks for coming. I thought we might pop across the road to the Bridge Inn, if you've got the time,' said Byrne.

'I can spare half an hour or so.'

'No urgent incidents to attend?'

'Not today.'

At the end of August, the leaves of the Virginia creeper on the walls of the Bridge Inn were just starting to turn a deep red. Inside the bar, they stood among a display of antique fire-fighting equipment and hundreds of foreign bank notes stuck on to the oak beams.

'Outside, I think?' said Byrne. 'Less chance of being over-heard.'

'We're not in a spy film, you know.'

She looked around at the locals in the public bar. 'I'd feel more comfortable.'

'All right.'

The riverside garden at the Bridge was big enough to accommodate a couple of hundred people, all under blue and gold Hardy and Hanson parasols. So although it was a Saturday lunchtime, there were plenty of tables free. Byrne chose a spot as far as possible from the pub, overlooking the Derwent and the older of the two bridges. For a few minutes they said nothing, but sat watching the ducks on the river and listening to the sound of the weir as they sipped their drinks.

Byrne fished into her bag. It was one of the most capacious bags Cooper had ever seen. He guessed it must contain her notebook, digital recorder, camera, phone, and whatever else the modern newspaper journalist needed.

'I brought you a copy of this week's *Eden Valley Times*,' she said. 'Just out. Hot off the press.'

'Oh, thanks. I suppose . . .?'

'We led with a story on the Savages, yes.'

'We don't call them that.'

'Don't blame me. It's what everyone is talking about. We just reflect the interests of our readers.'

'Right.'

She laughed. 'You're all the same.'

'Who?'

'The police. You look down so much on the media. Until you want our help with something. An appeal to the public, an e-fit of a wanted man. Oh, then we're all supposed to be on the same side. But when we want information from you, the barriers go up. Then you pull that disapproving face and say we're not helping the situation. You say we're sensationalising.'

'I don't have a disapproving face,' said Cooper. 'Do I?'

She took a drink to hide her expression behind the glass. 'Well, perhaps not as much as some I could mention. I've met Superintendent Hazel Branagh.'

Cooper stifled a smile. 'Oh, have you?'

'It was at some civic do. She was being all smiling and matey with the dignitaries, but when she found out who I was, she looked as though she'd just sucked on a lemon.'

'We're not all like that. But some police officers have had a bad experience with the press during the course of their careers. We learn to be cautious. We definitely learn not to say too much.'

217

'Or not to say anything at all,' said Byrne.

'Not quite, surely?'

She put down her glass and positioned it carefully on a coaster, wiping off a mist of condensation.

'My dad was a local newspaper journalist too. Old school. He ended up as a subeditor on the *Sheffield Star*. He once told me that when he was a trainee reporter, if he had the police stories to cover, he actually went round to the police station every morning and spoke to the desk sergeant. That was when there were such things as desk sergeants, of course. The sergeant would look in the incident book and tell him what had happened overnight. And because they spoke every morning, they got to know each other. So if the sergeant was busy, he just gave Dad the incident book to read for himself. It's a question of trust, you see.'

'That was, what? The seventies?'

'I suppose so. *Dixon of Dock Green* might still have been on the telly.'

'It wouldn't happen now.'

'Too true. The reporters on police calls now never see a police officer, let alone get to know one. They never go inside a police station, either. All they do is make a phone call and get a recorded message. There's absolutely no personal contact, and no trust. My dad pulls his hair out when I tell him what it's like now.'

'My dad would, too,' said Cooper.

She opened her mouth as if to ask him about his father. But perhaps she read something in his face, because she kept the question to herself. That required quite a lot of self-control for a journalist.

'Anyway, enough of that,' she said. 'I'm sure you don't want to listen to me moaning. This is what you wanted to see.'

She handed Cooper a clear plastic wallet containing a single sheet of paper and an envelope. The note itself was crudely written. He might actually have said drawn rather than written. It looked as if it had been scrawled in felt-tip pen by a clumsy child. Just one sentence.

'Sheffeild Rode,' he said thoughtfully.

'I know it's crude,' said Byrne. 'And illiterate, too.'

'Sheffield isn't all that difficult a word to spell, surely.'

'It could be written by someone whose first language isn't English?'

'Maybe. And what's this symbol?'

The note was accompanied by a rudimentary sketch – a short horizontal line with an arrow beneath it, pointing to the centre of the line. If it was supposed to represent a road, with a particular house indicated on it, the sketch was worse than useless. But perhaps it wasn't that at all. It looked more symbolic than representational.

'I don't know,' said Byrne. 'No one in the office could identify it.'

'And you didn't look it up?'

'We'd normally do a Google search, of course. But there's no way of entering a picture as a search term. No way that I know of, anyway.'

'No, that's right.'

'So without a clue what to look for, we were a bit stumped. That's why my editor agreed we should pass it to you. On the understanding that we, you know . . .'

'Get some information in return?'

'Yes. Or at least a bit of a head-start on the nationals when there's a breakthrough.'

Cooper nodded. 'I understand.'

'So, what are you going to do? Raid all the houses on Sheffield Road?'

He laughed. 'I would have difficulty justifying that on the grounds of an anonymous message.'

'Yes, I see the problem.'

'But we can get it forensically examined. Something might emerge.'

'I'll leave it with you, then.'

Cooper looked at her as she got ready to leave.

'You're not covering the show this afternoon?' he said.

'Oh, Riddings Show? That's today, is it? No, we don't have

time to cover things like that. We pay a village correspondent a few pennies to write down the names of all the winners. Names still sell papers, they say. If necessary, we give them a little digital camera so they can take their own photos, too. Much cheaper than sending a photographer out from Chesterfield. We don't have our own snappers in Edendale any more.'

'It's the way everything's going.'

'Oh, I know. We get policing on the cheap too now.'

'I won't argue with that.'

'Well, I'm sure there must be lots of things you should be doing. I bet some of the residents around here would be furious if they saw you sitting in the garden of the Bridge Inn having a drink with a journalist. They'd be writing to the chief constable in their scores.'

Cooper thought that was probably true. But right at this moment, he didn't care.

Byrne got up to leave. 'Will you report our conversation to your boss?'

Cooper hesitated. He couldn't mention his contact with the press to Superintendent Branagh. He'd heard her berate other officers for the slightest communication with the media, or for taking their claims seriously. He would risk being tainted by the meeting.

'I ought to.'

Byrne smiled. 'There are a lot of things we ought to do, Detective Sergeant Cooper. Sometimes it's much more fun doing the things we shouldn't.'

When she'd gone, Cooper checked his phone for messages, then decided to stay for a few minutes to finish his drink.

He opened the copy of the *Eden Valley Times* and flicked through the pages, glancing at the photographs. He wasn't interested in the lead story about the Savages. It wouldn't tell him anything he didn't know, and might well fill his head with misconceptions and half-truths.

Halfway through the paper, just before the property section, were the pages of community news. What was going on in the villages, in other words. As usual, that seemed to be mostly WI meetings and summer fetes, tractor rallies and fund-raising garden parties. But there they were, underneath next week's church services – a party of balsam bashers pictured by the side of Calver Weir. With their boots and waterproofs, packed lunches and water bottles, they looked ready for a happy day of non-native-plant destruction.

He peered more closely. The photograph was in colour, which ought to help identification. But this was the *Eden Valley Times*, and the colour register had been slightly off alignment when the page was printed. So everyone in the picture seemed to have a faint magenta shadow blurring the left side of their face. It was an odd effect, like looking at a 3D image without the proper glasses on. But Cooper recognised Martin and Sarah Holland, standing just to one side. Barry Gamble was over to the right, lurking close to a couple of Peak District National Park rangers who had posed in the foreground wearing red rubber gloves and clutching tall plants with pink flowers.

It was the expression on Gamble's face that grabbed Cooper's attention. Despite the off-register printing, it was clear that he wasn't smiling for the camera like everyone else. He wasn't looking towards the photographer at all. In fact, he had been caught in an unguarded moment as he waited for the click of the shutter.

In that second, Barry Gamble had turned his head to the right and was staring directly at the Hollands. And the look on his face told a whole different story from the accompanying piece on the benefits of balsam bashing. His expression was a mixture of loathing and triumph. He had the air of a man taking one last, gloating look at his intended victims.

19

Riddings Show was held on Froggatt Fields, right on the western edge of Riddings where it met the neighbouring village of Froggatt, another of the duke's creations, known for its quaint seventeenth-century bridge.

The show was said to be an offshoot of the village cow club, but there were no cows present now. Small-scale livestock shows had become far too complicated and risky to organise. They were too bound up in red tape and form-filling, too constrained by DEFRA regulations, too exposed to the possibility of another outbreak of disease. Foot and mouth, blue tongue, BSE – they had all contributed to the decline. Many village shows had never recovered from last-minute cancellation, and insurance premiums were beyond the reach of societies with limited sponsorship. Cloven-hoofed animals had become an event organiser's nightmare.

So Riddings Show had transformed itself into a more genteel August bank holiday occasion. Cooper expected there would be flowers, vegetables and handicrafts, with the only livestock being the ponies and riders in the gymkhana ring.

It had begun to rain on and off almost as soon as he'd left the garden of the Bridge Inn, and he needed his windscreen wipers as he joined the flow of traffic into the showground. When he drove through the gate on to Froggatt Fields, he was greeted by the smell of engine oil, and the chug of vintage farm equipment. There were a few nods to the show's agricultural origins after all.

The marquees and stands had been set up in the lower field, separated from the river by a line of trees. At the far end, the gymkhana arena lay in a natural hollow. As Cooper walked down the slope from the parking area, a brass band was playing a medley of James Bond themes. *Goldfinger*, *From Russia with Love*. The grass in the parking area had been mowed, but not removed, so the cuttings lay everywhere in deep swathes. They wrapped themselves around the tyres of the car, and covered everyone's shoes. He found himself wading through heaps of wet grass all the way down to the show ring.

He stopped for a moment to watch a children's entertainer in a sparkly blue jacket, who was talking to a dummy Afghan hound. The dog didn't answer, except by whispering in his ear. What did you call a ventriloquism act where the dummy didn't speak? He had no idea.

Cooper turned away. There were already too many people whispering to each other in this case. Why didn't everyone say out loud what they thought? It would make life so much easier. His life, anyway.

Carol Villiers was already on the showground. She was dressed off duty, in jeans and a T-shirt, with a jacket tied round her waist. She looked every bit the outdoor girl, the sun bringing out the colour in her face. Out in the sunlight, between showers, Cooper noticed how pale her eyes were. Sandy, as if they had been bleached in a desert climate.

They walked towards the long canvas marquee, where signs announced that it had just opened to the public after judging.

'I've heard you're engaged, Ben,' said Villiers. 'Congratulations.'

Astonished, Cooper turned and stared at her as if she were a witch. Psychic, at least.

'I haven't told anyone here about that yet,' he said.

'Well, someone has.'

'Blast. I didn't expect it to get round so quickly.'

'It's one of the perils of having a relationship with a colleague,' said Villiers. 'I should know.'

'I suppose so.'

Cooper realised this was going to take some getting used to. Once his engagement was announced, and was out in the public domain, it became real.

Inside the marquee, the long rows of tables looked spectacular. They were lined with all kinds of produce, from bottles of red sloe wine to jars of runner bean chutney. The scone classes seemed to have been particularly popular, and some of those extravagant flower arrangements must have taken many hours to create. Someone had even embroidered butterfly species around a cottage scene.

Cooper saw that the band was a local one, from Hathersage. Mostly middle-aged men, dressed in red jackets. Though a bandstand had been set out for them, they were playing inside the produce tent to avoid the rain. One of the musicians had stored his tuba case under a trestle table covered in mammoth cabbages and strings of onions.

'My brother used to be in a brass band,' said Villiers. 'Soprano cornet.'

'I'd forgotten you had a brother.'

'Charlie. You must have met him.'

'I'm sure I did. I just can't quite . . .'

'He only joined the band for the beer,' said Villiers.

At the other end of the tent, Cooper stopped to look at the winner in the photographic competition, a stunning close-up shot of frost on a barbed-wire fence. The photographer had caught the spikes of the frost mirroring the angle of the steel barbs. The clarity of the detail was amazing. Every facet of the ice crystals shone out of the picture.

Next to it on the table were entries in another photographic class – local scenes. Each entry was labelled with the name and village of the photographer, and one sprang out at him immediately. B. Gamble, Riddings. Of course. A keen amateur snapper like our Barry wouldn't have been able to resist showing off his talents in the local show.

Mr Gamble hadn't won a prize, though. Not even highly commended. His entry showed a corner of Riddings that Cooper wasn't familiar with. An ancient building with a corrugated-iron roof, moss growing on the stone walls, a door half covered in peeling green paint. No windows visible, so it was probably an old farm building. A lot older than most of the properties in Riddings. Perhaps it was a remnant of an agricultural holding that had stood in the village before the big houses were built.

Cooper guessed that Gamble had been going for an artistic statement about decay and abandonment. The building had reached a fairly picturesque stage of dilapidation. The weeds in front of it were dense and impenetrable. A bird had built its nest on top of a broken downspout. But he could also see why the photograph hadn't received even a commendation from the judge. The composition was all wrong. The angle of the shot was awkward, and the building itself was off-centre, part of it concealed by an ugly tree stump that had got in the way, as if the photographer hadn't noticed it. Cooper wasn't an expert, but even he could see that the picture would have been improved immensely if Gamble had simply moved ten yards to the right and got a few steps closer to his subject.

'Our Mr Gamble,' said Villiers, looking over his shoulder. 'Will he be here?'

'Oh, he wouldn't miss this.'

'A chance to observe his neighbours out in the open.'

'The same reason we're here, in fact.'

Cooper looked around, searching for the familiar faces of Riddings residents. The relationships and hierarchies were difficult to assess without seeing people together. He had been speaking to them only on their own territory, where they could present themselves in their best light, give an account of their relations with their neighbours that they wanted him to believe, tell him any story without fear of contradiction.

Outside the tent, children were running around with giant inflatable hammers their parents had won at a hoopla stall. Cooper and Villiers passed a vicar with cropped grey hair and a goatee beard, wearing muddy black jeans. A visitor had noticed his dog collar and stopped him: *We don't see a clergyman around here very often*. The vicar started to explain that he covered a huge area, stretching from Riddings and Curbar across a vast swathe of the Peak District to Great Longstone and Stoney Middleton. The sighting of a Church of England clergyman in an English village was becoming as rare as a working phone box.

The thought created a series of associations in Cooper's mind. Erin Byrne had mentioned that the phone calls to the *Eden Valley Times* had been made from a public call box somewhere. And one of the walkers Gavin Murfin had spoken to had mentioned seeing someone in the phone box in the centre of Riddings on Tuesday night, making a call.

It was a bit of a stretch. But it was one possible link in a case where nothing seemed to be connecting.

Nearby, an old Lister engine chugged, whirred, and belched out fumes. He saw that there were tractors, too. Not doing anything, just standing in a couple of rows like exhibits in a museum. One of the owners was leaning against his old grey Ferguson. In other years, Matt might have been here with his own Fergie. But not any more.

The first people Cooper recognised at Riddings Show were the Chadwicks. They seemed to have made a beeline for the book stall and snapped up all the Bill Brysons. Mrs Chadwick wore a blue anorak, and red cargo pants that stopped halfway up her calves, with white trainers. Her husband was in a green Craghoppers cagoule and matching straw hat. They looked as though they'd made a great effort to be casual. But William Chadwick wore a slightly hunted look, his eyes darting from side to side as he passed through the crowd, perhaps fearing to encounter a pupil or a member of staff from his school.

'Mr and Mrs Chadwick,' said Cooper.

They stopped, surprised. Mrs Chadwick almost dropped her books into the grass, but recovered her poise.

'Oh. It's . . .'

'Detective Sergeant Cooper. This is my colleague, DC Villiers.'

Mr Chadwick remained frozen, words failing him for a moment, anxiety filling his eyes. A trickle of perspiration ran down his temple.

226

'I'm really sorry to bother you,' said Cooper. 'I realise this is a social occasion. But there was something I wanted to ask you.'

'Well . . . go ahead.'

'Did you ever have any disputes with your closest neighbours in Riddings?'

'Neighbours?'

'Well, you live adjacent to the Hollands at Fourways, the Barrons at Valley View. Perhaps Mr Kaye at Moorside House?'

The Chadwicks looked at each other, but actually seemed relieved at the question.

'There was an incident with Jake Barron a while ago,' admitted Mrs Chadwick.

'It was silly really,' said her husband. 'It was at a time when I was feeling particularly stressed. Because of, you know . . .'

'The incident,' said his wife. 'It was a very difficult period, in both our lives.'

'I understand.'

'Anyway, the Barrons had a dog then.'

'Did they?'

'Yes, a Dobermann. They always had it out on the drive in a fancy collar, running about behind the gates. It used to bark incessantly.'

'The Barrons told us once that Dobermanns are emotionally sensitive,' said Mrs Chadwick. 'And if they're upset about anything, they bark. They claimed it was part of the animal's duty as a guard dog. We politely suggested they might take the trouble to train it properly, but they took no notice, of course.'

Chadwick nodded. 'Then one afternoon I couldn't stand it any longer. It was going on for hour after hour, day after day. It was intolerable. We shouldn't have to put up with that, should we? So when I saw him coming by in his car, I stopped him.'

'What did he say when you confronted him?'

'He became very aggressive. Started shouting and swearing at me. Threatening retaliation, just because I had the nerve to complain. Yes, he soon showed his true colours. The man turned into a foul-mouthed thug in front of my eyes. I've got to tell you, having them as neighbours has been like living next door to a family of yobs on a council estate.'

'Yet they've always thought they were so superior,' added Mrs Chadwick. 'It makes me sick.'

'But the dog isn't there now, at Valley View,' said Cooper. 'There was no sign of a Dobermann, or any other breed.'

'No. It went, about a month ago.'

The Chadwicks looked at each other again. There were moments when Cooper wished he had the power to read minds. He would really love to know what this couple were thinking right now.

'We heard it got sick and died,' said Mrs Chadwick finally. 'Sad for the animal, of course. But still . . .'

They were silent for a few moments, gazing at Cooper and Villiers as if they expected to be challenged.

'I suppose you think we shouldn't talk about the Barrons like this,' said Mrs Chadwick. 'In view of what happened, I mean.'

'On the contrary,' said Cooper. 'We much prefer it if people tell us the truth, instead of holding information back.'

They watched the Chadwicks walk off towards the marquee. A few minutes later, Cooper saw their daughter drifting through the showground, dark hair hanging over her face, her manner giving the impression that she was far too sophisticated for all this nonsense.

'Oh, hello,' she said when he stopped her.

'You're off to university soon, aren't you?'

'God, yes. I can't wait.'

'Is it that bad?'

'I need to get away. I have to get away from them.'

'From your parents?'

'Yeah. Well . . . from all of them. All the people here, in this place. Look at it. Our house is a like a prison inside a prison.'

She drifted away again, and was swallowed up by a group of young people. No doubt some of the same bunch that had been at the party on Thursday night.

The crowds were getting thicker now as the show became busier. The clothes on display were fascinating in themselves. Cooper saw pink wellies, white wellies with blue polka dots, wellies with roses on them. An incredible range of dogs was here at the show, too. Within a few yards he passed Great Danes, spaniels, pugs, golden retrievers, Airedales. There was even a St Bernard – and you didn't see those very often. No Dobermanns, though.

He looked at Villiers, trying to decide if it was a good time to ask her a personal question.

'I wondered,' he said. 'I thought you might have reverted to your maiden name when you came back here to Derbyshire.'

'I suppose I ought to,' she said. 'Yes, you're right, I should.'

'But . . .?'

'But?' She turned her face away. 'Well, Glen's name is the only part of him that I have left. How could I just throw that aside?'

There was nothing he could say to that.

'Let's try down this way.'

From his sign, Cooper gathered that the children's entertainer was called Doctor Woof. And the dog seemed to be called Trevor. Surely it would have made more sense if the entertainer's name was Trevor and the dog was Doctor Woof? But perhaps they had swapped personalities. The dummy certainly seemed to be the more lively of the two.

Doctor Woof was doing magic tricks now, and the kids were lapping it up. He'd gathered quite a crowd, and they could hear his voice repeatedly urging overenthusiastic children to stay in the prize zone.

Watching the entertainer in action, Cooper had the feeling of recognition again. He couldn't be sure under all that make-up and the false beard, but he felt this was someone he'd seen before. But to become a children's entertainer, Doctor Woof must have been CRB checked. If there was nothing found against him at the Criminal Records Bureau, then his own contact with him couldn't have been anything too serious.

After a while, Cooper found he could distinguish local residents from visitors. The locals wore outdoor clothes and sensible footwear, and tended to congregate near the gymkhana ring or the produce tent. Periodically they moved slowly up and down the aisle between the two, meeting each other and chatting in front of the RSPB stand. They seemed to be the local equivalent of Parisian promenaders. Couples met, air-kissed and chatted briefly. Then they moved on to the next encounter by the jam stall. A cry of *Give everyone our love!* drifted on the air behind them.

On the other hand, most of the visitors from out of the area seemed to have dressed in the confident expectation that it never rained in Derbyshire in August. But it was a bank holiday weekend, for heaven's sake. It always rained.

During the showers, they all milled around the tea tent, dodging each other with trays of tea and cakes. It was a peculiarly British thing, the way people were able to drink tea and eat ice cream while sitting in the rain, yet still seem to be enjoying themselves.

'Look at Mr Nowak,' said Villiers. 'No one is talking to him. They don't even seem to acknowledge his presence. I saw one woman speak to his dog, but not to him.'

'He came, though,' said Cooper.

'So why is he here? He must have known it would be like this.'

'To be part of the village, I think. To feel that he belongs.'

Villiers shook her head. 'Surely it just rubs in the fact that no one else thinks he *does* belong.'

'It's a very deep instinct, the urge to belong, the need to be part of a group. People will put up with all kinds of humiliations in their desire to be accepted.'

'Like initiations.'

'Exactly. It happens everywhere, from street gangs to the police.'

'And the military,' said Villiers. 'But sometimes they go too far, as we know.'

'Mmm. Are you thinking . . .?'

230

'That someone humiliated Mr Nowak a bit too much. It's possible.'

A hundred yards away, a man was shouting. At first Cooper thought it was part of the show. Another children's entertainer, perhaps. But this one sounded too aggressive. And that language he could hear wasn't suitable for children, surely?

'What's all the commotion over there?'

'It looks like Richard Nowak and Alan Slattery.'

'Had we better sort it out?' said Villiers.

'Give it a minute.'

They moved a bit closer, watching the angry gestures, trying to hear what the raised voices were saying. It was difficult to tell which of the men was the most irate, or what they were arguing about.

'Mrs Slattery and the Nowaks are direct neighbours too,' said Cooper.

'Interesting. Is this what you were hoping for, Ben?'

'Sort of.'

Villiers shook her head. 'In some of the countries I've served in, people are incredibly polite to each other,' she said. 'There's often a very elaborate system of manners, so elaborate that it becomes a ritual. And I think that's because those are large populations of people living cheek by jowl, right in each other's pockets. Sometimes you might have someone living literally on your doorstep. In those circumstances, you've got to have a way of masking the animosity that builds up between individuals.'

'But here, they don't seem to think it's necessary?'

'Well, they've got a certain amount of distance between each other. Or at least, the illusion of distance. And all that seems to have done is break down the barriers of courtesy. The animosity comes right out in the open.'

'It's a property thing,' said Cooper. 'Owning property is a very British obsession. And once you own it, you have to defend it against all comers. I've seen it so often.'

He didn't mention that he'd seen it in his own brother. Villiers hadn't asked about his family yet, but he was sure she

231

would before long. He was certain that she knew all about his father. Everyone with any connection to Edendale knew about the death of Sergeant Joe Cooper. In fact, he recalled her writing a letter, which had arrived just after the funeral. She was serving overseas somewhere then. He remembered opening the letter with its foreign stamp and discovering it was from his old school friend, offering her sympathy.

But she might not know about the more recent death of his mother. It depended who she'd talked to since she'd been back. It was strange to think that this person he hadn't seen for so long might know everything about him.

'I suppose it's why guns are illegal in Britain,' she said. 'Neighbours would be shooting each other every week otherwise.'

There was a final flurry of shouting, and some shocked gasps from onlookers.

'Uh-oh,' said Cooper.

'Incoming,' said Villiers.

And they both watched Richard Nowak sprinting frantically across the showground towards them.

20

Diane Fry gazed out through the windscreen at the streets of Sheffield. They were in an area of the city she didn't know at all. Firth Park. Narrow streets, endless rows of brick terraces. Satellite dishes sprouted in clusters from gable ends, wheelie bins stood on the pavement outside every front door. On the corner, a kebab and burger shop showed the only signs of life.

'What are they playing around at? It's like waiting for paint to dry.'

DI Hitchens was tapping the wheel impatiently. Fry could see that he hated not being in control. The operation was in the hands of South Yorkshire Police, and they were taking their time. Fair enough. They wanted to get it right.

'There's no hurry,' she said. 'We've got all day.'

'Sod that. I don't know about you, Diane, but I'd like to get some time off this weekend.'

Fry nodded. Station gossip had it that the DI's girlfriend was pregnant, and that she was pressuring him to make plans. That sort of thing was difficult to keep to yourself. It was true that he was less keen these days to spend more time in the office than was strictly necessary. Fry felt she ought to be able to sympathise. A work–life balance, and all that. But you probably needed to get a life first, before you could properly understand.

'They know what they're doing,' she said. 'They've done the surveillance, collected all the intel. Let them have their moment. We'll soon have ours.'

Down the street was a lock-up shop. This one looked as though it had been locked up for years. Steel shutters were drawn down over the windows and the front door. A delivery entrance in a side street was protected by locked gates, with a *No Parking* sign faded almost to illegibility. Behind the shop, a derelict building was starting to crumble, cracks splitting the brickwork, weeds growing out of the window ledges and between the slates in the roof.

Fry looked up. Dirty net curtains hung over the windows on the first floor. A broken drainpipe had left a dark stain down the wall. You wouldn't imagine that anybody lived there. But surveillance by South Yorkshire officers had confirmed that someone did.

Hitchens had begun to whistle under his breath. It was a habit that Fry found particularly irritating.

'It's time, surely.'

'Okay, here they come now.'

A van came down the street at speed. A marked police vehicle appeared and blocked off the junction at the top. Officers in black jumped out of the van. The strike team didn't bother with the steel shutters, but went straight for the gates. The padlock was snapped off, and they were into the delivery yard in seconds. Fry heard the battering ram hit the back door, and the shouts of officers as they entered the building, clattering up the stairs to the flat.

The radio crackled, but Hitchens was already out of the car.

'All right, they're in. Suspect detained.'

'Let's hope he's the right suspect,' said Fry, as they ran into the yard.

A door stood open on to a set of bare wooden stairs, the steps splintered and scattered with decades of dust. A stale smell oozed out of the flat.

Hitchens turned for a moment at the foot of the stairs.

'If one of the Savages had to live anywhere, this would be it.'

Red in the face and breathing heavily, Richard Nowak ran a few more paces across Riddings showground towards Cooper and Villiers, slowing down suddenly as he got nearer.

Cooper realised that Nowak hadn't been running towards them for assistance, as he thought. He hadn't even recognised them as police officers. He had been running away from the confrontation with Alan Slattery. That seemed out of character, from what Cooper had seen of him.

'Mr Nowak? Not enjoying yourself?'

He scowled. 'I must be a masochist, coming here.'

'These occasions can be difficult, if you don't fit in.'

'It's not the occasion that's difficult. It's the people.'

Nowak glanced over his shoulder. The sun was out now, and he was sweating. He wiped a hand across his brow, while he struggled to regain his breath. Cooper could see that Nowak's wife had stayed where she was, and was talking to some other women. Slattery had vanished, though. Maybe he had recognised the police when Nowak didn't.

'So what's your problem with Mr Slattery?' asked Cooper.

'It's *his* problem, not mine,' snapped Nowak. 'He had the gall to accuse me of making his mother ill.'

'Why?'

'He says I've been putting her under too much pressure.'

'I didn't know you had issues with Mrs Slattery.'

'Why should I tell you? It's nothing to do with the police. It's a matter of courtesy and reasonable behaviour.'

'Even so, sir. It would help if we're clear.'

Nowak let out a long sigh. 'Look, it's the way her house and garden have been deteriorating, ever since the old doctor died. She hasn't been carrying out maintenance at all. The fences are falling down, the trees are growing over our side of the boundary, and the weeds are waist high. We've been seeing rats in our garden, and I'm sure they're coming from

South Croft. She has a septic tank a few yards from the boundary, and it hasn't been emptied for years. It's just not acceptable. It's bringing down the value of our property. But when I speak to her about it, she just gets upset. And now I've got her blasted son on my case.'

'So that was what the argument with Mr Slattery was about just now?'

'Yes, of course. Why should I accept the situation, even if she is a widow?'

Villiers had been watching Nowak carefully. 'Are you feeling calmer now, sir?' she said.

'I'm fine,' he said sullenly. 'Fine.'

'So where were you running to?'

'To my car, if you must know.'

'I hope you weren't about to fetch a weapon to continue the quarrel?'

'Don't be ridiculous. I have my camera in the car. I wanted to show him the photographs I've taken, to prove what I was saying.'

'Perhaps it would be best to leave it for now, and let everyone calm down.'

'That sounds like good advice, sir,' said Cooper.

'Oh, for . . .'

Nowak walked away a few steps, then turned back.

'I want to be a reasonable man,' he said. 'I want to get on with my neighbours. But we came here to this village and they tried to push us around, because they think we're foreigners. They say to themselves, *These people don't belong here, they won't know their rights*. But I'm not stupid. I know my rights. And I won't be pushed around. It's something they have to learn about me.'

'A reasonable man?' said Villiers, as Nowak headed towards the car park.

Cooper shrugged. 'Perhaps. But what's reasonable?'

'The million-dollar question, Ben. It depends entirely on your point of view, doesn't it?'

'Entirely. If you're convinced that you're in the right, then everything you do is reasonable in your own mind. It might not seem reasonable to somebody on the outside. And certainly not to the person you're in dispute with.'

It was the middle of the afternoon now, and the show was in full swing. There were kids clambering all over the tractors, having their photographs taken yanking a steering wheel backwards and forwards. Members of the band were queuing at the tea tent for their refreshment break. Thirsty work, blowing a tuba.

'What's the name of that man with the sports car?' said Villiers.

'Mr Edson?'

'Do I see him flirting with Mrs Nowak?'

'Really? Where?'

'About two o'clock. Near the jam stall.'

Cooper picked them out. Edson was leaning casually on his shooting stick, smiling and talking loudly to Sonya Nowak. She seemed transfixed by what he was saying, but it might just have been politeness.

'Is that flirting?' said Cooper doubtfully.

'Watch,' said Villiers. 'He'll move a bit closer.'

Edson seemed to find something he'd said himself hilarious. He waved his shooting stick in an extravagant gesture, then planted it back in the ground again. Sure enough, he was now leaning an inch or two nearer to Mrs Nowak. His smile became broader, an eyebrow waggled. Cooper stared in horrified fascination.

'I would never have thought it.'

'She's quite an attractive woman. Don't you think so?'

'I . . .'

Cooper knew he shouldn't answer a question like that from another woman. He could never give the right reply.

'No?'

'If that's your taste. But him? I can't see what might attract Mrs Nowak even to give him the time of day.'

'Come on, Ben. Don't be naive. What's the greatest aphrodisiac in the world?'

Cooper sighed. 'Money.'

'Absolutely. People are so shallow, aren't they? The residents of Riddings are no different.'

'No different. Only worse.'

Russell Edson carried a shooting stick and wore a panama hat, no doubt direct from Ecuador. He wore rimless glasses, with his hair swept back, and a white scarf with tasselled ends thrown round his neck. There was a natural curl to his lip that Cooper found faintly disturbing. It wasn't so noticeable when he was looking at someone and smiling his polite smile. But it gave him a supercilious look the moment he turned away and his face relaxed.

In company, Edson talked all the time, seeming to have a strong opinion on every subject that came up. It was as if he needed to dominate with the sheer force of his personality. Between opinions, he smiled possessively at every woman within easy radius. Cooper supposed he was what the sociologists called an alpha male, the man with a single-minded urge to take over any group, the kind who always needed to have followers. He wondered if he himself was considered a challenge, whether he was supposed to be cowed by the display of dominance.

The other people drifted away as Cooper and Villiers approached. That was something you got used to, a reluctance on the part of the public to interact with the police, or even to stand next to them at a village show.

'It's a bit of a chore,' said Edson. 'But we have to be here, you know.'

'You don't like socialising, sir?'

'Socialising?' he said. 'Could you call it that? Everyone wants a piece of you, that's the trouble.'

Cooper stared at him, wondering if this man really did think of himself as the local squire, with a tiresome obligation to allow hoi polloi into his presence now and then.

'Your neighbours, you mean?' said Cooper.

'Neighbours, business associates, former so-called friends. Everyone.'

238

Glenys Edson had been listening to her son, eyeing him with a baleful expression.

'Even your children try to suck the life out of you,' she said. 'It's as if they want every last drop of your blood. They're never satisfied, never give up. What do *you* say, Russell?'

Edson looked angry. His face was flushed, his lips pressed tightly together. But he didn't respond to the comment, kept his mouth closed, apparently reluctant to argue with his mother in front of strangers.

Cooper and Villiers moved away, but had only gone a few paces when Cooper felt a touch on his arm. When he turned, it was Russell Edson again.

'I'm sorry about my mother,' he said. 'She didn't really mean anything by that last remark, you know.'

'It's between the two of you, sir. None of my business.'

To his surprise, Edson gave him a warm, grateful smile. It was if Cooper had just done him a huge favour.

'Thank you, Sergeant. If there's anything else I can do . . .'

'I'll let you know.'

Cooper saw one of the show organisers passing, a woman in a poncho with a rain hat and brown boots, and decided to introduce himself. Best to let them know that he and Villiers were here.

'The show looks busy,' he said. 'Good turnout?'

'Not bad,' she said. 'But it's difficult to keep things going. We're lucky that so many people give their services for nothing. We wouldn't manage without that. The children's entertainer, for example.'

'Doctor Woof?'

She nodded. 'He's not charging us a penny. He seems to do it for love. We hadn't even thought of getting an entertainer until he volunteered his services. It's wonderful that people want so much to be here at the show.'

A man in a cotton trilby had stopped nearby, seeming to overhear their conversation.

'Did you say you were police?'

'Yes, sir,' said Cooper.

'I don't mean any disrespect, but . . .'

Cooper sighed. 'I know, I know.'

Whenever the sun came out, he felt warm in his waterproof. People folded their umbrellas and carried them like swords. Entering the produce tent was fraught with danger as he dodged the lethal ferrules.

A line-up of classic cars was attracting attention. Cooper was surprised to see not only vintage Rollers and Humbers, but a yellow 1975 Hillman Imp. He dimly remembered a neighbouring farmer driving one of those when he was a child. He and Matt used to make fun of him whenever they saw it going past. They called it the sardine can. The Imp had looked totally cheesy then, back in the 1970s. Now it was a classic.

At the end of the row stood a Mark III Zodiac, with a sign appealing for spare parts. These cars must be a headache to keep running. And an immense drain on money, he was sure. He saw Russell Edson's name on a red 1967 MG convertible with big headlamps and indicator lights on the wheel arches. There was a man with money to burn, anyway.

'Mr Edson seems to be fascinated by the children's entertainer,' said Villiers.

'So he is.' Cooper frowned at the figure in the panama hat and white scarf. 'That's a bit strange. I hope it's not the children he's interested in.'

'It doesn't seem to be,' said Villiers. 'I've been watching him for a few minutes, and he hasn't even glanced at any of the kids.'

'Perhaps he missed out on magicians and clowns in his childhood.'

'And oh, look,' said Villiers. 'The missing element has made its appearance.'

She indicated a man in a black sweatshirt and a bright red baseball cap. He wore wraparound shades and a dark goatee beard shaved into an unnaturally geometrical shape. He was accompanied by a young blonde woman.

Cooper frowned. 'Who is that?'

'Ben, you're getting so out of touch.'

'Am I?'

'Luke Irvine would tell you straight away who that is.'

'Oh, wait a minute. Is it . . .?'

'Mr Terence Kaye, also known as Tyler Kaye or Tyler K.'

'Our missing celebrity. I wonder why he doesn't want to be known as Terence.'

'Yes, I wonder.'

'He's been abroad, hasn't he? Owns other homes some-where.'

'One in Florida at least, they say. He isn't seen in Derbyshire much during the winter.'

Cooper smiled. 'No, I can imagine.'

He could, too. A Pennine winter wouldn't appeal to the likes of Mr Kaye. Not when the wind howled over the edge and rain and snow blew down the hillside on to the houses of Riddings. Your outdoor swimming pool and barbecue patio weren't much use then. Your tennis court would fall into disuse, and the paddocks would turn into mud. Even in August, those shades Kaye was wearing looked out of place. If he was seen with them on in January or February, he'd be followed around by small children chanting and throwing stones.

On a word from Kaye, the blonde woman detached herself from him and headed towards Cooper. She was deeply tanned, no doubt from a Florida trip rather than any amount of time spent in Derbyshire. A dyed blonde, he guessed. Cosmetic surgery maybe. He couldn't really tell. He wouldn't even be willing to swear to her age.

He was interested to observe Carol Villiers bridle as the woman walked up to them.

'You're the police, aren't you? Detectives, yeah?'

'Yes, Miss . . .?'

'My name's Lisa. Tyler asked me to speak to you. He thinks you might want to talk to him. Someone has been up at Moorside House while he was away, looking for him.'

'It's just routine,' said Cooper. 'We're speaking to everyone in the area.'

'Well, he's only just flown in from the States. He gets really badly jet-lagged, you know. But he'll be happy to talk to you tomorrow. He has a bit of time before his new concert tour.'

'Are you Mr Kaye's girlfriend?' asked Villiers.

Cooper was surprised how much subtle meaning Villiers could get into the word 'girlfriend'. Lisa couldn't fail to detect it, too. She glanced at Villiers with undisguised hostility.

'Yes. So?'

'Nothing. Just asking. I hope you're happy together.'

The girl seemed to sag. For a second, Cooper thought she was going to cry. Instead her face seized up, fixed in a kind of comical expression of dejection. Cosmetic surgery, almost certainly. Botox froze the facial muscles.

'We've been together for months,' she said. 'But he's losing interest in me, I can tell.'

'Shame,' said Villiers. 'The loss of a meal ticket is always a blow.'

'What can I do to stop him leaving me?'

Villiers squared her shoulders. 'Tantrums, crying fits, emotional blackmail? The usual, I suppose.'

The girl drew back her teeth and snarled. 'I should have known better than to talk to the pigs.'

Cooper waited until she'd gone.

'That was a bit cynical,' he said.

Villiers shrugged. 'I told you, Ben. I've changed.'

A few minutes later, they stood on a clover-covered slope watching the gymkhana events, girls on ponies racing each other to collect upturned flower pots from posts.

A few of the older visitors looked as though they might have been members of the original cow club. Cooper noticed an old man in a tweed jacket and a brown waistcoat with a silver fob chain, untidy white hair stirring in the breeze. Despite his age, he had the keen gaze of a livestock man. Another old farmer in a suit and tie, with brightly polished leather shoes, was dozing off on a wooden chair near the pony classes.

A small girl with blond pigtails hanging from under her riding hat was seated on a dapple grey pony. The child screamed as her pony panicked and shied away from a judge trying to present her with a blue rosette.

They finally found the Gambles watching the gymkhana. From behind, the couple were hardly recognisable. Their chairs were pulled close together, and their heads were covered, hers by the hood of a cagoule and his with a tattered deerstalker instead of the cowboy hat. Even so, there was something about their posture that identified them to Cooper's eye. Perhaps it was the way they had huddled together and cut themselves off from the crowd, turning their backs deliberately to the rest of the show.

Cooper sat down in a chair next to Mr Gamble, while Villiers stood patiently behind their seats. Gamble barely acknowledged his presence with a twitch of his eyebrows.

'Interested in horses, sir?'

'Our granddaughter is competing.'

'Oh, really? Does she live in Riddings?'

'No, in Bamford. But they come from all over for this show.'

'I saw that you'd entered the photographic competition,' said Cooper.

'It's my hobby. I told you.'

'Well, one of them.'

'I didn't win,' said Gamble.

'I'm sorry about that. But it was a fascinating photograph. I was wondering where it was taken.'

'Are you interested in photography?'

'No, but I'm interested in Riddings. In everything about the place. And I didn't recognise the location in your picture.'

Gamble made a pretence of being engrossed by what was going on in the ring, applauding some child receiving her award. Cooper wasn't fooled. Not this time. He could practically see Gamble's brain working, trying to calculate the best answer to the question, maybe hoping Cooper would go away if he didn't reply for long enough. But Cooper wasn't going away.

'It's just some old farm buildings,' Gamble said finally.

'There are no farms in Riddings, sir. I imagine there haven't been any for quite a long time.'

'No, but there are still some derelict buildings. You just need to know where to look.'

'And where are these particular buildings?'

'On the outskirts of the village, under the edge.'

Cooper nodded. 'Perhaps I'll ask you to show me some time.'

Gamble scowled. 'I don't like being seen talking to you in public like this. People will think I'm in trouble.'

On the other side of Gamble, his wife made a small sound, a faint expression of incredulity. Cooper looked at her, saw her raise her eyes upwards in exasperation.

'I'm sure we can all be discreet,' said Cooper. 'Especially when we want to obtain information.'

He left Gamble muttering to himself, and Mrs Gamble hissing into his ear. That was one couple he was happy to unsettle.

The spell of sun had lulled everyone into a false sense of security. The waterproofs had come off, the umbrellas had been lowered, the ice creams were being handed round. The first big drops of rain hitting the ground caused a wave of movement across the showground as visitors ran for cover.

A gust of wind along the river blew sprays of water off the awnings of the stands. A few moments later, an even stronger gust dismantled the face-painting tent, tugging its pegs out of the ground and folding the canvas right over on to the popcorn stand. The sight seemed to have alarmed Doctor Woof, who had cut his show short and was packing up his gear as Cooper and Villiers walked towards his spot.

Now rain drummed on the canvas roof of the marquee, and water cascaded over the entrance flap, where straw had been strewn on the floor to prevent it from getting poached – churned up by thousands of passing feet.

The band was playing something more soothing now, but not a piece he recognised. He asked Villiers if she knew it.

'It's "Music of the Night".'

'"Music of the Night"? That sounds like something from Count Dracula. You know, when Dracula hears the wolves howling outside the castle. He says: "Listen to them. Children of the night. What music they make."'

244

'No, it's Andrew Lloyd Webber.'

'I was close.'

'You don't know *Phantom of the Opera*, then? You must be about the only person who's never been to see it.'

'Musicals aren't really my thing. Besides, you have to go to London.'

She smiled. 'And you could never do that. You're getting very provincial, Ben.'

'Getting? I always was.'

'I know. And I rather like it.'

When the rain stopped again, they decided to leave. As they walked back to the parking area, they passed small knots of people leaning on their umbrellas and shooting sticks, or picnicking under the tailgates of their 4x4s. All of them seemed to be too loud and too jovial, pretending that they were enjoying themselves more than they really were. Even a social occasion like this became a falsehood, a sham.

Cooper reflected that pretty much everybody he'd spoken to in Riddings had been telling lies about something. Lying when in doubt was a natural response, though. It seemed like a way to postpone trouble. Short-term thinking, of course. But everyone was guilty of that. Absolutely everyone.

Before they got back to the car, Villiers disappeared. Cooper found himself standing near the ice cream van. Frederick's, a local firm. He remembered his promise to buy Villiers a choc ice. But the van seemed to be advertising more exotic items. He had no idea whether she would appreciate a Festival Original or a Grande Chocolate.

For the last few minutes the band had kept returning to a few bars of 'We'll Meet Again', the Vera Lynn wartime hit. It was dropped in like a little bit of sentimental cream on the musical cake. The sound of it reminded Cooper of a sign he often passed for a farmhouse tea room, advertising *Tea and Nostalgia*.

Villiers caught up with him near the car.

'I won a box of Thornton's Continental in the raffle,' she said.

'Oh. So . . .?'

'So I could either take them home and eat them all. Or I could share them. What do you think?'

Cooper smiled. 'Sharing gets my vote.'

21

Robin Hood tourists. They used to be restricted to Nottinghamshire. They haunted Sherwood Forest, hoping for a glimpse of the Merry Men among the oak trees. Or they visited Nottingham Castle, signed up for a guided tour of the caves, and were amazed to find that the Sheriff actually existed. Occasionally, a few might stray into Derbyshire to look at Little John's grave in the churchyard at Hathersage.

But these people were a different kind. A different kettle of fish altogether. They weren't interested in bows and arrows, or men in green tights. Their obsession was with a more contemporary phenomenon: the developing twenty-first-century legends known as the Savages.

Cooper was frustrated by the number of vehicles parked all over Riddings. No wonder local residents got annoyed. There were constant trickles of people walking past Valley View and Fourways, pointing at the police tape, taking photographs on their mobile phones. And it wasn't because the village was quaint. Not any more.

He thought of the press photographers gathered outside Moorside House, and wondered if they were still there. If they'd been expecting Tyler Kaye to arrive, they had been right. Luckily, Cooper knew that he himself wasn't anyone the press would pay attention to. He was far too unimportant, not a face they would recognise.

E Division headquarters in West Street always seemed so much quieter at the weekend. Downstairs, the custody suite was still busy, of course. Uniformed officers on Saturday duty came and went, prisoners were processed, members of the public came into reception to visit the enquiry desk.

Upstairs, it was different. The incident room was manned, but Cooper's presence wasn't required. He wasn't even supposed to be in the office today. There was no sign of Hitchens or Branagh either, but that wasn't unusual at the weekend.

Luke Irvine was the duty DC. He looked up in surprise when Cooper and Villiers came into the CID room.

'Something up?' he said.

'No, no. Just wanted to check up on a few things.'

'Okay,' said Irvine uncertainly.

Watching him, Cooper was reminded of himself as a young DC, not quite knowing what was going on a lot of the time, and being reluctant to ask in case he seemed dim.

Villiers placed the open box of chocolates on a desk.

'This feels really decadent,' she said. 'Gavin will be sorry he missed it.'

'Not when it comes to a clash with the Rams at home,' said Cooper.

Villiers shook her head. 'Football. It's so sad.'

Cooper had begun making a list of names, consulting a file occasionally for one that he couldn't quite remember.

'There's no need for you to be here, you know, Carol. You can go home.'

'I know.'

He looked at her and smiled, reflecting what Diane Fry might have said to him in these circumstances. Something caustic and dismissive, no doubt. She certainly wouldn't have been here supporting him in some quixotic pursuit. A wild goose chase, she would have called it. And probably other things a lot worse.

248

Villiers peeked at his list of names. 'Well, from what we saw at the show this afternoon, there seem to be plenty of feuds and disputes going on in that village.'

'You're not kidding,' said Cooper. 'The Chadwicks and the Barrons, Mr Nowak and the Barrons, Mr Nowak and the Slattery family.'

'Mr Edson and . . .?'

'Well, his own mother, by the sound of it.'

'Is she his only family?'

'Hold on.'

Cooper called up the details that had been gathered on Edson during the early stages of the inquiry.

'Here we are. Russell Edson, of Riddings Lodge, Curbar Lane. A former building contractor, but he gave up the business after the big win. He's divorced, with two grown-up children. He lives at the lodge with his mother Glenys, as we know. His father died some years ago.'

'Divorced, eh? Did that happen before or after the lottery windfall?'

'Good question. It would make a big difference to the wife's divorce settlement, wouldn't it?'

'Absolutely. So what's the answer?'

'Before.'

'Unlucky. She's got to be resentful. Thinking if only she'd hung on a bit longer, all this could be hers.'

'It seems Mr Edson has one of the highest levels of security in Riddings, too. He possibly has the most money, and certainly the largest collection of valuables – the house is packed with them.'

'I wonder if he feels vulnerable. He might expect to be the next target.'

Cooper nodded. 'Yes, he might. Well, that's Edson. But the striking thing is that nobody seems to have had any objections to the Hollands. Not that we've heard about.'

'Interesting. So that leaves us without a motive for them being a target on Thursday night.'

'Ye-es,' said Cooper.

'I mean, we are thinking along the lines of someone in Riddings being responsible for these attacks, rather than the legendary Savages everyone else is out chasing? I have got that right, Ben?'

Cooper threw up his hands in submission. 'You'll say I'm mad, I suppose.'

'No, of course not.'

'Everyone else will.'

He looked over his shoulder, but Irvine was on the phone and paying no attention to them.

'Superintendent Branagh seems to like you anyway,' said Villiers. 'Unless you've got something on her?'

Cooper shook his head. 'I've just learned not to rub people up the wrong way all the time.'

'The way I do, you mean?'

'I didn't say that, but . . .'

'I'm getting on really well with Gavin Murfin, at least.'

'Are you?' said Cooper. 'I hadn't noticed. But, well . . . Gavin is okay.'

'And the youngsters are great.'

Cooper nodded. 'It's a good team.'

'I think I can fit in here, Ben.'

'I'm sure you can. I wasn't suggesting anything else.'

'I know I've come from a different background. Gavin's been a copper almost all his life, it seems. Luke and Becky are just starting out, so they have most of their experience to come. But me – I've seen and done things they never will, and to be honest I wouldn't ever want them to. That sort of experience leaves a mark on you. It can't be helped. Counselling only achieves so much. That's just the way it is. I'm sure *you* must see a big difference in me from the way I was before I joined up.'

'Not that much.'

'Oh, come on. I'm harder, more callous, less understanding of others. I'm sure that's the way it must seem.'

·'I—'

She held up a hand. 'No, you don't need to say anything.

There's no point in trying to contradict me. I know it's true. But I'm trying. I really am trying to get back into humanity, to join the everyday world like an ordinary human being again. I just need a bit of time. And perhaps a bit of help now and then?'

Cooper swallowed, touched by her confidence.

'You've got it, Carol. Any time you need it.'

'Thank you, Ben.'

She paused, scanned the CID room as if something had caught her attention. But there was nothing to see, except Irvine.

'So, Riddings,' she said. 'If your theory is correct . . .'

'It's not exactly a theory,' said Cooper hastily. 'Not a *theory*.'

'A feeling, then. An instinct?'

'Yes.'

'Well, that's good. You should trust your instincts.'

'Not everyone says that.'

She shrugged. 'But if your feeling is right, the answer lies among the residents of the village themselves. A personal motive for the attack on the Barrons – and perhaps on the Hollands?'

'I don't know. That could have been different.'

'Really? Well, we need a link, then. A definite connection. Somewhere there must be a name, or a combination of names, that explains everything.'

'Yes, you're right.'

Cooper frowned. He ran his eye down the list of names he'd just written down. It included everyone who lived or worked in the neighbourhood of the Barrons and the Hollands in Curbar Lane. Not just residents, but the housekeeper at Riddings Lodge, the cleaners, the man who maintained the drives. But there was still something missing.

'Luke,' he called. 'Did we get a list of employees from that gardening firm working Riddings?'

'Yes, it's here.'

Cooper scanned the list that Irvine gave him. Adrian Summers of AJS Gardening Services had listed half a dozen names, including two or three that sounded East European.

251

'Is this all of them?'

'Yes, why?'

'I'm wondering where Dave is,' said Cooper.

'Dave who?'

Cooper looked at him blankly. 'I don't know.'

'Dave?' echoed Villiers.

Cooper shrugged. 'A gardener, I think.'

It suddenly dawned on Cooper that he hadn't told Villiers about the letter he'd been given by Erin Byrne. She knew about the phone calls to the *Eden Valley Times*, but the letter had been lying on the back seat of his car, forgotten while they were visiting Riddings Show.

He ran back down to the car park to fetch it, feeling a mounting excitement that there might actually be a connection after all. On the face of it, the message seemed very trivial, even meaningless. But it must have some significance. Yes, it must.

'Well, I know that symbol,' said Villiers, putting her finger on the horizontal line with the arrow beneath it.

'You do?'

'It's some kind of surveyor's mark. The Ordnance Survey use it, and people like that. It's meant to indicate a point where a specific measurement can be taken. I think it's called a benchmark.'

'A surveyor's mark? That sounds educated. But the words themselves look as though they've been written by somebody illiterate.'

'I know. It's a puzzle. *Sheffeild Rode*? Which way is the Sheffield Road?'

'Well, from Riddings, it's over the edge,' said Cooper thoughtfully. 'Over the edge . . .'

'What?'

'That was originally the way to reach towns and cities to the east of the Peak District, for travellers and packhorse trains. Way back, before the turnpike roads were built.'

'They went over Riddings Edge?'

'Yes, over the edge, across the flats and on to Big Moor. Remember the packhorse way we used on Thursday night?'

252

'Of course. But across that moor? It's just a wasteland. No roads, no landmarks, no signposts, nothing but heather and bracken. How could that be the road to Sheffield?'

'Believe it or not, there were half a dozen trackways and trade routes up there, all converging on a pre-Roman road. It was a major east-to-west route through the Middle Ages, right up to the end of the nineteenth century. And it's not true to say there are no signposts.'

'Really?'

Cooper was staring at the symbol that Villiers had said was a surveyor's mark, and at the scrawled message *Sheffeild Rode*.

'And you know what?' he said. 'I think I've actually seen something like this up there.'

'On Riddings Edge?'

'Not on the edge itself – but behind it, out on Big Moor.'

Diane Fry had found that interviews often became a game of cat and mouse between interviewer and interviewee, a test to see which of them could make the other lose his temper. When a suspect was provoked to anger, that was when he gave the most away. Unless his solicitor was able to rein him in.

Mick Brammer had decided to decline the advice of his legal representative. He didn't know enough to appreciate the tactic of a repeated 'no comment'. He thought the fault wasn't his – so why shouldn't he say so?

'Ade signed me up for the job,' he said. 'It was just a one-off, that's all. Cash in hand, and nothing more said about it. Fair enough, I thought. You can't turn down a chance to make a few quid these days.'

Brammer was small and wiry, with quick, suspicious eyes and tattoos on the sides of his neck. Not the type Fry would have chosen if she was hiring a gardener. But for a burgling job? Yes, maybe.

'Ade? This would be Adrian Summers of AJS Gardening Services?' asked Hitchens.

'Yes, mate. Easy pickings, he said. And it would have been, too.'

'Until something went wrong?'

'Yeah. Well . . . I think that was it.'

'Are you sure? Did Adrian make a mistake? Or was it planned to end that way?'

'I dunno. I didn't expect it to go down the way it did. And I don't think the other bloke did either.'

'Who was this other bloke?' asked Fry. 'What was his name?'

'I don't know. I didn't ask.'

'That seems a bit unlikely.'

'No. You don't understand. It's best that way.'

Hitchens placed his hands on the table. 'Who was the client?'

'Look, mate, I don't know anything about that. It's no use you keeping on asking me.'

'Where did the instructions come from?'

'I can't tell you, mate. All I know is it was Ade who took me on for that job.'

'And what about the other jobs?' asked Fry.

He shook his head. 'I only did the one.'

Hitchens sighed. Quietly, so that the tapes in the interview room didn't pick it up.

'As you know, Mr Brammer, we have your DNA from the scene of the robbery at Hathersage last month. It was a match to a sample you gave when you were arrested for motoring offences in Sheffield twelve months ago.'

'Can't deny it,' said Brammer. 'DNA. So it was me, right? I was at the place in Hathersage. The banker bloke.'

'Mr Johnson.'

'Yeah. I was there to help take the stuff. I didn't agree to anything else.'

'Mr Johnson was injured in the attack.'

'That wasn't me. It was . . .'

They paused, waiting for a name.

'. . . the other bloke.'

Hitchens managed to stifle another sigh. 'Let's move on,

then. Let's talk about the robbery at Valley View, in Riddings, on Tuesday night this week.'

But Brammer was shaking his head vigorously, looking at his solicitor now. 'Not me. I wasn't there. I only did the one, the Hathersage job. I don't like the rough stuff. Too nasty, like. You can go down for a long time over that kind of business, can't you? So I told Ade I didn't want to know about any more jobs. It isn't worth it, for any amount of money.'

Fry and Hitchens exchanged a glance, and Fry nodded. Unfortunately, their suspect sounded as though he was telling the truth.

'Did Adrian Summers ask you to do any more jobs? In Riddings, particularly?'

'No, mate. Like I said, I told him I didn't want any more. So he never asked. I kept out of it. Good thing too. That was a bad business. Nasty stuff. It's not worth it.'

Word filtered through via one of the officers in the HOLMES incident room that a suspect was in custody. When he heard the news, Cooper was first amazed, then angry. His logical mind told him that his resentment was irrational, but he couldn't stop it welling up into his chest and making him feel light-headed with anger.

As soon as he saw DI Hitchens enter his office, he burst in without the barest suggestion of a knock on the door. Hitchens swung round in astonishment and alarm.

'Ben? What are you doing?'

'Why didn't I know about this arrest?' said Cooper bluntly.

Even to his own ears, his voice sounded too loud, and too aggressive. He saw the DI's face set into a rigid mask, and knew he'd already gone too far. But it was too late to step back now.

'You're not in charge of this inquiry,' said Hitchens.

'Even so – I should have known about this. I should have been told.'

'The operation was on a need-to-know basis. You've seen

what the interest from the press and public has been like? Well, the super is worried about leaks to the media. So a decision was made to limit the people involved. And that's the end of the discussion.'

Cooper felt a flush rising at the suggestion that he might be responsible for leaks. Then he remembered his meeting with Erin Lynch, and realised he hadn't told his DI about the letter. Perhaps it was best not to do it now.

But the surge of guilt only seemed to make him angry all over again. He was afraid he might not be responsible for anything he said in the next few minutes. So he took a couple of deep breaths before he spoke.

Hitchens raised a warning finger when he saw Cooper's expression.

'Don't push this, Ben,' he said.

Cooper shook his head. 'Was this arrest a result of the forensic evidence?'

The DI's face was still grim. 'Yes,' he said. 'A DNA match from Hathersage.'

'Hathersage? But not from Riddings.'

'No.'

Cooper's anger began to dissipate. Maybe he hadn't been proved wrong behind his back after all.

'So who . . .?'

'We pulled in a gardener working for Adrian Summers,' said Hitchens. 'A Sheffield lad.'

'I've seen Summers. Big shoulders, cropped blond hair.'

'That's him. He has a bit of a record. Nothing major, but some of his associates are interesting.'

'Can we tie him to the assault on the Barrons?'

'Not yet. Just the Hathersage job. But when we find him, we're definitely going to ask him some tough questions. He's got to be one of the Savages, though maybe not the leader.'

Cooper hadn't always had good experiences with gardeners. He still winced whenever he remembered a case a few years ago when he was still a hopeful DC. In the village of Moorhay, that was. He'd managed to make a fool of himself, and jokes about compost heaps had followed him around the division for months afterwards. In fact, given half a chance, Gavin Murfin would bring the subject up even now.

He turned away to the door, and managed a brief, apologetic nod that he knew wouldn't be enough for his DI.

'But it's never the gardener,' said Cooper. 'Never.'

It was no longer acceptable for the dead to be untidy. Civic orderliness, or health and safety considerations – whatever the reason, the headstones in the newest part of Edendale cemetery would never be permitted to lean, or grow mossy with age.

Sergeant Joe Cooper was buried in the new cemetery. He had no visible grave, only one of many headstones regimented into a neat row, with the grass around them mowed short and smooth. At the moment of his dying, when his blood had run on to the stone setts in Clappergate, he had left a stain that had taken weeks to remove. Sergeant Cooper's killing had darkened the reputation of the town. But now they had done their best to tidy him away.

Every time Ben came here, the row of headstones had extended a little further, as if his father was slowly vanishing into the distance. Not far away, in a more recent row, stood his mother's grave. Isabel Cooper might have expected to be buried in her village churchyard, like her parents, and her grandparents before them. But the churchyards were full. Now it was the new cemetery, or a trip to the crematorium. Those were the facts of death.

Normally the family came here in November, at the anniversary of their father's death. And lately they had been coming in September too. Cooper supposed they would stop coming one day, at some distant time in the future. He couldn't imagine when that would be, but it was bound to happen.

Today he had come for a different reason. This was something he could only do alone. He would never have an opportunity to sit down with his parents and tell them about his engagement.

Well, that wasn't quite true. They might never know now – but it didn't stop him telling them.

Every year, when he came here with his brother, the conversation seemed to follow exactly the same pattern. Their exchange had become a ritual, as much as the laying of flowers.

Three years, and it doesn't seem a day.

Matt's words couldn't help but sound trite. But Ben had never objected, just waited for the next part of the custom.

I still keep expecting him to appear. I think he's going to come round the corner and tell me to stop idling around. It's as if he's just been on night shift for a while.

Ben had always known it would be impossible to escape his father's shadow completely, unless he transferred from E Division. Sergeant Joe Cooper's memory would always be there, in Edendale, imprinted on the walls of the police station. Literally, in some places. In the chief superintendent's office at West Street, there was a large framed photograph of dozens of solemn men sitting or standing in long rows. They were the entire uniformed strength of Edendale section, pictured during a visit by some member of the royal family in the 1980s. On the second row, as a young sergeant, was his father. Downstairs, in the reception area, a memorial hung on the wall near the front counter – a plaque commemorating the death of Sergeant Joe Cooper, killed while on duty. Yes, he would always be there, cemented into the very fabric of E Division.

Eventually, in a few hundred years, Sergeant Joe Cooper's name might be worn away from this headstone by the winter frosts and the rains lashing down the Eden Valley. But for now, the letters were still clear and precise, with sharply chiselled edges. Life might be brief and transient. But death was written in stone.

Ben shivered. It was that cold shudder again. Perhaps it was just a result of standing on this hillside surrounded by death, an effect of all these graves around him. But he felt an uneasy sensation that somewhere out there, a disaster was about to happen. No, not quite that. It had happened already.

He spent a few quiet minutes standing by his mother's grave, thinking through everything that was happening in his life, hoping that she would understand. Then he walked back through the cemetery, reaching the exit just before the gates were closed for the night.

When he reached the car, he paused and looked back. He knew his father's grave would no longer be discernible from here. It had long since merged into the anonymous rows of headstones, swallowed up among Edendale's dead.

In his flat at 8 Welbeck Street, Cooper had finally fallen asleep in his armchair in front of the TV, with his cat purring in the crook of his arm, well fed and content. When his phone rang, he jerked awake in panic, knocking the cat off the chair in a protesting heap.

'Yes?'

'Sarge, it's Luke Irvine.'

'Oh, Luke. What is it?'

'Reports are starting to come in of another incident. I thought you'd want to know straight away.'

'Not in Riddings?'

'No. Further away, on the other side of Edendale.'

'Can it be connected to the other attacks in our inquiry?' asked Cooper.

'I don't know at this stage. But everyone in the division is jumpy. The DI is on alert, maybe even the superintendent.'

'Everyone knows it's impossible to predict where and when the next attack will be.'

'If that's what it is.'

'What do you mean? Is this an aggravated burglary, or not?'

'There are no details yet, Ben. Just the 999 call so far. We'll have to wait for the FOAs to report in. Sorry, that's all I have.'

Cooper saw that he had another call waiting.

'Got to go,' he said. 'Keep in touch if you get anything more definite, Luke.' And he pressed the key to accept the new call.

At first there was only silence on the line. No, not silence – a series of strange, disturbing sounds thudding and yelping in the background. Noises he couldn't identify, but which made his heart lurch and his throat constrict with fear.

'Hello? Hello? Who is that?'

Finally a voice, barely distinguishable. It sounded muffled, oddly choked by distress and panic.

'Ben? Ben, you've got to come to the farm.'

'Kate? Is that Kate? I can barely hear you. What's happened? Is it one of the girls?'

'No, no. It's Matt.'

There was a long pause on the line, with Kate quietly sobbing, and Cooper's mind racing as all the possibilities went through his head. He was picturing an accident with a piece of farm machinery, his brother trapped and crushed under a toppled tractor, his leg caught and mangled in the blades of a combine harvester. His thoughts moved so rapidly that they'd flashed through all the scenarios and reached the scene in hospital, Matt on a trolley in A&E, being wheeled straight into theatre for emergency surgery to save a severed limb. He felt sick with the immediacy of the horror and pain and blood that he knew awaited him at Bridge End Farm.

Time must have stood still for a moment, because it all went round and round inside his head before Kate finally spoke again and dropped the bombshell that turned Cooper's life over.

'Ben,' she said. 'It's Matt – he's shot somebody.'

22

Sunday

The light of dawn came slowly to Bridge End Farm. The hills to the east hid the morning sun and kept the farm in shadow, even while the valley below it was already bathed in light. Ben Cooper shivered in the chill of the paddock behind the house. Within the next hour or so, the dew would begin to evaporate, forming a mist between the dry-stone walls, leaving him floating in space, half in sun and half lost in a haze.

He'd just finished helping Kate to pack up the car and drive away from the farm with the girls, still dazed and tearful with incomprehension. She was taking them to her sister's, who lived over the hills near Holmfirth.

After a mad race from Edendale, Ben had arrived at Bridge End just as the ambulance departed. He had been in time to see Matt, too, handcuffed and being guided into the back of a police car. His brother had looked pale and dishevelled, unshaven and somehow smaller and older than he had ever appeared before.

In the darkness of the early hours, the lights of emergency vehicles filling the farmyard had turned the scene into a stage set. Bridge End had looked alien, an artificial setting for a TV melodrama. For the first time, the farmhouse he'd grown up in looked totally unfamiliar, a mere façade under flickering stage lights. At that time of night, the blinding flicker and glare had emphasised the depths of blackness beyond the farmyard, reinforcing the impression that all these people were simply actors. Somewhere out there in the darkness was the real world, where this kind of thing didn't happen.

No wonder he found it impossible to believe the official account of the night's events. Somebody must have made it all up. It was one more incredible story released on the world, with the inevitable tragic outcome.

It was only when Kate had told him the tale herself that he was forced to accept the truth. His sister-in-law was a real, living person, a victim dragged into the drama against her will.

'It was about midnight,' she'd said. 'We were in bed, asleep. Well, I'm not sure Matt was asleep. He's been sleeping very badly recently, you know?'

'Yes, I know.'

'Anyway, he got up, without me noticing. I woke a few minute later, and realised he wasn't there. I thought he'd just gone to the bathroom. But then I heard noises . . .'

'Outside? Or in the house?'

'No, outside in the yard. I knew there were people out there. And suddenly I was frightened. I jumped out of bed to go to the girls' rooms, to see they were all right. But then . . .'

'Then?'

'I heard the shots.'

As he watched the sun come up over the hill, Ben realised finally how exhausted he was. His skin felt dry and gritty, as if he'd been wading through sand. His eyes burned, and a dull ache throbbed deep in his skull. The exhaustion wasn't just physical, though. It was emotional, too.

Ben had always sensed the police service being blamed by members of his family for the death of his father. Now the police were taking the blame for the arrest of his brother. And he had become part of the police. As far as his family and their friends were concerned, he *was* the police.

The one thing he couldn't do – couldn't possibly do, in any circumstances – was let his brother get sent to prison. The prospect was unimaginable. He couldn't be seen to stand by as that happened, let alone appear to be helping the process along.

He would have to resign from the force before that happened. Yes, his job was important to him. But family came first.

Bridge End Farm inextricably tied the Cooper family together. It had played that role for generations. For Ben, these trees and slopes were as familiar as family photographs. Barns where he'd played as a child, fields where he'd lain in the sun through his school holidays.

But tonight, standing in the yard at Bridge End had been like finding himself marooned on an island while the whole world rushed around him on important business that he had no part in. For the first time he became aware of how the family could be ignored in situations like this. The SOCOs and uniformed officers were inclined to treat them as if they didn't exist. They seemed embarrassed to be spoken to, even avoiding eye contact, as if they were visiting a leper colony.

Dealing with the family was the worst job in a murder case. Worse than handling a dead body, more difficult than seeing the blood or sifting through the mess for evidence. Raw emotions from living people were much harder to cope with. Everyone said it. He'd said it himself. He'd never realised that it might be so obvious to the family that no one wanted to have anything to do with them, and didn't want the trouble of explaining what was going on to people who might be in an emotionally fragile state. From this point of view, it was much more convenient to pretend the family didn't exist, to walk around them without acknowledging them and tell yourself it was a question of professional detachment. The danger of getting too involved. That was what officers shied away from. But how did you judge where the fine line lay between detachment and insensitivity?

'They're only doing their job, I suppose,' Kate had said, as if reading his thoughts.

Ben could tell she was trying to rationalise her own feelings. She didn't want to make a scene, but could feel herself right on the edge.

She had rested against his shoulder, dabbing her eyes with a tissue. She looked terrible.

Guiltily, Ben remembered what he'd said to Carol Villiers just a couple of days before. *When people get as jumpy as this, something bad is likely to happen. You'll see, there'll be an idiot who decides to take the law into his own hands, and a random passer-by will get hurt. It's inevitable, the way things are going.*

'I don't know what to do,' said Kate. 'I just can't see what there is I can do. How do I support Matt right now? How do I support him and the girls at the same time? Ben?'

He didn't really know how to answer her. What were you supposed to say in these situations?

'What are they saying happened exactly?' he asked.

She wiped her eyes again, and took a ragged breath.

'It seems Matt saw these two men coming across the paddock towards the house. They say he took the shotgun from the cabinet, loaded it and went out to challenge them. Then he fired at one of them, and hit him. But, Ben, they're saying he shot the man when he was already running away. Shot him in the back.'

'Matt wouldn't do that,' said Ben. 'He wouldn't shoot someone unless he had to, unless he was driven to defend himself or protect his family. He wouldn't have shot a burglar who was running away. He's my brother. I know he wouldn't do that. So I'm with you, Kate. I'm on your side.'

Kate had looked at him then through red, swollen eyes.

'That's the trouble,' she said. 'I'm not sure.'

'What do you mean?'

'I hate to say it. It . . . it sounds so disloyal. But with the state of mind he's been in recently, I think Matt actually could have done it.'

Even now, hours later, Ben still recoiled at the shock of that tentative confession from his sister-in-law. He was very fond of Kate. In fact, he'd always liked her, ever since the time he first met her, his older brother's new girlfriend, brought home to meet the parents. She had always seemed so balanced, so supportive. He'd often envied his brother, felt Matt had found exactly the right partner. He'd wondered many times if he would ever find someone like Kate.

But for her to tell him that . . . It showed what a degree of trust she had in him. He had a suspicion that she would never dare say it to anyone else. She probably shouldn't have said it to him, in the circumstances. And wasn't it ironic that she seemed to trust him more than his own brother did?

He wondered how Matt was coping right now. Not well, that was certain. He could barely imagine his brother in a police cell. It was a picture that just didn't make any sense, an impossible optical illusion, like one of those paintings by Escher, where stairs ran upside down. It did not compute. Of all people, Matt was made to be outdoors, not to be locked up away from the daylight.

There were some choices you made that you could never go back on. A split-second decision that changed your life. That moment for Matt had come when his finger tensed on the trigger of the shotgun. Once the hammer had begun its acceleration towards the firing pin, there had been no going back.

Some time early in the morning, Superintendent Branagh had made an appearance at the farm, looking grim-faced.

'You can't be involved, Ben,' she said. 'You know that, don't you?'

Cooper couldn't remember her ever calling him Ben before.

'Yes, ma'am,' he said.

'We're bringing in a DCI from Derby to head the inquiry. It will all be handled properly.'

'He'll need local liaison.'

Branagh shook her head. 'Not you, anyway.'

A bit later, when he saw Diane Fry walk into his field of vision, Cooper blinked and looked at her wearily. Perhaps he ought to be surprised to see her here at the farm. But nothing made any impact on him any more, after the night he'd just gone through.

'Ben,' she said.

'What are you doing, Diane? Aren't you off back to the working group?'

She hesitated. Cooper had hardly ever seen Fry hesitant about giving a reply. She was always ready with a sharp comeback, or a quick put-down. Why should she hesitate? What was it that she was reluctant to tell him?

'I've been given another assignment,' she said.

'Oh?'

Cooper was staring at her, trying to get her to meet his eye. But she looked deliberately away from him.

'You can guess what it is,' she said finally.

His eyes seemed to have trouble focusing on her now. She seemed even more unreal than any of the other individuals coming and going in the farmyard. For a moment he wondered if he might actually be hallucinating and had imagined her.

But then he nodded.

'Local liaison,' he said, 'for the DCI from Derby.'

'Right first time.'

Fry had been told to meet the team from Derby at the entrance to Bridge End Farm. She had visited this farm just once before. Not that she remembered a great deal about it. One farm was pretty much like another, wasn't it? Mud, more mud, and all those pervasive animal smells that seemed to cling to your clothes for weeks.

When she'd come here previously, Ben Cooper had actually been living at the farm. His mother had been alive then, too. With Matt Cooper's two daughters, that had meant three generations of the Cooper family making their home together. For Fry, it had seemed strange to see people doing that willingly. In her experience, it was something a family did only when it was forced on them by necessity.

But the Coopers had always been a type of person beyond her experience. Who knew what went on in a close-knit family group like that, with their own peculiar ways of doing things? Especially out here in these remote farmsteads, where no outsider could have any idea what was going on, and shotguns were so readily available. Perhaps it shouldn't be too

266

surprising that a man like Matt Cooper had ended up shooting somebody. Maybe the real surprise was that it didn't happen more often.

A couple of cars pulled into the gateway of the farm. The team were arriving from Derby. She'd been told to expect a DCI Mackenzie, and it looked as though he'd brought a couple of bag carriers for moral support.

As he walked into the yard, the DCI skidded on a wet cowpat and twisted his body awkwardly, grimacing in pain as he tried to keep his footing. He was wearing the wrong kind of footwear for this job. Fry had remembered to pack her boots in the car before she left.

Fry introduced herself, and Mackenzie shook hands. He was a big man, over six feet tall and wide across the shoulders. A bit top-heavy, perhaps, carrying too much weight above the belt to be fast on his feet. He gave her a shrewd stare, weighing her up in that way an experienced officer did, even with a colleague.

'You've familiarised yourself with the reports, DS Fry,' he said.

'Of course. I've read everything. The entire file, such as it is at this stage.'

'So what's your initial assessment?' he said. 'What would have been the scenario?'

'Well, first of all, there's a context of aggravated burglaries in this area, as I'm sure you know. A whole series of them, including serious assaults and one homeowner left dead.'

'Yes. So it's likely we have a member of the public who is on edge. He's been made anxious by reports of incidents in the area.'

'Exactly.'

'The suspect is . . .?'

'Matthew Cooper, aged forty. A farmer.'

'Family in the house?'

'A wife and two young daughters. So he would be protective.'

'Naturally.'

267

Fry waited for the next question.

'And the circumstances at the time of the incident . . .?'

'It was dark, of course,' she said.

Mackenzie turned round slowly, did a full three hundred and sixty degrees as if searching for something on the horizon.

'And no street lights out here,' he said.

'Obviously.'

Fry looked at the city DCI, irritated to find herself having to explain the obvious facts about the countryside. No, there are no street lights. Yes, if you've noticed, there are fields, and cows and sheep. It's a farm. What a surprise.

Mackenzie tilted his head slightly to one side to look at her.

'We have to get this one right,' he said. 'I'm sure you know that, DS Fry. Our task is to balance the requirements of justice and the rights of the individual. It's going to be a fine line we're walking together.'

'Yes, sir,' said Fry, regretting how stiff she sounded.

He nodded. 'All right, then.'

'The National Farmers' Union say that people living in isolated rural properties face particular problems when it comes to crime.'

Mackenzie smiled. 'You might want to try telling that to people on my patch in the city.'

'It's true, though. All those CCTV cameras have been having an effect on crime prevention and prosecution rates in the towns and cities. Thieves are looking at rural areas for softer targets. Well-planned and opportunist thefts are increasing.'

'I've seen the statistics.'

Fry gestured at the farmhouse. 'If you live in a place like this, in the countryside, you have to be aware that you're a potential target. Especially if there are portable things like power tools and generators lying around in outbuildings.'

Within the past few months, E Division had taken part in Operation Solstice, aimed at tackling the theft of high-end four-wheel-drive vehicles from farm premises. A total of twenty Land Rover Defenders alone had been reported stolen in the High Peak and the Derbyshire dales in the first six months of the year. A professional gang had been stealing the vehicles to order, with willing foreign purchasers just waiting for delivery.

Some of this stuff was big business. Organised crime. Not just the kind of petty theft that officers from D Division might imagine.

'These farmers, they have some kind of Neighbourhood Watch scheme, don't they?' said Mackenzie.

'Farm Watch.'

'That's it. Still, this isn't about crime prevention, not any more. We're dealing with a point of law here. Did you happen to read that up while you were looking through the reports?'

Fry bristled at the insinuation that she wasn't familiar with the law.

'The Criminal Law Act 1967 provides that a person may use such force as is reasonable in the circumstances in the prevention of crime,' she said.

'Almost word perfect. But it's up to the courts to decide what can be considered reasonable force. Not us. Right?'

She didn't reply, and Mackenzie looked at her sharply.

'Right?'

'Of course, sir.'

Fry knew that the Court of Appeal had set precedents that governed the modern law on belief: *A person may use such force as is reasonable in the circumstances as he believes them to be.* To gain an acquittal, the defendant must have believed, rightly or wrongly, that an attack was imminent. A man about to be attacked didn't have to wait for his assailant to strike the first blow or fire the first shot. Circumstances might justify a pre-emptive strike. Even if you sought out the confrontation that provoked the aggression. The crucial factor was that you were defending yourself.

But in this case, the victim had been shot in the back. An open-and-shut case? Or was it more complicated than that?

'And then we have the IP,' said Mackenzie.

'The injured party is Graham Smith, from Chesterfield. Previous convictions for burglary and theft.'

'We got a call from the hospital a few minutes ago. I'm told Mr Smith has just come out of theatre from five hours of surgery to have pellets removed.'

'He hasn't been interviewed yet,' said Fry.

'No, but FOAs spoke to his son, who was with him at the time.'

'Craig Smith, aged seventeen. He has a slight leg wound, but is otherwise uninjured.'

Mackenzie nodded. 'Craig claims that he and his father were hunting rabbits on the farm.'

'They didn't have guns with them, did they?'

'No.'

'Or dogs?'

'No.'

'They weren't hunting rabbits, then.'

'You sound very sure of that, DS Fry.'

'It's obvious, isn't it?'

Mackenzie smiled. 'Let's see what the evidence tells us, shall we?'

Although there was a suspect in custody and not much doubt about his involvement, the standard forensic procedures were being put into place. Shotgun pellets were being collected, tweezered out of wooden fence posts where necessary. Unburned powder was being sought, so that chemical analysis could indicate the manufacturer of the ammunition and possibly match the box of shells found in the gun cabinet in the farmhouse.

Scenes-of-crime had already observed from an initial examination that there were no discarded cartridge cases, nor any sign of a wad, the plastic insert that sat on top of the powder charge and contained the lead pellets. The wad was fired from the gun and cushioned the pellets as they went up the barrel, keeping them in a tight, uniform mass until they left the muzzle. As the shot pattern expanded, the wad peeled back and fell to the ground.

'Our ballistics expert says the wad usually falls within a radius of fifteen to twenty-five feet of the muzzle,' said

270

Mackenzie, surveying the farmyard. 'So the discovery of a wad would have given a general indication of the position of the shooter. If a shooter isn't familiar with shotgun shells, they might pick up a discarded shell casing but not realise they should also look for the wad.'

He looked at Fry for a response.

'Yes?'

'It seems this shooter has left neither.'

Fry didn't bother to point out that some of the ballistics inform-ation was unnecessary. It wasn't the first incident she'd dealt with involving the use of a shotgun. She knew that spent plastic casings were printed with the name of the manufacturer, along with details of pellet size and load, powder charge and gauge. Also, when a firing pin hit the metal primer to detonate a charge, the impression it left was unique. It could be used to identify the specific weapon, like matching a fingerprint.

All of this scouring for evidence at the scene might seem unnecessary in the circumstances. But nothing would be missed in this case. Every t would be crossed, every forensic detail covered.

Fry looked round. At least Ben Cooper had gone. Someone had finally managed to persuade him to leave. That was a relief. Cooper had the irritating habit of seeing a good side in everyone. It was a weakness when you were part of the crim-inal justice system. In this situation, it was a positive liability.

Ben Cooper had showered, shaved and changed at his flat in Edendale. He fed the cat, took two paracetamols, and drank three cups of coffee. It didn't make him feel much better.

When he climbed into his car, he looked slowly around Welbeck Street for a few minutes before turning the ignition key. He still felt dazed, and strangely detached from reality. The feeling was a bit like waking up with a hangover. His head ached and his thoughts were fuzzy. He couldn't quite be sure whether what he'd been doing last night was real, or part of some awful nightmare.

His car radio was tuned to Peak FM. When he switched it on, he was just in time to hear the local news bulletin.

A man is under arrest after two people suffered shotgun wounds at isolated farm premises near Edendale.

The incident happened at just after midnight today. A forty-two-year-old man and a seventeen-year-old youth received injuries and both were taken to hospital. The youth was discharged after treatment to a leg wound, but the man is detained with injuries to his back and shoulder.

A local man is in custody and will be questioned by the police during the day. Inquiries are ongoing to determine the circumstances around the incident, and anyone who has any information that would help the police . . .

Cooper switched off the radio. He didn't want to hear any more. Please, no interviews with the victims' family, the nosy neighbours, or the spurious pundits who were always dragged out to discuss a subject they knew nothing about.

He turned things over and over in his head. What should he do? Who could he turn to? He knew he needed to talk to someone about Matt, and tell them things they might not know, before the situation went too far. Before there was no going back.

Obviously, Diane Fry was the last person he wanted to speak to, especially about a situation like this. He shouldn't actually speak to any officer involved in the inquiry. He ought to go through his own DI, and hope that information would filter through.

Meanwhile, there was still the family to consider. Kate was still at her sister's with the girls. So at least he wouldn't have to face that prospect yet – the accusing stares and the even more unnerving silences. Because he was completely sure that Amy and Josie would blame him for what had happened to Matt. After all, it was the police who had taken their father away. And Uncle Ben was the police. Simple.

The trouble was, he could sympathise with that view. At times like these, it was helpful to choose simple logic when deciding who to blame. Everyone would be taking sides, one way or another. All convinced they were right, and refusing to accept any contrary argument – even if they knew nothing about the case. A simple black or white. If only everything in life was so clear-cut.

A couple of neighbours had agreed to look after the livestock at Bridge End for the time being. There were plenty of farmers who owed Matt a favour. And there was no doubt which side of the argument they fell on. Any one of them would have done the same, they said. Simple.

Cooper pictured Bridge End Farm full of strangers, picking over the lives of his family. He imagined Diane Fry, who knew more about him and his family than was really good in the circumstances. He tried to remember what he might have told her over the past few years, whether he'd been too honest.

Yes, Diane Fry was the last person he wanted to speak to.

Cooper picked up his phone and dialled.

'Diane? It's me. Yes, I know. But don't hang up, please.'

Fry was standing by the back door of the farmhouse when Cooper rang. Even without his name coming up on her screen, she would have recognised his mobile number straight away. They had called each so often when they worked together.

She hesitated with her finger over the reject call button. He shouldn't be phoning her, not now. He shouldn't be trying to influence the inquiry. Proper procedures had to be followed, a complete forensic examination of the scene and interviews with witnesses. She mustn't let Cooper try to put preconceptions in her mind.

Fry looked up to see where the DCI was. She felt sure he was somewhere in the house, perhaps upstairs checking the view from the bedroom window where Kate Cooper had been. One of his DCs was in the yard, watching the forensic team at work.

She pressed a button. 'Ben, you shouldn't be calling. Give me one good reason why I should talk to you.'

'You won't understand the evidence,' he said.

'Won't understand? Who do you think you're talking to?' Fry saw the DC glance towards her. With an effort, she lowered her voice. 'Ben, this is wrong.'

Cooper heard the warning tone, but wasn't deterred. He tried to get the words out as quickly as possible while he had the chance.

'Did they find any cartridge cases or wads at the scene?' he said.

'Not so far.'

'Foxes were Matt's main worry. They're getting overconfident these days since the hunting ban, so he often gets close to them. He would have gone for cartridges with a big load, and big pellets. Something like Express Super Game firing number one shot. It makes for a humane kill.'

'Express Super Game? Yes, they found an opened box of those in his gun cabinet.'

'You see? He was never planning to shoot a person. It wouldn't have crossed his mind.'

'But if he's disposed of the cases and the wad . . .'

'The only people who leave their cartridge cases on the floor are those who can afford to employ someone else to pick them up. And plastic wads can be lethal to livestock if they fall on grazing land. So Matt would automatically pick up the cartridge case and the wad. I don't care what else happened, he would have picked them up. Didn't he tell you that?'

'He's been telling his interviewers that he can't remember. He doesn't seem to be able to remember much at all, if he's telling the truth.'

Cooper bit his lip, holding back the automatic response. There was no point in saying that of course his brother was telling the truth. Matt was a man incapable of lying. He wouldn't know how to start, even to save himself. But the inquiry team had to find that out for themselves. Hearing it from his brother would only prejudice them against the idea. It was all about balance and fairness.

His emotions told him it wasn't fair at all. But his training told him this was the way it had to be.

'I'm telling you, Diane, he picked up the cartridge case and the wad. He wouldn't even have been thinking about it. He would do it instinctively. You'll find them in his pocket. And another thing . . .'

'No, stop.'

'Matt had been called away to deal with some stray sheep last night, and he hadn't finished washing the yard. He would have left the job until morning. No choice, really.'

'It doesn't . . .'

'Think about it, Diane. Just think about it. That's all I ask.'

As he ended the call, Cooper heard the echo of desperation in his own voice, and wondered what Fry had made of it. Probably she would treat his call with nothing but contempt. But he had to try.

DI Hitchens met him at the top of the stairs in West Street, no doubt having been alerted by someone that Cooper was on his way up.

'Ben, I know how difficult this must be for you,' he said. 'You've got to take some time off. Go home and support your family. Everybody will understand.'

Cooper hesitated only for a moment.

'Thank you, sir. But no. The division is too short-staffed as it is, with everything that's happening right now.'

'We'd cope without you for a while. Seriously, Ben.'

'No, it's fine. I'll stick with the job.'

Hitchens frowned a little now. 'Okay. Well, it's your decision. If you've got work to clear up, do it. But stay away from your brother's case.'

'I—'

The DI held up a hand. 'I know – you'll tell me that goes without saying. But I have to say it anyway. It's important, Ben. Important for everyone concerned, I mean. Do you understand?'

'Yes, I understand. There is one thing I'd like to ask, sir.'

'What do you have in mind?'

'I'd like permission to interview Sarah Holland again.'

Hitchens opened his mouth to refuse, but hesitated. Cooper knew that if he'd asked Superintendent Branagh, the refusal would have been immediate. But the DI was a different matter. They'd worked together for a long time, and Hitchens had surely learned by now that Cooper's instincts could often be trusted.

Nevertheless, Cooper kept his fingers crossed out of sight until Hitchens answered.

'Okay, Ben. In a day or two, yes? And do it sensitively. Who will you take with you?'

'Carol Villiers.'

The DI nodded. 'Are you happy with her?'

'Perfectly.'

Some of the team were at their desks in the CID room when he walked in. Becky Hurst, Gavin Murfin. He could sense their embarrassment, their difficulty at not knowing what to say to him. For once, Murfin was without a wisecrack or a cynical comment.

They were all good people. But who could he actually rely on for help? At one time he might have gone to Diane Fry. Despite their ups and down over the last few years, Fry had come through when he needed someone to believe in him. Now, she had pretty much written him out of her life.

In the end, he couldn't stand it any longer. He picked up his jacket and went down to the car park. Back out in the open air, he stopped to take some deep breaths. He heard a footstep behind him, and turned to see Carol Villiers.

'Ben, you look dreadful,' she said.

'Oh, thanks.'

'Is there anything . . .?'

Cooper kicked at a loose stone, turned, and walked away a few feet. He stared unseeing at the rooftops of Edendale spread out in front of him, then walked back again. He was feeling lost.

'I don't know what to do,' he said. 'What do other people do at a time like this?'

'Focus,' said Villiers. 'Focus on something useful, a practical objective. Think about how you can help your brother and his family.'

'The family. Yes, Amy and Josie. Oh God.'

'Ben . . .'

'Okay, yes. Focus on something. But what?'

'Well, how about this? There was another incident on Tuesday night, somewhere on the outskirts of Sheffield. Dore, I think. The MO fits the Savages exactly. Word is that South Yorkshire have made some more arrests.'

'Tuesday night? Close to the time of the attack on the Barrons?'

'Close enough to make it impossible for the same offenders to be responsible for both. Even Robin Hood and his Merry Men couldn't be in two places at the same time.'

'No.'

She patted him on the shoulder. 'So it looks as though you were right. Your feelings were spot on. Congratulations.'

'Thanks,' he said.

Villiers was looking at him as though she expected jubilation. And he supposed he should be pleased, ought to be experiencing a sense of vindication right now. But the feeling didn't come. Inside, he just felt dead. Being right no longer gave him any pleasure.

23

Even more than the neighbouring villages of Curbar and Froggatt, Riddings was dominated and constrained by its edge. There was nowhere in the village that the edge wasn't visible, except from inside the houses – and only then in a room where the windows faced away from it.

To Cooper's eyes, the people here seemed to have tried to keep the world out, in their own way. Maybe at a subconscious level they saw the edge as a form of protection, a psychological barrier. It symbolised their desire for privacy.

Yet the world couldn't be kept out, could it? You could never escape it, never get away from people altogether. No gates or fences would keep them at bay. The world was right here, in Riddings.

In some villages he knew in Derbyshire, superstition would be taking hold by now. Grandmothers would be trotting out well-worn stories of past supernatural events, and aged regulars in the local pub would be retelling folk tales about hobs and demons, hideous creatures who came down from the moor at night to spread terror and destruction among God-fearing folk.

But the inhabitants of Riddings weren't the type to give in to superstition. They were more likely to put their faith in burglar alarms and electronic gates. Right at this moment, the residents were probably phoning each other to discuss the employment of private security guards. Their demons would be kept away by a man in a uniform with a two-way radio and a German Shepherd. If they were lucky.

Cooper looked at his phone for the hundredth time that morning. It had become a compulsion since leaving Bridge End Farm. It was far too early for any news, of course. He didn't even know who he was expecting to call, or what he was hoping to hear. There would be no news yet. All he could do was wait. And waiting, as everyone knew, was the most difficult thing in the world.

He had to try to think about something else. That was the only way.

'Let's try to get things into a logical order,' said Villiers. 'Focus, remember? If you're going to be here, Ben, then concentrate your mind.'

'Yes, you're right. I'm okay. Let's do that.'

'Let's start with Tuesday night, then – and the Barrons. Why would anyone attack them, if it wasn't a robbery?'

'They had fallen out with the Chadwicks. Jake Barron had an unpleasant confrontation with William Chadwick.'

'And we know Chadwick has a temper, from the incident at his school,' said Villiers.

'He admits he was under stress at the time he spoke to Jake.'

'Absolutely. But the Barrons had also been involved in a long-running dispute with Richard Nowak.'

'Mr Reasonable.'

'So he says. That's not the impression he gives, though.'

'He has no record of violence,' pointed out Cooper.

'True. But there comes a point when anyone might cross the line.'

That was true. Cooper had seen it many times – examples of perfectly ordinary people who had lost perspective and cracked under intolerable pressure. No one was immune. No individual could be sure that they would never find themselves in those circumstances.

'Their dispute was over the piece of land in Croft Lane. But it had been settled in court.'

Villiers shook her head. 'Not to Mr Nowak's satisfaction.'

'Okay. But the Barrons' closest neighbours are the Hollands at Fourways, Tyler Kaye at Moorside House, and Russell Edson at Riddings Lodge. Mr Kaye wasn't even in the country. And no one seems to have anything against the Hollands.'

'Not that we know of. Not that they're telling us about.'

'All right.' Cooper glanced automatically at his phone, then shoved it deliberately into his pocket. 'And of course we have Mr Gamble.'

'Ah yes, Barry Gamble. If I've got this right, at the time of the attack Mr Gamble is out nosying around the village, as is his habit. He's close to Valley View when he hears a suspicious noise. He sees a light on – and because of his previous observations, he knows this is unusual.'

There was a sceptical tone to her voice as she spoke the last sentence, an upward inflection that made it sound more like a question. Cooper realised she had put her finger on a point that had bothered him very early on in the inquiry.

'He couldn't possibly have seen the light from the lane. I checked that out. He must already have gone on to the Barrons' property.'

'And maybe he was already in their garden when he heard the noise,' said Villiers. 'But he doesn't want to admit that.'

Cooper nodded. 'I think it's very probable.'

'What is Mr Gamble up to, then? Is he a voyeur, a peeping Tom? Hoping for a glimpse of Zoe Barron in a compromising position?'

'Possibly. But I think it's more he's just obsessively nosy. He seems to have appointed himself as a one-man unofficial Neighbourhood Watch. Except he's keeping surveillance on the local residents, instead of watching out for potential intruders as he would have us think.'

'He spends an awful lot of time trying to keep an eye on what his neighbours are doing.'

'He gets around the village quite a bit. He claims to be watching out for intruders and so on. It sounds like a reasonable excuse just now. But Gamble knows these tracks around here better than anybody. I bet if we mapped them in detail, it might be surprising how many properties they border.'

'Well, he's the man who would know about any disputes between his neighbours, if anyone does.'

'Right.'

Cooper thought about the neighbouring families in Riddings. They were all here in the village – all those nightmare neighbours that people talked about. The noisy ones who played loud music or left their dogs barking all day, the aggressively territorial ones who argued over boundaries, the obsessively nosy ones who watched every movement you made, the lazy or inconsiderate ones who brought down the value of your property. All human life was here, in its own way. The amount of money some of these individuals possessed made no difference, except on the surface. Underneath, they were still just animals, marking their territory and screaming at intruders.

Villiers was in full flow now. Cooper could see that she was trying to distract him, to occupy his full attention with her precise rundown of events in Riddings. And he had to admit that she was succeeding. For a few minutes, he'd forgotten what might be happening at Bridge End, or in an interview room at West Street. He fingered his phone in his pocket, then abandoned it again as she continued.

'So,' said Villiers, 'whatever the reason he's there, our Mr Gamble pulls his cowboy hat down over his ears and bravely goes up to the house to see if there's anything wrong. He looks through the kitchen window . . .'

She paused, and frowned.

'Yes?' said Cooper.

'Why didn't he knock on the door?'

'Good question. I'd say he didn't want the Barrons to know he was there, wouldn't you?'

'Do you think there might have been bad blood between them and Mr Gamble too?'

'Almost certainly. They must have been aware of him hanging around. And with the children in the house . . . well, parents get wary. Protective.'

Cooper swallowed. It was bound to happen that small things would remind him directly of his brother's situation. There were obvious parallels between the attack on the Barrons and the incident at Bridge End last night. The difference was that in the first case the householders had become the victims of violence. Matt had not let that happen.

Villiers was watching him carefully. She didn't miss much.

'We're thinking that if Mr Gamble had made a nuisance of himself previously, he might have been nervous of encountering Jake Barron. Yes, I see that. But when he looked through the window and saw Zoe's body, he still didn't knock on the door, did he?'

'He told the officers who responded to his 999 call that he was frightened the attackers might still be on the premises,' said Cooper.

'Mmm. That's reasonable, I suppose.'

'Well, he couldn't have known who'd attacked her. It might have been her husband, for all he knew.'

'Perhaps.'

Cooper was interested to hear the doubt in her voice again.

'And then there's the call itself,' she said.

'He claimed he couldn't get a mobile phone signal at Valley View. That's quite feasible in this area. But I suppose it's equally likely that he wanted to get away from the scene, for his own safety.'

'Because the attackers might still have been around, yes. But it still seems a bit odd to me that he would run to Riddings Lodge.'

'I guess he went there to use a landline to make the 999 call, as he said – or else he was seeking safety and ran to one of the nearest properties.'

'Mmm. He would have run to Russell Edson for protection, you think?'

'He wouldn't be my choice,' admitted Cooper. 'But he must have known that Tyler Kaye wasn't in residence. So it was a rock or a hard place. There was nowhere else to go.'

Villiers smiled. 'You're making a good job of justifying his actions.'

'Just trying to put myself in his place.'

'Very good. And who else was out and about that night, apart from Mr Gamble?'

'The Chadwicks were up on Riddings Edge, watching for the Perseid meteor shower. The Hollands had been balsam bashing and called in at the Bridge Inn for a few drinks on the way back. The Edsons had been out for dinner at Bauers restaurant.'

'But they were back home when the attack took place.'

'Obviously.'

Villiers held up a finger. She had a bright, animated expression on her face, like a primary school teacher trying to enliven a class of sleepy children.

'What else do we know about Tuesday?' she said. 'Around the time of the attack on the Barrons?'

'A party of walkers saw someone in the phone box, a few yards from Valley View.'

'That's right.' Villiers looked round. 'Well, it's a place to start.'

The phone box in the centre of the village was one of the old red ones designed by Gilbert Scott. As a result of a decline in their use, they were preserved in many areas for purely decorative purposes. Cooper crossed The Green to peer through the windows. Yes, totally empty. Stripped of its phone, coin box, information panel, everything. No one used public phone boxes any more. They were heritage.

'Who would be standing in the phone box, then?' said Villiers. 'Not some visitor who thought there was going to be a phone in it. They'd be straight out again.'

'Of course.'

'Could someone have been sheltering? Was it raining?'

'No, it was fine. It had been for days.'

'But all the residents of Riddings must know there's no phone in that box any more, so . . .'

'Right. The only reason anyone would stand in the box

283

pretending to make a call was to prevent the walkers from seeing his face. He didn't want anyone to be able to describe him later on. If he hunched over as if he was making a call, all they would see would be his back.'

She shook her head. 'That doesn't mean it was someone local, though.'

'I think it was. I think it was the person who was on the Barrons' property that night. Someone who lives in Riddings.'

'But why would he do that? The walkers would have had no idea who he was. Besides, if he lives here, he had every reason to be on the road.'

'It might seem that way to someone else, from the outside. But when you're feeling so conscious of what you've just done, you don't want anyone to see your face. You imagine that your guilt will be written clearly in your expression. The desire is to get away and hide from the world.'

'How do you know what goes on in someone's mind in those circumstances?'

'I've talked to people,' said Cooper. 'I've asked them. Ordinary people, not those hardened to killing. The ones who didn't expect it to happen, and weren't prepared for it. It's not difficult to understand, if you have enough imagination.'

'So who, then?'

Cooper didn't answer her question directly. He was thinking it through in his own mind.

'I mentioned it to Mrs Gamble. She knew straight away that there was no phone in the box, but she didn't say anything about it. Why?'

Villiers nodded. 'Because she guessed who it might have been.'

'Yes.'

'Her husband, you mean.'

'More than likely.'

'What's the strength on Gamble? Have we got a case?'

'Not one the CPS will run with.'

Cooper ran his mind over the things he hadn't done. There were so many, it would make a long list.

'Did we ever get forensic results from Gamble's clothes?' he said.

'Not that I know of.'

'The report ought to have arrived by now.'

Villiers pulled out her phone. 'I'll call Gavin and get him to check.'

Cooper looked up at Riddings Edge. The hillside up to the edge looked almost impassable. It was too steep, and too scattered with huge lumps of rock, some of them half-worked millstones. A long strip of birch woodland clung to the upper slopes. Birch was a pioneer species – the first tree to colonise bare ground like the lower slopes below Riddings Edge.

He didn't know how long he'd been staring, but he suddenly realised that Villiers had been speaking to him.

'Oh. Sorry – what did you say?'

She looked at him strangely. Was that a hint of pity? Or just friendly concern?

'Gavin has just gone through the forensics report for me. The fragments of gravel stuck in the soles of Mr Gamble's boots match the gravel on the Barrons' drive. Some of the vegetation that had attached itself to his jacket was from a blackthorn bush similar to the one growing against the Barrons' back wall.'

'Blackthorn? Ouch. The spikes on those things are lethal.'

'And lots of other stuff. Pine needles, thistle seeds, rhododendron twigs . . .'

Cooper nodded, absorbed in a thought of his own.

'I wonder what's in there,' he said.

'In where?'

He looked at her with a smile. 'Let's see if we can take a look.'

'No, it's Barry's shed,' said Mrs Gamble. 'I never go in there. Every man needs a shed, so they say.'

They were at the back of 4 Chapel Close, standing in the small garden, so different from the acres of grounds surrounding some of the other properties in Riddings. Almost half the space was taken up by the wooden shed, with only enough room left for a patch of grass and a single flower bed.

'And I suppose he's out of your way when he's in there,' said Cooper.

She smiled. 'Yes, that's true. I can't deny it's a relief sometimes. We've been married quite a long time.'

'But you don't have any contact with him when he goes out to the shed,' said Villiers. 'You can't see him from the house, can you?'

'No. In fact often I don't really know where he is. I just like to think he's in his shed.'

Cooper looked at the padlock holding the hasp. 'Do you know where the key is, at least?'

'No.'

He looked at her sharply. 'Are you sure?'

She sagged a little, unable to withstand even the slightest pressure.

'All right,' she said. 'There's a spare. Barry doesn't even know it exists.'

When she had fetched the key and the padlock was opened, Cooper stepped into the shed, hesitating as his eyes met the darkness inside.

'There's a light switch to your left,' said Mrs Gamble.

'Thank you.'

'So this is his den, is it?' asked Villiers.

'I suppose you might call it that.'

On the shelves of the back room were an incredible variety of items. Polished stones, fossils, lumps of weather-worn wood, cones, feathers. And sitting in pride of place, like an evil presence, was a sheep skull. Its bones were bleached white, its jaws and grinning teeth still intact.

Cooper had seen many skulls from dead sheep. They lay around the fields, were often left perched on walls or gate posts. Sheep were suicidal creatures, after all. They died in the most unlikely of places. But their teeth tended to fall out, their

286

jaws became dislocated, they crumbled in time. They were rarely as intact as this one.

'What is all this stuff?'

'His collection.'

'A collection of what? This is just junk.'

'Souvenirs. Mementos. Little things he's picked up on his travels.'

'His travels?'

'His walks, I mean. Around Riddings, mostly. He calls them his patrols. I know some people think Barry is a bit odd. But it keeps him out of mischief.'

'Oh, does it?'

One other item caught Cooper's attention. It was a rough pentagram shaped out of twigs. He'd seen this sort of thing left at stone circles, like the one on Stoke Flat. There were often other tributes left, too – flowers, candles, a few old coins. Of course, it was a hangover from a more superstitious era, but it suited the atmosphere of the place. When travellers crossed these moors before the erection of guide stoops, they were living in a different age – a time of darkness and fear, a world of witches and gargoyles. Any token or charm that might help was worth trying.

Speaking of gargoyles . . . He turned back to the doorway.

'Mrs Gamble, where *is* your husband?'

'Do you think she knows more than she's telling?' asked Villiers, as they drove away from Chapel Close.

'Oh, yes,' said Cooper. 'But so does everyone else around here. That's always the way of it. No one wants to tell you more than is absolutely necessary.'

'I suppose it's human nature. If someone wants to tell you everything, you can bet there's something wrong with them.'

'That's right. The nutter who sits down next to you in the pub. He's the only person who ever wants to tell you everything about himself.'

They found Barry Gamble right where his wife had

suggested. He was taking photographs of the edge from a children's play area behind the village. To Cooper's eye, it seemed that he was trying to get just the right juxtaposition of sheer rock face in the background with an empty swing in the foreground. He couldn't quite think what that was supposed to symbolise.

'Oh, what now?' said Gamble when he saw them.

'Mr Gamble, we had the traces on your clothes analysed, you know.'

'Well, I supposed that was what you must be doing. I didn't think you just wanted to try them on for size.'

'It's obvious from those traces that you must have been on every property in this part of Riddings. Without the permission or knowledge of the owners, I would imagine.'

'No one sees me.'

'Do you really think so? Even after Thursday night, when you were seen by those kids hanging around their party at The Cottage?'

Gamble shuffled in embarrassment. 'Yes, well that was unfortunate. But usually . . .'

'Unfortunate? You could get yourself into a lot of trouble.'

'Think about your wife,' added Villiers. 'What did she have to say to you after Thursday night?'

'She told me I was too old for this nonsense. *This nonsense.* I ask you. Besides, I'm not the one showing my age. I said, *Take a look in the mirror, Monica. That's no spring chicken you see.*'

Villiers looked up from her notes. 'And how did she take that comment?'

Gamble grimaced. 'Oh, she didn't take it well. She didn't take any of it very well at all.'

'I think you must be very familiar with all the lanes and tracks in this area,' said Cooper.

'Yes, I am. I can't deny that.'

'Even some that no one else is aware of?'

Gamble fidgeted with his hat, worrying at the beads around the brim. Cooper felt an urge to grab it off his head and hurl it across the garden. But that would be silly and childish, not the actions of a responsible police officer. He might get someone else to do it instead.

'There are a couple of old trackways that have been there for hundreds of years,' said Gamble. 'Worn away and sunk into the ground. None of these people round here either know or care about them.'

'I might want you to show them to me some time soon,' said Cooper.

'I can do that. I suppose you'll be around.'

'You can bet on that.'

'So, what do you know of any feuds or disputes between residents in Riddings?' asked Villiers cheerfully.

Gamble's eyes gleamed. 'Oh, well. How long have you got?'

He began to reel off details. Gamble might seem a bit vague about some things, but his brain was like a well-organised filing cabinet when it came to the activities of his neighbours. He knew all about the court case between Nowak and the Barrons, about the confrontation between William Chadwick and Jake Barron over the dog, and about Richard Nowak's complaints against Mrs Slattery. He had observed every last second of the argument between Nowak and Alan Slattery at the show on Saturday.

Unfortunately, his litany ran out before he'd told Cooper anything he didn't already know.

When he'd finished, Gamble smiled at them with satisfaction.

'I'm glad to help,' he said.

'What about the Hollands?' asked Cooper.

He shrugged. 'They keep themselves to themselves, pretty much.'

'You missed out on Thursday night, then,' said Villiers.

'What?'

'When the Hollands had an intruder at Fourways.'

'You know where I was that night.'

'Yes, we do.'

Cooper studied him thoughtfully, reflecting that if it hadn't been for the teenagers and their pursuit of him on Thursday,

Gamble might actually have been on hand to witness the incident at Fourways. It certainly wasn't like him to have missed something. What a pity he hadn't been there to tell the story.

'And Mr Edson?'

Gamble sniffed, and tugged at the brim of his hat.

'Him? No chance. Can't get near the bugger.'

'So that's it,' said Cooper when they left Gamble to his own devices and the attentions of his wife.

'Not quite,' said Villiers. 'There's your message.'

'What?'

'*Sheffeild Rode*. And the surveyor's mark. You had an idea that you'd seen it somewhere.'

'Of course.'

Cooper looked up at the Devils' Edge, shading his eyes against the brightness of the sky. Had he just seen something drop over the edge? He couldn't be sure what it was. A climber? A bird? He had no idea.

He scanned the face of the rock, trying to pick out a movement. But there was nothing. Whatever he'd seen was gone now, either vanished into a crack in the stone or lying motionless and too well camouflaged.

With a shrug, he went back to the car. The Devil's Edge was full of illusions. He mustn't let his imagination lead him astray. There was far too much tendency for that to happen already.

'You've got your boots, then?' said Villiers.

'Always.'

Her phone buzzed. 'Hold on a second.'

Cooper watched her face closely as she took the call, seeing her expression change. The animation faded, and was replaced by concern and despondency.

'It's Gavin. There's been a call from the hospital,' she said.

'The hospital? That means bad news,' said Cooper.

'Yes.'

He closed his eyes in pain, as all the emotions of the past twenty-four hours rushed back into his mind. The man who'd been shot by Matt last night must have died from his injuries. It was the worst possible news. It meant that Matt might face a charge of manslaughter, at the very least. Or the case could become a murder inquiry. It raised the stakes to a whole different level.

'Yes, it's Jake Barron,' said Villiers. 'They've turned his life-support machine off. He never regained consciousness.'

24

It was amazing how different the landscape on the edge was from the White Peak country below it. Down there were green fields carved by limestone walls, wooded valleys with clear streams, a distinct sense of a place formed by human activity. None of that was present on the moors. Almost all signs of human occupation had been wiped out. Big Moor had reverted to a wild place.

Cooper unfolded his Ordnance Survey map of the White Peak. Previous generations of inhabitants had certainly used their imaginations. All along these edges, rock formations had been given evocative names. Many of them spoke of the dark imaginings of people who had been obliged to find their way across these moors in fog and snow, and maybe at night too. A traveller crossing Big Moor on the way from Sheffield would have to identify a specific rock from a distance if he was going to navigate his way safely through the bogs. It would have been an essential skill for the preservation of life and limb, not to mention the ability to arrive at the right spot for a steep descent into the valley.

How would you pass on instructions for a crossing like that? Only by describing the shape of a rock in terms someone else would recognise. The Eagle Stone, the Toad's Mouth, the Three Men. A traveller would have watched for the moment when a shape became recognisable, like a sailor scanning the coast for the glimpse of a lighthouse. He would be waiting for a giant black toad to open its mouth, for a monstrous bird to spread its wings on the horizon.

No wonder, in those superstitious times, that stories of monsters and demons had thrived. A packhorse lost in a bog could have been swallowed by a serpent. A man falling to his death from the edge would have been led astray from the path by an evil spirit. It wasn't so difficult to believe when you could see those monstrous shapes in the desolate landscape. Things that were moving, changing. Practically breathing.

'There are still traces of the old packhorse routes somewhere on these moors,' said Cooper. 'Tracks and hollow ways. It's funny to think how localised people were back in those days. They knew nothing about the geography of neighbouring valleys. And that was because of the moorlands that separated them. They were pretty inhospitable places.'

'I know villages around here where you're still considered a foreigner if you're from the next valley,' said Villiers.

Cooper smiled. 'A foreigner? Practically an alien.'

He was tending to forget that Carol Villiers was local too. He'd become used to having to explain these things to outsiders who knew nothing about the area. But Carol understood.

'All that travellers had to guide them at one time were the natural rock formations.'

'The Salt Cellar. That was always my favourite.'

He nodded. 'That's further north, on Derwent Edge.'

It was true that some of the rocks on the eastern edges had less sinister, more domestic names. The Wheel Stones, the Cakes of Bread, the Salt Cellar. A few of the meanings were too far lost in time to be explained. Take the Glory Stones, or the Reform Stone. What glory did they refer to? What long-forgotten reforms? You could write a book about these stones, and unravel an entire layer of Derbyshire history just from their names. For all he knew, someone might have written that book already.

In the Middle Ages, the only exceptions a traveller might stumble over were the crosses set up by monastic landowners.

These weren't just an aid to travel; they marked the boundaries of property and reminded everyone of the power of the Catholic Church. Monasteries had felt it important to mark out their territory, even out here on the moors. An ancient cross base and the stump of a shaft were all that remained of the Lady Cross on Big Moor.

But guide stoops had been erected following the dissolution of the monasteries and the Civil War, to help all the extra trade generated by an improving economy. Derbyshire was slow to follow orders from central government – which was pretty much in character, he supposed. And in the end its guide stoops had been erected in a hurry, early in the eighteenth century.

Cooper knew he'd seen some of these stoops. He'd passed them when he was out walking, had stopped to look at them out of curiosity, and had their history explained to him. They were inscribed with the names of the nearest market towns in each direction, to help guide those travellers venturing into the wilds of Derbyshire.

He looked at the symbol on the message again, and the scrawled inscription, *Sheffeild Rode*. A guide stoop, then. But which one?

The path from the car park above Riddings passed the first guide stoop within a few yards. It was positioned just above the road, over the first stile – a tall, rectangular block of stone, well embedded in the ground. Carved from the local gritstone, it stood about five and a half feet high, and was a foot wide on each of its four faces.

'This is a guide stoop?' said Villiers, running her hand over the rough surface.

'One of them.'

This stone was in too exposed a location, though, and had suffered badly from the weather over the last three hundred years. There must have been lettering cut into each of the faces, but the stone surfaces were totally eroded and the inscriptions illegible. All Cooper could make out was a 'V' sign on one face.

He pointed at the OS map.

'We need to follow this track to the next one,' he said.

Sheep sheltered under a hawthorn tree, the ground beneath it worn bare by their hooves. In places, the bracken came up to Cooper's shoulders. But the masses of heather were coming into flower, turning the more distant hills into a purple haze.

They crossed a muddy stream on a bridge made of planks covered in wire mesh. A steep climb past the old walled enclosures brought them to a modern signpost at the top, pointing the way to White Edge and Birchen Edge.

Looking back, Cooper could see thirty or forty beehives sheltered in the lee of a wall in one of the enclosures. When he stood still, he became aware of the buzzing all around him. Thousands of honey bees were humming through the heather.

In the middle of the moor, there were no extraneous sounds, only the closest thing you could ever get to silence. The stillness made him more aware of the life stirring under his feet as he walked. Birds and rabbits scuttled away from his approach. The sweet scent of the heather blossom rose into the air with every step.

There were many boggart holes in the bare earth. Some of them looked deep, dug by animals into the shallow peat. Reddish-brown soil had been kicked out of the larger holes. You could put your arm right down into them, if you weren't too worried about what you might touch. This was adder country, after all.

'This place is full of legends, you know,' he said.

'Nice things, legends. I like 'em.'

'You know about hobs, Carol?'

'I know you have to show them respect, or they cause mischief in the house.'

'You got that from your grandmother?'

'Of course.'

Not too long ago, a bowl of cream would have been left on many Derbyshire hearths to ensure that the hobs did good for the household. Of course, many people believed that a hob's real home was out here, in the wild landscape. There was a

Hob Hurst's House in Deep Dale, and another on Beeley Moor, just to the south of here.

Over there was an area called Leash Fen, said to have been a community the size of a small market town. There was nothing to be seen now. According to the stories, the town had sunk into the bog, and vanished without a trace. It sounded unlikely, until you went up there. In the winter, with your feet sinking deep into the ground, your trousers wet up to the knee, it was possible to imagine the fate of Leash Fen. If you had the imagination, you could even picture the ruins of the stone houses lying mouldering under the ground as the bog deepened over the centuries. In fact, there were probably other things under there too. Animals that had strayed off the track, a crashed Second World War German bomber, and maybe the odd hiker who had never returned home. Cooper wondered if global warming would dry out the bog one day, revealing all the buried secrets of Leash Fen.

They walked across the moor, following a faint track through the heather, until they came to another guide stoop. This one was smaller, less than three feet tall, possibly only the top half of a broken stone.

Cooper recalled that there was supposed to be one that had been damaged by gunfire when the military were training on the moor during the war. He felt that was further on, though – in Deadshaw Sick, near Barbrook Reservoir. This one had just fallen or been broken accidentally. It was probably a common fate for moorland stones. Yet the inscriptions were clear on each face. *Chasterfield Road, Hoope Road, Dronfeld Road.* The way the names of the towns were spelled must have reflected the accent of the stonemason, he supposed. None of the men who chiselled the letters on these guide stoops in the eighteenth century would have been entirely literate. Yet each of them had their own ideas about spelling. This one knew how to spell 'road', at least.

'Not this one,' he said.

'How many more are there?' asked Villiers.

'I'm not sure. A lot of them will have disappeared over the

decades. But at one time they would have been all over these moors. They were the only means the packhorse men had of navigating their way across, especially when there was snow on the ground to cover the trails.'

Cooper imagined the immense task it must have been to get these guide stoops into position. A full-sized stone had to weigh around four hundred kilos. Once they had been shaped and inscribed by the stonemason, they had to be transported from the mason's yard, brought as far as possible by horse and cart, then probably dragged by wooden sledge and manpower to their final position.

'In that case, we could spend all day out here.'

'No, I don't think so,' said Cooper.

He turned his body through three hundred and sixty degrees, trying to orientate himself. He could picture the old packhorse men doing this, too, taking their position from the sun or stars, or from a distant landmark.

Over that way, if you took a route directly across the moor, you would enter South Yorkshire and emerge in woods near the hamlet of Unthank. But in the other direction, you were in Derbyshire, the Derwent Valley – in the villages below the edges.

'This way,' he said. 'It shouldn't be too far.'

After five more minutes of walking, Villiers stopped and pointed across the moor.

'Is that one over there?'

'Yes, I think so.'

They could soon see a full-sized stone, standing straight and upright. For Cooper, it was as welcome a sight as it might have been for many weary travellers crossing this moor. When they reached it, Villiers rubbed a patch of lichen off the inscription.

'It's a bit eroded, but . . .'

'What does it say?'

'*Sheffeild Rode*. This is it, Ben.'

She looked flushed and excited, like a child who'd just won a treasure hunt, or discovered a hidden Easter egg.

They walked round it, exploring the wonderful tactile surface of the rough gritstone, tracing the letters on each of the four faces. *Bakwell Rode, Tidswall Rode, Hatharsich Rode*. And most carefully of all, they studied the symbol chiselled into the stone below *Sheffeild*. The horizontal line and arrow. The surveyor's benchmark. The mason's spelling had been eccentric, but the 'Rode' was consistent. And the inscription on that face was exactly as it had been reproduced on the message sent to the *Eden Valley Times*.

'Brilliant,' said Villiers. 'I'm so glad we found it.'

But Cooper was shaking his head.

'What's the matter?'

'It's the wrong way round,' he said.

'What?'

Cooper had orientated himself at the last stone, and had retained his sense of direction as he covered the last few hundreds yards across the moor. He knew which way was which.

'The route to Sheffield would be that way, to the east,' he said. 'This guide stoop needs turning ninety degrees to be pointing in the right direction. I suppose it must have fallen over and been replaced at some time. And whoever repositioned it didn't worry too much about getting the direction right.'

'Well, they don't exactly serve a useful purpose any more, do they? I mean, nobody is likely to follow their directions.'

'No, they're just history, I suppose,' said Cooper. 'Another part of our useless heritage.'

Villiers ran a hand over the eroded stone. 'So the Sheffield road . . .?'

'Isn't the Sheffield road at all. The hand is pointing south instead.' Cooper turned round to face the other way. 'It points downhill, look. Directly towards Riddings.'

He gazed down the slope. Nothing looked quite so dead as dead heather. Though it was probably only last year's growth, the stems of the dead plants already looked fossilised, dry and skeletal, their brittle stems crumbling under his boots. They were petrified, as if they were already on their way to becoming the next layer of peat.

'And I think that could be the packhorse way,' he said.

From the guide stoop, there was a clear route winding its

way down the hillside. Overgrown with bracken and reeds, it looked hardly more than a rabbit track. But for the route to have remained distinct even during the summer, there must at least be well-compacted earth, or more likely stone slabs laid on the ground to make it passable in wet weather. Otherwise the undergrowth would have covered it completely in time.

With his back to the guide stoop, Cooper let his eye follow the line of the track downhill. It curved between the scattered rocks, taking a circuitous route that avoided the steepest parts of the slope.

'Is that what you'd call a road?' said Villiers, when he pointed it out.

'Some people would. If they used tracks and old pathways to get around this area. That looks almost like a three-lane highway.'

She shrugged. 'I suppose we should follow it, then?'

Towards the end of the track, just before they reached the outskirts of the village, they stumbled across an area enclosed by half-tumbled stone walls and fractured lengths of barbed-wire fencing.

'Wait,' said Cooper.

Through the undergrowth he'd glimpsed the remains of an ancient building with a corrugated-iron roof and no windows. Moss grew on the stone walls, and a crooked door was half covered in peeling green paint. The weeds in front of it were dense and impenetrable, and a bird had built its nest on a broken downspout. He was looking at an old farm building, a lot older than most of the properties in Riddings. It was Barry Gamble's artistic statement about decay and abandonment.

And now Cooper could see why the composition of Mr Gamble's photograph had been all wrong. There was a reason why the angle of his shot had been awkward, with the building off-centre. The photographer had been unable to move those ten yards to the right and take a few steps closer to his subject. He had been prevented by the barbed-wire enclosure.

Inside the enclosure, Cooper saw a pair of brick slurry pits, which must have lain disused for decades. They were over-grown with willowherb and full of a dark, oily sludge, choked with old tyres and covered with green scum. He dreaded to think how foul that sludge would smell, once you broke through the crust on the surface. Matt would never have let any part of his land get like this.

Cooper leaned over and looked into the nearest pit. There was one clear patch on the surface, where something had dropped through the scum and vanished into the murky depths. A small cloud of mosquitoes hovered over it.

For a moment, he stood quite still, oblivious to anything else around him. The moor seemed to recede as if it was no more than a landscape in a dream. For a second he'd slipped back into the real world, the one inhabited by all those people down there in Riddings.

He looked towards the village, and saw the distinctive roof of one of the houses very close to the bottom of the track. His mind filled rapidly with images. The body of Zoe Barron, her blood staining the tiles. The fragments of gravel scattered across the Barrons' lawn. The white handprints on their back wall. Gardeners, a grey woollen fleece, and a gust of wind blowing canvas over a face-painting tent.

Then he shook himself. He felt as though he'd just woken up and found the nightmare was real. He took a step back-wards, and almost bumped-into Villiers.

'What's the matter?' she said. 'Ben? What is it?'

Cooper could barely answer her. After everything that had happened this week, it was as if his mind had suddenly cleared. The fog had lifted, the mist had finally been burned away by the sun. He still didn't have the proof, of course. But like those white chalk marks on the rock faces of the edge, he realised that there were one person's prints all over this case.

'We need to get some equipment up here, and empty out these slurry pits,' he said.

'Oh my God, Ben. Are you serious? You are going to be *really* popular.'

'I know. Trust me, I know.'

25

Diane Fry stood in the farmyard at Bridge End, watching the activity still going on. A tractor had been reversed out of the way to give the forensics team room to work, and a ballistics expert brought in from the Forensic Science Service was faffing about in the yard in his scene suit. To one side stood a trailer full of fresh manure, which no one had wanted to move. Nearby, a cat sat on the wall, washing its paws calmly, as if waiting for the next stage of the entertainment.

Fry had supervised a neighbouring farmer who had come to deal with the cows, taking them round the back of the milking parlour to avoid crossing the ground in front of the house. That would have made DCI Mackenzie *really* unhappy, to see a herd of cattle trampling his crime scene. Considering that possibility, Fry almost wished she'd allowed it to happen.

She looked around the yard again, picturing the scenario of last night's shooting. The victim, Graham Smith, had been hit by a single shotgun blast in the middle of the yard. Blood splatter on the ground had been indicated by a series of yellow plastic evidence markers. The preliminary theory was that Smith had been shot in the back while running away from the farmer brandishing a shotgun. And no evidence had so far been found to contradict that theory.

According to the ballistics man, the lead shot used would have had a muzzle velocity of more than thirteen hundred feet per second. Fry knew that that could make a terrible mess of a human body at close range. Further away, the damage was serious, but more widely spread. Individual pellets became embedded under the skin – but provided the face wasn't hit, it might only be a question of scarring once the pellets were removed.

But if the pellets missed their target and travelled even further, they would become scattered and lose their velocity, causing minimal damage. Eventually, the shot would fall harmlessly to the ground.

Fry stood in the doorway where Matt Cooper would have emerged from the house, an old jacket and a pair of jeans pulled over his pyjamas. He would probably have fired from here, if he'd been defending his property. But perhaps not if he'd been pursuing an innocent victim who was already fleeing. No cartridge case or wad had been found to show where he was standing when he fired. But the victim had been hit in the back, so it was obvious, wasn't it?

She studied the surface of the yard around the area of the yellow markers. Then she took one final glance around the outbuildings, the parked tractor, the trailer full of manure, the cat grooming itself.

Finally, she sighed. Of course, she felt under no obligation to try too hard to find evidence clearing Matt Cooper. And yet . . .

Fry looked at Mackenzie as he walked gingerly along the edge of the yard, skirting the smellier areas. She remembered seeing the DCI slip on a cowpat as he came into the yard, twisting his body painfully as he tried to keep his footing.

'What are you thinking about, DS Fry?' asked Mackenzie as he came nearer.

'Cow muck.'

'Well, there's plenty of it.'

'And it's slippery.'

'Yes. So?'

'I'm thinking that if Graham Smith slipped as he was running away across the yard . . .'

Mackenzie looked at her more closely. 'It's possible. I did it myself.'

'I know you did, sir. I saw you.'

'What are you suggesting?'

'Matthew Cooper has been saying in interview that he thought one of the intruders was armed, hasn't he?'

'Yes. But as you know, they weren't in possession of any firearms. And nothing has been found at the scene.'

Out of the corner of her eye, Fry could see the FSS man removing his scene suit and packing his gear, getting ready to depart. Job done, then? Well, perhaps not.

'Take a look over here,' she said. 'Would you, sir? Please?'

'Why, what have you found?'

'I could tell you what I think we'll find. But you should see it for yourself.'

Mackenzie crossed to the trailer with her, wrinkling his nose at the increasing pungency of the smell as they approached. Fry pulled on a pair of latex gloves, ignoring the odour and the cloud of flies that rose from the manure. She began to shake loose some of the straw.

'I don't know what on earth you're doing,' said Mackenzie. 'Is it some kind of rural custom?'

'It's all a question of trajectory and velocity,' said Fry.

'Oh?'

'Well, mostly. There's also the complication of people who see only what they want to see, and ignore anything unpleasant.'

A black pellet dropped into her gloved hand.

'Is that it?' said Mackenzie.

'No,' said Fry. 'There'll be more shotgun pellets over this way.'

'Where?'

'In the trailer.'

'But it's full of . . .'

'I know. So?'

The DCI grimaced. 'How did they get here?'

'Some of the pellets missed their target,' said Fry. 'At that

303

range, you wouldn't miss. Not unless your target moved suddenly.'

'I see.'

'And now, given the velocity and trajectory, we'll be able to calculate exactly where the shooter was standing when he fired.'

Mackenzie bent to look at the pellet in her hand.

'I'll get the ballistics expert back.'

He called over one of his DCs to send him after the forensic scientist, who was probably washing his hands before departure.

'By the way,' said Fry, 'when they searched Matt Cooper in the custody suite, was there anything in the pockets of his jacket?'

The DC checked his notebook. 'I can tell you that.'

'Let me guess,' said Fry. 'A seventy-millimetre cartridge casing, and a plastic wad.'

'Yes, exactly right.'

Fry nodded. A sea of conflicting emotions was seething inside her. She loved those moments when she was proved right. Everybody did, didn't they? It was pretty much what she lived for, that brief surge of adrenalin and excitement that made her heart quicken and her breath catch in her throat. But the credit in this instance wasn't hers. Not truly. It belonged to the same person who had so often snatched the glory from her in the past. Even now, when he shouldn't even have been speaking to anyone involved in the investigation. How did he manage to do that?

An incongruous shape caught her eye. Something round and shiny, a curious object to be nestled in a heap of cow manure. Fry reached in a hand. It was fortunate that she was still wearing her gloves. She took hold of the object and drew it slowly from the manure. It kept coming – more than three feet of it; a length of pale, smooth wood sliding into the light and becoming thicker as it emerged. A baseball bat.

'Well I think that's pretty clear,' she said. 'Don't you?'

*   *   *

An hour later, DCI Mackenzie was preparing to leave the farm. Before he got into his car, he turned to Fry with an ironic smile on his lips.

'You're a real farm girl, aren't you? A proper expert in rural life. I was thinking of offering you a job with my team in Derby, but you're obviously more at home here in the country.'

'What?' said Fry, outraged. *'What?'*

Mackenzie laughed as he opened his car door, wiping the soles of his boots carefully on the grass.

'Look at this stuff. I don't want to take any of this back to the city with me, do I?'

Fry stood stunned as Mackenzie and his team left the farm.

'A farm girl? *Me?'*

At West Street, Cooper had just returned from a session with Superintendent Branagh and DI Hitchens, justifying the exercise to empty and examine the slurry pits outside Riddings.

In any other inquiry, it would have been out of the question. But these were no ordinary low-priority burglaries they were dealing with. This was a high-profile case, and for once the budget had been stretched. It was important to be seen to be doing something, and officers with shovels and expensive machinery were just the ticket.

Gavin Murfin was very subdued today. Cooper looked at him, aware that Murfin wasn't on the rota for duty this weekend.

'Should you be in, Gavin?' he asked.

'No, but they couldn't manage without me.'

'Overtime, then?'

'Oh? It hadn't even crossed my mind.'

'Yeah, right.'

'Well, I'm here to help, anyway.'

'Thanks, Gavin,' said Cooper.

'First of all, there's a message for you. William Chadwick phoned. He and his wife want to talk.'

'Oh, good.'

'Do you think they might be involved in some way? In connection with the deaths of the Barrons, or Martin Holland?'

'Not really. I did think at one time of finding out about the incident at Chadwick's school. Checking out the family of the pupil involved.'

'Oh, in case it could have been a revenge attack that went pear-shaped? They just got the wrong house?'

'Valley View is directly across the lane from the Chadwicks. I thought if the attackers were coming into the village by an indirect route, they might easily have got confused.'

'It's possible. But . . .?'

'I didn't bother checking in the end. It doesn't seem necessary now.'

At The Cottage, Cooper was invited into a sitting room somewhere in the depths of the barn conversion, with French windows looking out on to a large pond surrounded by reeds and oriental grasses. There was no sign of the herons today. Had they been scared off, or had they simply exhausted the available supply of fish?

Marietta Chadwick did most of the talking. Her husband sat fidgeting with anxiety, wiping the sweat from his forehead.

'This isn't a place where we expect violence to happen, you know,' said Mrs Chadwick. 'It's rather beyond our experience.'

'Not for all of you.' said Cooper.

'I'm sorry?'

'Some of the residents in this village are probably more familiar with violence than you might think.'

'I don't know what you mean.'

'Never mind.'

She twisted her hands together nervously. 'I'm just trying to explain why we . . . well, why our initial response might have been the wrong one, in retrospect.'

'Oh?'

'We didn't want to put ourselves forward, that's the truth

of it. We've got so used to trying to keep a low profile. Just in case, you know.'

'There's really no need to make excuses, Mrs Chadwick.'

'I wasn't . . . Well, anyway . . . it's about Russell Edson.'

'Oh?'

'We've never been happy with him. Such an odd man. That Barry Gamble is odd, too, of course – but in a different way. We've always thought he was harmless. Not everybody agrees with us, though.'

'Mr Edson?' said Cooper, trying to steer her back on topic.

'Edson, yes. Well, he's a complete pain in the neck, to be honest. Have you seen his place? Of course you have.'

'It's well protected.'

'He uses that CCTV system like a surveillance network. We imagine him sitting inside the house, watching his monitors twenty-four hours a day. If you do the least thing on that lane, he sees you and comes out to object. If you park your car with its wheels slightly over the verge, or let your dog go to the toilet on the grass, or even pick a blackberry off the hedge . . . The smallest thing, and he'll be out shouting that it's his property and you have no rights. He's a very rude person. Very arrogant.'

'It's a wonder no one ever punched him on the nose,' said Chadwick.

'William,' said his wife warningly.

'I'm speaking metaphorically, of course.'

'Oh, his metaphorical nose,' said Cooper. 'I see what you mean.'

'Also, he wants to cut down that wonderful monkey puzzle tree,' said Mrs Chadwick.

'Does he? I thought he was quite proud of it.'

Mrs Chadwick shook her head. 'He has no feeling for anything if it gets in his way. He wants to clear the view of Riddings Edge from his terrace.'

'I see.'

'Those trees are dying out in their native habitat, you know. Climate change is causing forest fires in Chile.'

'That's very interesting. But . . .?'

She nodded, and looked at her husband. Cooper had the feeling they must have discussed this long and hard, maybe all week. Had it taken them five days, ever since the death of Zoe Barron, to make their minds up about what to do? What had convinced them in the end? he wondered. Another death? Or two, even. The deaths of Martin Holland and Jake Barron had intervened.

'We didn't come forward before, because it seemed to us that it would only complicate matters,' said Mrs Chadwick. 'The situation here is worrying enough, after all. And we kept hearing that police resources were overstretched. We didn't want to distract you from doing your job with irrelevant information.'

'When you say "we" . . .?'

'Bill and I talked it over, of course. And . . .'

'Who else?'

'Well, we discussed it with one of our neighbours.' She pointed vaguely to the north. 'Mr Nowak, at Lane End.'

'This *is* about Tuesday night?' said Cooper impatiently. 'The time of the attack at Valley View.'

'Yes. There were people in the village that night, you see. Oh, I know that sounds strange. There are always people in the village. And it's not always clear why. But these were different.'

Her husband couldn't resist butting in.

'Russell Edson used to have parties, you know,' he said. 'All kinds of people came then. But they haven't taken place for a while. That's why we noticed, I suppose.'

'Did you see any vehicles at all?' asked Cooper.

'Nothing unusual.'

'That's not the same thing.'

'Well . . . one. Though the vehicle itself wasn't unusual. We see it in the village all the time. But it was a bit late for it to be around.'

'A bit late?'

Mrs Chadwick looked at Cooper rather too brightly.

308

'Yes, late. After all, you don't do much gardening in the dark, do you?'

When he got back to his car, Cooper wondered whether to return to the office. There was a nagging voice at the back of his mind – a constant muttering of anxiety, a fretful whisper reeling off all the possible developments at Bridge End he should be worried about. But he knew that if he stopped to listen to it, he would never do anything else. He had to find something to occupy his mind. Carol Villiers had been right. He had to focus, and stay focused.

A call came in before he could make up his mind what to do next.

'Gavin? Have you got some news?'

'Yes. I was feeling particularly spiteful today, so I decided to check on Mr Edson's alibi for Tuesday night.'

'He was out for dinner,' said Cooper.

'Yes.'

'You checked up with the restaurant? What made you do that?'

'I don't like him. Is that a good enough reason?'

'It'll do for me, Gavin.'

'When we visited him, I remember him being very specific about what he and his mother ordered. Migratory ducks and all that.'

'Yes, he was.'

'To me that suggested a very good memory. Or more likely that he'd made a note of it, so that he could sound totally convincing if he was asked about it later.'

'Gavin, sometimes I love your appalling cynicism.'

'It gets results,' said Murfin modestly. 'See, by doing that, he wasn't actually telling us a lie. Only by omission, anyway.'

'Go on, then. What was it he omitted to mention?'

'That it wasn't just him and his mother who were supposed to be eating at Bauers that night. They had a table booked for three.'

'Oh, really?'

'They know Edson well there. *He dines with us often*, they said. So I asked who else was in the party. The head waiter sounds the sort of bloke who clocks everything.' Murfin laughed. 'A bit like an upmarket Barry Gamble, I suppose.'

'Yes, Gavin.'

'Anyway, there was no third person. A table was set for three, but it seems the third person never arrived.'

26

At Riddings Lodge, Cooper found only Glenys Edson at home. In the room packed with antiques, he saw that the glass table was damaged. A jagged crack ran right across it from one edge, shattering the perfect reflection.

'An accident,' said Glenys Edson, before he had even asked.

'What a shame.'

'These things happen.'

Cooper glanced at the tapestry, remembering his conversation with Gavin Murfin. *You can't just sit and do nothing for hour after hour, day after day. You'd go mad. You'd start tearing up the furniture.*

'I'm sorry, I don't know when Russell will be back,' she said. 'He's taken the car for a spin.'

'The Jaguar? No, of course not. The MG convertible.'

'That's right.'

'Do you know where's he gone?'

'I have no idea.'

'Mrs Edson, I need you to talk to me about your son. And about Tuesday night.'

She shook her head. 'I'm not telling you anything. Not without Russell here. You'll have to speak to him.'

'On Tuesday night, you visited Bauers at Warren Hall. You were dining in the restaurant there. Who else was supposed to be with you?'

Mrs Edson drew herself up as stiffly as she could. 'I'm afraid that I'm not going to be answering your questions.'

'You know this is a murder inquiry?'

But he could see that meant nothing to her.

'You'll have to arrest me then,' she said. 'Otherwise, Detective Sergeant, I'll ask you to leave.'

Frustrated, Cooper peered through the gates of Riddings Lodge as he used his phone to call the office. He got through to Gavin Murfin.

'How are they getting on with the slurry pits, do you know?'

'They've got two pumps set up to remove the liquid, but there are several inches of thick mud at the bottom, which is slowing the job down. I'm told the smell is appalling.'

'Oh, I can imagine.'

'In fact, we're starting to get complaints from the residents in Riddings,' said Murfin. 'I guess the wind must be blowing in the wrong direction.'

'I hope to God they find something,' said Cooper. 'Otherwise they're going to throw me into one of those slurry pits.'

'We've found the van, though.'

'The gardener's van? AJS Gardening Services?'

'That's the one. Dumped in a lane behind Riddings. No sign of the owner, Mr Summers. Luke Irvine is there.'

Cooper was at the location within a couple of minutes. The doors of the van had already been opened. In the back, among the gardening tools, he found a small pile of stainless-steel posts, each measuring over three feet long. They were the kind of thing used for preventing parking on grass verges. Very popular in Riddings.

He picked one up and slapped it against his palm.

'These must weigh about eight pounds each.'

'Good enough for the job,' said Irvine.

'A bit unwieldy, I would have thought. But if that was what came to hand . . . a thing this size would certainly strike fear into your victim.'

'What are they exactly?'

'These are the posts they embed in the ground to stop people parking on the grass,' said Cooper.

'So they are. I tripped over one the other day.'

'And I parked up against one. I don't know if these are the exact posts used in the attack on the Barrons. But somewhere in Riddings, there'll be at least one with traces of Zoe Barron's blood on it.'

Since Edson had left the Jaguar behind at Riddings Lodge, Cooper called in and asked for the search to be extended to the car. He remembered the thorough cleaning it had received earlier in the week, a handyman in waterproof trousers working away on the bodywork under Edson's eagle eye. If any evidence was available to be found, the interior was likely to provide more traces.

Cooper thought about the handyman. He had been checked out, like everyone else. But every job here was contracted out. Someone came in to do the cleaning, the gardening, to wash the car. There was a man to fill the swimming pool, and another man to rake the gravel. And teams of small, soot-blackened children to sweep the chimneys, too.

Well, maybe not the last one. But it was a close-run thing.

Gavin Murfin turned up among a team of officers who were arriving to begin a search of the grounds. This could be a long job, unless they had a stroke of luck.

'It's amazing,' said Murfin. 'I suppose Mr Edson didn't think we would check his alibi. He just couldn't imagine us going to Warren Hall and asking about his dining arrangements. It took them completely by surprise when I phoned.'

'I don't think he's been living in the real world,' said Cooper. 'Some of these people in Riddings have probably been used to it all their lives. Being comfortably off, I mean. But something happens to people when they suddenly have unimaginable amounts of money. It seems to be too much for the mind to take.'

'You know what? I think I might lose touch with reality too, if I woke up one morning and discovered I'd won millions of pounds.'

'I agree,' said Cooper. 'I've often thought winning the lottery was the worst thing that could happen to anybody. Buying a ticket every week is like playing Russian roulette.'

'Well, it didn't do Mr Edson much good, in the end.'

Cooper looked back towards Riddings Lodge. He could only see the roof from here, the late-afternoon sun reflecting from the dormer windows. He was reminded of that glimpse of Chatsworth House a few days ago. Some properties looked magical from a distance. But not so good close up.

'Actually, it's an older story than that,' he said.

Murfin took no notice of the comment, as he often did. If it was too difficult to think about, he didn't bother. It was a sensible attitude, one that had probably helped him get through life so far without going mad.

'This Russell Edson,' said Murfin. 'I was always a bit troubled about him, like. He gives off the airs and graces, but everyone knows his situation. All fur coat and no knickers, my old mother would have said.'

'What?'

'It means all show. Outward appearance, with no substance underneath. Someone who pretends to be wealthy or important, when actually all they've done is learned how to present themselves. What you find underneath doesn't match what you see on the surface.'

'All outward appearance. You think so?'

Murfin was warming to his subject now. For once, he wasn't eating, or even chewing. Cooper realised that he was serious, might even be excited about the job now that things seemed to be going their way.

'Listen,' said Murfin. 'My dad worked for a company once where they were up against a serious business rival. One day, the rivals put personalised number plates on all their vans. I thought that was pretty impressive myself. But Dad told me that when you saw someone put personalised plates on, you

314

knew they were in trouble. In business, you have to pretend you're doing well. You've got to find some way of putting out a message, like. And he was right, too. The rival firm went bust a few months later.'

Cooper turned at a sudden flurry of excitement in the grounds of the lodge. One of the officers in the search team had raised a hand, and had become instantly the centre of attention. He was standing near the long rhododendron hedge that marked the boundary of the property.

'Sergeant Cooper!' the officer called urgently. 'Over here.'

'What is it?'

'There's a body.'

It lay half on the lawn and half under the rhododendron bushes. Legs in brown corduroy trousers, torso in an old brown anorak. Cooper knew who it was before he had seen the face. Barry Gamble. Lacerations on his face, thorns embedded in his flesh, the hair on the back of his head matted with blood.

Cooper and Murfin stood watching as the scene was taped off.

'He was attacked from behind,' said Cooper. 'From the way he fell, it looks as though he was running, and pitched forward on his face when he was struck.'

'So he was running away from someone.'

'Seems like it. Someone a bit quicker on his feet than he was, too.'

'Do you think someone caught him snooping again, and overreacted?' asked Murfin.

Cooper nodded. Gamble had seen something, without doubt. What it was, he hadn't been telling. At least, he hadn't told the right people. Talking to the wrong person might have been what got him killed.

'You know what?' said Murfin. 'Some people would give anything for their last testament not to be "found wearing a brown anorak and brown trousers".'

Cooper remembered that Gamble was a keen amateur photographer, and that Riddings was his chief subject.

Somewhere there ought to be photographs. Lots of photographs.

At Chapel Close, Monica Gamble had already been informed of the death of her husband, and a female officer was sitting with her. Monica didn't look quite as shocked as many people would in these circumstances. Perhaps living with Barry for all those years had led her to expect an outcome like this.

'I'm sorry, Mrs Gamble,' said Cooper, 'but we have to take a look in your husband's shed again.'

'I don't know what you expect to find in there. It's just rubbish.'

'Not to your husband, perhaps. I think Mr Gamble knew a lot of things he wasn't telling.'

'Of course Barry knew things. He knew things about everybody. It was his interest. All right, his obsession. But he never meant any harm. Never.'

'Why didn't he just come to us with his information?' asked Cooper. 'It would have been so much simpler.'

'After the way he'd been treated?' said Mrs Gamble. 'He knew he was under suspicion from the start. It was obvious none of you believed what he was saying.'

'Well, that was because he was lying,' said Cooper. 'Mrs Gamble?'

She nodded slowly. 'What is it you want particularly?'

'Your husband's camera. And any CDs, memory sticks or storage devices he might have kept his pictures on.'

'Will it help?'

'Yes, I think so,' said Cooper.

There were so many uses for a laptop these days that Cooper carried one in his car. He opened it up and loaded the memory card from Barry Gamble's camera.

The card held about two hundred pictures. The first were shots of the derelict farm building and the two abandoned slurry pits, no longer simply suggestive of picturesque decay, but carrying a greater significance.

And there, of course, was the guide stoop. It had been photographed from all angles, with each of its faces depicted and the inscriptions clearly legible. *Sheffeild Rode, Hathersich Rode*. One of the pictures showed the stone in the foreground, with the slurry pits behind it. It was as though the stoop was pointing towards the exact location where Zoe Barron's phone and wallet would be found. *Sheffeild Rode*.

Cooper wondered if the next step in Gamble's campaign of anonymous communication would have been to send a copy of this photograph. The last stage, just to make the point clear for those who were too dim to put two and two together.

He didn't intend to go through all two hundred images on the memory card. He sorted the files into date order and looked for shots that had been taken on Tuesday.

From that night, he had expected pictures of the Barrons. But the shots he found weren't of Valley View, or its grounds. They had been taken nearby, yes. But the house they showed was Riddings Lodge.

Cooper scrabbled around until he found a copy of the Riddings map. It seemed that the only spot where Gamble could have got some of these views of Riddings Lodge was right on the boundary between Edson's property and the Barrons'. There was only a narrow strip at that point where the two properties bordered each other. To the west was the Hollands' garden at Fourways. Eastwards, there was only the rough sloping ground at the base of the edge. The rock-strewn heath cut a slice between the manicured lawns and almost looked as though it ought to continue along the boundary line as far as Croft Lane.

Eagerly Cooper swung round to his screen and called up the aerial view. When he zoomed in, it became obvious. There was more than just a boundary line between Riddings Lodge on one side, and Valley View and Fourways on the other. The satellite image had captured a wider, darker area that connected the base of Riddings Edge with Croft Lane.

A sunken lane, surely? But why hadn't it been visible on the ground?

Then he remembered the dense rhododendron hedge, yards and yards of it along the bottom of Edson's garden. He'd stood and admired it from Edson's lounge. He recalled thinking that many keen gardeners would have tried to get rid of the shrub. Rhododendrons sucked minerals out of the soil and prevented anything else from flourishing near them. But Edson hadn't cared about that. He had no interest in gardening. He probably never went near the hedge – not near enough, anyway, to see that it hid the remains of a sunken lane under its dense foliage.

But Barry Gamble had known about it. Gamble had sneaked into the old lane to take photographs of Riddings Lodge. He still had rhododendron twigs sticking to his fleece days later. But why did he want to photograph the house so secretly?

Cooper turned back to the photographs and scrolled through them. Figures started to appear now. Glenys Edson taking a stroll in the garden. The housekeeper, Mrs Davies, walking round the house. Mrs Davies pictured talking to the odd-job man, whose name Cooper had forgotten. There was Russell Edson himself, standing in the conservatory, apparently doing nothing. Waiting, perhaps.

And who was that? A younger man, talking to Edson. Now there were several shots, taken by Gamble in quick succession. The two men seemed to be arguing, judging by their arm gestures. Finally there were two frames capturing Edson and the other man coming outside, stepping out of the conservatory and turning towards the garage on the other side of the drive. A moment later and Gamble would have lost them from sight. But those last two frames were good ones. Edson was clearly recognisable in both, his hair swept back, his expression upset or angry – Cooper couldn't be sure.

And the other, younger man? With a jolt, Cooper realised now that he'd seen him before. Edson hadn't been joking when he'd said he'd got a man in. This man might have been called in to do the gardening. But he'd come even further into Edson's

318

life, judging by the close, affectionate embrace that Barry Gamble had captured in the very last frame.

It was funny how a photograph could strike so much more directly to the memory. Perhaps there were too many distractions when you met someone on the street, or saw them at a showground. The voice might sound familiar, the mannerisms might ring a bell, but the brain just didn't have enough focus to put the features together and make that leap of recognition. Yet when you sat down and studied a photo of the same person, suddenly it was all there.

Cooper jumped at a loud rapping on his window. His heart pounded in shock. He must be in a more nervous state than he'd thought. Normally he would have noticed someone approaching his car. Normally he wouldn't have reacted as if he'd been shot.

He looked up to see Carol Villiers' face pressed against the glass. He unlocked the door, and she jumped eagerly into the passenger seat.

'Just wondering,' she said. 'We haven't spoken to Sarah Holland again. Or to Tyler Kaye at all. Weren't we going to do that today?'

'It's not necessary.'

'I see.'

She produced her notebook, and Cooper watched her expectantly. He recognised an element of teasing in her tone. He probably shouldn't allow that. But he let it go, because he knew she had something he wanted.

'Did you know there were fifteen complaints to the district council about neighbour nuisance?' she said. 'But none from Russell Edson. And none about him either.'

'There must be some other motive,' said Cooper. 'Maybe disputes that end in court aren't the problem. There could be one that everyone is keeping quiet about.'

Villiers beamed. 'You're right. How come you're always right, Ben?'

'I can't explain it. It just comes naturally.'

'It's all in the breeding. I see.'

319

Cooper closed his laptop. He was learning that he couldn't hurry Villiers when she had something to say. The more important it was, the longer she seemed to take getting the information out. She liked to savour the tastiest titbits before she released them.

'So there was some kind of dispute between Edson and the Barrons?'

'Absolutely. But not over anything so trivial as the ownership of a bit of land. This was about money. A large amount of money.'

'Ah. Now that's getting to the real life blood of Riddings.'

'Yes. And to follow your analogy – our Russell was bleeding profusely. It seems Mr Edson has been spending an awful lot of money on legal fees, without the dispute ever coming to court. He hired private detectives and paid for surveillance. He must have collected a mass of information, everything that could be known about the Barrons. He was like a jealous husband digging up dirt on his wife's lover.'

'What?' Cooper felt confused now. 'He didn't have a wife. Was he interested in Zoe Barron?'

'No, in Jake.'

'Eh?'

Villiers laughed. 'Not like that. No, Mr Edson was interested in destroying him.'

Cooper gazed at the stone houses clustered in the centre of Riddings. The quaint narrow lanes, the old horse trough, the neat grass verges, the Union Jack flying at the crossroads. Beyond the centre lay the large, expensive properties, with their pony paddocks and landscaped gardens. It was a place for the upwardly mobile, in more than one sense. Property prices in the seven-figure bracket, and a long drag up that hill without a car.

Yet in another sense, this village was still a jungle – dark and wild, crawling with primal instincts.

'This has taken some digging out,' said Villiers. 'Gavin has helped me to tap into all the best sources. It's amazing what you can come up with when you start piecing bits of information together. But it's all there somewhere, waiting for someone to put two and two together.'

'Tell me,' said Cooper. 'I can't bear this.'

'Okay, here goes. Jake Barron had persuaded Edson to put a lot of money into the carpet business. And when the company went bankrupt, Edson realised he'd lost it all.'

'Bankrupt? I thought the Barrons were doing well?'

'No, they just tried to give that impression.'

'Oh, personalised number plates. I see.'

'What?'

'Nothing.'

'Well, it seems they had decided to expand the business just at the wrong time,' said Villiers. 'They bought out another firm with stores in Ireland. Paid through the nose for it, too. At the time, they said it was a perfect fit to grow the business. But they didn't know the recession was about to hit. And it was worse in Ireland than here, as you know. The economy was decimated. The Celtic Tiger rolled over and died.'

'So the Barrons overstretched themselves.'

'By a long way. They had a bit of a cushion to carry them through for a while, but they couldn't survive forever waiting until the upturn came along. They'd taken out a massive loan from their bank for the purchase, and it was being called in. The bankers couldn't see any prospect of a return on their money, so they pulled the plug. I'm told the chain of carpet warehouses is only days away from going into receivership.'

'I must say, Jake Barron didn't seem to be suffering from the effects of a financial crisis,' said Cooper.

'That must have been what infuriated Edson most, seeing the Barrons still spending money when he was about to lose everything.'

'Yes, I can imagine.'

'Jake was a smart businessman, you see,' said Villiers. 'He moved all his assets into his wife's name before the crash came and the crisis became public. The house was entirely hers, for a start. Yes, a smart businessman, Jake. But Russell Edson wasn't. He was just a jobbing builder who got lucky.'

'And then very unlucky.'

DI Hitchens was smiling when they met him near the horse trough in the centre of the village. It seemed like the first time he'd done that all week.

'Well, Ben – it looks as though you've come up smelling of roses. Unlike some of the officers in the task force.'

'Sir?'

'They recovered a couple of items from one of the slurry pits. An HTC android mobile phone, and a purse containing a hundred and fifty pounds in cash.'

'Zoe Barron's property.'

'Yes. But I don't understand . . .'

'What?'

'Well, why would they just dump their haul? Including the cash – that doesn't make sense. Even if they were afraid of getting caught, they would keep the cash, wouldn't they? Or stash it somewhere at least. Somewhere they could recover it later, I mean – not a slurry pit, for heaven's sake.'

'Doesn't it seem likely that those items were taken to distract our attention from something else?'

'But from what?'

'From the real motive for the attack.'

'The real motive?'

'Oh, yes,' said Cooper. 'What about Russell Edson? Any sign of him? If we don't find him now, we'll have a problem. There's a mist coming down, and it's going to be dark soon.'

'Well, we've found his red MG. It's been left up at the car park by Riddings Edge.'

27

Cooper loved the transitional nature of dusk. He liked the way the colours changed, and the world slipped into shadow. It was fascinating how a figure moving in the distance could become smaller and smaller, fainter and fainter, until it was no longer a movement but a trick of the light.

At the car park below Riddings Edge, the only light seemed to come from within the mist itself. It was as if it had swallowed light from the day and was leaking it slowly back into the valley.

Apart from Russell Edson's red MG, there were only a couple of vehicles still in the car park. Late-evening walkers? Photographers hoping to capture a sunset? Or maybe it was something more. From here, Cooper couldn't see Riddings at all. Instead, he was looking down towards the River Derwent, and beyond it a small hump of land that hid the larger village of Calver.

A gnawing in his stomach, which he'd thought was anxiety or fear, suddenly resolved itself, as he realised that he hadn't eaten anything all day. He was starving. He had a vivid image of a pub that stood in the middle of Calver, overlooking the cricket field. A sprawling Georgian inn, said to be haunted. It was a pub, not a fancy restaurant, but it did good food. A lot of their produce was sourced from the area, and local people left bags of plums, pears and rhubarb at the back door, which was one of the reasons home-made desserts were always available.

It was the sort of place Cooper would choose to go to like a shot. But not Russell Edson. No home-grown rhubarb pie for him.

He tried Edson's mobile number again. It was engaged, as it had been for some time.

Villiers and Hitchens arrived in the car park. A marked police car went past with its lights flashing, though Cooper couldn't guess where it was heading.

'Russell Edson?' said Hitchens. 'This is a firm suspect?'

'Mr Edson is much too respectable to get his own hands dirty, of course,' said Villiers. 'So he must have contracted it out. Got a man in to do the job.'

'In a way,' said Cooper.

Villiers looked at him curiously, but he kept his face as straight as he could.

'There's very little daylight left,' said Hitchens. 'I think we're going to have to leave it until morning, Ben. We can't risk officers up there in the dark. They would all get lost and break their legs. The compensation payments don't bear thinking about.'

When Hitchens turned away to respond to a call on his radio, Cooper looked up at the edge and saw a figure. Not an outcrop of rock this time, or a trick of the light – but a human figure gazing down towards Riddings.

'Carol,' he said, indicating the spot.

'I see him. Is it . . .?'

'I think so.'

He tried the number again. And this time it rang.

'Mr Edson? Where are you?'

'Ah, Sergeant Cooper. Where else would I be? I'm on the edge.'

'Stay right where you are.'

'Only if I choose to, Sergeant.'

Cursing under his breath, Cooper began to climb the path from the car park towards the edge. Villiers fell in behind him.

By the time they reached the moor, it was totally dark. The lights from Riddings and the other villages in the valley failed to reach this far. Besides, the sky overhead was black with clouds, which blotted out the stars and any moon there might have been. It wasn't a night for watching meteor showers.

As the thought went through Cooper's head, it began to rain. Heavy drops were suddenly beating on his shoulders and soaking his hair. He'd come without a waterproof, but there was no time to go back. Villiers, of course, had been much more sensible.

'If I can get close enough, I'll try talking to him,' said Cooper. 'But I don't want to alarm him too much. He might be in a dangerous state.'

'You mean you want me to stay out of the way, in case I frighten him,' said Villiers.

'Not exactly. But I think we can do this without fuss. He just needs approaching the right way.'

'All right. I'll take the other path and go round.'

'Can you find it?'

'I'm like a cat in the dark.'

Villiers vanished into the darkness, swishing through the wet bracken. Cooper continued up the path alone, placing his feet carefully out of the streams of water running down from the edge.

Normally, the night was the perfect time to walk on the moor. Out here in the dark, you could experience the place properly. Your eyes had a chance to adjust to the darkness, free from the glow of city lights. But you needed to use your night hearing too, and your other senses. The moor became a different world then. Its size was measured as much by sound and smell as by sight. You became more aware of the hum of life around you. Not human life, but the sound of the natural world stirring in the safety of darkness.

Cooper looked up as he walked. The sky . . . well, the sky was so much more visible than during the day. It dominated the moor, weighed down on him as he walked. All the time he was conscious of its glittering black canopy hanging over his head and swirling on the horizon. Out on the moor at night, you soon became aware how big the sky was. So much bigger than your own little world. So huge that it put everything beneath it into perspective.

Cooper was well aware that some people never looked up at the sky. It just didn't occur to them to step out at night into an empty landscape and gaze at the stars. It was no wonder they failed to keep their lives in proper perspective. Small things seemed to take on an enormous significance for them. A momentary offence became a matter of life and death. An insult was the last straw. And the outcome could be disastrous. Tragic. If only they would all stop occasionally and look at the night sky, just take a few minutes to count the stars and reflect on the millions of solar systems they represented. The mind reeled at the immensity of the universe. The soul was humbled at an individual's insignificant place in it.

That was one of the reasons he had never thought the Chadwicks capable of acting against Jake and Zoe Barron. They had spent their time watching the Perseid meteor shower, up here on the Devil's Edge in the darkness. No perceived insult or offence from their neighbours could seem important enough to them after that.

Moths appeared suddenly in front of his face, fluttering out of the night. His ears told him that invisible sheep lay breathing and cudding in the heather. A gust of wind rattled through the bracken like an approaching train, blowing a squall of rain against his face. But there was nothing to worry about here. None of those things was a threat. It was only the imagination that turned them into something quite different.

After a few minutes, his feet hit rock, and he knew he was near the edge. Stepping more carefully now, he felt his way between the boulders until a view opened up in front of him. It was a panorama across the Derwent Valley, deep pits of blackness with the lights of villages here and there like clusters of beads strung up the hillsides. From here, he could see right up to the ghostly gleam of the limestone quarries in Middleton Dale.

For a moment he experienced a surge of panic as a wave of dizziness swept over him. He didn't normally suffer from vertigo. But the sudden drop appearing beneath his feet had thrown him off balance, mentally as well as physically. He swayed a little on the balls of his feet, held out his arms to steady himself. The sensation was like solid ground lurching beneath his boots, as if the horizontal rock shelf had tilted towards forty-five degrees in an effort to tip him off the edge into the valley. For that second, he'd thought he was about to join the dead sheep, broken and bloodied amid the wreckage of millstones. But gradually the world was righting itself, his balance steadied and he knew he wasn't going to fall.

Cooper felt the sweat dampening his forehead as he took a deep breath. That was definitely a primal fear, the terror of falling from a great height. The edge was a place that seemed to exploit that fear. His footsteps had been led to the drop as if by some unseen temptation.

The moor might look bare and empty in the cold light of reality. But in the minds of the people who'd travelled across it, there must have existed a dark forest of superstition, a psychological world inhabited by trolls and demons, crowded with all kinds of dangers that lurked in the darkness. Their consciousness would have been full of stories of death and madness, tales of ghosts and cut-throats, fear of storms and fog and sucking bogs. Above all, this would have become a mythical landscape where you might encounter terrible beasts.

Yet if there were demons on Big Moor, he hadn't seen them. The Savages had become as mythical as hobs. But what about the evil at work down there in Riddings? Were those devils human? Or just a part of the landscape?

His mobile phone rang. Just one ring, then silence. Cooper looked at the display, and recognised the number he'd dialled only a few minutes ago. That was clever. Edson had called his phone to establish his position in the darkness. Now he knew exactly how close Cooper was.

'Don't come any nearer, Sergeant.'

Cooper stopped, peering into the night.

'There's nothing to worry about, sir. I just need you to come with me.'

'I'm fine here, thank you.'

'Mr Edson . . .'

'No. Stay where you are.'

As his eyes adjusted, Cooper began to make out the shape of the man a few yards away. He couldn't be sure from here, but it looked as though Edson was standing right on the edge, on the very rim of a flat, rocky outcrop jutting out into space. His figure was outlined against the distant lights somewhere up the valley. Around him was nothing but empty air.

Cooper wiped the rain out of his eyes, and pulled his jacket closer around him. He was starting to get very cold, and the throbbing headache was returning. He knew that if he stayed motionless too long in this wind and rain, exhaustion would begin to get the better of him. He could feel it now, surging in waves through his veins.

This mustn't take too long. The only thing he could do was distract Edson's attention, or try to get him to talk.

'Mr Edson, you're not a rock climber, are you?' he said.

'Me? Good heavens, no.'

'Much too dangerous for you, I suppose?'

'I can't see the point of it. Why do you ask?'

'We found magnesium carbonate in your car.'

'Magnesium . . .?'

'It's used sometimes in taxidermy, for whitening skulls. You don't go in for taxidermy, do you?'

'No, of course not. Stuffing dead animals?' Edson stared at him. 'Sergeant, have you lost your mind? What on earth are you talking about?'

'The other most common use for magnesium carbonate is in the form of a chalk. It's useful as a drying agent for the hands. To help the grip, you know. It's used by most often by gymnasts and weightlifters. And by rock climbers, of course.'

'I don't know how it could have got into my car. That's a bit of a mystery.'

'Well, perhaps,' said Cooper.

328

Through the rain, he saw another figure approaching along the edge. Not from the direction of the car park, but from the packhorse route. Villiers had worked her way round, finding her direction across the moor, even in the dark.

A blast of wind buffeted the edge, and Cooper had difficulty keeping his feet. Edson swayed and held out his arms to balance himself. He was wearing a long black coat, which flapped angrily in the wind. The downpour was becoming torrential now. It pounded on the rocks and cascaded over the edge, forming instant waterfalls.

This had to be done more quickly. Cooper knew he had to try to keep Edson talking, giving Villiers the chance to get into position.

'We found Barry Gamble's body,' he said. 'Was Mr Gamble trying to blackmail you, sir. Is that what it was?'

Edson laughed. 'Oh, he tried. In a very roundabout way. He was wasting his time with me, though.'

'Because of the money, you mean?'

'The lottery money? It's all vanished. Extravagant expenditure, a series of bad investments. I had to mortgage the house to release some capital, and now I can't make the payments on it. Everything will have to go. No, there's no money left, not a penny. I'm up to my neck in debt.'

'So the big lottery winner is broke?'

'Absolutely stony, I'm afraid.'

'A whole series of mistakes, Mr Edson.'

'Mistakes? Yes. Too many to count.'

Shivering, Cooper moved a few paces closer, feeling the rock carefully underfoot with each step. He saw Edson turn, and could sense the man looking at him through the rain.

'It's a pity I told you that Barry Gamble came to Riddings Lodge that night,' said Edson. 'You didn't know about that until I mentioned it, did you? Gamble hadn't let on.'

'No, sir, he hadn't.'

Edson shook his head. 'Strange man. I didn't expect him to be the sort of person to keep a secret. Just one more mistake.'

Finally, Cooper felt close enough to hold a proper conversation,

329

instead of shouting against the noise of the wind and rain. He could almost see Edson's eyes, just a glimmer of white in the darkness.

'So what happened, Mr Edson? Why did it go so wrong?'

'I'm not sure where it all went wrong. Oh, I didn't know enough about money from the beginning, I suppose. I certainly didn't realise how quickly it would disappear. And I was a fool to trust Jake Barron. But after that . . .'

A few more steps, and Cooper was close now. He could see Edson smiling sadly. Yet his expression also seemed to reflect a sort of satisfaction, as if somehow things had actually gone the way he expected.

'After that was when everything really started to fall apart, surely?' said Cooper. 'The death of Zoe Barron wasn't part of the plan, was it?'

'What?'

'I think you just wanted to punish the Barrons. But you hired the wrong people. You'd heard about the Savages and how they got away with their crimes. You figured another attack would just be put down to them. But the people you hired weren't professionals like the Savages. These boys were complete amateurs. They had no idea how to do the job right. They didn't know the way to hurt someone without killing them. They didn't know what to do to make it look like a genuine robbery. A mobile phone and a purse? What sort of haul is that? Right there, when you made that decision – that was your worst mistake.'

Edson took a step closer to the edge, wiping the rain from his face. The wind whipped round him, lashing his hair, flapping his coat open like the wings of a bird.

Cooper began to move towards him, but saw how slippery the wet rock was. He was afraid of startling Edson and making him lose his footing. The edge was too high, the drop too steep and sudden. Making a sudden move would be dangerous. He looked past Edson, met Villiers' eye, made a small gesture to keep her back.

'It's very good,' said Edson. 'Your story, I mean. All those

330

things that went wrong. I think it's probably very accurate, in a way. An example of bad planning. Yes, it was an appalling decision to employ amateurs. It's always better to spend a bit more money and use professionals. You get what you pay for, after all.'

'Yes, that's true.'

Edson paused, and looked out over the dark valley.

'There's only one problem with that story, Sergeant Cooper,' he said. 'The person who hired those thugs to attack the Barrons – it wasn't me.'

With a loud crack, a slice of rock shifted, dropped, then slowly peeled away from the face of the edge.

Cooper saw Russell Edson held for one second in mid-air, his arms outstretched, his coat flapping around him like wings. He was a huge black bird, screaming and screaming, a creature fighting against the blast of the wind and the pull of gravity. His last moment was only a flicker of movement, a dark thrashing against the sky.

And then he began to fall.

28

Tuesday

On the eastern edges, car windscreens flashed in the sun, like secret signals being sent across the valley. There would be no climbers on the Devil's Edge today. The rock faces were too wet, and there was too much police activity. Parties of gritstone addicts took one look and went further north, to Froggatt or Stanage.

But at E Division headquarters in West Street, Edendale, plenty was going on. The August bank holiday weekend was over, and Ben Cooper was at his desk, chest-high in paperwork. Who knew there would be so many forms to fill in when you'd just been involved in a fatal incident?

He'd told the whole story to Liz the day before, emptying out his feelings to her all day long, it seemed. And she'd listened to him for hours, as the bank holiday crowds thronged into the Peak District around them, intent on squeezing every last ounce of enjoyment from the scenery, from the picturesque villages, the stately homes and heritage centres. It had meant, for once, that Liz didn't talk only about the wedding. He cared about her deeply, of course. Yet he was already starting to feel exhausted by the subject.

Wearily, Cooper stopped for a moment to gaze out of the window of the CID room at the rooftops of the town, longing to be out there in the open. But he was stuck here for quite a while yet, head down, repeating details he'd already given several times over.

At the same time, he was waiting impatiently for something to be decided. And waiting, as everyone knew, was the most difficult thing in the world.

'Daydreaming, Ben?'

He started, and turned to find Diane Fry at his shoulder. She had never lost that ability to creep up on him when he wasn't expecting it. It was a trick that made him feel particularly vulnerable.

'Oh, Diane.' He stood up eagerly. 'Is there any . . .?'

'News? Yes, the CPS have made a decision. Quick work, for them. But they've established precedents in the last few years. Similar cases, with similar reasons for their decision.'

'What decision?'

'No prosecution,' said Fry. 'Not in the public interest.'

'Oh, thank God.'

'I'm pleased for your brother, Ben.'

'And it's a victory for you too.'

A shadow passed across her face. 'A victory of sorts,' she said.

'No, you did a really good job at the farm,' said Cooper.

'Average, I thought.'

'Well, anyway . . . Thanks, Diane. I just wanted to say that.'

'I didn't do it as a favour to you.'

'I'm sure you didn't. But I'm saying thank you nevertheless.'

Cooper wondered why it always seemed to end up like this between them, why even saying thank you had to sound like an argument.

'You know, when you first came to E Division,' he said, 'I really thought we would be able to work together.'

'It's too late for that now. There's one DS too many in Edendale. A team can only have one leader.'

'What went wrong, Diane?' he asked, hearing the echo of a question he'd asked Russell Edson not so long ago

'Wrong? I couldn't say.'

Cooper gazed at her, but she looked away. To his ears, her answer seemed to mean 'I don't *want* to say'. Perhaps she just liked to give the impression that she knew more than she was telling. On the other hand, he couldn't resist a nagging suspicion that she *did* know something he didn't.

He was sure of one thing, though. He would never find out what it was unless he asked her exactly the right question.

'You had a tough one in this Riddings place, from what I hear,' said Fry. 'Too many people with malicious intent. Whether there's a prosecution or not, it never makes for a good outcome.'

Cooper wondered if that was a subtle dig, some oblique reference to the Bridge End Farm incident.

'Matt was a different case,' he said.

'I know the difference,' said Fry. 'There are people who think they're doing the right thing, protecting their families. And there are others who know that what they're doing is wrong, but don't care. I met one of those not very long ago, in Birmingham. He was as close to me as your brother is to you, genetically speaking. In other ways, we were worlds apart. But he's gone now.'

'Oh, you mean your biological father. He's still alive, though, isn't he?'

'Yes, as far as I know. But to be honest, I wish I'd killed him.'

'Not really,' said Cooper, shocked that she could even contemplate the idea.

'Yes, really.'

He began to feel angry. 'If both your parents had died, you wouldn't even think of saying that.'

She looked at him then, a mixture of emotions passing across her face. He wondered which of them would win. But this was Diane Fry he was talking to.

'I suppose I ought to apologise,' she said.

'Oh, don't feel that you have to.'

'We're so different, you and me. I'll never understand your world. And you, Ben, will never understand mine. I'm not going to apologise for that.'

'That wasn't . . . Oh, never mind.'

'I am sorry about your parents, really. I imagine it must have been hard.'

'Yes. But it's only an effort of the imagination with you. You don't really *understand*, do you?'

Fry was silent for a moment. 'I don't think I ever did,' she said. 'That's one thing you're right about.'

He searched for something else to say. But he saw Gavin Murfin watching them from across the room, and only one thing came to mind.

'So were there any repercussions for you, Diane? I mean from your own, er . . . incident in Nottingham?'

'I received words of advice.'

'Lucky.'

'Oh, yeah.'

Cooper watched Fry walk away. He hadn't asked her whether she had been successful in obtaining a transfer, or finding another job. He knew she'd been looking for a few weeks now. If she did, though, he would be the last person she told.

Well, one thing was certain. When she did go, Fry would be remembered. Though maybe not for the right reasons. Murfin still talked about the battered chips he'd seen in the Black Country, when he was there with Fry on an inquiry. He'd been trying to persuade his local chippy to make them for him ever since. Luckily for his arteries, they'd refused so far.

Fry paused in the doorway, caught once more in the act of passing from one place to another. It was the way that Cooper would always imagine her.

'By the way,' she said, 'who have you got in Interview Room One?'

'It's my Riddings suspect,' said Cooper. 'Name of Edson.'

In Interview Room One, Cooper sat down next to DI Hitchens and regarded the man across the table. He was accompanied by his solicitor, and he looked relaxed and confident.

Cooper recognised that look. It was in the eyes and mouth mostly. Without the make-up and the false beard, the similarity was obvious. His hair was dark, but swept back just like his father's. It was the same sardonic eyebrow, the same supercilious curl to the lip.

For Cooper, the surprising thing was that he hadn't recognised this man when he'd seen him with Adrian Summers last week. Thursday, that must have been, not long after he'd visited Riddings Lodge for the first time. He'd experienced a feeling of recognition, but it hadn't clicked into place. It was a problem when you saw people out of context. In the end, it was only Gamble's photograph that had made everything fall into place. But at least he'd found his missing Dave.

'You are David Edson,' said Hitchens, opening the interview with the tapes running. 'The son of Mr Russell Edson, of Riddings Lodge?'

'The same.'

'We understand your father was a very wealthy man. A big lottery winner?'

'He certainly was. And here I am, struggling to scrape a living.'

'As a children's entertainer,' said Cooper, 'if I'm not mistaken.'

The eyebrow lifted and the curl came to the mouth as David Edson smiled.

'Oh, you saw me.'

'Yes, of course. No one at Riddings Show could have missed you. The famous Doctor Woof.'

'Well, that's just a little hobby of mine. Not what I do to make a living.'

'Especially when you don't charge for your services, but volunteer to do it for nothing.'

'True.'

'I wonder what you have in your past, Mr Edson.'

'I'm CRB checked, you know. I couldn't work as a children's entertainer if I wasn't.'

'Yes, we're aware of that. But that's not what we're here to talk about. We're here to discuss two murders. Those of Jake and Zoe Barron.'

As the interview went on, David Edson's façade began to crumble. Cooper was glad to see it. His attitude was all show, after all. Just like his father's.

In the end, Edson ignored his solicitor's urgent advice, and blurted out the one thing that was most important for him to say.

'I thought that killing them would make me feel better. But it didn't.'

Carol Villiers was the first to congratulate Cooper. The rest of the CID team milled around in celebratory mood, their paperwork forgotten for a while.

'You were right on that one, Carol,' said Cooper. 'What infuriated the Edsons most was seeing the Barrons still spending money when they were about to lose everything. But David was the most infuriated. He was filled with rage. He blamed Jake Barron for his father's situation.'

'That's a bit like a jealous lover, too, when you think about it,' said Villiers.

'How do you mean?'

'Well, instead of blaming his father, he blamed the object of his father's obsession. He took the view that Barron was ruining his life, and his future prospects.'

Cooper nodded. 'Yes, Barron was draining off all the money that should have come his way. David had built all his expectations on that money.'

'So it was David who hired Summers, knowing that the job would be blamed on the Savages.'

'Yes. And there was never any intention to steal anything, just to grab a couple of things to make it look like a burglary. They went through a gap in the fence to get to and from Valley View, then up the track to dispose of the haul. They spent the night in Edson's garage, then drove their van out next morning.'

'Meanwhile, his father and grandmother calmly went off to have dinner at Bauers,' said Villiers.

'It must have been quite a shock for Russell to find Barry Gamble turning up on his doorstep that night. Gamble had figured it out. He wasn't stupid. He knew all about people. And why wouldn't he, when he spent so much of his time watching them?'

'He'd been spying on the Edsons, then.'

'Of course. Though he probably wouldn't have called it that.'

'How did you know what Gamble had been doing, Ben?'

'In the first place, from one of his souvenirs,' said Cooper. 'A monkey puzzle cone. They grow on trees like the one in the garden at Riddings Lodge. That has to be where he picked it up. Mr Edson told me himself that there isn't another tree of that species for miles. Why do you think Gamble ran to Riddings Lodge first when he discovered Zoe Barron's body?'

'Because he knew Edson was responsible?'

'Well, not until he saw the light on. And not the light in the Barrons' kitchen; I mean the light in Edson's garage. The photographs confirmed it, of course. He'd snapped Edson with his son, David.'

'No one even mentioned that David Edson was in the village,' said Villiers. 'In fact, no one mentioned him at all. That was suspicious in itself, looking back.'

'One person mentioned him,' said Cooper.

'Oh? Who?'

'His grandmother, Glenys. I thought she was talking about Russell. And Edson let me go away with that impression. But she wasn't. When she spoke about children trying to bleed the life out of you, she meant David. She knew David was trying to drain off all the money for himself.'

For Edson, it had been a last desperate stand, as if he could protect what he'd owned by fighting with his neighbours. But he was aiming at the wrong target. Like so many people, he was his own worst enemy.

Cooper had never got the chance to talk more to Russell Edson about how the chalk traces came to be in his car. Of course Russell wasn't a climber himself. But Cooper had wanted to say: *We could ask your son, perhaps. Because he is a rock climber, isn't he, Mr Edson?*

'Some time ago, David Edson was climbing on Riddings Edge with a friend when he fell from the face and struck his head on the rock.'

'He was the climber who did a highball off Hell's Reach and nearly died?' said Villiers.

'Yes. It was a close-run thing. He lost consciousness and went into a fit. He was stabilised by paramedics and a doctor from the mountain rescue team, then airlifted to Nottingham to be treated in the neurological unit at Queen's Medical Centre.'

'But he recovered.'

'Yes. Later on, he gave a big donation to the mountain rescue people. And he went back to rock climbing.'

'Those white handprints?' asked Villiers. 'There was never any explanation . . .'

'David Edson was back climbing on Riddings Edge that day. I imagine he looked down from one of those spurs of rock on the edge, and saw how easy it would be to get into the grounds of Valley View. You can't appreciate that from any other point – certainly not from anywhere in the village. You need to get the perspective, you see. You've got to achieve that bird's-eye viewpoint you can only get from the edge. So you might say it was the Devil's Edge that put the idea into his mind. It presented him with the temptation, just when he was most open to it.'

'That must have been earlier in the day, during daylight.'

'Of course. At the end of his climbing session, David went back down the edge. But instead of returning to his car, he tested out the route on the ground. No doubt he took note of the derelict farm building and the slurry pits, and figured out how he could use them. Then he got as far as the back wall at Valley View, and pulled himself up to look in.'

'And that was when he left the handprints.'

'Yes.' Cooper looked at the clouds rolling in across the horizon. 'In a way, he was unlucky. Unlucky that the weather

339

stayed good for a few days. Rain washes the chalk off. Those handprints will be gone now.'

'And he acted really fast, didn't he? He signed up Adrian Summers as his accomplice and they did it that night.'

'One thing they didn't reckon with was Barry Gamble,' said Cooper. 'He was right on the spot.'

'Nothing like a bit of good surveillance.'

'And then Summers got greedy. Well, he'd been getting away with it for weeks, and he was being built up as a folk hero, some sort of Robin Hood figure. He must have started to believe his own press, and thought he was untouchable. After he'd done the job with Edson, he saw an opportunity and two nights later decided to check out the neighbouring property. The Hollands were never involved in anything. Martin Holland was an incidental death.'

'Collateral damage,' said Villiers.

'Summers is in custody anyway. They scooped him up in Sheffield, along with another accomplice.'

'So the Savages' time is over.'

'I wonder, though,' said Cooper.

'What?'

'Whether David Edson ever did recover fully from the head injury he suffered in that fall from the rock face. A good defence lawyer will be able to come up with medical evidence to show that he's been left with a degree of permanent brain damage – enough to change his personality and impair his judgement. He'll get manslaughter on the grounds of diminished responsibility.'

'Well, that's the way it goes.'

'Yes, it is,' said Cooper. 'That's exactly how it goes.'

'Russell and David Edson are no one's idea of folk heroes,' said Villiers. 'But they're not complete monsters either.'

No, thought Cooper. Who needed monsters and devils, when people had so much evil in them?

'Well, anyway,' he said, 'everybody else in Riddings deserves a medal.'

'What for?'

'For not having murdered Barry Gamble.'

Villiers laughed. 'Or any of their neighbours, in fact.'

'Despite the provocation.'

'At least those other monsters are off the streets,' said Villiers. 'The Savages, I mean. Now people can live their lives without fear again. No need to worry about being attacked in their own homes in the middle of the night.'

'We always have monsters in our lives,' said Cooper. 'But sometimes the monsters are ourselves.'

It was difficult to understand all the bad things that happened in the world. But you had to make the attempt – it was part of the job. Sometimes, though, the only way was to find the evil inside yourself, and use it.

Cooper doubted if he would ever go back to the eastern edges with the same feeling about them. The Devil's Edge had not only provided a backdrop, a barrier, a protection, a perspective. In the end, it had also given him the clues he needed to the secrets of Riddings.

Diane Fry let herself out of the custody suite on the ground floor, and crossed the walkway to enter the main building. She was oblivious to the weather, or her surroundings – at least, as far as it was possible not to be aware that she was in Derbyshire, in the middle of the Peak District, surrounded by these rural wastelands.

She was thinking of one thing – DCI Mackenzie's parting shot, aimed at her as he left Bridge End Farm. *A real farm girl, aren't you?*

She wondered why she didn't feel more resentful. Helping Cooper's family had lost her an opportunity to transfer to the city. Okay, Derby might not be the biggest metropolis in the world, but at least it would have been a route out of this backwater. Somehow even that had gone wrong.

She walked back into the CID room, looking around hesitantly as if she wasn't quite sure where she was. She approached Cooper's desk.

'Your brother is just being processed out of the custody suite,' she said. 'I thought you'd want to know straight away.'

'Great. I'll take him home.'

'Oh, okay. I'm sure that will be fine, Ben.'

'Thanks . . .' he began.

But Fry held up a hand, placed it between them like a shield. 'There's no need,' she said. 'Really. No need at all.'

A few minutes later, Cooper waited while his brother shook hands with Fry. That was something he'd never expected to see. But nothing was the same now. His family had come pretty close to the edge themselves.

Matt walked down with him to the car park and got into the passenger seat of the Toyota. Ben said nothing, and his brother looked at him as he fastened his seat belt.

'I was just saying thank you,' he said. 'She did a good job. That other bloke from Derby knew nothing. If it had been left up to him, I reckon I'd be spending the next ten years of my life in a prison cell.'

'Yes, it's fine.'

'Because they kept you out of it, didn't they, Ben? You weren't allowed anywhere near the investigation. That's what they told me. Conflict of interest and all that.'

'That's right, yes. Conflict of interest.'

'Because if you had got involved, it might have prejudiced the outcome. The Crown Prosecution Service could have gone ahead with charges just to show there was no favouritism to the family of a police officer. That's what they told me.'

'Yes, that can be a problem.'

Matt shook his head in despair. 'It's all been such a nightmare from the start. It's appalling, the state the countryside has come to.'

Ben thought of Riddings, and how different it was from the way he'd always imagined a village should be. He supposed a place like that was a particular form of twenty-first-century Britain. It still retained the superficial appearance of a village, right down to the horse trough and the smell of manure. But the horse trough was a relic of the past, just like the empty phone box.

It was sad to see a village where farming had so thoroughly disappeared. In fact, it couldn't really be called a village at all, could it? It was just a façade, a surface veneer of nostalgia. It was probably a symptom of things to come, a time when thriving rural communities would be a distant memory. A trace of a field pattern and an abandoned slurry pit on Big Moor.

He read the latest text from Liz on his phone. *R u ok?* Then he switched on the CD player, needing to fill the car with sound. In Riddings, he'd picked up a favourite Show of Hands album called *Roots*. Just the right thing to remind him that he was still in the countryside, not some outer suburb of Sheffield. Now, when he restarted it, the fourth track came on: 'Country Life'. The vocals were Steve Knightley at his angriest on the hypocrisy of attitudes to the countryside. Cooper had chosen it because he remembered that it contained a verse inspired by the devastating foot and mouth outbreak:

> *Picture postcard hills on fire*
> *Cattle burning in funeral pyres*
> *Out to graze they look so sweet*
> *We hate the blood, but we want the meat*

But the lines that struck him now came at the end of the first chorus. They seemed amazingly appropriate:

> *One man's family pays the price*
> *For another man's vision of country life*

Ben thought of Zoe and Jake Barron, and Martin Holland, and of Barry Gamble. Even of Russell and David Edson, and poor old Glenys, all the other people who'd been affected by the events in Riddings. Every one of them had clung to their own vision of country life. In some cases, it was a vision of escape, or a yearning for peace and quiet. In others, it was a chance to act like the country squire.

The coffin of our English dream
Lies out on the village green

He started the Toyota, and drove slowly towards the exit. Before he reached the barrier, he saw Fry's black Peugeot a few yards ahead, standing at the kerb on West Street. He wondered what she was doing, just sitting there in her car. What was she waiting for?

And then he saw the answer. Carol Villiers ran down the steps from the double doors at the front entrance. Without a glance towards the car park, she went up to Fry's Peugeot, opened the passenger door and got in. Fry turned her head and said something. Again, that private communication between them, a moment that he wasn't allowed to share. What were they talking about? Where were they going? When had they arranged this meeting?

It shouldn't bother him, but it did. He felt a sharp stab of anxiety, an uneasy sense that something was going on he didn't know about. And perhaps he would never find out what it was.

Although the barrier was up to let him drive out, Ben sat quite still, holding his breath, making no attempt to leave the car park as the Peugeot drove away down West Street.

'So it's good that you didn't get involved,' Matt was saying. 'You left it up to Detective Sergeant Fry, without any interference. I'm glad you felt you could trust her.'

'Oh, yes,' said Ben, as he watched Fry's car disappear into Edendale. 'That's very important, isn't it? Trust.'